To all my ....
at Dove's Rest. Enjoy and
God bless you! Suzy

Rel Fict
$5.00

The Summers Bluff Saga

Suz Dempsey

WESTBOW
PRESS®
A DIVISION OF THOMAS NELSON
& ZONDERVAN

Copyright © 2016 Susie Dempsey.

All rights reserved. No part of this book may be used or reproduced by any means, graphic, electronic, or mechanical, including photocopying, recording, taping or by any information storage retrieval system without the written permission of the author except in the case of brief quotations embodied in critical articles and reviews.

This is a work of fiction. All of the characters, names, incidents, organizations, and dialogue in this novel are either the products of the author's imagination or are used fictitiously.

WestBow Press books may be ordered through booksellers or by contacting:

WestBow Press
A Division of Thomas Nelson & Zondervan
1663 Liberty Drive
Bloomington, IN 47403
www.westbowpress.com
1 (866) 928-1240

Because of the dynamic nature of the Internet, any web addresses or links contained in this book may have changed since publication and may no longer be valid. The views expressed in this work are solely those of the author and do not necessarily reflect the views of the publisher, and the publisher hereby disclaims any responsibility for them.

Any people depicted in stock imagery provided by Thinkstock are models, and such images are being used for illustrative purposes only. Certain stock imagery © Thinkstock.

ISBN: 978-1-5127-4539-9 (sc)
ISBN: 978-1-5127-4540-5 (hc)
ISBN: 978-1-5127-4538-2 (e)

Library of Congress Control Number: 2016909465

Print information available on the last page.

WestBow Press rev. date: 11/1/2016

Contents

Part Two: San Francisco

Part Three: Jake

Part Four: Sentimental Journey

To my husband, Mike, who knows me the best, loves me the most, and made this book possible. My love and thanks!

Part One

Summers Bluff

Chapter 1

Summers Bluff Plantation February 1870

It was a delightful, sunny, spring-like morning, just like a thousand others before it, but for some reason, each one seemed significant to Emma Summers that year. The unseasonably warm February weather was already showing signs that the day would be a scorcher. Emma thought it would probably reach near eighty degrees before noon unless she missed her guess.

The cold, long winter had seemed to drag on forever, and warm weather had been long in coming. Though it had been considered a mild winter, compared to some in recent memory, it was still good to feel the sunshine, warm upon her bare arms. Her mama and Granny Thornton would be fussing at her when they saw her skin begin to bronze, but for all that, she would continue to spend most mornings out of doors.

Emma loved to spend the first part of the morning in her garden. The daffodils, one of her favorite flowers, had bloomed just that week; those happy-looking yellow flowers were nodding their heads, glistening with the dew of the early morning.

Emma normally gathered flowers for the breakfast table, as the conservatory kept flowers in bloom all winter long.

This morning she would pick some of the fragrant daffodils from the outside garden, situated along the south side of the house. She loved this the best of all her chores; it was one she had taken upon herself. She cut the daffodils at the last minute and put them in water in the cool springhouse until the breakfast hour.

Emma had loved early morning for as long as she could remember. The captivating twilight time between the light of crepuscule and that of dawn told her that God was on his throne and all was well with the world. She could be alone in the quiet, feeling grateful for her blessings and giving thanks, as she contemplated the day before her. The house would be quiet for a little while yet, though the plantation was already a flurry of activity. Emma was always up before any other member of the family, besides her papa, Josiah Summers, master of Summers Bluff.

Emma was content with her lot in life, all things considered. She had much to be thankful for, and that day she experienced a sense of well being, as she sat there in the sunshine and contemplated her life. That contentment was not to say that the Summers family had been untroubled. After all, were they not just on the other side of the awful Civil War?

Yes, they had known their share of trouble and heartache, to be sure. But she was nineteen, healthy and some considered her a beauty, what with her thick, fiery, auburn tresses and her emerald eyes that sparkled with merriment, as she laughed and played and got on with her life.

She was maybe a bit on the tallish side at five-seven, but that was a matter of taste, as were the freckles sprinkled across her nose that became even more prominent as she spent time in the sun.

She was quite slender, but well rounded in all the right places. Her husky voice made her sound maybe a bit more mature than she really was, but her voice was her own and she felt at home with herself, for all that.

Perhaps the reason Emma was such a happy, confident young miss was because she had been loved all her life and treated well by those she loved. In turn, she had always appreciated and loved those in her small world and had never had cause to know jealousy, strife, or envy. She also had no reason to rebel or fret, as after the long war, peace ruled once again in her father's house.

Yes, Emma knew who she was and knew her place in the scheme of things. She had many friends and was usually in the midst of the social circles that were comprised by the people of standing in the community. She looked forward to attending many more activities since the advent of warm weather, but she had always been happier at home than anywhere else. *Yes, I enjoy the outings to the theater, concerts, and cotillions, as well as to other plantations for holidays and celebrations, yet I'm always eager to get back home to Summers Bluff.* She wondered why that was when most of her friends lived to go to town.

Summers Bluff plantation, which started as a rough, one-storied log cabin, now boasted a typical white-columned colonial home with well-appointed outbuildings. It was perched along the bluff of the Savannah River, southwest of Savannah. Home to the Summers family for four generations, it was known for producing some of the finest-quality cotton and rice in the South. Emma's family had also been known for their Christian hospitality and genuine goodwill for all four generations of plantation living. Emma felt that after such a tragic war that had caused the upheaval of their lives and very existence, things were finally becoming somewhat normal again.

As normal as it could be with her brother, Fletcher, having been reported killed in that awful war. She wondered how the South, or North for that matter, could ever function with so many men lost and their families left so desolate. Never mind how the nation could ever cohere again; could they ever be able to forgive and be brothers again, or would it end up in a vicious cycle of suspicion giving way to frustration and fear giving way to anger and more distrust?

Callers had started coming around when Emma was fifteen. While some came with romantic notions, many just loved Emma's sincerity, friendliness, and ease of conversation. The young bucks knew she could be trusted with their secrets. She knew how to listen and was genuinely interested in what they had to say. She always told them what she thought about whatever was on their minds. Since she had no real romantic interest in any of them, she had been able to cultivate rich and comfortable friendships with all of them.

Even all her friends' beaus would visit and ask her what they should do in one situation or other with their ladies fair. Yes, she had plenty of visitors and plenty of opportunities for romance, but none from the quarter she wanted and hoped for.

The young women in her circle of friends knew of her friendships with their beaus, but Emma didn't evoke their jealousy for all her beauty and poise, because she showed kindness, love, and loyalty to them all in many ways and many times over. She was loath to flirt for the sake of flirting, and so was held in high esteem with both genders of friends.

Later that morning, Emma felt the stifling heat as soon as she entered the stand-alone brick kitchen on the backside of the house. "Granny Thornton! It's becoming a scorcher today. It's just too hot to be roasting those hens!" cried Emma. "Mercy me, but even Papa said one of your delicious cold plates would do nicely for dinner this noon."

Old Granny just nodded her head and kept on basting her birds, as she considered what would be good to serve for the supper meal. She decided that she would serve a cold plate of leftover hens from dinner for the evening supper, and said so.

Of course, Bessie was the cook and Granny the helper, but old Granny did whatever she felt up to, and making decisions was mainly what she felt up to these days. Bessie loved the old soul and always had let her have her way, saying, "That's good, Granny. There'll be plenty of chicken left over from dinner with just the three of 'em now."

Granny had been her papa's nanny, as well as her brother's and hers, and was the oldest person on the plantation. She still took a hand in seeing after them, as they all certainly still needed her presence in their lives, as she was thought of as family.

Granny hummed her hymns and wished she could see just a little better. Her old eyes had been failing her of late, but she never let on, because there was plenty of time to worry the missus over something like that. *I'll jest keep on keepin' on till I drop, I will. Jest like me granny did and her granny afore her,* she thought, grateful to still be of use in her dotage.

But all in all, I've given life a pretty good run, haven't I? Isn't me back still straight, and haven't I the most part of me own teeth left in me mouth? And who had nary a white hair on her head till long past her fiftieth birthday if it wasn't me, ol' Granny Thornton?

Yes, that birthday had been more than thirty years ago. So what if her eyes fuzzed a bit and she had to have Bessie thread her needle more oft than not? Worse things were happening to people all round her, so she would not be feeling sorry for herself one bit. She would carry on the best she could. *Have we not come through the awful war but half a decade ago, and are we not doin' fine as ever ye please these days?* she asked herself, as she continued her musing.

Ah, but there it was! All of us had not come through the war, had we now? 'Twas the young Master Fletcher— he had not come through the war. And that sad it was. Sad enough to break the strongest heart, she mused.

Granny Thornton could recollect it as if it had been but yesterday, as she remembered the letter that had announced Fletcher had been killed. *The master and missus, who never did a bad thing in all their born days, were brought low by that tragedy— ol' Granny can avow to that,* she thought. She shook her head in the sadness she always felt when thinking of the young one.

She could remember the first news that came back in '63 was that the young master's name was to be found on the missing list in the *Tribune.* Worrying about his safety had been their lot in life since the beginning of the war. That was until that overwhelming next letter had arrived announcing his death, and then worry had turned into a disbelief that had been like a pall that settled over the plantation. Nary a dry eye was to be seen around the place for days.

Granny Thornton let her mind wander as she basted her birds. She had always said Master Fletcher was most beloved, man and boy, and there was no one who could tell her differently. *It seems so long ago that he was lost to us, and still, 'tis like we're expectin' his footfall in the hall or on the stairs, but it never comes, mores the pity,* she thought as she turned her attention to her cooking.

When Emma thought Granny had not heard her, she asked with a hint of concern, "Did you hear me, Granny?"

"Missy, don't you be worryin' none about ol' Granny. I can take the heat, I can, 'cause me bones are always cold these days. I'm after bastin' these hens, and when they're served, your papa will be thankin' ol' Granny, I'm thinkin'. I raised that boy from a pup, and well ye know it. I reckon I always know what he likes after all these years! Why, the young master loved them as much, too!" she said, the sadness still in her old eyes. Granny had been deeply hurt over Fletcher's death and still spoke of him most days.

Yes, Emma remembered how her brother could put away Granny Thornton's cooking. He always did her table justice—breakfast, dinner, and supper. He was the last one to ever be late to the table, and he had rarely needed to be called.

"Yes, Granny, he did love to eat your cooking," she allowed. Emma saw the sadness and patted her shoulder, as she hurried from the kitchen to gain the privacy of her own room. *To escape the heat 'cause it makes my eyes water*, Emma told herself.

Once in her room, she crossed over to the mantle and picked up a picture of Fletcher in his Confederate uniform. She missed him every day of her life. After all this time, she still could not believe he was truly gone, as she brushed away an unbidden tear. But she had never believed he was dead somewhere, probably because there had been no funeral. That she had not seen his face in death was why she still had hope of seeing him again.

Well, the report of Fletch's death could have been a mistake. Why, with the carnage and chaos of that horrid war, who could be sure of every soldier's fate? And were there no errors in their record keeping, pray tell? Of course they could have made mistakes! After all, they were just men, and tired, and hungry, and defeated men at that.

She put down the picture and tried to turn her mind to other matters. She could do that now. Not in the beginning, but she could now. Ah, the beginning — after the awful shock of the news— but no, she wouldn't think on that now. It was too fine a day. She straightened her shoulders and shook off the memory of that awful time. She would think of nothing, save what was immediately before her. Surely, the past was as dead as were all the good men who had fought that horrible war, never to return home. And she knew tomorrow, no doubt, she would have enough to worry about, come to that.

Chapter 2

he cotillion is taking place in Savannah this Saturday. Isn't that the most awaited and frivolous event this spring? Emma asked herself, trying to work up some enthusiasm for it. With so many friends and acquaintances killed in action, to say nothing of the many maimed, a ball in her opinion wasn't necessarily the best place to try to carry on a semblance of past festive traditions. It was more likely to have just the opposite effect. It would make all the more evident how many young men in their prime were missing. But, society didn't like change, and the sooner they could get on with some of their traditions, the better they would like it, and the more control over their circumstances they would think they had.

However, it would be splendid for all the young belles just coming of age and attending their first ball. They had no fond memories of the grander balls of the past before the war, and would have no reason to see it in a lesser light as those who could remember. Emma had come of age during the war, but had not been presented at the cotillion after her seventeenth birthday, as she normally would have done. She had refused to be presented after news of her brother's death and had agreed to do so only at the cotillion the previous Christmas.

Her parents couldn't blame her when she had refused to be presented right after they had learned of Fletcher's death. It was all they could do to get through the normal daily routines the year after Fletcher had had been reported killed, so they had thrown themselves into doing what it took to make the plantation prosper once again. After the first year's harvest was sold, Josiah Summers was able to replace some of the milk cows, chickens, and hogs that had been taken during the war.

Many of the cotton-producing plantations around Summers Bluff had been sold off, mostly due to unpaid taxes that had increased. Northern bankers were buying up mortgages and calling in notes. A great deal of land had been divided into small farms and was being worked by freed slaves and poor whites—sharecroppers for the new owners—and all of them growing cotton.

The demand for cotton had been high after the war since Southern cotton had only been available in greatly diminished amounts for the five years of war, due to Northern blockades. However, the overabundance of cotton produced after the war resulted in the soft price of cotton they were now dealing with.

Josiah had had the wisdom to rotate and fertilize his crops long before it had become customary. With so many small farms growing cotton, rather than food, it left the food supply in dire need. Josiah had seen the benefit of diversifying and planting more food crops and less cotton to meet the growing demand for food, which yielded higher prices for his crops.

He took what little money he had left, after replacing the livestock and planting mostly food crops, and bought the best-quality cottonseed he could and planted just a few acres of cotton. From what he had heard tell, those few acres would yield enough high-quality cottonseed from the first harvest to plant several more acres the next year. After a few years of that, if the price of cotton had improved, he planned to plant more cotton using this high-quality seed, but that would be depending upon the food situation.

He had seen fields of cotton produced by the high-dollar cottonseed; it had produced much superior cotton, with larger bolls and more bolls on each stem, than the seed they had been forced to use during the war. Not that it had mattered all that much then, as the Yanks were as apt as not to set cotton fields ablaze on their march through the South. But it looked like he would be sticking to growing food crops for a while yet.

With having milk cows again, Josiah sold the excess milk, butter, and cheese from the creamery and meat from their slaughterhouse. He had realized high profits from those endeavors for the past four years.

The cotillion was upon them, but Emma still was not anticipating it as much as others were. She wasn't quite sure why that was, because surely every young miss loved to dress in their finery, go to a ball and be merry, while handsome young bucks danced with them or admired them from the sidelines.

Usually, Emma thought.

As some situations tend to be eclipsed by others, so it was that all thoughts of the cotillion had been overshadowed by the fact that the day after the ball, Emma's parents planned to take their first journey since the war. Emma's mama, Miss Tilley Summers, was the daughter and only child of Judge Wainwright and Judith Callaway of Callaway Court in Philadelphia. Grandfather Callaway had suffered a stroke, and even though he seemed to be on the mend, Grandmother Judith had summoned them, and they had felt the need to go. Miss Tilley had not seen them since the war had been declared nine years before, so a good visit with her parents was long overdue.

They planned to visit her people there in the place where she had been born, reared, presented, and married. For all the pomp and circumstance that Miss Tilley had known at her own debut, she had realized that she would not have been able to provide the same for Emma in turn, had she chosen to come out when she had been seventeen. So it was just as well that she hadn't wanted to be presented then.

Not that her dear child cared one fig about that, but Miss Tilley certainly had. But now she could finally once again afford the kind of finery Emma would wear to the upcoming cotillion, just as she had for the last Christmas cotillion when she had been presented.

Emma had simply not wanted her parents to go on this proposed journey. Of course, she wanted her mother to see her parents again, and they all had been concerned for Grandfather Callaway. Not being a self-centered girl, she couldn't understand why she didn't want them to go. She called it just an uneasiness that seemed to hover over the very thought of their leaving. She knew it was unreasonable to feel like that, but she couldn't seem to help herself.

She knew she would miss them terribly, probably because ever since Fletcher had been reported dead, they had scarcely let her out of their sight and she would be lonely without their nearly constant company. It had been kin to a miracle that they had even consented to go up North without her in the first place. Had it not been for her grandfather's stroke, she knew they wouldn't have gone then.

The prosperity of the plantation had made the trip to Philadelphia possible. Emma's parents were also planning to purchase more furnishings for the plantation similar to those that been destroyed or stolen during the war. It had been a downright shame how the Yankees had pillaged, plundered, and destroyed, but of course there had been exceptions. And mind, no doubt the Rebs had done their share of the same in the North, as well. Then, too, some things seemed to have just walked out of the house all by themselves.

That they had been subjected to such an insult as people—guests or even kin—coming into their home and leaving with a priceless canvas rolled up in their trunks or other valuable objects was unthinkable. But the unthinkable had happened and some precious things had vanished.

Emma had speculated numerous times what else could be the cause of the disappearances just at the outbreak of the war, but had not come up with any answers. They had missed several small things, and no one had gotten to the bottom of it.

However, her papa would never hear of a thought that any of the friends or family members, who had stayed with them from time to time, would have done such a thing. Nor could he imagine anyone about the place being so discontent as to go to thieving. He had liberated his slaves some years before and still had prospered enough to take good care of them and to live well besides. He had always maintained that it must have been someone local who had taken advantage of them having guests to cover their misdeeds.

But later, after enemy troops had been in and out of their home, their valuables had been taken or destroyed, leaving them with practically a house devoid of all but the bare necessities. After the war they had been fortunate enough to buy some things from other plantations at auction, and also from others in town who had fared a bit better.

But hopefully, her parents would find some of their very own belongings in the North. Hadn't they heard of just such a thing happening recently to one of their neighbors? Couldn't the same thing happen for her parents?

Emma knew she would have to keep herself busy while they were gone to help pass the time before their return. She had already seen to her wardrobe; it was in order for the coming summer's outings. Everything was far from the way it was before the war, but they were comfortable enough to have nice clothing once again, and she had her share. She didn't need anything else, but custom demanded a few new gowns each spring and fall. Now that they could afford them, her mama would no doubt see she got them.

Miss Tilley had planned to have them made up North and get them back home in plenty of time before Emma would need them for the coming social whirl of summer. One minor advantage was that none of the young misses from around there would have the same gowns as she would. Not that Emma was all that vain, but even though fabrics in Savannah were beautiful enough, the dressmakers there did not have the creativity the dress shops in Philadelphia and Boston had.

Mama loves to shop, and the hats she'll bring home for me will be exquisite, Emma thought. She had strong feelings of love and affection for her mama. *Hats are always mama's weakness. Everyone knows that,* and chuckled at the thought. Yes, Miss Tilley's only daughter would have the loveliest hats around, and what girl or woman couldn't use another lovely hat?

Her thoughts ran to her mama. She always enjoyed her mama and was proud of her, knowing that even though she loved to shop and live well, she was not a frivolous woman. *Mama is a smart woman who has a deep faith in God and in her marriage. She surely takes her mothering to heart. She adored Fletch, as she adores me, and has raised us as the good book said. I still remember the evenings we all would sit in front of the fire and read the bible. Fletch and I learned so many bible verses that way.*

Yes, her mama believed that everyone should be guided by their beliefs, so there should be no great difference between their internal beliefs and their outward behavior. She had always said that while a body had the opportunity, he or she should do right and love well while it was called 'today.' She would say that death would come to every mother's son and usually long before it was welcome. Therefore, people should live in such a way that when that day came, they could meet it without regrets.

Yes, her mama was nothing if not diligent, and she took all her responsibilities seriously. Nonetheless, she lived life to the fullest in the joy of her salvation and the gladness of a clear conscious and a made-up mind.

Papa agreed with mama's philosophy; he always allowed that you couldn't live wrong and die right and that dying right was the main purpose for living, from the human point of view.

She couldn't think about her mama without her thoughts turning to her papa. *Yes, papa has surely suffered more than anyone else on the place since we lost Fletcher. He was the son and heir, and they had a wonderful rapport in every area of life. They worked and played together, walked the fields, hunted in the woods, and prayed together until it was as if each were a mirror image of the other in the things that mattered.*

When papa's disbelief in Fletcher's death finally gave way to his acceptance that he was truly gone, he had sunk into a valley of despair so deep that we worried whether or not he would emerge from it with his mind intact.

They all could easily remember the time when Josiah Summers had come out of the study one day during the midst of that trial and demanded to have a long-overdue conversation with his heir. They were all beside themselves, knowing that their worst fears had been realized and that his mind had gone for sure. *That was until he looked at me and said, "Come, daughter, we have things to discuss about your plantation."*

We needn't have concerned ourselves unduly, because he hadn't become lost in his despair. He had merely shut himself away for a bit and had withdrawn from the living only to grieve for the dead. But for all that, surely he had been letting the Lord heal his broken heart, too, as he had come out stronger and had determined to go on with God, just the same as he had done when God had given him the son in the first place.

She faced the memory with a renewed determination to be all she could be to her papa, whatever that might demand of her, or however long it took. Still, she knew that could never make up for the loss he had suffered by losing Fletcher.

Chapter 3

Whenever Emma made the trip to town or anywhere else, her best friend, Kitty Thornton, always accompanied her. She and Kitty, being the same age, had been raised together, and seeing as how Granny Thornton was Kitty's grandmother, they were always together.

Kitty was her best-loved, bosom friend in the world. She was smart and funny, as all the Irish had their own sense of humor. She was as pretty and petite as Emma was pretty and tall. She, too, was redheaded and had a temper to match, but she was kind and good to everyone, in spite of the spitfire she could muster if called for.

She had spent her formative years in Ireland, but had come over to live with her granny when she was eight. She had never lost her Irish speech or mannerisms, since her granny still spoke and acted in the old way. She was a delightful girl and was fiercely loyal to Emma. They lived in splendid harmony as they thought the same on just about everything. Granny used to allow that they were more identical than twins.

Big Joe was the stable master at Summers Bluff and they didn't call him 'Big' for nothing. He was the biggest man anyone in those parts had ever seen. He had taught both the Summers children and Kitty to ride when they had been little bitty things. When they were older, he taught them to care for their mounts. He was patient and witty and more like an uncle to them than the stable master, and all the children adored him. They called him the 'gentle giant'. The gaiety and laughter they all had shared had been wonderful times in a childhood free from worry or cares.

If their mama or Granny Thornton had known what all he had allowed them to get away with, Emma knew they would have been in their places in the corner repenting and thinking about how they should have acted right.

Big Joe had a real knack for caring for sick animals around the plantation, which was probably due to his deep compassion and love for all living things, especially the horses. Josiah Summers had a good many horses. Fletcher had started accompanying him to Kentucky on buying trips when he was young, maybe around ten. Josiah had wanted to teach him everything he could about every aspect of plantation life, and so he passed on all of his working knowledge to his son, as his father had done with him.

Josiah and Big Joe had put a lot of time and energy into the horses and into teaching Fletcher, and both enterprises had paid off handsomely. Because of his deep love of horses and riding, Fletcher had paid attention and had learned quickly. By the time he was finished with his regular schooling, he was considered somewhat of a connoisseur of horseflesh.

Big Joe had known what the horses wanted or needed before they had, and he'd passed on that ability to Fletcher. By the time he was full grown, Fletcher could see a horse in the field and know that it was ailing, and after a quick look, he could usually tell you why, and knew what to do about it.

Emma's brother could also hold his own whenever he was bargaining with dealers and other horse buyers. He could keep his head during a feverish horse auction, regardless of how much he had wanted a particular horse. But by looking at him, you would have thought he couldn't have cared less about it.

But he was Josiah Summers' son. He had always maintained a calm, respectful spirit. That self-control had caused all who knew him to have confidence in him, and that in turn had bolstered his confidence in himself.

He and Big Joe had a mutual fondness and respect for each other that had continued until Fletcher went to war. Later, after he had been reported dead, Big Joe had fond memories of Fletcher, as if he had been there in the flesh. The boy had truly been mourned since the news of his passing.

After Fletcher was grown, unless Josiah or his son was driving the buggy, Big Joe had always been the family driver on Josiah's standing orders, as he was the best there was.

Big Joe had proven himself years before on the day Miss Tilley and the children were on an outing. The weather had turned nasty and wet, and they were on their way home. Another buggy tried to pass them just before the creek, but the driver was going way too fast, considering the condition of the roadway.

While passing them, the horse of the other buggy had shied at the upcoming covered bridge and the buggy had slid into theirs, forcing them over a small embankment. Their buggy had overturned and had landed partly in the water.

Most of them had been thrown clear and hadn't suffered any real harm, as they had landed on a soft, sandy area, but Emma had been trapped inside the buggy. Without stopping to collect himself, Big Joe had waded into the water and had turned the buggy right side up and pulled Emma to safety before the others had even gotten to their feet. So it was that her papa had never let anyone other than Fletcher or Big Joe drive Miss Tilley or the children anywhere on any outing when he was not present.

It had been that way concerning Emma from her first outing without her parents. Big Joe would probably drive her honeymoon carriage to a steamer bound for somewhere in Europe, or some other faraway port, when the time came.

Not that Emma was anticipating marriage anytime soon. After all, she was only going to be twenty come September. It was true that many of her friends were already engaged, and some even married with children, but Emma was in no real hurry. She considered marriage a forever thing, and besides, there was nobody of her acquaintance with whom she was considering marriage. Pastor Jake came to mind and held there for a long moment.

Truth be told, Pastor Jake Jackson was the one she had wanted to come calling. Although he had been a frequent visitor at the house for the past two years, whenever he called, he had talked more with her parents than with her. Emma had been as patient back then as a seventeen-year-old could be, while Pastor Jake was as conscious of her age as he was of her beauty, and so had held his peace. She couldn't quite figure out why he hadn't seemed to want to court her, and she wondered if he would ever get around to it. While that was painful to her at times, she still had a certain hope for a future with him.

But thinking of Jake Jackson was something she tried not to spend too much time doing. She figured she'd have plenty of time for that once he declared himself to her, but it was nearly summer, she was young and carefree, and had the rest of her life to think about marriage.

Chapter 4

Philadelphia September 1865

A reddish-brown-haired, well-built young man with emerald-green eyes and a pensive look stood in the doorway of a farmhouse in the countryside outside Philadelphia. He looked down the lane thinking that he should be going somewhere, but he couldn't quite think where.

His wife, Elizabeth, came up behind him and gently laid her hand on his arm. He turned and looked into her soft-blue eyes, and the sad look that she knew all too well crossed his face again. She knew how much he loved her, but she also knew that he was a haunted man.

One of the soldiers, Private Charles Purdue, who had brought him down the lane to her door a year earlier, had gone to a military officer's academy in that area, but the war had broken out before he could finish his training. He had been from a well-off Southern family and was acquainted with Elizabeth McWilliams, as they had moved in the same circles of society during his schooling.

Elizabeth was a Southern lady, who had married a Yankee before the war, and that she was a Confederate sympathizer,

Charles knew to be fact. They both had been present at several social functions where there had been many and long discussions about the issues threatening to lead to war. She was not outspoken in her support of the South, but any Southerner could tell she sympathized with them, by the looks she gave at some of the comments she heard, and also by what she did not say.

Charles felt she could be trusted and that hers were the best accommodations Fletcher could hope for in his situation. Charles told her that the soldier lying before her had escaped, along with them, from the horrid Union prison camp some miles from her home. Charles said that he had been wounded during the escape two nights previously and that he was in no condition to travel farther.

She had reluctantly agreed to take him in. Her farm was isolated, and she could always pass him off as a relative if need be, maybe as a cousin from back home who had come to help her with the farm after her husband had died in the war. The gunshot wound he had sustained could be passed off as a hunting accident if need be. Yankees would know that it would have been nearly impossible for him to have gone home while the war was raging. Yes, that would probably be believable sometime in the future, if necessary. One could only hope.

After they had helped her get him into bed, they were off again in haste. They told her his name was Fletcher and that he was from Georgia and then they were gone.

She wasn't looking for trouble with the Yankee army, but she couldn't send a Southern gentleman in his condition back to that awful place. That winter would find thousands sleeping in tents in the cold Philadelphia camp, just as they had done the previous winter. Word was that the water there was not fit to drink, food supplies and medicines were next to non-existent, and disease was rampant. Due to their general poor health and lack of food and blankets, some soldiers had frozen to death the previous winter. The same fate would no doubt await the soldiers again during the upcoming winter. Yes, she would be glad to keep him there as long as he needed her.

When he had awakened he couldn't remember what had happened to him. In fact, he couldn't remember anything of his past. He remembered things, but not events or people. Not his name or where he was from, although his Southern drawl told him it was somewhere in the deep South. That he was an escaped Confederate soldier he didn't doubt, especially after Elizabeth had enlightened him as to what she knew of him. She had told him he was from Georgia and that his name was Fletcher, but that meant nothing to him. At least it was a beginning, something to go on sometime in the future when the war was over and he would try to find his way home.

He had no idea, however, how he would reestablish his identity and find his home and family, but he somehow knew he had faith in God, who would tell him what to do when the time came.

Chapter 5

The cotillion had proved to be a diversion from plantation life for Emma, but somehow it had seemed rather empty and shallow all the same. It had been a beautiful event, to be sure, with all the young maidens dressed in all their best finery and the young men looking so handsome. The men who still could had whirled the ladies around the ballroom till all hours, amid the laughter and great conversation that everyone had enjoyed immensely.

But surely, there is more to life than dancing and flirting. Of course, it had been fun trying to flirt with Jake Jackson. If only he would flirt back some. For the past two years, she had been sweet on him, and she felt he was just as interested in her.

As he was the pastor of their church and a single man, those facts were uppermost in his mind. He conducted himself with high honor and didn't make it a habit of showing any of the women special attention.

However, there were times when she would feel his eyes upon her and when she sought him out, he actually had always been looking at her. Many long, deep looks had passed between them. Love looks, if what she had seen between others was anything to go on.

At those times, he would approach her to show her he knew what she was thinking and let her know he felt the same. He wanted to spend time with her, but someone would always ask her to dance or ask to fetch her a drink. And the other girls would come and talk to her just so they could gush over Jake.

It wasn't easy for an honorable man to find private time alone with a woman. He always let her know he resented those interferences as much as she did by the helpless look of frustration on his face. He had danced with her once and told her he was sorry his winter schedule had kept him so occupied. He had told her that when spring had fully arrived and warmer weather set in for good, he would be freed up and hoped that she would be, too. Emma had taken that to mean that they would start a courtship soon, and had been thrilled at the prospect.

She could get lost in the looks he had given her, because she knew he didn't know how to flirt, and even if he did, he still wouldn't have. His adoring looks were coming from tender emotions deep in his heart that he couldn't hide. She was nineteen years old, but part of the problem was that she didn't really know how to flirt either. If flirting meant giggling and fanning herself and batting her eyes, she'd be loath to do that, so she guessed she would just have to forget flirting!

But if he didn't declare himself soon, she told herself that she might be driven to declare herself to him, heaven forbid! She knew how to speak the truth; surely, speaking the truth in love couldn't be that much different.

Emma's mama and papa were leaving the next day for Philadelphia and beyond, and she would keep herself busy overseeing the plantation while they were gone. It ran like a well-oiled machine, needing little attention from her; at least that had been the case when her papa was there.

Jefferson Lewis would probably think it a mere nuisance that Josiah had placed Emma in charge of the plantation while he was away. She didn't think Lewis was one to take instruction from a woman. But he knew her papa would be obeyed and dared not resist. However, should anything go very amiss, she basically would be there to notify her papa and get his instructions for Lewis.

It wasn't that she didn't know about plantation life, for she did. For years, she had tended the flowers, helped tend the fruit trees, and knew how to care for the vegetables in the conservatory. She had also assisted her mama with whatever was needed inside the house. She had watched and later assisted Big Joe and Fletcher with the foalings, and also when the goats had been born. She knew how to oversee their former slaves, that she had known and loved all her life. Every aspect of plantation life was Emma's propensity.

But her main responsibility for the past three years had been to keep the accounts and handle the money, which she did to her papa's satisfaction. She knew the prices of all purchases and pretty much when supplies needed to be restocked. She watched Josiah make arrangements for shipping cotton and rice and knew about making said transactions.

Josiah oversaw her work, to be sure, explaining the whys and wherefores of the decisions he had and would make, as he had been training her for the responsibilities she would inherit once he was gone.

Emma had proven herself deft with figures and knowledgeable about business principles and would rank her alongside the smartest business minds in the North, where much being heard of the suffragettes making political speeches and running their own businesses. Of course, women could match wits with men in the business arena, given the chance, not that most women wanted to. However, the good Lord had given wisdom to male and female alike, and women had been matching wits with men in the marriage arena for eons. Women had also been managing large plantation homes and castles and the like for centuries.

But all the same, women like Miss Tilley worked hard. They had made their homes places of peace because they understood what their main abilities were as women. They provided the kind of comfort and support their men needed for them to be able to handle the cares and disappointments of life, including reversals in finances, crop failures, depravities of war, and the likes.

Her mother always told her that just as surely as a structure needed good support, so did a marriage. Just as such support was under the structure and didn't show, so must the support of a good woman be kept inconspicuous, even though evidence of that support could be seen all around in their peaceful, daily lives.

Her papa, well aware of his wife's support, was unlike most men, in that the majority of them believed a woman's place was in the home, and even most women would agree with them. Due to such thinking, women had little opportunity for advancement in the public forum, whether they were in the North or the South.

Someday women, who don't have a man like Papa to provide for them, would no doubt sooner or later be thrust into responsible positions, Emma thought. *The war has surely meant that women have had to become more self-sufficient while they worked to keep businesses and homes intact while their men were off to war.*

Josiah cherished a good mind and sought to cultivate it in both his children. Emma had been trained and nurtured in business principles by a man who recognized her good judgment and business acumen. He had been truly thankful for her help since Fletcher was gone.

He took comfort in knowing that when he passed on, he wouldn't be leaving a helpless daughter to struggle alone with the burdens of a large plantation with no understanding or hope of success. Knowing his dear Miss Tilley wouldn't be much good at what would be facing her after his death, he counted on Emma to bridge the gap and run the place as he had. Hopefully, that would be a long time off, but one never knew.

Chapter 6

The front door chime sounded. Emma heard the voice of their nearest neighbor, Cal Morgan, her father's solicitor, who had come to call. She knew he had been aware of her since she was sixteen, as he had tried to court her when she was nearly seventeen and several times since. She had not cared for him, to say the least. For all the manners he always displayed, she knew he wasn't what he seemed to be. He had changed of late; he had become much more hardened in his tone and more impatient with her refusals of his marriage offers, all while being soft-spoken and polite in front of her parents.

Hypocrite! she thought while stamping her foot. *If only papa would find another solicitor!*

Even his reputation with his slaves had left much to be desired. She knew he had changed, or more likely, since she was grown, she was seeing him as he really had been all along. His momentary politeness in front of people would not have stood the test of a courtship. Of that she was certain.

Her papa hadn't had much to do with Cal; he had always dealt with his father for all his legal needs since becoming master of Summers Bluff, but he could probably see right through Cal, nonetheless. Certainly, he didn't know about the proposals, as she had chosen to not even recognize them.

While there was much more to Morgan than met the eye, one thing she did know was that Morgan was not the fine, upstanding Southern gentleman he acted and was purporting to be. In truth, she had no idea what kind of man he really was, but she felt that if she were favored from above, she would never have to find out.

She determined to make her escape out the morning room French doors onto the verandah, but before she could, she heard Jesse May saying, "Yes sir, Mista Morgan. Miz Emma surely is ta home. She's yonder in the morning room with her flowers. I'll just take you in."

"No need, Jesse May, I know the way. Go back to your chores now."

The gall of the man! Emma thought. She had not heard his footsteps stop at that exchange, so she could just imagine his long stride closing the distance between them before she could reach the doors. Sure enough, he called out, "Why, Miz Emma, a lovely morning, isn't it? And what a picture you make, you with your flowers and all," he gushed.

She merely nodded in acknowledgment of his presence.

"I came by to inform your father that I will be by later this afternoon to fetch them to Savannah to catch the steamer north. Should be fine weather for our trip."

Emma was taken aback. "*Our* trip? Are you saying you are to accompany mama and papa to Philadelphia?"

"That's right, I am." Cal answered with a smug, self-satisfied look. "You know I am a patient man, Emma." He used her given name alone, without the required "Miss" or her permission to do so. "But I have asked you more than once to do me the honor of making you mistress of Morgan's Creek," he said. "So while you are considering it, I thought this would be a wonderful opportunity for me to meet your Philadelphia relatives and be of whatever assistance I can to your folks on the trip."

She couldn't respond. She was speechless with fury at his presumption. He had pushed himself in on her parents and Philadelphia relatives and was assuming much to think she would ever consider marrying him.

He hurried on, undaunted. "I also think it a fine idea to replenish some of my own treasures that were lost to the enemy during the war. I wouldn't want you to feel my home inferior to that which you are accustomed."

What nerve! He's going to sweet-talk mama and papa and all the Callaways so they will all want me to marry him! I don't know what it is, but there is a darkness about him, she thought as she fiddled with the flowers. *I have never trusted him!*

"Well, I surely will inform papa of your message," finally finding her voice. She had decided it best not to acknowledge his ridiculous comment. "I pray you all have a safe trip."

"Yes, indeed! I wouldn't want anything to happen to any of us now, as you and I are sure to be coming to an understanding soon, if you will." He seemed to sneer.

It was all she could do to control an outburst. *Like I would sit across the breakfast table from you every morning for the rest of my life, not to mention other things I would have to do!* She quietly but firmly replied, "Sir, I have never led you to believe I am entertaining the proposals of marriage you have given me on a few occasions now. In fact, I have discouraged you at every turn and have refused outings with you or even carriage rides on Sundays. We are not close to an understanding unless you have finally come to understand that I will not marry you!" Her voice trembled with the impotent fury she felt.

"Come, come, my dear. You are overwrought. What with your parents leaving you here while they are gone, you have worked yourself up into somewhat of a frenzy, I fear."

"Mr. Morgan, I have not worked myself into anything! I am as clearly, and as simply as I know how, telling you that I refuse your proposals. All of them! Please refrain from ever mentioning this to me again, as I will take it as an affront should you be so inclined. I'm sure you wouldn't want me to burden Papa with all of this."

She flounced from the room leaving him seething in her wake. She was grateful for one thing. If he were in Philadelphia, she would not have to worry about him calling on her while her folks were away.

She was glad Aunt Caroline would be arriving that day to be her chaperone. She was her papa's sister and lived on up the river a ways in the old Summers family home place that great-grandfather Summers had grown up in. It was now occupied by their grandfather's sister, great-aunt Arabella and her family.

Her papa's sister, Aunt Caroline, had lived with them in the big old house ever since her parents had passed away long before the war, as she had never married. Aunt Caroline would be glad of the opportunity to spend time with just Emma for the duration of her parents' journey.

Having Aunt Caroline here will be the best consolation I could have during my parents' absence, she thought with a half-smile. She still wished they weren't going.

She had left the room before she could have seen the flash of pure anger and hatred that contorted Cal Morgan's features. Had she seen that, she would have known that he would never take no as her answer.

It's just a matter of time, my insulting Miz Emma Summers, until I see you humbled and groveling to marry me! he thought. *Threaten me, Cal Morgan, with telling your papa of my interest in you? We'll see about you telling Josiah anything. Because of those haughty words, my dear, life as you know it, has just fallen to pieces!*

Chapter 7

*L*ittle more than a fortnight after her parents had left for Philadelphia, Emma received a long letter from her mama telling her that they had arrived safely and that all the family had wished that she had come with them, as they would have dearly loved to have spent time with their only granddaughter.

Her grandfather was as well as could be expected and except for the weakness of his right lower limb, he was recuperating. Grandmother Judith said that he had been grieving and pining to see his only child, and was elated when he saw his dear daughter's face, confirming the necessity of her decision to visit.

Miss Tilley told Emma all the family news and stories. She also told her about hearing of several lovely paintings and other treasures for sale that she knew Emma would welcome to their home. She wrote that the next day they were going with Cal Morgan to a small town a few miles outside Philadelphia to investigate reports of more available treasures.

She told Emma that they had just seen a theatre matinee performance of the new moving pictures that was all the rage. The performance only lasted a few minutes, but nevertheless, she had marveled at her experience of seeing pictures move, as had all the other theater patrons.

She related that after the matinee performance, they had all gone to the Emporium for a bite to eat. She described the delicious fare offered to customers in the soda fountain area of the store and said there were always people standing in line waiting for food service. My, but she reckoned they made a handsome profit on that novelty idea of serving food where they shopped. Indeed, the savory aromas wafting through the store made it almost impossible to leave without sampling the fare.

As to the suffragettes, they were still making speeches championing their cause. Talk was reaching them of women now in the Eastern law schools, so presumably there would one day be female attorneys and possibly even female judges, if one could imagine such a thing.

Her letter continued to say that her mother had heard of the many wonderful things going on in New York City, if one could believe them. They said that there was talk of building a railroad of some kind that required the train to travel completely underground! It would carry passengers quickly and unseen to their destinations. Without the gridlock of so many wagons and other means of commerce needed to service so large a city, to say nothing of the carriages used in personal travel to contend with on the streets, one could cross the city in an unbelievably short amount of time.

"Could anyone imagine such a thing?" her mama had written. She wrote that she herself would be afraid to enter such a contraption and would continue to choose the carriage as her means of conveyance.

She related many other interesting tales of happenings in the North. Just hearing from her mama was a breath of calming peace stealing over her. Emma had always loved to hear her mama speak, and as she read her words, she closed her eyes and nearly heard her mama's voice.

Aunt Caroline is so much like mama, even though she is papa's sister and not mama's, she thought, as her aunt sat spellbound while Emma read the letter aloud to her.

"How nice to hear from Tilley and Josiah and to find all is well!" Aunt Caroline remarked. "I know it is hard to wait to hear from loved ones that they have arrived safely at their destination, but I know they have been busy," she said.

"Tell me something, Emma. Do you think you will want to travel somewhat before you marry?"

"I should say I very much want to travel!" Emma replied. "Why, the man I marry could be a dreadful homebody and refuse to leave kith or kin to travel. No. On second thought, I would never marry anyone who refused to travel. It is so enlightening! New faces, new customs, new everything! I wouldn't want to travel continuously, mind you, as some seem to do, as I would never want to live anywhere but here. Of course, I haven't traveled farther than Philadelphia, and that was nine years ago! Why do you ask, Auntie?"

"Well, I am not old, but I do think if ever I am to travel, it should be soon. I'm the maiden aunt, after all, and that should count for something, as I can't just up and light out on my own. Perhaps we could travel, say to Europe together, you and I?"

"Why, Auntie! Of course, I would love to see the world with you! I can think of nothing greater! You know if only..."

"If only what, dear?" she asked. Then it dawned on her what Emma meant. "Oh, you mean if only Fletcher could have been here to go with us it would have been perfect? Yes, indeed, that would have been wonderful. I know how much you miss him," she crooned. "We all do, dear, but...well, we must make do, mustn't we? Don't be sad, little Emma." She patted her niece's hand. "Things will get better."

Little did she know how much time would have to pass or how much worse things would have to get before that prophecy would be fulfilled.

Chapter 8

*J*ust as supper was finishing, another summons came from the front door. *Who can that be?* Emma thought. She peered out the window. "It's Jamison from the postal and telegraph office," she said in bewilderment. "Lo, Auntie — seldom have we had two messages in the same week let alone the same day! What do you suppose it means? I do hope all is well," she murmured more to herself than to her aunt. She had a presentiment of something looming so monumental in front of her that it could swallow her up; something so much more immense than herself.

"Well, dear, if you'll open the door, we shall find out. Since you know it is just a lad, no need to stand on formality and wait for Jesse May," her aunt said.

"Yes, of course." Emma moved slowly to the door and opened it. A palpable fear fell upon her heart at the solemn and frightful look on young Jamison's countenance. He was blinking rapidly and looked for the world and all as if he would bolt and go back the way he had just come any second.

O Lord, what has happened that could make him look so fearful? Emma compelled herself to remain calm, but failed miserably. She couldn't speak; she just stared at him. Her sudden pallor, speechlessness, and tremors frightened the young man even more than he already was.

Aunt Caroline approached. "Young man, what news is this that you have brought us?" When he faltered, wringing his hat in his hand, she said more forcefully, "Out with it, young man, if you please!"

Young Jamison tried repeatedly and finally blurted out, "Ma'am, it is the worst possible news. I—I don't know how to tell you!" he stuttered, apparently failing to realize for the moment that he wasn't supposed to tell them, but to hand them the telegram.

Aunt Caroline looked at his white face and realized he could neither tell her the news nor hand her the telegram. She took the envelope from his shaking hand and saw that it was addressed to Emma. With an intense dread and fearful heart, she read,

"Tragic news Stop Buying trip necessitated overnight stay in country inn Stop Inn burned in the night Stop Neither Mother nor Father escaped Stop Am returning with them immediately for funeral Stop With deep sorrow Stop Cal Morgan."

Having read the telegram, Caroline Summers did something she had never done in her fifty-two years of life. She dropped to the floor in a dead faint.

Jamison, good boy that he was, had prepared himself for hysterics from the women, but not unconsciousness. He called for help, and Jesse May, running into the room and assessing the situation, fetched the smelling salts from a side table. They attended her and got her up and over to the sofa.

As if caught in a nightmare, Emma tried to run away from this scene, but her limbs wouldn't carry her a step. For what seemed like an eternity, she stared at the hateful yellow paper. She finally stooped and picked it up with icy fingers.

Chapter 9

*I*t's odd the things that one thinks of in the midst of a crisis. Emma remembered that when they had received word from the commander of Fletcher's regiment about his death, the hideous news had been on ordinary white letter paper.

If such awful news had come on ordinary white paper, then what dreadful news would present itself on this yellow one, known for bearing the news of the most devastating emergencies and tragedies? She read the inconceivable words with fear and trepidation. She read, but couldn't comprehend it. She read it again, and as it made sense, she trembled at those horrid words.

No! Not this! Noooooooo! Not this! No, no, no! Fletcher and now mama and papa! In a horrible fire! Oh, no! Oh, please, God! she screamed, internally.

"Help me, Jesus!" she whispered, nearly inaudibly. An enormous, immediate weakness settled upon her, at which, her knees threatened to no longer hold her upright. The thick blackness that had descended upon her, threatening to engulf her, finally succeeded.

When Emma came to, Jamison was cradling her head in his hands, and Aunt Caroline was waving the smelling salts under her nose. She sat up slowly. Everything came back to her. *Surely this cannot be real. Oh, Mama, my dear, sweet Mama! Papa! Papa! What shall I do without the two of you? You never prepared me for this … how could you have? How shall I live without you?* "Oh, Lord! Oh, Lord! Oh, Lord!" was all she could say.

Sometime later, when she had wept all she could, the doctor had been summoned and gave her a sedative. Granny and Aunt Caroline had put her to bed. When she calmed down some, she felt herself drifting to sleep. She suddenly had a question. *Cal? Why this dreadful news from him? Why not Grandfather Callaway?*

She prayed that the news of her parents' deaths had not given him another stroke. *No, we would have heard of that by now had such an awful thing happened. Morgan would have sent word,* she reasoned. She could only imagine how Morgan would have usurped Grandfather's rightful place to notify his granddaughter of her parents' death. *Of course, Morgan would be that possessive!*

All the grief that she was experiencing and her intense dislike of Morgan somehow merged in her mind, and all the pain of that devastating experience would forever be connected to Cal Morgan. Something akin to hatred in her, flared up against him in that moment.

Chapter 10

The bright sunlight streamed through the window of Emma's bedroom. She awakened and wondered what time it was, and glancing at the clock, saw it was ten o'clock. Why, *I've slept the whole morning away! When have I ever slept so late?* She felt a growing uneasiness. In the space of a heartbeat, she remembered what was wrong.

Oh, no! She remembered that the funeral was that afternoon. She had received the life-shattering news of her parents' death the previous evening; Morgan had sent the telegram from a port relatively close to Savannah. Now all she could do was wait for the ship to bring her parents the rest of the way home for the last time.

Emma had been given the sedative and that had kept her in the bed since shortly after she had received the life-shattering news. But she was awake now and wondering how she would ever get through the ordeal of the funeral and burial of her beloved parents.

Kitty had been looking in on Emma all the morning, and had taken up a position on a chair in the hall, waiting for her to awaken. When she heard Emma cry out, she summoned Granny Thornton and the others. When they entered her room, they found her totally shaken, as if the news of the loss of her parents had just been broken to her.

They hurt so badly for her and comforted her the best they could. Knowing where her strength would have to come from, they laid their hands on her and prayed. Bessie led the group. "Lord, you see our little sister here. She's hurtin' real bad and she's needin' you now like she ain't never needed anythin' before. You will help her, we know. But if you want to use us to comfort her some, we thank you, Lord, 'cause this is a mighty big time a trouble. In the name of Jesus we pray, amen."

When Emma had collected herself and Kitty had finished her toilette so that she was at least presentable, she learned her pastor had called on her last night and again this morning. She could not even imagine how she would get through this horrible time, but her mind was too foggy to even try to figure out what needed to be done or how to do it.

She had no proper mourning clothing, but Bessie had brought her one of her mama's black gowns. She was just a bit taller than her mama, but otherwise, the gown fit her slender frame. Never having seen herself in black, she was startled when she caught a glimpse of herself in the mirror hanging over the upstairs hall table when she automatically checked her skirt in the petticoat mirror below it. She swallowed with difficulty at both the unreality and the enormity of what was taking place. She steeled herself to carry on and made her way to the parlor to meet her pastor.

Jake Jackson had started praying for Emma and heading for Summers Bluff the moment he had done what was necessary to arrange for the funeral for the next day. He had been smitten with Emma for a couple of years, but he had been falling in love with her since a few months back at the Christmas Cotillion. That was when he realized that Emma was nineteen now and that she had grown into a beautiful young woman. He had let all guards down and had fallen hopelessly in love with her.

She and her family were among his regular church attendees, and he had found her to be a well-respected and kind-hearted young woman. He took note that she knew how to conduct herself appropriately, unlike some chits who couldn't put a sentence together without giggling or flirting and making a man uncomfortable.

She sang in the choir, donated her time and efforts working in the Ladies' Missionary Society, and helped whenever she could with whatever social functions were going on at the church.

Of course, he appreciated her gentle womanliness, to say nothing of her beauty. After all, he was her pastor, but he wasn't blind! Sometimes, he wished she would flirt with him more, as that would give him the confidence he needed to ask such a gorgeous woman if he could court her.

Yes, Emma Summers is a paragon of the ideal pastor's wife, he thought. What amazed him was that she seemed to care for him, as well. He had never seen her with a beau on any outing; she had always been in a group. Jake remembered the meaningful looks the two had shared at the Christmas cotillion, when Emma had been presented to society, and many looks since.

He had been unusually busy that winter; the majority of his time had not been his own. He had cared for the elderly and sick in his flock, and they were scattered all over the county, so he hadn't seen as much of Emma as he had hoped for.

But every time he saw her, he had come to care for her more. He had every intention of proposing to her that spring. Though he felt she cared about him, he had not seen her return his feelings as much as he had hoped she would. But, she was young and perhaps was just waiting for him to step up. He prayed the summer outings would give him opportunity to press his suit and win her hand.

It had been difficult to find any time to woo her at public assemblies, but he had been waiting until his time was once again his own during the hazy days of Savannah's summer to see more of her privately in the hopes of offering a proposal. He had been counting on a late summer or early fall wedding, and even though the next winter would still see him busy with the needs of others, he thought he might well be coming home to his wife at night.

Had he known about her parents' trip to Philadelphia before the last moment, he would have taken his chances of speaking to her papa and proposing before they left so he could have spent time with her as her fiancé during their absence and get to know her better. Her parents had planned to stay in Philadelphia until after the celebration of the resurrection festivities. But he had waited too long. Now he could not pursue her until her mourning period was over.

Jake had been looking forward to the summertime for many reasons, but he knew now the summer would be hurtful for her. She would be doing alone those things she had always done with her family. His goal was to be of help to her in the midst of this storm. He had prayed repeatedly for her to receive strength.

Now that he was face to face with her, noting her pallor, which stood out all the more against the color of such a gown, he took in her swollen, red eyes that testified to the fact that she was still in the throes of deep sorrow. He felt it to the quick, as her pain could never leave him untouched.

He took her hand and supported her elbow, leading her to the sofa. She had an unstable gait brought on, no doubt, by the shock of the tragic news and the sedative she had been given the night before.

He offered her his heartfelt condolences and confirmed to her that all the necessary arrangements had been made. Having seen that the announcement of their deaths had been broadcast and the funeral arranged, he wanted to be on hand should she need him. But by the time he had arrived at Summers Bluff the previous night, Emma had already taken the sedative and had gone to bed. She thanked him as well as she could for both visits. She was so grateful that he had come, but could barely get the words out.

Jake allowed her to speak when she could and remain silent as the need presented itself. She wept quietly, first with quiet sniffles, trying to control herself, but then she gave way to soul-wracking sobs. She was so vulnerable right now, but still Jake needed to take her in his arms to comfort her. For more than that he knew he could wait.

As he held her, Aunt Caroline quietly sat beside her holding her hand and allowing her own tears to course freely down her face. Only God could really help these precious ladies in their grief, but he would stay close to them all the same.

Chapter 11

The ship carrying the remains of the two people she loved most in the world arrived in the wee hours of the morning. The coffins holding the remains of her parents had been taken to Jake's church, where the funeral would be held later that morning. It occurred to her that their bodies would be marred beyond recognition and that the caskets would have to remain closed. She knew she would be denied the comfort of looking one last time on their beloved countenances, just as had been the case with Fletcher.

Emma felt that she wouldn't have been surprised in the least to hear that all the cows and other animals on the plantation had died, too, or that a sudden, terrible wind had blown the house down about her.

For mercy's sake, Lord, what kind of Job's plague am I in the middle of? Am I being punished? If that's the case, what have I done? She wasn't demanding that God explain himself, but merely prayed for enlightenment.

She received the answer to her prayer when Jake reassured her that God didn't kill family members to punish sin or transgression. That aside, he wondered what she could possibly have done that was wicked enough to deserve such a sentence of punishment from a good and benevolent Father, as losing both of her parents on the same day in a tragic manner. She knew in her heart that was true, but her mind was being tormented by grief and the need to know why.

All Savannah turned out on that warm, but windy March morning for the double funeral of some of the city's most beloved neighbors and friends. Jake accompanied her from the plantation to the church and didn't leave her side for a moment, except to deliver the eulogy.

Judge Joseph and Isabelle West, her papa's best-loved, lifelong friends, had been there to meet her at the church. The judge took her hands and tenderly drew her to his breast, where he wept right along with her, as did the majority of those in attendance.

The talk of their untimely deaths had been on everyone's lips. Josiah had been born and raised on the plantation, as his father and forefathers before him. He had taken a Yankee bride, to be sure, but she had turned out to be the jewel in his crown. Kind to the poor, she was, and known for her healing balms. She was never too tired or occupied to attend the sick on the plantation or on the neighboring estates. Matilda 'Miss Tilley' Summers would be missed as much as her Georgia-born-and-bred husband.

Many were the sincere accolades that Josiah and Miss Tilley received that day; while they couldn't hear them, their daughter certainly could and did. She was grateful that the people of Savannah had known, loved, and appreciated her parents so much. She got through the impossible ordeal of the funeral with the help of the Lord, Jake, her friends, and Aunt Caroline.

She felt that all she had been doing since receiving the devastating news was weeping or sleeping. However, since the funeral and hearing all the people's praise of her parents, she had cause to remember how strong and good her parents had been.

In the days and weeks ahead, she succeeded in shaking off the overwhelming despondency that had nearly done her in those first few days after she had received the telegram. She disciplined herself to think of how her mama and papa would have wanted her to conduct herself. She would not disgrace their memory by overmuch sorrow to the point of people thinking she had no faith in God or any hope.

She realized she had been close to where her papa must have been after Fletcher had been reported dead. She felt that if she didn't leave that sorrowful and despairing place quickly, she might never be able to. She had her faith and her friends, and she knew this would not be the last time she would be called upon to put her personal grief aside for the good of those around her. She rose admirably to the occasion.

Work was a healer, and she threw herself into the work her papa had trained her to do, body and mind. There was no one else but Emma to do it, so she did it. She placed her soul in the mighty hand of God, where she knew it would be safe. She let the rest roll on by her just like the rolling Savannah River.

Chapter 12

*I*t was not a fortnight later that Cal Morgan paid a call at Summers Bluff. Aunt Caroline was sitting in attendance upon Emma and wouldn't be persuaded to leave them alone, even for a few moments of private conversation, but sat across the room with her knitting. Cal lowered his voice so she couldn't easily pick up his words. But all the same, she could tell from the reaction he was getting from Emma that whatever he was saying was having a negative effect upon her. *The odious man! I can't see why she lets him come around. I'll have to take it up with her when he leaves.*

After some moments of conversation, Morgan produced some papers and handed them to Emma. She heard Emma audibly gasp and saw her put her hand to her mouth as she read them. Then she exclaimed, "This can't be true!"

Emma's aunt laid aside her knitting and crossed to where they sat. She demanded to know what was wrong. Emma had not the force of spirit to keep anything so unpleasant from her, and so handed her aunt the papers.

Caroline Summers read them and was aghast. "What nonsense is this? Why, Josiah Summers would no more borrow this much money from anyone than I would, much less from anyone like — well, anyway, he wouldn't have done it!"

"Madam, I don't wish to contradict you, certainly, but you hold his very notes. Surely, you recognize your brother's hand?"

"Yes, of course. This looks like his hand— but *is* it?" she asked.

"I'm sure I do not understand your inference, madam. If not his, then whose hand could it be?"

"Well, I can't rightly say, but I certainly can say whose it is not, and it is not Josiah's! I don't believe a word of these notes!"

"Madam, I assure you I have none but the best of intentions regarding the repayment of these notes. As you are no doubt aware, I have fondly hoped that one day your niece would consent to my making her the mistress of Morgan's Creek, and of course, should she consent to our marriage, these debts would naturally be cancelled to my wife."

"Your wife! I most certainly am not aware of any such thing! I have not heard of any such leanings on Emma's part!" she said in utter disbelief. She turned to Emma. "*Do* you have any such leanings, my dear?"

"Nay, Auntie, I do not and have told him so on several occasions. I have implored him not to mention it again," Emma said forcefully.

"Why, you blackguard! Coming here and the funeral not two weeks hence, and you ask her to be your wife when you know it's downright indecent in polite society to pursue her, with Emma yet in deep mourning! You seem to forget, sir, that she has lost not one, but both her parents! Furthermore, according to what she has just told us, she has asked you not to persist in your attentions. You should be horsewhipped, that's what!" she all but shouted at him.

"Very well, madam. Be that as it may, concerning the debts of Mr. Josiah, I assure you these notes will surely have to be dealt with sooner or later." For the life of him, he didn't know how he kept from shouting at them or worse, but he knew his day would come.

"I cannot see any other way of her paying them off," he said. "Even if there were sufficient cash on hand to cancel the debts, that would rob your niece of any money she would need to see to the running of the plantation," he wheedled.

"If they are not paid off, I would have no other choice but to lay a claim against the plantation, and it would have to be sold for repayment. She will surely see this great property of hers on the auction block before the month is out," he prophesied, finding it harder and harder not to raise his wicked hand against them right there and then.

"That being so, madam, you should encourage her to come to her senses and see that the only sensible way out, and for her own good, mind you, is to allow me to care for her in the manner to which she is accustomed."

He turned to Emma, a facsimile of a smile on his face. "Miz Emma, dear, surely you will change your mind after a good night's sleep. Pray take a drop of brandy wine to calm your nerves."

"She doesn't take strong drink, my good man, and nothing is wrong with her nerves that getting to the bottom of this won't cure. Good night to you," she said dismissively.

After a long pause, he said, "Fare thee well, ladies. I will return at a more suitable time."

He left the plantation in a barely controlled rage. *Caroline Summers will rue the day she ever had the audacity to speak so disparagingly to me! Time will come, so much sooner than they think, for me to show them with whom they are dealing! I'll make sure it's slow torture. As my wife, I will have many years ahead to make Emma pay!*

Chapter 13

Pennsylvania 1869

Remembering back when Fletcher had first come to her house, Elizabeth could well recall all the hardship it imposed upon her. What with caring for the homestead, keeping firewood chopped, cooking, washing the clothing, and trying to stay out of the soldiers' way, Elizabeth had cared for Fletcher's head wound, which healed rather quickly. She had realized his biggest problem had been the loss of blood.

She hadn't enough of the good, nourishing food that he needed for healing, and was fearful for his soon recovery. After all, the war had gone on for so long and people all over were hungry. She had fretted and prayed over him and did all she could for him that needed to be done.

When he was totally well, except for his memory loss, she found that she had cared for him as her patient until she had come to care for him as a man. She had realized the possibility that he might already belong to some other lady, who even at that moment, could be pining for him somewhere in Georgia. That had been a constant threat hanging over her head. She had tried to ignore her feelings until she realized that he had the same feelings, but like her, was trying to push them aside.

After months of struggle not to become involved, the two had fallen deeply in love, even though there was the threat that he might not be free. They decided to face that issue after the war; hopefully, his memory would return to him by then. He prayed daily that he had not done wrong to anyone.

Just a short while after Fletcher realized that Elizabeth was the only one for him, they were quietly married by an elderly preacher who had been in her area and had stopped by to pay his respects, as usual. He was a true man of the cloth, and after hearing their story, he told them he could be trusted not to reveal Fletcher's identity.

They decided to take their chances on happiness and deal with whatever awaited them after the war. That was when they would be able to do all they could to find out his history. After all, there was a very real possibility that he might never recover his memory or that he would recover it only to find that he was a man free of any romantic entanglement whatsoever.

Even back then there had been a sense of urgency in Fletcher that would not be held at bay for long. Until the war was over, they had not been able to travel openly in any kind of safety, and so the only thing they could do back then was to wait, hope, and pray for a better day and that God would grant a speedy end to that awful war.

"Fletcher is the only name Charles Purdue gave me as yours, love. He didn't say who your people were or exactly where you lived, except that you lived in Georgia. I come from Atlanta and know many people in Georgia, but I am of no help to you, because I have never heard of a Fletcher family. I don't even know if Fletcher is your given name or family name," she said. "Time will tell us all we need to know. I have faith in that, Fletcher."

Yes, it had been a time of struggle with many things back then in '64 when he had first come to the farm as a wounded soldier. Now the war was long over and he was still wounded, although not physically. No, his wounds went deeper. His memory had not returned and by not knowing who he was, he was still a haunted man.

Chapter 14

Jefferson Lewis stood on Emma's front verandah and twisted the chime. It was eight o'clock in the morning and he wasn't alone. When Jesse May opened the door, Lewis advised her that Sheriff Oaks wanted to see Miss Emma about an urgent matter. Jesse May hurried off to tell Missy that the greasy sheriff and that shifty Lewis was out front and that the sheriff didn't look none too happy.

Emma told her to fetch them some lemonade and tell them she would speak to them on the verandah presently. She didn't think her papa had ever trusted their overseer, Jefferson Lewis, any more than she or her mama had. A guarded look would come to her papa's eyes whenever he came to the house for a consultation.

He had been taken on only because Dan Sheridan, the previous overseer, had left during the fighting, as he was a retired army officer. He had been killed in late '64 and there wasn't an abundance of good, loyal men to replace him in that position. So many good men had been killed in the war or had arrived home broken and maimed. For that reason, they had carried on with Lewis, hoping that sooner, rather than later, they could find a more suitable person for the job.

That Jefferson Lewis was a sly one, as Kitty had said, was no exaggeration. His reputation did not stand him in good stead with many people. Kitty told her many things that her mama didn't seem to know about him—things that Kitty had learned by overhearing the women talk when they didn't know she was around.

So, Lewis and the sheriff are calling together at this hour, are they? Emma mused. She knew as sure as she knew her own name what the call was about. Cal Morgan had no doubt gone to the sheriff over the 'bad' notes he was holding and saying they were her papa's.

She knew her papa would never borrow that much money; he wouldn't have done it even in the lean years or during the war. Not to say that loans were easy to get during the war. Fact is, no Southern landowner could easily qualify for a loan. Nobody knew if landowners would be able to keep their lands after the war, especially if the South were to lose, God forbid.

All their valuable possessions had been confiscated or destroyed by the enemy early on in the war, but even if they hadn't been, there had been no money for people to buy much more than food to keep body and soul alive, let alone buy any valuables that might have been sold off to pay taxes. Neither would any bank lend money on land already encumbered.

Oh, well, she thought, *I might as well get this over with*.

The men rose when she swept onto the veranda. Lewis leered at her as if he could eat her with a spoon. Sheriff Oaks, the coward, seemed embarrassed by his mission of having to extort money from a woman, but he managed to muddle through, nonetheless.

"Now see here, Miss Emma," he began, "I don't want to cause you any hardship or suffering, but I have no option, but to come here and speak with you about a matter concerning business dealings between your papa and Cal Morgan."

"Yes, Sheriff Oaks?"

He began to fidget, but he blurted out what he knew about the notes Cal held. "Miz Emma, Cal is right that the notes must be settled, and I—"

"Excuse me, Sheriff, but I will go to the bank this morning and settle with Morgan."

"You will, Miz Emma? But I thought—"

"No, Sheriff, no need to think. All will be taken care of today. Be so good as to have Mr. Morgan meet me at the bank at eleven sharp. Good day, gentlemen."

She left them standing with their mouths open. They wondered what Morgan would have to allow on hearing those words. They knew he didn't want to be paid off in cash. No, they knew he had other plans for the beautiful and desirable Emma—and Summers Bluff.

True to her word, Emma arrived at the bank at ten forty-five and waited for the bank president, Jim Grant, to assist her in withdrawing her funds. Both of his clerks were busy with other customers, and as Grant's door was open a wide crack, she decided to just announce herself and get this over with. But what she heard as she approached the door astonished her. Morgan was inside with the sheriff, Lewis, and Grant, talking freely about the notes.

"It's all right, gentlemen," Morgan said with a chuckle. "Not what I wanted, but certainly what I expected. She will use her cash to pay me off, but I will have her just the same. Once she pays me, she won't be able to run the plantation on her beauty alone. Tell me, Jim, how much has she left in her account?"

"Let me see, Morgan. Uh, ten thousand and two hundred dollars."

"Well, that's good. I might as well make me a couple more 'bad notes' from Josiah Summers while we're waiting for her!"

All four men laughed at that remark.

Lewis piped up. "And I thought I's a crook when I 'liberated' a paintin' here and there from Summers Bluff, along with some other good stuff, before the Yanks got to 'em!"

Jim Grant retorted, "The Yanks treated us well if you'll but recall, gentlemen. We got our share of the proceeds from the paintings and baubles from many of the plantations around here when we sold them for the occupying Yankees.

"Well, gentlemen, I needed the money to afford to marry the beautiful Emma," Morgan said sarcastically.

"Well, boss, she don't seem to cotton none to the idea from what I kin see," Lewis said. He took a risk to needle Morgan, and no doubt thought he could get away with it, being in the presence of the others. Morgan must have given him one of his deadly stares for his trouble, because his laughter ended abruptly without the other men joining in.

Morgan replied in the coldest voice anyone had ever heard him use. "She will be my bride soon or she will lie alongside her loving parents before the month is out!"

Chapter 15

Pennsylvania 1870

Elizabeth had seen the obvious concern and a preoccupation that was clearly troubling Fletcher. His restlessness had been increasing by the day, and she knew it had to be dealt with soon. However, she had been dreading it. Whatever conclusion he came to, it would definitely mean a change in their happy existence. She thought the only way she could help him was if she brought it up herself.

"Fletch, the war ended five years ago now, and you've been restless and agitated for the past six months more than usual. I know it's because you're worrying over not knowing who you are. Of course, we don't have much money since the war took such a toll on everything. You'll allow that by the time you arrived, the Yankee troops had conscripted everything I owned down to the last egg on the place," she reminded him.

Fletcher simply nodded and held his own counsel. She continued, "So many have barely existed throughout this long war, but the past five years that have followed have been so much better for us. But still you're not happy here," she reasoned.

When Fletcher remained silent she became even more concerned. Her fear must have been apparent, as Fletcher reached for her hand, apparently wanting to console her.

"Darling, if you feel you have to look for your roots in Georgia, I'll stay here so you can do what you need without the expense or hardship of having me along. What do *you* suppose should be our next step now?"

Fletcher had been wondering about that for months. He looked at her another long moment. "Elizabeth, I have given what I'm about to say a great deal of thought and prayer. I haven't done much else lately except think. But please don't agree or disagree with this until you have given some earnest thought to what I am about to suggest."

She tensed with apprehension at the seriousness she saw on his countenance.

This is why he has been so restless of late. Is now the time he's going to say good-bye to me? It has been as plain as plain that he is troubled and has had something on his mind he's been keeping to himself. If he chooses now to tell me that this is the time he has to go, I don't think I can bear it!

He noted the sudden look of alarm on her features and hurried on. "Darling, what would you say, and would you even consider, maybe selling the farm and moving away with me? Before you say anything, please hear what my thinking is. If we were to sell up, we could go down South and stay as long as we'd need to. I wouldn't be leaving you here alone, and I wouldn't be down there alone."

He waited for her to comment, but when she just waited for him to continue, he said, "Surely, somebody down there will recognize me by face if not by name, and I can find work there easier than a Reb could up here. But if you won't go, I'll stay here, for I won't consent to go without you," Fletcher said, with emotion clearly displayed on his face.

Elizabeth was startled at his mention of selling the farm, but very moved at his determination not to leave her, even temporarily. She thanked the Lord that it was just selling up that had been on his mind, although the thought had never occurred to her. She had always known he would make a trip to Georgia, but she had always pictured him returning to her at the farm.

"Sell the farm? I'd never thought of that, but I can see your point. If moving down South will allow you to find out who you are, then, of course, I'm all for it. I already know *what* you are—a fine, honest, and gentle man." She smiled and her relief was evident. "I've always been concerned about you going alone to face whatever awaits you, so I suppose selling up would be the best solution. Actually, I think it's an inspiration! Of course, we'll sell the farm! Just as soon as I can talk with Mr. Riley, because I know he has wanted this farm for years. Maybe now's the time, love. Hitch up the buggy. Let's go see what he says."

Chapter 16

*E*mma was absolutely and utterly stunned! She had just been ready to storm the office and confront him on those forged notes when she heard his threat on her life, and was very glad she had shown restraint. At this new side of Morgan coming to light, she felt herself grow cold and knew she was in the presence of absolute evil.

Suddenly the whole meaning dawned on her. Her father had never borrowed money from that filthy pig, just like she had known all along!

Why, that devil forged Papa's name, and he's not a bit worried about them knowing about what he's done! Nor does he care if they know what he's planning to do to me if I refuse him again. I knew he was evil!

So, Sheriff Lewis and the banker have been in on this with him, and not only this business. They were in cahoots with the Yankees, too! Traitors! she screamed to herself!

She knew what they were for certain now, and murderers into the bargain. If he could throw around talk of killing her in such a casual manner, it must be talk they're used to hearing, Emma realized.

I must think. Think, Emma! What shall I do? If I give him the money I have in the bank, he is right. I can't run the plantation without money.

Plantation? What plantation? I can't run it with all the money in the world from the grave! I have to face facts. If I stay here, I have to either marry him or die. Either way, I'm a dead woman. Think Emma! Calm yourself and think. You have to face them in a minute. Okay, what is first? Focus, Emma!

Okay, first, I can't stay here. That's right. Okay, if I have to leave I must get the money out of the bank now. That's right. Get the money and leave. Third-

Figure the rest out later when you're out of here, she commanded herself.

Knowing now what she must do, she willed herself to walk to a clerk on the far side of the room, closest to the main door, and asked him to please alert Mr. Grant to her presence in the bank. She steeled her face. She would reveal nothing of what she had heard of this evil plot even though she realized she was shaking like a leaf in a storm and must have been pale. She took several deep breaths to calm herself. She had to look as though she had just arrived, so she stayed at the clerk's worktable while he summoned Grant.

Grant came out and rushed over to her with hand outstretched, as if he were greeting his best friend. She allowed him to take her hand and express his joy at seeing her again, though regrettably under the circumstances. She accepted his greeting without demur and preceded him into his office.

She nodded to the sheriff, Lewis, and Morgan and even managed a slight, pasted-on smile. Cal at once noted her pallor and shakiness and asked if she were well.

She choked back a barbed retort. Speaking slowly, she settled for, "Well, gentlemen, it is a sad day for me to be involved in such a distasteful matter as the one before us here today. I have never been called upon to handle such a matter as this, as I am but a woman, pray remember," she said, trying not to scream, but instead, to look pitiful and weak to disguise her trembling. "But we are here to proceed with the business at hand. I have decided to first withdraw my funds, if you please, Mr. Grant."

"Of course, dear lady. I have them right here. How much do you wish to withdraw today?" he asked.

She appeared to be a bit bewildered about that, as if she were uncertain as to how to proceed. "Well, how much do the notes come to, sir?"

"A little over five thousand dollars," he answered, throwing a meaningful look at Morgan.

Emma didn't miss the look. She emitted a gasp, which she really felt, but also thought that had been a convincing touch. "Very well. I will withdraw all the funds in my account today, if you please." As soon as he handed her the money, she placed all of it in her reticule and drew the strings closed. She thanked them and headed for the door.

"A moment, dear lady!" Cal Morgan said. He had a look of incredulity on his twisted face. "I was informed that you wished to clear up the matter of your father's debts today. Is that not so, Sheriff?"

"To be sure, to be sure, Mr. Morgan!" the sheriff vehemently assured him.

She took a moment or two as she forced herself to look from one to the other of them, while she was seemingly considering something.

She willed herself to appear calm. She finally spoke, saying, "Well, gentlemen, I have just decided that the best thing I can do right now is to wait and see, Mr. Morgan, if you really intend to see my plantation on the auction block before the month is out," she said smoothly in a tone as respectful as she could manage, as she moved out the door.

She knew she had infuriated Morgan, which wasn't wise, as she had just learned that he was a much more deadly foe than she had hitherto realized. But maybe by inferring that she would wait to see what he was going to do, just maybe, it would give her some time. He wouldn't be expecting what was beginning to formulate in her mind.

It took all the strength she had to take her next step and to keep walking. She felt the look of fury and hatred emanating from Morgan through the open office door. She finally exited the bank and leaned against the wall for support.

Big Joe came to her side and assisted her into the buggy. As hurriedly as the horses could manage, they headed for home and Aunt Caroline.

Chapter 17

rriving at the plantation, she entered the front door with a shout and Bessie, Jesse May, and Kitty, came running. Even Granny Thornton and Aunt Caroline came in as quickly as they could without submitting to a full gallop.

"Mercy me, child, who's after ye? Ye a comin' in here shoutin' with such a wild look in yer eye?" Granny Thornton said with evident concern.

"Follow me," Emma cried.

When they all were assembled in the library, she told them what she had overheard at the bank and what her future would be if she stayed there.

Disbelief and unreality seemed to be the prevailing emotion they all were feeling as they listened, but the more she related of what had transpired, the emotion turned from disbelief to anger that turned into fury. Then their fury gave way to unfathomable fear. Those four men involved in this atrocity, to their shaken minds, seemed an unstoppable force of evil that threatened their very existence, and Emma's very life for certain.

But Emma continued on with what she had heard. When Granny Thornton learned of Lewis's part in stealing their valuables, she asked, "Ye mean to say that them there pictures and stuff that just walked out had Jefferson Lewis' legs under 'em? I've always known he was a villain!"

"Yes, Granny, that's what I mean to say. I have to tell you all the plans I felt impressed to make on the way home from the bank. I've done a lot of thinking and praying in a hurry. I mean to fight fire with fire, and when I do that, somebody is sure to get burned. Pray that it is not me." She was fuming as she unlocked the drawer to the desk and drew out the deed to the plantation.

"I am sending Big Joe right now with the deed to the plantation, which I am signing over to Judge West," she said, as she picked up a pen and signed the deed. "I have told Big Joe to tell him that I know he and papa were closer than kin, and when Big Joe tells him what is happening here, he'll take the deed that is made out to him and record it at the land and deed office as his own this very day," she advised them.

"That will give him time to sell everything and get the best price, much more than I could have gotten had I tried to stay here until I could sell, what with Morgan just waiting to do me in. Or the judge might even decide to keep it. Even if he just sends me a down payment on the plantation, it will more than meet our needs until he can settle up," she told them. "When I get to where I'm going, I will let him know, and he will send a letter of credit to the bank there for the difference. Big Joe will be back long before dark, so we will be ready to leave here when he is ready."

She received nods of understanding all around.

"Bessie," she continued at a feverish pitch, taking her hands, "you have your family, and they will provide for you. I thank you with all my heart for all y'all have meant to us all these years. Papa emancipated all his workers long ago, as you all know. You and the other workers are free to go wherever you need to, but I pray y'all will stay and work here and help see to the land until the judge sells the place, but after that, you are free to stay or go as you see fit."

They were watching her with their mouths hanging open in disbelief.

"Granny Thornton, you are too old to be hiding and running. It'll break my heart to leave you, as sure as I'm standing here, but I'm taking you to Savannah, and the judge will make arrangements to care for you and Kitty as long as you need a home. I know there are just the two of you now, excepting a couple of cousins in Virginia, if I recall. Never fear, as I won't see you unprotected."

Granny raised a bony finger and said she wouldn't leave her no matter what the reason. Emma reminded her that if she took her along, she would have to travel slowly and chances were that Morgan would probably catch up to her if she did that. That sobered her. Granny reluctantly agreed to go with her to Judge West when they left the plantation later that day.

They tried to push down any fears that were shadowing their hearts and threatening to consume them, as they packed only what they would absolutely need on their journey. Their closets looked as if nothing had been removed.

Emma had never been a grasping or selfish girl, but looking around her at all the things she had taken for granted all her life, assuming that she would always have them around her, had been thoughtless on her part. *Mama and papa were going to bring more things back for this lovely home. Now I'll never see what they chose. I'll never again awaken in the room that I have awakened in every day of my life these nineteen years.* No doubt she would have appreciated them more if she had but known that she would not always be there.

I must go to mama and papa's room! I want to be in the place where I have been comforted by visits to their room all my life. How

I, as a child, would fly to the fainting couch where mama used to have her lie-downs. I would fall on her bosom, and she would dry my tears. This is hateful, hateful! But Emma, get a hold of yourself. You don't have the strength for all this right now. Think of mama when you get out of here.

They knew they would be missed come morning, but they decided they would try their best to act normally for the rest of the day and not let on to anybody what was happening. Maybe that would give them the few hours head start they needed.

They took their mourning clothing with them, but decided to dispense with wearing them on their getaway journey that they were anticipating. Morgan's bunch would certainly be looking for her and Aunt Caroline in mourning attire. It was nearly more than they could do to leave them off, sound reasoning though it was.

You'll do a lot of untoward things that don't set well with a conscience; things that would turn people over in their graves if they knew. But when it comes to life-or-death things, what do social customs mean? Emma asked herself. *Mama would go right along with this if she were here, because my love for her isn't tied up in the color of a dress; nor hers for me, if it comes to that.*

Chapter 18

Big Joe was back from town and Judge West had decided they would be safer leaving Savannah by ship than any other means of travel. He had procured passage with a captain, who was a good friend and ally. The judge had told Big Joe to tell Emma to arrive at the docks around dawn, but hadn't mentioned where she would be going. They would approach Savannah from the southwest and thereby arrive at the docks by the appointed time. The captain would also alter the names of the passengers without blinking an eye.

Granny Thornton had packed enough food to last a week. They would be plenty glad of it when they had to deal with ship's fare, but right then they assumed that food would be the least of their problems for the next few months. Nobody could even think of supper, though Granny had it ready, as she had always thought food was the answer to all life's problems. Besides, what would the others on the plantation think if they didn't smell supper cooking?

The happenings of the past few hours had devastated this frightened little group of women. They were on the run from the meanest threat they had ever known and weren't ashamed to admit they were shaken to the core. They were rapidly making plans to leave their beloved Summers Bluff, the place where they had lived all their lives, and Granny was eighty years old. That was a long time to live in one place. She was too old to think of leaving it, considering she was nearing the end of her earthly journey. Her dreams of sitting on the veranda in the old rocker and gazing out over the land she had loved for so many years were going up in smoke before her old eyes.

Well, whatever will be will be, Granny thought. *The good Lord knew this day would come upon us, and he knows what's breakin' our hearts this very moment. We've nothin' to fear from those heathen devils in town! He knows jest what to do and will surely lead us on out of here in safety or me name's not Kathleen Thornton!* Her heart believed that, but her mind had to be reminded of it often.

They knew Lewis would stay in town most of the night drinking and gambling and would be fair done in by the time he reached the overseer's quarters. Still, they would not leave until he was safely in his quarters for the night and passed out in an alcohol-induced, deep sleep for fear he might pass them on the road, or see them leave, or notice the buggy gone.

Big Joe would cover the horses' hooves with burlap just before leaving to quiet the noise, and he would remove anything on the carriage that might rattle and give them away. Given that the roadway was basically sandy loam would help keep down the noise.

Finally, the dreaded hour came. Big Joe slipped in the kitchen door and motioned to them that it was time to go. Emma had thought to make one last pass through her beloved Summers Bluff and hesitated to follow them, but the urgency on his face bid her to make haste.

She glanced around the comforting old kitchen. She remembered all the times that she, Fletcher, and Kitty had eaten cookies and had drunk cold sweet milk there on hot summer days. The joyful times they had known, when they had trudged in out of the wet and cold on winter days, flashed through her mind. Granny had scolded them, saying that they would catch their deaths, but she had served them hot chocolate and buttered biscuits at the kitchen table, while she lovingly fussed over them.

Yes, she would miss the place, and so much the more, given she had no idea where she would end up or what she would have when she got to where she was going. But Big Joe's eyes were pleading with her to leave. With a final, lingering look, she bid her home adieu. She knew real panic at that moment and wondered for the hundredth time if leaving like this was faith or foolishness. But the Lord knew she had come too far to back out now. Big Joe picked up her carpetbag, while she picked up her skirts and quickly fled the kitchen.

Chapter 19

As they crept away from Summers Bluff, they refrained from talking or making any other noise, especially as they came close to any place that was occupied, though each of them sat back from the road a distance. They took the seldom-used cattle trails as much as possible until they gained the main road, fearing detection at any moment.

As they neared Savannah, Granny spoke with her granddaughter in a low tone, and the others knew something was going on. Before they arrived, Kitty informed Emma that she was going to go with her, at Granny's insistence, as she had felt that Kitty would be needed to take care of Emma.

Granny had reasoned that the judge would take care of her for as long as need be, but she had a presentiment that it wouldn't be too much longer anyhow. At the same time, Granny had known that with her gone, Kitty would be all alone in the world. But, she also knew that if she went with Emma now, as long as Emma Summers had breath in her body, she knew her Kitty would be looked after. Yes, that would suit her. She couldn't ask for more.

Thoughts of being followed then and in the near future were uppermost in their minds that night. They knew they would have to travel under aliases to make sure Morgan didn't find them.

They considered it for awhile and finally came up with new names for themselves. Kitty chose Lilly, Aunt Caroline would be Sadie, and Emma would be Victoria. They would all share the family name of Harris, with Kitty posing as an Irish cousin.

Morning was dawning when they arrived at the docks. They were relieved to see Judge West waiting for them. He hurried over and his own hired man saw to their baggage, instead of using the regular dockhands. The women were well veiled and hopefully no one could give a good description of them, should they be asked.

He introduced them to the captain, who seemed a pleasant fellow despite his scruffy appearance. "Me good ladies!" he bowed. "A pleasure to prove a comrade in arms with ye! Ye cannot do better than meself in keepin' your women folk safe aboard this ole tub, Judge. The *Neptune* be a sturdy vessel, and I'll take 'em to 'Frisco safe and sound or me name's not Ira Flynn!" He bowed to the women. "Aboard, fair damsels. We've a wee ways to go and 'tis full daylight now. We'll leave as soon as we get ye aboard, for we must be makin' the tide."

The judge ascended the gangplank with them. He encouraged them to find quiet lodgings at first until they found an appropriate house in which to put up, once they had learned their way around the city.

He advised them to consider changing their names, at least until they were out of danger, and he assured Victoria that he would mail her whatever documents would be needed to substantiate a name change once she got to San Francisco.

They apprised him that they had already changed their names and gave him the names they had chosen. He said he would confirm with the ship's registry at the port authority when he was ready to send the documents to be sure of the spelling of their names. He suggested they all begin to use their new names immediately, lest anyone aboard hear their true ones.

He spoke very seriously. "Surely, Cal Morgan would not let you make a fool of him like this and get away with it. He will know of your leaving by this very morning and will be checking all possible means of transportation out of the city."

He advised her that as Morgan would be hunting her down and that she needed to be aware that her description would not fit just anyone. He felt sure she would be remembered for her unusual beauty, height, auburn hair, and such vivid green eyes. Therefore, for the voyage and beyond, she should be as inconspicuous as possible.

He further assured her that he would make it his business to be alert and keep up with any travel Morgan might be inclined to make, and would notify her if he learned that he was headed anywhere near San Francisco.

He told Emma that when she arrived in San Francisco, she was to check the telegraph and postal office for any 'will-call' mail addressed to a Mr. M. W. Brown. He also told her not to contact him unless it was an emergency, and then she was to telegraph him and identify herself as Mr. Brown, a businessman and write the telegram as a business inquiry. He would understand and respond in kind. He knew Morgan had his ways of finding out information.

He then told her Big Joe had told him that she had withdrawn all of her money from the bank and since they would not need any more money on the voyage, suggested he send a letter of credit in the amount of the sale of the plantation to the largest bank in San Francisco and she agreed. Judge West bid them farewell and quickly left the ship, his heart heavy with concern for their safety.

A part of her heart was breaking at the enormity of her decision to leave her papa's home for the last time and hie off on her own for the very first time. She would have to become the provider for

Aunt Caroline and Kitty, as well as herself, with no earthly idea of how to do that. Yes, she had learned business principles and was skilled in numbers, but she wondered who besides her papa would give her the opportunity to prove that.

She was understandably grieving to have to leave her lifelong home in that fashion, the graves of her parents and it had also been painful to her that she hadn't had a moment to say goodbye to any of her life-long friends, never mind that she probably wouldn't ever see them again.

Once again thoughts of Jake Jackson flooded her mind, adding to her dire misery. *Will I ever see you again, Jake? How could I?* she thought adding despair to her misery.

The ship was heading out; this was really happening to her. With a sense of utter disbelief, she watched as they eased away from the dock. She was suddenly reminded of the conversation she had had with Aunt Caroline the night the telegram had arrived about her parents.

Aunt Caroline had asked her if she wanted to travel before she settled down and married. She had answered that she certainly did. Well, they had both expressed a desire to travel and see the world together. Not a fortnight later, they were on their way.

I am really underway to parts unknown with Aunt Caroline and Kitty! I'm nineteen years old, an orphan, and homeless. I am also probably wanted by the law for not paying off those forged notes of Morgan's. I am certainly wanted by Morgan, to be done to death by his own hand, she thought. She shook her head in disbelief of what was happening to her.

She pushed those thoughts aside. *No, not with Aunt Caroline and Kitty! Remember: you are Victoria, and you are en route to San Francisco with Aunt Sadie and Lilly.* It was going to take some time to remember to use their assumed names all the time.

If Emma Summers had ever been so weary, she didn't know when. So many emotions were fighting for expression; she was grateful to be escaping, sad to be leaving, but elated at the idea of never seeing Cal Morgan again.

She was exhausted with the unbelievable day she had just experienced, not to mention not having slept since the night before last or of having so much anxiety of not knowing what lay ahead. Her deep grief for her parents had just begun to lessen to a somewhat tolerable level and then all this had come upon her. She wondered what unearthly thing might happen next. *Will I ever feel safe again?* she wondered as she looked out to sea.

Chapter 20

The noise of merrymaking by the other passengers aboard, who were waving and making their farewells to their loved ones on shore, was too much for Emma. She needed some peace and a quiet place to endure this momentous occasion.

Leaving the rail where everyone else was enjoying making their farewells, she went to the opposite side of the ship to be alone for a few moments. She noticed an inbound vessel still a little ways out making toward the dock where they had just left. It was a steamer approaching from the north. She noted that there didn't seem to be many passengers pressing the rails presently.

Her thoughts turned to the incredible day she had just had, and she still couldn't believe the deadly, preposterous conversation she had overheard in the bank. That conversation was seared in her memory for all time. She wondered if the fear it had caused would ever go away. *What kind of man would murder the woman he wanted to marry if she didn't consent? To what lengths will he go to find me? Will he ever let this go?*

The fear the answer to that question produced in her was nothing short of debilitating. She knew the answer! She felt herself close to tears and wondered if she would make it out of Savannah harbor without disgracing herself after all. Her weakness demanded that she find a place to sit; choosing a nearby crate, she gratefully sat.

If only papa had lived, he would have cleared all this up. We would all be together instead of the three of us being on the fly like this with no concept of the place to where we are headed. She felt like a young, untested girl who didn't know how to act in a time of crisis. If only she had Abram's faith when God called him to leave his home and all he knew and go to an unknown country. At least she knew her destination was San Francisco. *That's something,* she supposed.

The others joined her. By their countenances, they looked as exhausted as she felt. Aunt Caroline suggested they pray before starting on such a long, hazardous journey. She asked the Lord to clear Emma's mind to know His, and to take away their cares and fears. She asked that He grant them journey mercies, for which they would be forever thankful.

Prayers over, they stood and Emma was about to suggest they get some rest when turning, she glanced again at the small, inbound steamer they were very closely passing. Green eyes, not unlike her own, were plainly staring into hers. She would have known those eyes anywhere in the world! But at the moment, she felt so otherworldly and weak that the voices around her faded and ceased, the sea disappeared, and utter blackness descended upon her.

Fortunately, the crew was busy with the work before them, and other passengers were busy with good-byes. Only Aunt Sadie, Lilly, and the captain witnessed her pass out on the deck in front of God and those green eyes.

Chapter 21

*I*t had been a week since Elizabeth had sold the farm. She and Fletcher—Mr. and Mrs. F. Connor Sullivan—were on the deck of the *Newark* making their way south to Savannah. Since Fletcher hadn't known what his last name was, he had chosen F. Connor Sullivan to use until such a time as he discovered his own.

All he really knew was that he loved his wife, Elizabeth, more than he could imagine, but he was on his way to Georgia to find out if there had been another woman before the war, whom he had loved just as much. All he knew to do was to trust God to make his path clear and lead him where he needed to go.

Elizabeth snuggled closer into his arms. He kissed the lips she had momentarily lifted to him. He still couldn't believe his great blessing, as to have had the favor of finding so beautiful a woman, widowed and alone on a farm where his fellow soldiers had left him to recuperate!

What are the odds of something as perfect as that happening? he wondered. Surely, that was a good sign, a sign of good things to come. Whatever they found awaiting them in Georgia—well, whatever would be, would be.

They had departed from New York aboard the *Newark,* which had been a decent steamer, and the voyage had been a good one, but had become distinctly more pleasant once they had reached the warmer Southern climes.

As the *Newark* was approaching Savannah, fear and trepidation tugged at Fletcher's heart. He couldn't know what was awaiting them in Georgia. But the choice had been made to face the future and it was too late to turn back.

As their steamer entered the harbor, another vessel had just eased away from the dock. Fletcher noticed the fine lines of the vessel and had remarked that they didn't make sailing ships like one that anymore.

His attention was suddenly drawn to a lovely woman aboard the vessel with the saddest green eyes he had ever seen. She was staring at him as they moved in opposite directions. She lifted her hand to her mouth and the look on her face changed. It was as if something had gone terribly amiss. The middle-aged woman beside her turned to see what she was staring at so intently. The older woman beside her recognized him immediately. She gasped, "Fletcher! Oh, my dear boy!" The beautiful young woman with the green eyes emitted a moan and momentarily collapsed. The older woman stumbled into the arms of another young woman who was standing beside her, as pale as the other two, looking for all the world as if she had just seen a haint!

Elizabeth gripped Fletcher's arm so hard that it had become painful. Never had they imagined in their wildest dreams that he would be recognized before he had even gone ashore! "What can we do, Fletcher?"

Fletcher had no earthly idea. He could scarcely fathom what was happening. He could only call on the Lord to see the matter through. *Who is the lovely lady with the sad eyes? Why was she so agitated upon seeing me that she swooned? Even the lady with her had to have recognized me from her reaction and calling out my name!*

Captain Flynn had been greatly perplexed when he saw the young miss swoon; the older lady had nearly done so. Thankfully, they had not caused a stir among the other passengers, nor had the crew noticed them, as they had been working at the rail on the other side of the ship. He went to give them his assistance, but she was already up. The older lady had recovered herself, too.

"Is that the lad from whom the young miss is trying to escape?" he asked Lilly, as she was the only one still able to answer him, even though her hair fairly stood on end.

"Not a bit of it," she stammered, "That's the brother of the young miss, come back from the grave, he has!"

When Emma was able to focus again, she cried out, "Where is he? Where is he?"

Aunt Caroline, calmer at that point, said, "Patience, my love. Don't fret. We haven't lost him. We will surely be returning to the dock, and he will join us. Never fear, my dear girl, never fear. All will be sorted out, you'll see! Everything will be all right." But, indeed, she had no idea if anything would be all right ever again after the day they had endured.

Captain Flynn, recognizing the women's distress, looked across at the lad. Even he could see the resemblance and the distressed look on the faces of the young man and the woman beside him. He ordered the boat put about back to shore.

Only God knew what the outcome would be of this predestined meeting of both sets of brilliant, emerald eyes.

So much for not disgracing myself before getting out of port, Emma thought.

Chapter 22

When the passengers of the *Newark* had disembarked, the women braced themselves for what would come next. As if all that they had endured that day wasn't enough, what if the man they had seen aboard the *Newark* wasn't Emma's brother? She wanted that man to be Fletcher. No. She *needed* that man to be Fletcher.

She didn't know what would happen to her mind if she found out that he was someone else. Or worse, what if that man had left the dock before they identified him? She was most perplexed by the fact that Fletcher had seen her, Aunt Caroline, and Kitty as clearly as they had seen him, but he hadn't responded to them at all. He had merely reacted to her swoon, to hear Kitty tell it, and that was just by way of concern that he might have shown for any woman he saw collapse in front of him.

Emma began to pray. *Lord, I have endured hardship as a good soldier. I have never blamed you for any of my troubles, for I know you are a good God. But I need that man to be my Fletcher! I do not think I could endure it if it turns out to be someone else!*

Upon docking, crew had been sent ashore to secure the young man's trunks and fetch the couple aboard. The steward was sent to amend the ship's passenger registry from the small party of three to one of five, and for him to find out the name of the young man and register the party under that name.

The register soon reflected a party of five sailing under the name of Mr. and Mrs. F. Connor Sullivan. The registry now listed the three Savannah women as Victoria, Sadie and Lilly Sullivan.

Fletcher and Elizabeth were nearing the *Neptune*. The three women aboard the vessel breathlessly waited for the young man to come aboard. As for Fletcher, he seemed to be in a daze; he was simply following behind their trunks.

Elizabeth's heart was breaking in two. She had witnessed the tall, elegant young woman with the auburn hair have such a shattering reaction to seeing Fletcher. She would have to have been someone very important in his life. *But pray God not his wife!*

Fletcher and Elizabeth walked up the *Neptune's* gangplank as if they were approaching something worse than death, whatever that was, and knew their lives had changed forever; whether for good or evil, only time would tell!

When the steward had conducted them to Victoria Sullivan's cabin and knocked on the door, it was immediately opened by the auburn-haired damsel herself. They were ushered inside and Elizabeth had never been prouder of Fletcher than she was at that moment. He extended his hand to the young woman and introduced himself as Connor Sullivan, whereupon she unexpectedly flew into his arms.

"Oh, it *is* you! It's your voice, my love! It really *is* you!" She burst into uncontrollable sobbing. The older woman patted his arm while he was holding Victoria up. It was evident to him that she would have collapsed had he not.

Elizabeth merely looked away at the emotional scene. He held her until her tears were spent and she pulled away to look into his dear face. "I can scarcely believe what I am seeing with my own eyes!"

Aunt Sadie said, "Well, my boy, they told us you were dead! And your name is Fletcher. Is there a reason you are using the name Connor?" she asked.

Fletcher implored her with his eyes to understand and stated, "Madam, I have a condition called amnesia. I know some things, but I cannot remember people or past events from earlier than when I awakened after escaping a Union army prison camp in the winter of sixty-four, but not before sustaining a significant gunshot wound to the head, causing my present condition. I only knew my name was Fletcher, but not whether it was my first or last name. I decided to use my initial and take the name Connor Sullivan after a name I had read in a book until I discovered my full identity. May I know who you are, ma'am?"

"My poor boy, of course, you may. I am your papa's sister, your Aunt Sadie. And this heartbroken child in your arms, well— she is Victoria— your dear sister."

Fletcher was looking at this beauty, whose green eyes were red and puffy from weeping. "My sister?"

"Yes, my boy, your dear sister, Victoria. She has never really believed you were dead, you know. She always maintained it was faulty record keeping or some other mistake. She couldn't accept that you were gone. And this is your cousin, Lilly."

Victoria gave him a tumultuous smile. She turned to Elizabeth and quietly said, "Fletcher, won't you introduce us to this beautiful lady beside you?"

"Why, of course! I am in a daze. Elizabeth, dear, how remiss of me!" As he moved her to his side he said, "Aunt Sadie, Victoria, Lilly, this is Elizabeth, my wife."

They all three exclaimed at the same time, "Your wife?

"Oh, Elizabeth, my dear, we are so thrilled to make your acquaintance! Image Connor with a wife!" Aunt Sadie said. Only the Lord knew the relief he and Elizabeth felt upon learning that Victoria was his sister.

"Yes, just imagine! Elizabeth, I can scarcely take it in. You see, until just now, I was the only one left of my direct family line except for Aunt Sadie, and now, not only do I have my brother again, against all odds, but a sister, too!" Victoria exclaimed, her voice full of emotion. "God has been gracious to us. Although you may not agree when you hear the news I bring you." she said with a shudder.

As they were seated in the privacy of their stateroom, Victoria began her story. "You may not remember us yet, dear brother, but just a fortnight ago, our dear mama and papa were killed in a fire in a country inn outside Philadelphia. So many things have gone wrong since then," she told him and again shuddered.

"You need to know immediately, Fletch, that we are on the fly to escape certain death if we remained in Georgia," she continued as well as she could. "You may not know this about me yet, but I assure you that I am not given to fainting, hysterics or other flights of fancy, although I have swooned twice in as many weeks, but I am not embellishing this tale. If anything, I cannot adequately express to what depth of evil this will go in future, but this is what is happening to us now. I can scarcely credit it myself," she said, watching the emotions play over Fletcher's face.

"I'll try to finish this quickly since you have been so kind not to ask questions. I'm sure there will be plenty you will want to ask when I've finished," she said. "Cal Morgan was Papa's solicitor, and for the past two years he has been after me to marry him. I heard him remark just yesterday that I would be his wife or I would lie alongside mama and papa before the month was out."

She saw bewilderment and a touch of anger on her brother's face, though she could tell he didn't remember Morgan or anyone else she was mentioning, but any true Southern gentleman would have felt anger at even a stranger being subjected to what Victoria was sharing with him, let alone something like that happening to his sister.

"You see, after Papa died, Morgan came to me and showed me notes he held, which Papa had supposedly signed, for over five thousand dollars. It was my intention to meet him at the bank to settle the 'debt,' but while I was in the bank awaiting Mr. Grant to handle the withdrawal of my money, I overheard Cal Morgan, our overseer, the Sheriff, and the president of the bank in his office talking freely about the notes, if you can imagine it!" she fumed. " Morgan actually bragged about forging Papa's signature on those notes and even forged more of them while I waited to settle up with him!"

"That's when I overheard him threaten my life if I didn't marry him even after he knew I was intending to settle up with him. I knew then that it didn't matter what I did, he would marry me or I would be dead. I knew I couldn't stay there and survive." She shivered at the thought.

"I had to think of something to give me more time, so I withdrew all the money from the account, but refused paying off the notes. I left them standing there thinking I would be waiting at the plantation to see if they really would put my home on the auction block," she related, still experiencing a feeling of disbelief in her own words.

"I supposed they never thought I would up and leave the place I loved better than any other, at least not that quickly. They probably thought they had time to deal with me another day. Morgan had planned to secure the plantation by placing liens on the property and then give the legal notices of the impending auction. I knew I wouldn't feel safe until there were thousands of miles between me and that man."

"That's an amazing story, sister!" Fletcher exclaimed. "I can't tell you how it pains me to know what you have endured these past few weeks!"

"Well, that is not all the story, Fletch. And by the way, the names Auntie used to introduce us are assumed ones so Morgan can't easily find us. I am Emma Summers, but I use Victoria. This is your Aunt Caroline Summers, who uses Sadie, and this is our childhood friend, Kitty Thornton, posing as our cousin, Lilly. It seems we all have taken your last name of Sullivan, at least for a while.

Since you are registered as Connor for this voyage, I think you had best continue to use that name. In fact, we need to use it even among ourselves, even when we are alone. One never knows who is listening. It's also a good idea to stop using our real names, because we might forget and call each other's real names at maybe a critical time So, I will begin to call you Connor, don't you agree?" she asked.

Connor agreed, as he realized that an unusual first name like Fletcher would be remembered. Given his association with the women of his family, who were under assumed names, he couldn't take a chance of giving them away because of his name.

"I know you must find this all terribly muddled, Connor, but since you are just now learning our names anyhow, just learn our new ones!" she said with a twinkle in her eye and a touch of amusement in her voice, which earned her a chuckle from him.

"I will try to remember that you are Connor. You do realize it will be much harder on me to remember your new name, as you have been Fletch to me all my life. Starting now, I'll do better.

And I will finish my story as clearly as I can. You see, today I signed over Summers Bluff." Seeing his confused look, she said, "Our family plantation. I signed it over to Judge West, Papa's dearest friend, who arranged passage for us on this ship to San Francisco, which is where we are headed in case they didn't indicate that when they ushered you aboard. And the captain can be trusted." She looked deep into his eyes. "So you see why I had to do what I've done, don't you, Connor?"

He nodded his agreement, nearly unable to speak, what with so many emotions riveting his mind from the story he had just heard.

"I had to get out with as much as I could as quickly as I could. But believe me, I would never have thought to sell your inheritance had I known you were alive," she said. Connor patted her hand and assured her she had done well.

"I know only that you and Elizabeth are gifts from above," Victoria said with emotion barely under control. "And that just seeing your face, even if you don't rightly remember me, has turned my life that seemed filled with insurmountable despair into one of joy and gladness — and hope!"

"Sister, I am glad you have experienced joy in our reunion, even if I don't remember you. At least I know we are none of us without family." He looked at his sister and aunt. "Or friends!" he said as he looked at Lilly. "Surely, I will begin to remember with y'all to guide me and remind me of what my life used to be."

"Of course, you will remember! I'll help you, and so will Auntie and Lilly!" Victoria said. "The most urgent thing of the day was to get away from Morgan and his gang, which thankfully we have now done. And the plantation will not be auctioned off, as Morgan thought it would be, for him to buy for pennies. The judge will sell it off for the best price it can bring, and we will start anew. All in all, an incredible day!

"Brother, I know this is a lot for you to take in right now, but during the voyage, we can share with each other about what has been happening to you both and all about … well, everything. You know, Fletch—no—Connor. I must remember to start calling you that!" she remonstrated with herself. "Mama and papa like to have died when they got the letter from your commander, telling of your death." She saw the sadness on the faces of everyone and decided talk like that could wait. "But that is over. You are here. You and Elizabeth!"

"Incidentally, Connor, where were you all that time after you escaped?" Aunt Sadie asked.

"My farm was outside Philadelphia," Elizabeth said.

"Philadelphia! Why, Connor! Callaway Court, the estate of dear mama's parents, was right there in Philadelphia! You were within a few miles of them the whole time!" Victoria exclaimed.

"Oh, Connor! Now that I have found you, you must stay with us. I need you, my brother. We all do. I don't think I can handle all this alone any longer. Not when you're here back from the dead, as it were! If you were to return to Georgia, why, there's no telling what Morgan would cook up against you. You'll stay with us when we reach San Francisco, won't you, Connor?"

Who would have ever thought, as dastardly as the events of this day have been, that it could ever have ended as outstandingly as this? Victoria asked herself. *It just goes to show that miracles can and do strike as suddenly as disasters!*

Chapter 23

So Fletcher Summers is my full name. At least I know that much, he thought to himself, still trying to make sense of all that had happened. He knew that this dazzling beauty was his baby sister, and that this kindly lady with her was his aunt, and that Lilly was a childhood friend.

He also had felt a sadness he didn't understand when he was told of his parents' deaths. He also knew that some of the worst fears that he had harbored in his wasteland of foggy past events had come to pass.

Yes, his worst fears had just become a reality. He would never again know his parents in this lifetime, and he no longer had a home awaiting him when he recovered his memory. *Anytime a man loses his parents and an inheritance, whether he remembers it or not, is cause for sadness.*

He had always imagined that he would one day be returning to a family home and be surrounded by a loving mother and father and other loved ones, welcoming him home, but now he realized that to be a fantasy that would never change. That part of his life was gone forever, never to be gotten back again. Even if he regained his memory that day, it wouldn't change his circumstances.

He did, however, realize these honest, God-fearing women needed his help. Of course, he would be overjoyed to stay with them in California. What else would family do? It was obvious that they sincerely wanted and needed him to stay with them and he was overjoyed to be in the midst of family again.

Connor exchanged looks with Elizabeth, whose smile of relief said it all. These women were overjoyed at learning Elizabeth was his wife. They certainly would not have been had he been involved with someone when he went off to war. They were both so grateful that they had no more to fear from that quarter.

Elizabeth, on the other hand, wondered what was wrong with the ladies in Savannah that a catch like Connor had not been reeled in ages ago. But their loss was her great blessing.

Connor smiled at them. "Yes, of course, we will stay with you, Victoria," he agreed, "and Aunt Sadie and Lilly. We will go with you to San Francisco and become Californians together. So much I still don't know, but with my four girls helping me," he took in the lovely ladies before him, "the sky is the limit!" His laughter was infectious.

He would get his sister out of harm's way, and learn so much that he still needed to learn about himself into the bargain. Surely, it wouldn't be long before his memory came back since he now had his little family to help him.

This was a new season in all their lives; they would begin anew in an adventuresome land where they would become stronger and learn to love each other all over again while they put down roots together.

Victoria smiled, and her smile seemed to release all the pent-up fears of the future she had harbored since her parents' deaths.

She turned and looked out the porthole as the town of Savannah and home receded far into the distance. Gone was everything she had put her hopes and trust in for her entire life. Her loving parents were gone, her beloved Summers Bluff was gone, her friends and her dreams of the future were all gone.

Thoughts of Jake Jackson filled her heart at that moment; she realized there had been one man of her acquaintance she could have seen herself married to. In all of her misery in thinking of things that could never be now, she had begun to think of all the 'if onlys' in her life. If only!

If only Jake had declared himself before this tragic episode in my life, what would my life have been like had I married him? If only I had declared myself to him! No, mama would have had my hide and well she should have, because that would not have been right. But no, no, in all reality, Morgan would never have allowed me to marry Jake! She just knew that.

She knew she had been wrong about something else, too. Everything was not gone that she had known all her life; she still had her unshaken faith in God. It had sustained her when she faced her grief alone in the night. Yes, Jake had helped her, as had her best friends, and those friends had been they of her own household. But, it was the Lord's comfort that had ultimately dried her tears and allowed her to put one foot in front of the other and still be in her right mind.

No, all was not gone from her life, but she thought it best not to dwell on Jake; she was too fragile just now. Besides, the reality was that she was on the fly, and he had his church and flock to care for. She couldn't have put his life in danger; she knew what Morgan would have done to him if he had declared himself. Jake would have resisted Morgan, and would have paid the price.

She didn't know what was in store for her, but she knew God had given her brother back to her within mere moments of missing each other for the rest of their lives. Had they not been at that railing or had either of them been merely looking the other way, they would have literally been ships that passed in the night.

Yes, God had allowed that man that she had seen on deck of the *Newark* to be Fletcher! To be given her brother back at such a critical, strategic time in her life, and in such a supernatural set of circumstances, had to be a sign from the Lord. He had seen what she needed and had not let her down.

She again recalled, with amazement, her conversation with her Aunt Caro—Sadie, when they had discussed seeing the world together. She had told her it would have been perfect if only Fletcher had been there to accompany them. *And now he is! Surely there is purpose in all that!*

They were all deep in their own thoughts as the *Neptune* maneuvered far out into deep waters. Despite all of the things that had happened, they were still hopeful about the future. Yes, Summers Bluff and Savannah were forever behind them. They were on a voyage to a new land, and were determined to forge ahead to meet life, however it would come.

The captain told them they should reach their destination by sometime in September. *Ah, September. September is good, isn't it?* Victoria loved the changing of the seasons, and autumn was her favorite time of year. She wondered what it would be like in San Francisco in September.

It was also her birth month. She had come into the world on the twenty-fourth of September, and hopefully, she would come into her new world in time for her birthday. That was significant to her, just like those lovely spring mornings back in her garden had somehow seemed so significant to her back in February. She hadn't known then that they would be her last mornings in a place that she had lived and loved, but God had, and therefore had called attention to them so that she would take special note to enjoy them while she could.

Only God knew what tomorrow held for them, what September would bring to them, but time would tell. They knew one thing: they all knew they wouldn't have to face one more day alone.

Chapter 24

*J*ake Jackson was beside himself with concern over Emma's disappearance. She had gone missing three days earlier without a word or a sign to him that anything was wrong. Try as he might, he could not bring up any memories of conversations he had had with her that would even remotely suggest she was in trouble or danger.

True, she was still grieving the loss of her parents, but surely, she would not have deliberately struck out on her own without a word of good-bye. He was deeply in love with her and they were going to marry as soon as her mourning period was over, weren't they?

He was blaming himself for not taking better care of her. He blamed himself for not declaring his love for her when he'd had the opportunity, when it would have done some good, before Josiah and Miss Tilley had gone up North. If only he had any kind of warning from the Lord, he most certainly would have.

He tried to puzzle out why he had not received any warning whatsoever about what was troubling Emma or why she had left so suddenly. He knew perfectly well that the Lord speaks to his children and looking back, they can usually see he was trying to prepare them in some way before an unseen tragedy or hurtful event occurred. *Hadn't Emma kept saying that she hadn't been able to help herself feeling a dread about her parent's trip? She had been warned of an impending attack. Why had I not been warned about her leaving?* It perplexed him greatly that he had had no warning at all.

He knew Emma loved Summers Bluff better than any other place. *How could she have ever left it voluntarily?* That was the question that was bothering him the most. He had a million questions, but nary an answer. *Where is she? Is she well? Where are the others: Big Joe, Aunt Caroline, Kitty, and Granny? Did someone take her and the others away by force for some evil reason? No, surely not! Are they being treated well? Surely not, if they had been taken against their will in the first place!*

Questions hounded him night and day. He had seen Judge West several times in the past three days, but the judge had seemed as confused as the rest of them as to where she might be.

Judge West had seen the on-going state of mind Jake was in over worrying about Emma's safety, and so had revealed the part of her story about selling the farm to him, and saying she would contact him where to send the money from the sale.

Then was the first time Jake had known any relief whatsoever, as at least she was safe in as far as it went, and had not left by force. Whether she was, indeed, safe remained to be seen.

The judge had said that he could not tell him where she was presently, as he said he did not know. Actually, he did not know exactly where on the ocean she was, so that was technically true. But, had he known just how badly Jake Jackson was hurting, he would have told him all.

Jake had some semblance of pride left, and if she had not wanted him to know, he couldn't blame her, or the judge, or anyone but himself. He could have been married to her now, if he hadn't put every other obligation first. Hindsight was clearly identifying his taking his time in courting her as the cause for him not being a married man right then.

At least he now knew she had not been taken by physical force, but mental force was something else again. It was obvious that something she greatly feared must have been behind such a drastic decision to leave a beautiful, prosperous and generationally held land. She was afraid of something big enough that would cause her to also leave the man she loved without a word.

He wanted to think he knew Emma's heart, if not her mind, when she had made her decisions to take off on such a wild tangent. Emma Summers' heart was such that she wouldn't cause anyone to worry unnecessarily if she could in any way avoid it. That was truly her heart. She would put herself out gladly rather than inconvenience others. He had witnessed that time and time again.

And yet this lovely, young woman had sold her most valuable possessions and had gone off to places unknown without a word to anybody except Judge West. *Why did she not come to me? What could have possibly caused her to hie off like that alone in the dead of night? Will I ever have answers? Not the longest day I live will I let this go!* he vowed.

He reasoned night and day and had finally admitted to himself that he didn't have the money to go off haphazardly searching for her when he didn't have any idea where to search. The judge was having private detectives do that, and he finally decided he could only wait and see what developed. When they found her, he could decide then what his actions would be.

He also realized that even if he had had the money to go looking for her, he could not leave his sheep unattended, especially with no other pastor to step in and take his place. The Lord had given him the solemn trust of caring for their souls, and he didn't have any release or peace to do otherwise.

He couldn't understand what was happening or why, so he just had to take it by faith that God was still in control and would work it out for everyone's good someday. He just hoped it would be sooner, rather than later.

He didn't know how people went about their daily lives with such losses in their hearts. He understood a little bit now about how Emma had felt when she had lost her brother and her parents. *Does that kind of hurt ever end?* he wondered. He banished that thought. He may have to endure for some time, and it wouldn't do to become a victim of these circumstances, or to be defeated at the onset. No, he would carry on, stay where he had been placed, and be faithful. Some things were out of the hands of men.

If Emma had left because she was not supposed to marry him, what then? No, that would be such insult to injury. She wouldn't ever be fickle. His fragile state of mind would not permit that thought. Nothing had changed between them except geography. They were still Emma and Jake. *She will be waiting for me somewhere. The Lord will surely lead me to her!* He had always been strong mentally. He had to believe that. So he believed. Emma's leaving had been the worst thing that he had ever had to face.

"Emma! Oh, Lord, how I miss you, my love! Forgive me for not being there for you when you needed me the most! Wherever you are, please forgive me and know that I will always love you and that I will come to you the moment I know where you are. My heart is true, and I won't change my mind. It would take a true act of God to get me to forget you, and I can't even imagine that," he spoke to the empty room.

"Lord, you are going to have to help me! I cannot endure this on my own. I know I must, but I want to give you the honor and glory for everything in my life, or as to Emma, not in my life at the moment, but I can't give it to you unless you help me!" he cried.

"I have answered your call. I am staying at my post. But I ask you to strengthen Emma and me, for I know she is unhappy wherever she is. I know she loves me as I love her. Forgive me for not being diligent enough to her needs. Keep us in your hands for this journey!" he prayed as sincerely as he knew how.

The rest was up to a higher power, a power he had trusted all his life; a power that evidently had a greater plan and purpose for his and Emma's future than he had realized. But he would have to take this journey one step at a time and alone.

For the sake of sanity, he would somehow have to get a grip on himself. He would have to take one day at a time. *It may only take a few days to find Emma and therefore, I have no real need to despair! I can endure a few days, can't I?*

But the suffocating pall hanging over him warned him it would be more than a few days, maybe months, even years! What would he do then? No, he couldn't allow his mind to go there. That was a dangerous place to dwell. With some things, nobody but the Lord could help. But he knew, as incomprehensible as it was, that whatever would be would be.

Chapter 25

"I don't care what you think!" shouted Morgan. "I am telling you all that I want that witch found! She's not getting away with this! Not ever will I let her go unpunished!" he ranted.

"But boss, we checked ever'where. The whole mess of field hands are where they should be, and exceptin' Big Joe, the old granny hag, and that grandkid of hers, all of 'em's accounted for," Lewis said. "Don't know where they could be a headed as we went down ever' road out of the plantation, and not one neighbor or worker saw anybody leavin'. Not even anybody on your own spread saw a thing, and they'd a had to a passed right by your place! Wh—"

"Shut up and listen to me!" Morgan interrupted. In the height of his fury, the veins in his neck were distended and his face was red and contorted. He lifted Lewis by his shirtfront until he was nearly on his toes and yelled, "I'm no fool! I don't care what anybody says! Some body saw something! Find out who saw what and get back in here. Tell me what you find out, Lewis, and tell me soon, or I promise you they'll be talking about what I did to you for a long time to come!"

"Will do, boss," he said, grateful to be getting away from the evil force emanating from Morgan not to mention the evil stare he was known for and had been giving everybody since the moment he found out the chit was gone.

Lewis's thoughts raced. *Like I can find someone who's just up and gone like so much smoke. Nothin' to go on, nobody to squeeze, no place to turn. No tellin' who he's a gonna shoot before this here mess is over with! How in the world am I supposed to find out what the boss couldn't find out?*

Lewis knew Morgan surely didn't get his information by asking nicely, either. *That's the truth. Why, if he even suspected that somebody knew anythin' and hadn't told him, they'd be lucky to walk away from the conversation, let alone with any front teeth left in their mouths,* he thought, remembering such incidents he'd witnessed from Morgan's past dealings.

I kin rough somebody up with the best of 'em. But I don't think anybody seen 'em pass. He had remembered that everybody had been scared out of their wits and shaking like a wet hound when they had busted in asking each one about it, but they had the look of truth in their eyes, for all that.

I jest can't seem to find out anythin', and we know everythin' that happens in this place! Somebody's head's a gonna roll, and I shore hope it ain't mine!

Cal Morgan had seen fit to personally question Judge West, just to see his reaction when he told him of Emma's disappearance and asked whether or not he knew where she had gone.

"What in heaven's name do you mean gone?" asked the judge, jumping to his feet. Cal hesitated. Seeing the judge's astonishment, he was satisfied he had been genuinely surprised by the news.

Seeing Morgan's hesitation, the judge exploded. "Well, don't just stand there, man! Explain yourself at once! What do you mean coming in here telling me that Josiah's young girl is missing? How could she be? When did she disappear? Whe—"

"Hold on, Judge," Cal said. "I need to show you some notes her father signed showing that I had loaned him money on several occasions. They are perfectly legal and in order. That is his true signature and will stand up in court."

"You young scamp, how dare you? Don't you dare tell me what will or will not hold up in a court of law!" he bellowed. "I'm a judge, for pity's sake! Now you will explain to me what those notes could possibly have to do with that girl's disappearance!"

"Well, it's like this, Judge. I have greatly admired Miz Emma for a while now. After her folks passed away so sudden like, before Mr. Summers had an opportunity to cancel these notes, I again proposed to her, assuring her that these notes would certainly be cancelled for my wife. However, sh—"

"Sir, are you telling me, a judge, that you blackmailed that girl into agreeing to marry you?"

"Not at all, Judge, not at all. I had proposed to her before. Naturally, I knew that if she attempted to pay off these debts, it would leave her without funds to operate the plantation, in which case she would lose it. I explained all that to her, but she insisted yesterday that I meet her in the bank with the notes so she could repay the loans. I was there with Sheriff Oaks, Jefferson Lewis, and Grant, just to be sure that what all was happening there was clear to her understanding."

"And did she agree to marry you, or did she pay off the notes?" he asked in growing frustration.

"Actually, she did neither, Your Honor. She withdrew all her money from her account and simply placed it in her reticule and left the bank. That was the last any of us saw of her."

"Well, how in thunder can a lone woman like Miss Emma Summers just up and disappear? Just you tell me that if you can!"

"Well, that's just it. She wasn't alone. Two of her house maids and her driver, Big Joe, are also missing."

"For pity's sake, man, Big Joe could never be missing!" he exploded. " He's the hugest of men, measuring at least near seven foot, and people notice him *everywhere* he goes! You know that! Who else is 'missing'?"

"Nobody has seen Miz Emma's aunt, the old granny, or her granddaughter since yesterday. Lewis said everything was in order, though, when he went to bed last night."

"Well, what are you doing here? Why are you not out looking for her if you care so much for her that you want to marry her?" The judge shook his fist at him. "What has the sheriff done to find her? Tell me that! Have all the field hands been questioned? Surely, somebody knows something!" He pounded his fist on the desk so hard that his clerk came running to see why a dignified judge was shouting and pounding like that, which none of his clerks had seen or heard before.

"Yes, of course, all measures have been taken to question everyone whether they are apt to know anything or not. We have also questioned all the clerks at the railroad depot about passengers going to Atlanta, Charleston, and beyond. We've checked passenger lists for all those, as well as all ships that left port last night. I tell you they've just vanished!"

"Well, I for one just don't believe it. She would have no reason to. If she did this because of money, she knew I would have lent her enough for the plantation once she paid you off. She knew that, surely. What other reason could she have?" he asked in bewilderment.

"Really, I can't think of one. On the trip to Philadelphia, her father had given me his blessings to ask for her hand. He was even going to speak to her about accepting my proposal. But then the fire—"

"Yes, yes, that dreadful fire." The judge slumped back into his chair, looking sad and regretful. "I'm sorry, my boy, for my unfortunate reaction here today, but you must appreciate what a shock this has been to me. Her father and I were the very best of friends since boyhood. Josiah and his whole family were like my own kin, and them dying like that a mere fortnight hence— well, it's still so raw." He shook his head in grief.

Suddenly, he looked as if a thought had just occurred. Jumping back to his feet, he exclaimed, "I can't think why I never thought to tell you this at first, but I suppose I was so downright overcome with news of Emma's disappearance, that this never entered my mind until right now," the judge exclaimed.

"I certainly should have mentioned it sooner, for this is important, but Big Joe came here last night with a signed deed to Summers Bluff plantation. I was asked to buy it from Emma, and I recorded the deed in my name just this very morning, in fact. I won't tell you what she sold it to me for. That's our business."

Noting the look of utter disbelief that flashed across Morgan's face at such news, he hurried on. "But I surely asked him, 'Big Joe, is everything all right out there?' Big Joe just grinned at me and said, 'Shore 'nuff, Judge.' The judge forced a slight smile and continued. "So naturally, I didn't suspect anything was amiss."

He continued his story. "She had told him to tell me that she just didn't think she could carry on further without money, as she was fixing to pay off some unexpected notes, and that the responsibility of such a large plantation was also wearing on her, so…" he shook his head at the pity he felt for her, "I just thought she was exhausted from all the mental worry she has been through in the past five years, and her nothing but a child," he lamented. "I supposed that some small notes she'd come across had her concerned."

Judge West saw Morgan's unbelief give way to malice and hatred as it fully dawned on him what Emma had pulled off.

"Nevertheless, she needed money and was using the plantation as collateral for what I was considering a loan. I tried to send the deed back to her, but she had told Big Joe that if I did that, he was not to accept any money. I was proud to help her. I assumed she would keep on working the land and when she got rested and her grief had lessened, she would buy back the place when she could. Well, that was my thinking, but now …," he said, shaking his head in supposed bewilderment.

"Maybe she figured she needed the money to pay you off before she decided not to," he speculated. "Or maybe she knew she was leaving and had no intentions of ever buying the place back!" he said, still sadly shaking his head.

There was nothing Morgan could say or do in answer to this incredible information that the judge had just given him concerning what Emma Summers had done to him.

Oh yes, I have underestimated the chit, for sure. But I won't make that mistake again, he thought, while trying to hold his fury in check in front of the judge.

"We both knew that Josiah had said that with Master Fletch gone, if anything should happen to him, or should the plantation ever get into trouble or became too much for Emma, she was to sell the land to me," the judge said. "Josiah knew it would bring enough to keep her in comfort until such time as she would wed, and surely that would not be long in coming. But if you hear anything, anything a tall from her, you let me know immediately or I will know the reason why!"

"Why, of course, Judge. Of course!"

Cal Morgan was seething in his dilemma as he left Judge West's office. *Well, I am sure now that the old man is as in the dark as I am. Nevertheless, I'll keep an eye on him. But if he were trying to hide anything, why would he have divulged that business about him buying the plantation? Yes, she is a witch and no doubt about it, but she'll not withstand me again! Up and sold it right out from under me as cunningly and deceitfully as any blackguard! She will rue the day she decided she could hold her own against Cal Morgan!* He was shaking with rage and a determination for revenge.

Well, that was certainly enjoyable! Judge West laughed out loud as he watched Morgan climb into his buggy and lay the whip to his horse. *I pray that I live to have the pleasure of laughing in his wicked face just as I'm laughing right now! Yes, Judge West, you can still strut and shout as well now as you did as a trial lawyer some years back!* His shoulders fairly shook with his laughter.

The judge thought that even if he did say so himself, that it had been a stroke of genius to tell him about the sale of the plantation. *He would have found out about it anyway had they tried to place a lien on the place in order go ahead and auction it off, as surely as they would have done to satisfy those forged notes. Then he would have wondered when all that had transpired about me buying the place.* He smiled to himself.

"*This way, it shows that I had nothing to hide from him, and it also stopped him from putting a lien on the place to force a sale,*" the judge thought, still remembering the exact moment Morgan had realized that his fat was in the fire.

Thank the Lord that Emma has had the presence of mind to outwit him a get away! He tried to bamboozle her, but she used the same chicanery on him and got away with it! She surely is a force to be reckoned with!" he chuckled, remembering how infuriated Morgan was when he stomped out of his office.

He could have strangled Morgan with his bare hands when he had been lying to him about how Josiah Summers had given him permission to wed that beautiful girl of his. Like he would have let that lowdown trash touch one hair on her head. *Knowing that he had threatened to kill that child and then to sit there and tell me how much he cared for her had been pert near more than I could stand!*

Remembering those three women's fear when he had left them alone aboard that ship, he sobered up. *I declare that he will swing for this before it is all over!* But he feared it was far from over. "Yes, mark my words, he will hang before it's all over, and hell will not be hot enough for the likes of him!" he prophesied aloud to the room in general and to himself in particular.

Again, picturing Morgan's face when he had realized that he had been flimflammed by a mere slip of a girl, he chuckled and said out loud, "I know this is far from over, but my, my, my! That *was* refreshing while it lasted!"

The End of Part One

Part Two

San Francisco

Dedication

To my sister, Judy, who believes in
me and is my dearest friend.
To all my Sisters in Christ, who
love a clean mindless romance.
This one's for y'all.

Prologue

Savannah, Georgia 1870

Pastor Jake Jackson was still beside himself with concern over the seeming disappearance of Emma Summers. She had gone missing three days ago without a word or a sign to him that anything was amiss in her life. Other than the obvious horrible grief she was living through over losing both her parents a mere fortnight before.

Yes, he knew she was still grieving that loss, but surely she would not have deliberately lit out on her own without a word of good-bye to him. He knew she cared for him, and he was deeply in love with her. They were going to be married just as soon as her mourning period was over, weren't they? Of course, they were! Wherever she had gone, when her mind was more settled, she would contact him and he would go to her and make her his wife. Surely, the Lord would see to that.

He was blaming himself for not taking better care of her. He blamed himself over and over for days now for not declaring his love for her when it would have done some good, before Josiah and Miss Tilley had gone north to Philadelphia. If only he had any kind of warning from the Lord he most certainly would have done. He knew that God speaks to His children. Yet he had not had any warning whatsoever, and that fact was bothering him more than he could say.

Jake's congregation had also been outraged at Emma's disappearance, just as he had, as all of them had known and loved her all of her life. Her disappearance had caused heartbreak among her friends all across Savannah, as first her brother had been killed in the war, then both her parents had been killed in a tragic fire, and now they were stunned when Emma and her aunt had gone missing.

Had they not known the integrity of heart with which the entire Summers family had shown with the workers on the plantation, those with whom they conducted business, and closest friends alike, they would have sworn they were living under a curse. However, they had known how much they loved the Lord, and how they all had lived righteously before Him. Even so, they also knew that bad things happen to good people all the time, as it rains on the just and unjust alike.

They knew there was more to the story than was meeting the eye concerning Emma's whereabouts. Yes, truth will out someday, they reckoned amongst themselves. Until then, Emma, Caroline Summers, old Granny Thornton, Kitty, and Big Joe would be in their constant prayers.

Something had been behind this sudden and drastic action on Emma's part to up and sell her beloved Summers Bluff plantation. Judge West had seen the state of mind that Jake was in from worrying about her safety, and had revealed the part of her story about selling the place to him, and her saying she would contact him where to send the money from the sale of the property. With that revelation at least now he knew she had not been kidnapped or otherwise physically coerced into leaving.

Jake could not know that Emma was using the name Victoria Sullivan, her aunt Caroline was being called Sadie, and her friend, Kitty, was now posing as Cousin Lilly. Nor did he know his lifelong best friend in the world, Emma's brother, Fletcher, whom he thought to have been killed in the war, was alive. Not only that, but he had been reunited with Emma and was traveling with her to help make a new life in sunny California. Had he but known that, he would have been much comforted by the knowledge, and very much less concerned about her safety.

Jake knew it would be just a matter of time before she contacted him. He knew that someday he would know all. He had no idea when, but he could wait. Yes, he could wait for Emma, however long it took. In the meantime, he would carry on with as much dignity and faith as he could muster. He determined he would be there awaiting her contact. *Yes, Emma, I will come to you the moment I know where you are!*

Chapter 1

*V*ictoria and the others had been traveling aboard the *Neptune*, making its way from Savannah, down around the tip of South America, and back up the West Coast to San Francisco. Having spent the best part of six months sailing to get away from Cal Morgan, they were now nearing the end of their long voyage.

They had made several ports of call in South America to drop off cotton, and other supplies from Savannah, and to take on fresh and dried fruit, dried beef, coffee, and other goods that would be delivered to San Francisco. Several times they had been forced to hold up in port to weather violent storms, prolonging their journey. They were young and healthy and had endured hardship like good soldiers, but were very glad their journey was drawing to a close.

During the long, monotonous journey, the family had ample time for many long conversations about things in Connor's past in hopes of helping him regain his memory. Connor did not recall any of the specific stories the women had shared with him, but just hearing about them made it seem like they were implanting memories. Just knowing the same things that they recalled gave him hope that one day they would become more than mere stories to him.

Since they were all using assumed names to thwart being found by the Morgan bunch, during their long months at sea they had pondered and discussed the prospect of permanently giving up their time-honored name of Summers. They assumed they had now successfully escaped Calhoun Morgan. They wondered if it were safe enough to resume their rightful names once again once they landed in San Francisco.

Their quandary was that Southern people did not easily do such a thing as to give up their generationally established good names, at least not in that year of 1870. They had come through the Civil War with nothing much but their good names, and even this temporary name change had cost them plenty of guilt and shame, necessary as it had been.

They had finally decided on the side of wisdom and prudence that they would still have to use the name of Sullivan until this ordeal with Morgan was truly over. They had realized that it would still be folly to resume using even their given names. A tall, auburn-haired woman of means called Emma, newly arrived in San Francisco, living with her Aunt Caroline, and having a maid called Kitty, well it wouldn't matter what the last name was, it would not be difficult to read between those lines. Even if their enemies thought Fletcher dead, a name like his wasn't common. It could cause curiosity, especially given his close association with the ladies.

There was also the difficulty of the other passengers and crew aboard the *Neptune*. They had followed through with using the assumed names during the voyage so that if anyone was ever questioned, all they would remember is that the Sullivan family of five had made the journey. That would agree with the ship's registry, and it would be said that none of them had been in deep mourning. Although the chances were slim, yet not impossible, that later on they might come into contact with some passenger or crew, and in that event, they would be better off still being known by the names they had used aboard ship.

So it was determined that they all would remain Sullivans until Morgan and his bunch were brought to justice. Then too, a household of two female cousins, a brother and sister-in-law, and an aunt, all living together under a name other than Summers would give pause to anyone looking for them.

Also, after nearly six months of addressing each other in their assumed names, they were comfortable with them now, but remembering them in a time of excitement or crisis might be another matter. They would have to school themselves not to answer or react when they heard someone speak their real names, as they would most probably be speaking to someone other than themselves.

Connor was hopelessly in love with his beautiful wife, and as the voyage progressed he found that he dearly loved his newly found sister, aunt and 'cousin' as well. Who could help but love those kind, adorable, and beautiful women? Victoria, Aunt Sadie and little Lilly, with their bright eyes, big smiles, and true hearts. They may have had tears in their eyes occasionally, as they lamented their circumstances, but it was certain they would also have a smile on their lips, and a hope in their hearts for what awaited them on the other side of the voyage. They were just those kinds of women, and Connor loved them for it.

Yes, the Sullivan family was growing closer every day. Connor was beginning to realize how much his going to war, and subsequently having been reported killed in action, would have so hurt his gentle and loving sister. Should anything happen to her now he knew he would be devastated. If he could have remembered her from childhood, how much worse would that have made losing her?

Yes, loving sometimes leads to pain, as it well might in this case, but it will well be worth the suffering. No, I wouldn't trade my position in this family now for anything else I could imagine! he mused.

Chapter 2

When they reached the Bay of San Francisco, 23rd September, it was a marvelous sight they beheld! So much was to be seen in such a grand place that they could scarcely catch their breath, let alone be patient for the ship to dock. They had made port late in the afternoon. But to be done with the long, hazardous journey, and to set foot on dry land would be a wonderful thing after so many months at sea. Gazing around them, they could scarcely believe their eyes. The Bay of San Francisco boasted dozens of ships of every size and description, unlike the much smaller port back home in Georgia. Why, they were beholding a city at least five times that of Savannah!

Captain Flynn had told them there were over one hundred fifty thousand people living in San Francisco then. Although the gold that had been discovered in forty-eight, and the rush of forty-niners had given way somewhat, he claimed that the added mining of silver, and other minerals in the valley, was now full blown making more fortunes than could be imagined.

What an exciting day it had been! The most exciting Victoria could remember having in a long, long while, apart from discovering Connor standing on the deck of the *Newark* nearly six months earlier. But that day could hardly be called exciting, even for all the excitement they had experienced after finding Connor alive, but what could they call the rest of the heartbreak they had endured that day?

No, not exciting, to be sure. It was a fearful, hurtful, time of fleeing for one's life, releasing one's lifelong home and friends, and lighting out for parts unknown in fear and trembling. Finding Connor alive, although suffering from amnesia, was the only bright spot in that otherwise terrifying day. But after finding Fletcher, the overwhelming emotion that had overcome them all was a deep reverence and thankfulness to God, for they had been given an incredible opportunity to be united once again. They had certainly cheated death, and Victoria couldn't help but regret all the wasted time spent in the agony of grief that she and her dear parents had suffered needlessly in thinking Fletcher dead.

Looking at the city from the bay, they found so many diverse types of homes that it made the city a sight to behold. Besides the normal dwellings, there were vast numbers of buildings that boasted three, four, and even five stories with columned porticos on many of the large buildings, attesting to the prosperity of the city. Some homes were rough and small, but others were like palaces of gingerbread. Still others were beautiful, romantic mansions of the bay-windowed Italianate architecture that were situated facing the bay. The Lord had surely brought them to a promising and prosperous looking place to begin again.

The prevailing atmosphere around them on that soft, warm, September day was one of gaiety and liberation; they all sensed it until every last one of them felt simply giddy. They were experiencing joy and true happiness that day, which none of them had felt or expressed much of during the long months at sea.

Contentment was the most any of them could have hoped for, but today reminded Victoria of when they were all growing up before the war. They were a carefree lot back then, the three of them. Fletcher was a bit more serious than the two girls, who giggled more than any five girls they knew back in Savannah. But despite all of his responsibilities on the plantation, he did have fun growing up. Especially, when he was with Jake Jackson or the girls.

Yes, they were happy once, a long time ago before…well, before a lot of things. But they all were worn out with being sad and having terrible things happen to them. Somehow they knew this was another opportunity to be joyful again, and they intended to grab all the joy they could, and to do it with both hands!

Growing up, Victoria's brother had the ability to fool her time and time again with his mischief. How she had missed his laughter when he had gone to war. She thought never to hear it ring out again. But now she thought, *That's like the time when we thought mama had gone to town, but she had only gotten halfway to the road when she had turned around because she had forgotten her gloves. She caught us just as we were skipping our studies and heading for the swimming pond. How we had laughed over that when we came out of our corners, where we had been sent to meditate on how to behave ourselves when mama left the house.*

When Granny Thornton heard what the three of us had done, she said, "It just goes to show ye that ever' good-bye ain't gone, is it now? I'd be recollectin' that in future, I would!"

Well, neither is my brother's laughter gone, and once we find our routine, his memory will surely start to come back. Then we can share our memories once again. *They will be twice as precious then.* She added out loud to herself, "Truly, Granny, ever' good-bye ain't gone!"

The first thing they were concerned with was finding lodgings. They supposed they could find a good hotel without any difficulty and could look for a permanent residency a bit later on. Surely, people here advertise accommodations in a city of this size.

Having a porter locate their trunks, they asked a cabby on the docks to take them to a respectable hotel in a nice area. He said he knew of a boarding house in a nice part of town that had only one other boarder presently. The unusual vacancy was due to a family that had been living there while their new home was being built, and since the house was now finished, they had gone to their new abode just that day.

The Sullivans didn't think they were interested in a boarding house, but the cabby advised them to reconsider. As good shelter was hard to find, what with cold weather nearly upon them, so many lodgings had already filled, with more people looking for permanent housing every day. He told them that since it was late in the day, they would be arriving around supper time wherever they went, and should they decide to go to Stanhope Street, they could be assured of finding that all would be ready for them at Killian House.

"How do you come to know so much about this establishment," Victoria asked the cabby.

"Well, miss, you see it belongs to my niece, Maude. It's her place and she is one of the best cooks in town, if I say so myself. Not that she does the cooking, mind, but she has taught her cooks well, has Maude. Besides, this is a noisy town, all right, but it's quiet over there with no building going on about the place. It's in a more established part of town, you might say, so everything is already built up about it. Not that Maude needs to have boarders. No, no, not at all. Her Caleb, God rest his soul, left her enough that she is comfortable off now," he told them.

They didn't want to seem rude, but just the same, thought it would be advisable to have him take them to a hotel. After all, they were not used to life in a big city. Who hadn't heard tales of fraud, robbery, and the likes? He graciously accepted their rejection of his suggestion, and proceeded to take them to a hotel that was well placed in a respectable and affluent part of town.

When Connor approached the registry desk asking for accommodations for a family of five, he was met by a wide-eyed stare by the reception clerk. He then informed Connor that the railroads were holding a convention in the city to discuss both sides of the issue of one of the railroads possibly selling out to the other. People had come from all parts around to listen to the arguments. Many people of means had invested in one or the other railroads and wanted first hand information, as they had a dog in that race. "That being the case," he informed them, "it is nigh on to impossible to find a room for one in any hotel of any size or reputation, let alone for five!"

Just then, the cabby came in carrying some hand equipage. He was recognized by the clerk and addressed. "My good man, why haven't you told these people about the home on Stanhope Street? Are there no rooms available there either?" he asked, perplexed.

"I did, guv'nor, but they preferred a nice hotel, so to speak."

The clerk told Connor that the Killian House on Stanhope Street was well known in the city, and that it was a beautiful, well-run establishment. He assured them that they would be well situated there.

That seemed to settle it for everyone, since they didn't seem to have any other options, and so agreed to be taken to the Stanhope Street dwelling. They only hoped they were not making a mistake by going to a private home, instead of the hotel they had imagined.

Victoria thought maybe it wouldn't be so bad after all. Perhaps a woman who was well known, and who had boarders, would know a bit about what was going on in town. She might be able to guide them in what areas to stay away from, and what areas they should look for more permanent accommodations when the time came. But for tonight, they looked forward to a good cook's supper table and a hot bath afterwards.

The cabby, whose name they had learned was Samuel, had been true to his word. The Killian House was situated in a neighborhood that was nicer than most, where the bay-windowed Italianate architecture was prevalent. It was in front of one of these mansions that Samuel had drawn up the horses and stopped. The home was on a lovely, tree-lined street on one of the several hills of San Francisco. It was a three-storied, cream-colored façade with terracotta tile roofing that blended in nicely with the other homes around it. It certainly qualified as a mansion, and they could only hope that it was as nice and homey on the inside as it was beautiful on the outside. The interior of houses had a way of disappointing one, when much was expected from a beautiful exterior.

Samuel led them up to the front door. He told them there was also a private back entrance where there was a stairway leading directly to the second and third stories. He said another one led downstairs and opened onto the beautifully landscaped garden. Victoria was delighted to hear about the garden, and made a mental note right then to visit it at her earliest opportunity.

Upon entering the atrium, they found they needn't have worried about the inside of the home. The large atrium held lush palms, tropical plants, and flowers all around. Beyond, they could see luxurious furnishings, very well appointed, and done in a most tasteful manner that befitted a mansion such as that one. Introductions were made all around, as Connor presented his Sullivan family.

The proprietress, on first impression, seemed a sympathetic and gentle lady of about fifty years, who had maintained her neat figure and good looks, just as Aunt Sadie had done. She informed them that she was particular about whom she accepted into her home, and that she would require references as soon as possible.

Connor assured her that he perfectly understood the advisability of references, and assured her that theirs would soon be forthcoming. He informed her that a judge, and long time friend of the family, would be sending references by wire just as soon as he knew where to send them. Mrs. Killian was satisfied and it was left at that, as she could easily discern what manner of people stood before her.

She told them that she had been hoping for another family of lodgers, as the one that had just left had been so delightful. She expressed her obviously sincere hope that they would be comfortable and content in her home, and would want to stay on awhile. She asked them to lay off their light wraps and hats in the adjoining cloakroom, and then proceeded to show them to their quarters.

While the ladies removed their outerwear, she looked at Connor and asked, "Where are you from, Mr. Sullivan?" Since she had asked him, he took his wife's arm and answered that they were from Pennsylvania. He hadn't really felt the need to explain where the ladies had begun their journey, for she had not specifically asked about all of them. The less said about Savannah, the better.

Victoria looked around her lovely quarters, after having lived six months aboard the *Neptune*, and immediately felt like she could love this home. She had made up her mind not to compare any living arrangements they may come up with to the plantation, where she had lived in splendor all her life, as she had felt that none could compare favorably with Summers Bluff. She wondered for the thousandth time when and where they would eventually have a home of their own again. But for now these accommodations were much more welcoming and beautiful than she could have imagined, and they were very much appreciated.

The delicious aromas emanating from the kitchen announced that the evening supper hour was approaching, reminding her that she was quite famished. It smelled like pot roast and gravy, with all the trimmings, and there was nothing she liked better!

Chapter 3

fter they had been shown to their rooms, they had quickly refreshed themselves by washing up a bit. They hadn't bothered to dress for dinner, as Mrs. Killian had said there was no time to make a toilette. They hurried down to the formal dining room where the other boarder was already seated.

As they entered the room, he rose to his feet and introduced himself, as Maude was speaking with a maid at the moment of their entrance. Paul Cabot was probably in his late twenties or so, rather good-looking, having a medium build, sharp eyes, thick black hair, and a small mustache. He had very little to say throughout the course of the meal, and seemed to have trouble handling any direct gaze from the four women at the table.

As is the way with spirit beings, some things are picked up in the spirit without any words being exchanged or actions noted. It was not like any of the Sullivans to make snap judgments, especially ones that put others in a harsh light without benefit of time to reveal their true personalities, but with Mr. Cabot, they were willing to make an exception.

Shiftless, Victoria thought, immediately feeling guilty for making such a snap judgment.

He gives me an odd feelin', that'un does, thought Lilly.

Aunt Sadie was busy with her own thoughts. *I wonder a seemingly particular woman like Mrs. Killian trusts him enough to keep him as a boarder.*

Connor was thinking, *He's one to keep my eye on around the women folk.* Elizabeth felt he was a cold man, despite the affable smiles he gave them when he introduced himself. He definitely seemed to be a contradiction. She hoped he would not be the fly in their otherwise perfect ointment.

The small group chatted pleasantly over the extremely well cooked supper, and Mrs. Killian had managed to put them entirely at ease in her home. She related something of her life in San Francisco before the passing of her husband, and what her life was now that she had been widowed for a few years. She said that she had not been raised with wealth, but that Mr. Killian had been a very successful businessman in the fur and trapping trade, buying and selling furs, and supplying food and other necessities to the trappers.

Later, he had benefited greatly as a supplier to the gold miners. He eventually made his fortune, even more so than many miners, who picked and panned in the gold fields for years, never hitting a big strike. Toward the end of the war he had been killed when he'd been thrown from his stallion. Fortunately for Miss Maude, as she preferred to be addressed, his assets had more than carried her through the six years hence. It could be presumed that there was still a very nice, large nest egg in the bank. If a fortune could rightly be called a nest egg, as she had sold off the business concerns and had realized a handsome profit.

True to Samuel's word she did not have to accept boarders, but after a few solitary years, she found that she was lonely in her big house on the hill, and wanted to see it come back to life. She loved people, and the near empty house was so large and lonely for so few occupants as just her and the servants. She wanted friends who would live in it with her, even if they started out as her boarders.

She was grateful for her prayers being answered by such a nice, young family as the Sullivans moving in. But especially was she grateful for Sadie, who was about her own age. They would have many things in common, and surely, would become fast friends. She hoped so. She'd been so lonely since Caleb passed, and the last family who boarded with her had a growing family, which took up too much of their mother's time for them to become really close friends. She had high hopes for Sadie becoming just such a friend. Maude had no way of knowing how many lifelong friends Sadie had given up when she left Savannah, or how much she had missed them the past six months, or just how much she longed for close friendships again.

They all went to bed that night content and happy that they had come so far without mishap. Now when they had finally arrived, they had been blessed with a good home, and a good mistress, in this peaceful abode. They all were thinking that God had been so very good to them. They were filled with thankfulness, as they drifted off into a deep and restful sleep for the first time in a long time.

As Victoria was drifting off to sleep, she wondered where they would find a church to attend before Sunday. Thinking of church, she naturally thought of *him*... those big, brown, love-filled eyes looking into hers, and wondered what Jake was doing right then.

She prayed that some day she would have the opportunity to sit down with him and explain everything. She knew he must be worried about her. Despite all of the good reasons she felt she had at the time to keep from involving him, she knew that he would have been deeply hurt. But time would heal his heart, and she preferred to have him hurt for a season, rather than dead forever. She prayed that when he found out everything that he would understand and be able to forgive her.

Chapter 4

$\mathcal{L}$illy quietly entered Victoria's room, and finding her still asleep, she cried, "Happy Birthday, 'Cousin'!" plopping down on the bed beside her. "It's time to rise and shine! Ye've a beautiful day for yer twentieth birthday!"

Victoria thought a moment and said, "Yes, of course! It is the twenty-fourth of September now, isn't it? Funny, after so long of not caring about birthdays, now on my twentieth one I can't wait to see what this day brings. I haven't been excited about a birthday since Connor went off to war!" She wouldn't understand until later the significance of this very birthday, and the sweet memories it would bring in future.

"Thank you, 'Cousin'," Victoria told her, as Lilly tidied up the room. When Victoria was ready, Kitty would help her with her toilette, as she had a way with hair. Then they would go down to breakfast.

"Are the others awake?" Victoria asked.

"And why not? It's been daylight this past hour. I heard 'em stirrin' a while back," Lilly answered. "How did ye sleep in yer new home?"

Victoria answered in the affirmative, as she had slept like the dead. "And you?" Victoria asked her.

"Ye know me, miss, I kin sleep anywheres. Never been a fussy sleeper," she answered. "So what's our plans for today, me lady?"

"Plans!" Victoria repeated, as she savored the word. How long had it been since she had been able to plan a day, rather than just survive it?

The Sullivan women had long discussed what they would like to do upon arriving in San Francisco. They found they wanted what they had missed the most: the simple, every day things that they had taken for granted all their lives; the things that people miss so much when they are taken away. Things like having a hot, luxurious bath whenever they wanted. After being aboard a vessel with privacy being kin to non-existent, enough could not be said for having wonderful privacy once again. To sleep in a nice bed that didn't sway with every roll of the waves was a real blessing, too. Things uppermost in their minds were things like having some fresh, home-cooked food again, not to mention the replacement of their threadbare wardrobes. Before they could establish a normal daily routine they would have to go shopping, as they had planned. Now they were finally on dry ground and could begin to fulfill those plans.

Yes, we can plan. We can live and do what we like in this huge city! I feel safe for the first time since dear mama and papa passed, she thought.

Finally answering Lilly, she replied, "I suppose we will unpack and get ourselves situated. Today is…let's see…Saturday. Yes, Saturday, September 24, 1870. We should see what church Miss Maude attends and perhaps plan to visit with her tomorrow. I'm sure we would all benefit from services more than anything else we could do. What say you, Lilly?"

"Yes'um, I surely am ready to be with other believers in a real church after half a year's journey with heathen sailors. At least the captain was a friend of the judge and made 'em leave us alone," she replied with a pout of her lower lip, recalling the looks and murmurs they had received from the crew.

They finished their morning toilettes, and on their way to breakfast, met the others in the hallway. They had been on their way to Victoria's room to extend to her their very best birthday greetings. That done, they all went to the cozy breakfast room, where they enjoyed the crispy-fried bacon, scrambled eggs, hot scones, fruit, tea, and very lively conversation.

It was a wonderful birthday breakfast, especially with the fresh fruit, but they certainly needed to stretch their limbs and see some of the city while they walked off the delicious meal. They agreed to try to find the church Miss Maude attended, where they would be visiting on the morrow. Victoria, Lilly, and Aunt Sadie were left to explore the church on their own, as Elizabeth and Connor seemed to be resting after breakfast.

Miss Maude attended the Harbor Mission, which she explained was a cross between something like the Evangelical Baptist and a Pentecostal Church. It was located just about a six-minute leisurely stroll from the mansion and was a pleasant, two-storied edifice made from beautiful red brick.

It was Saturday and probably nobody would be about. The doors likely being unlocked, as was the case, they took the opportunity to see the interior. Since there was no one about, they took their liberty to spend a few moments at the altar giving thanks again for all the storms, rough seas, fevers, home-sickness, and bad food they had experienced aboard the *Neptune,* which the Lord had brought them safely through.

Their prayers finished, they were rising from the altar, when they realized a man had entered a side door across from the altar, and had been quietly watching. He apparently had seen the ladies praying, and had stood still awaiting them to finish. When they arose, he was taken aback by the tall one's beauty. He quickly came forward to greet them, and identified himself as the pastor, Mark Angelos.

He was a handsome man of about six feet, with dark locks and eyes, and was of an olive complexion. He was probably around twenty-eight and seemed to have a sense of humor about him, as he had a ready laughter. Although he was a perfect gentleman, most sincere, and certainly not flirty in the least, still he seemed to have a constant sparkle in his dark eyes that one was bound to notice.

They chatted for a few moments and he seemed to be an all around pleasant gentleman. He gave them the time of services, expressed a desire to see them in the morning worship, made his farewells, and was gone, headed in the direction of the residence off to the left side of the church, which was presumably the parsonage.

Well, that was an unexpected and pleasant exchange, Victoria thought. He had not made mention of wife or children, she noticed. Yet, surely an attractive man of his age was surely taken.

She did so dislike mishandling the truth of their prior home, but there was nothing to be done about it. She didn't exactly lie when she intimated that her people were from Pennsylvania as, indeed, were her grandparents and her mama. Certainly Connor and Elizabeth had lived there. She didn't see the wisdom of enlightening him as to the Callaway connection in Philadelphia, and certainly not the connection in Savannah.

This living with alias names, and a certain amount of elimination or evasiveness of their past, could get confusing and frustrating, but the less said was the less to keep track of. She would have to warn the others of that, too.

Mark Angelos had been the pastor of the Harbor Mission for the past five years, and theirs was a mixed congregation of all ages. While there had been an abundant number of young ladies attending, none were of the caliber of the one he had just spoken with. Ever since he had become pastor he had been extremely careful of even hinting that he was looking for a wife, for obvious reasons. He did not want the usual round of dinner invitations extended him from anxious mothers wanting their daughters wed. For that reason, as was his custom, he had only seen women from the church on social occasions in full view of everyone in attendance.

Now that the lovely Victoria Sullivan was staying with his good friend, Miss Maude Killian, the possibilities of a more serious social life had just become a reality for him. He had been incredibly drawn to those green eyes that he instinctively knew would dance and brilliantly shine at her amusement and good pleasure.

And that abundance of auburn hair! He had always loved the look of a redheaded woman, but had not personally known any before now. And he never could see a tall man like himself with a small, petite woman. He had always pictured a woman taller than most, as the one of his dreams.

It sounded silly to Mark's own mind when he thought about it, but when he had heard her somewhat husky voice it had nearly done him in. Maybe his lack of social life was showing, and that is what had inspired his much detailed thoughts of what he would want in a woman when the time came.

As appealing as her voice was, one thing puzzled him though, as he wondered just where in Pennsylvania they had managed to pick up their Southern drawls.

Victoria had started her voyage with accepting the irrefutable fact that any hope of romance with Jake Jackson was gone forever.

Change can be slow and painful, but once that had been settled, she had spent the next six months successfully pushing down all feelings and thoughts of him. Anytime a thought of Jake had crossed her mind, she had pushed it away immediately. While that had left a void on the inside of her, it had been preferable to the pain she had endured at first.

Now she was comfortable with life, without any uncontrolled longings for something or someone she couldn't have. She could tell that she had matured through the extreme circumstances forced upon her of late, starting with the death of her parents. She no longer felt like a victim of those circumstances. No, she had taken the options open to her, and now she was her own woman, making her own life with the Lord as her guide.

Pastor Angelos was the kind of man that left an indelible impression behind. *What a fine specimen of a man!* she thought, as they left the encounter. She knew she was feeling a bit giddy, and could only imagine what her mama would think of her thoughts! He did have the dark looks that women swoon for, after all. Not to mention his personality and humor, which had immediately put them all at ease. It was like he really wanted to speak with them, not just fulfill an obligation. And what about that sparkle in his eyes when he laughs?

Oh, don't even start with that! she chastised herself. No, this time it would be different! She would guard her heart until another man, who might cause her breath to catch, had declared his feelings for her. She didn't want another half way love affair, only to be lost before it really had even begun, leaving her hurt, confused, and in despair. After all, she was no longer the same carefree debutant as when she gave her heart so freely, and childishly, to a man who had never spoken the words.

Chapter 5

After the dinner repast, Victoria had made her way to the garden she had been told about, while the rest of the house was quiet with everyone presumably resting. The conservatory was average sized, compared to the size of the home, but much smaller than the one at Summers Bluff. She admired the dwarf fruit trees, the big leafed banana trees, lovely ferns, and beautiful tropical flowers, some the likes of which she had never seen before. Of course, there were all the common vegetables, too, being as there was an outside garden beside the conservatory, with it boasting some of the same things as the conservatory, only on a larger scale.

The outdoor palms around the estate were huge. The landscaping itself was remarkable. Much tier work had been used to accommodate the gently sloping or sometimes rolling terrain, which had an outstanding positive affect. Common railroad ties had been used as retainers, where all manor of flowering ground cover had been used to nearly hide the tops of the ties, with the plants draping themselves beautifully over the sides.

All in all it was a work of art, nevertheless, she would presume it to be fairly easy to maintain. Even so, the garden would require a loving and constant hand. She wondered if it would be intrusive to offer to help Miss Maude with the flowers while she was in residence. She would think about it and perhaps make the offer if such an opportunity afforded itself. She needed something useful to do as soon as possible, given the long, empty days she had endured aboard the *Neptune,* with nothing more demanding to do than the care of the clothing and oneself.

All of a sudden, she knew she was being watched. It started with a prickling on the back of her neck. Her mouth went dry and she had trouble swallowing. Should she try to run, she wondered whether or not her limbs would even carry her, as a sudden weakness had suddenly descended upon her. *No, it's better to act as natural as possible*, she thought.

She recognized this feeling as the same terror she had felt when she had overheard Morgan declare she would be dead within the month unless she agreed to marry him. As terrified as she had felt she knew she had to face him and his cronies but a moment later. Therefore, she summoned all the strength she could, and had been able to put her shakiness down to her embarrassment in having to settle her papa's unpaid 'debts'.

This time she was experiencing an unknown fear. As she was facing the windows in the conservatory, she casually looked up to see if there were any reflections of someone behind her. She had looked up just in time to see a flash of clothing, but couldn't discern anything else. There were too many large plants staggered throughout the conservatory to have a clear view of someone exiting. She was sure she had been watched, probably for some time, and had just become aware of her personal surroundings when she had felt the cold dread.

She thought she would have to tell the others about her experience. But what could she tell them? Someone beside herself had been in the conservatory? Perhaps even someone who had plenty of good reasons to be there. No, she couldn't make something menacing out of a sudden fear she had felt. After all, her experiences back in Savannah could be clouding her mind even now. She had felt the brunt of how hateful evil men could be when their façade was removed. Those fears were still very close to the surface. Besides, she had not fully rested and recovered from the long sea voyage, physically or emotionally. She chastised herself for her cowardly reaction. Then she just felt shame of being so afraid of seemingly nothing. Nevertheless, something told her to keep her eyes open in future. Even though she had felt it irrational she felt that something menacing could very well be afoot in the house.

After her constitutional in the garden, she returned to her room to set her clothing in order, only to find that Lilly had already been hard at work on them. "Lilly!" she exclaimed. "If you are to be a member of this family, you can no longer serve as my maid! I realize you have to stay busy to be happy, but maybe you can take up a hobby, like painting with watercolors, or even knitting.

We will have to use the same washerwoman that Miss Maude uses. Another thing, young miss. You won't be calling me 'Your Lady' or 'Miss' anymore, either, just like you couldn't on board the ship. I suppose now that we are back to a somewhat normal routine of living, you just thought to return to the way things were in Savannah. But I am Cousin Victoria to you now, and you, dear Lilly, have become a lady of leisure; a necessity in order to preserve our identities."

"Well and fine! Those things be fine for the evenin's by the fire, but what am I supposed to be doin' with all the workin' hours, pray tell? Besides all the gallivantin' goin' on around here, that is. Why, the missus has had two callers already this day! Do the fine ladies of San Francisco have nothin' to do then, I ask ye?" Lilly demanded to know, standing there with her hands doubled into fists and firmly placed on the sides of her waist.

Victoria laughed out loud and then stopped. They looked at each other and then both burst into merriment that was overheard clear down the hall by Connor and Elizabeth.

"She's a fine woman, don't you think, Elizabeth?" he asked, pulling her over to him, as he stood before a large bay window, watching the comings and goings down below. The street was fairly busy with the neighbors taking their constitutionals, and with the nurses airing the babies in their perambulators.

"Well, they both are, but I'm assuming you mean your sister?" she asked, as she laid her head on his shoulder. He nodded his assent, and she said, "You know I do, Connor Sullivan," she said, looking deep into his captivating green eyes. "How could she not be, coming from any family that produced a man like you," she murmured. She reached up, put her arms around his neck and slowly kissed him with a passion she felt down to her toes. It was full of the kind of passion that they had not shared much since they had left the farm, for obvious reasons.

Connor responded with a series of deep, ardent kisses that she couldn't get enough of. It seemed he couldn't either. He reckoned that he girls would just have to explore the city on their own that day.

Chapter 6

After the Sunday service, the Sullivan family and Miss Maude were discussing their worship experience over the buffet of excellent baked fish with creamy lemon sauce, roasted chicken, boiled potatoes, green beans, with plenty of fresh corn, a garden salad congealed in gelatin, and the meal was topped off with slabs of bread slathered with freshly made butter. Earlier, they had caught the wonderful aroma of the peach cobbler, made with fresh peaches, baking for dessert.

Fresh! Fresh! Fresh! It was so marvelous to have really *fresh*, home-cooked foods again after nearly half a year at sea! The Sullivans had eaten sparingly of the ship's fare, and their weight had diminished during their sea voyage. They could well afford to eat all they wanted of such delectable and exquisite food as was set before them that day. Everyone was certainly doing justice to the lovely buffet.

There were also guests at the table, unmarried, elderly sisters, June and Belle Daugherty. "Miss Maude's Sunday buffet is noted to be everyone's favorite and is always outstanding," June told them, as she explained that they were frequent guests at the mansion.

"It is always a treat to finish a wonderful church service, and then gather around an inviting table laden with wonderful fare, such as this one always is," Belle chimed in, reaching for her second slice of bread.

They used the time to discuss their impressions of their first time being in services in a real church after so long at sea. They were excited, nay thrilled, with the Harbor Mission experience, so much so, that they were endeared to Pastor Angelos immediately. They were so inspired with his sermon content and delivery that they felt the Harbor Mission would be their home church.

The friendly congregation was responsive in their worship, and the pastor preached a sure word of truth from the Bible. There were many young families in attendance, indicating that the church would continue to grow and, no doubt, retain the second and third generation of worshipers, as well.

Victoria still didn't know the marital status of Pastor Mark, since no one had seen fit to remark upon it. She hadn't noticed him with anyone at the service, but certainly didn't feel at liberty to come right out and ask Miss Maude about it, no matter how curious she was to know. She decided that she would just have to wait until the subject came up naturally.

She didn't have long to wait as Lilly asked the table in general, "So tell me, is Pastor Mark a married man then?"

Miss Maude looked at her with an amused look on her face, that the others shared, and replied, "No, not the last I heard, missy" which drew laughter all around, but Victoria let out a deep sigh of relief, just the same.

Lilly blushed, and began to protest. "Ye know I wasn't meanin' a thing by that question, do ye not?"

Miss Maude assured her that they were only teasing, but still, he was a good man, and if she should become interested, there was certainly nobody stopping her. "He has been at the church for nearly five years and no young miss has captured his eye yet, and after all, he does possess much to recommend him!" she said, with a twinkle in her eye.

Paul smirked at their conversation, not so that anyone noticed, as they were all looking at Lilly. *I will have to take to going to church and keep an eye on this Angelos fellow after this,* he thought to himself in disgust.

Connor had so appreciated services that morning, and had once again implored the Lord for a positive change in his memory. Something about his relatives seemed to spark some bond that they had all shared, even though no specific memories were forthcoming. It was like a memory would be just out of his conscious reach, and that if he turned the right corner, or opened the right door the past would come flooding back to him.

He was stuck in a kind of limbo. He was certainly in the 'meantime' of his life. Not where he had been, but not where he was hoping to go. He was learning patience, because he was discovering that the 'meantimes' of life were always mean times. On occasion, he felt as though he would never remember anything from his past ever again. But other times like today, when everyone was so full of life and well being, he felt that he could receive a miracle at any moment, and have his past simply unfold before him. He could only hope!

They relaxed in the parlor after the buffet, and planned what they would do the next day.

It was decided that they would begin the exploration of their new city. They loved the ocean and thought it delightful that after leaving a city on the Atlantic Ocean, they were now situated in a city on the coast of the Pacific Ocean. It was their understanding that there were wards and districts, and that they could get a simple printed layout of the city from the municipal agent.

They would start at the dressmaker's shops around Kearny Street and they would be basically looking at fashions in the windows. They didn't know exactly what was in style, or at least, what the stores were carrying in this part of the country. They would need to know, so that when they went to the modiste in a few days, they would have some idea of what they wanted. They also had planned to visit a large hotel tearoom just so they could see what the ladies were wearing.

That would keep them occupied for a while, and they would take the horse-drawn public cars, rather than a carriage, so that they could see so much more of the city. They would disembark to further explore any place that appealed to them. Such a simple thing as shopping, but what anticipation they all had for the morrow!

Chapter 7

"Connor! Did your hear me?" Victoria asked the next day, as they began their outing, and were riding in one of the horse drawn cars. Answering, Connor said, "I'm so sorry, sister, but truly I did not. What was it you said?"

"Well, I asked what you thought of any business prospects that we might consider. Do you think there are many to be had that would keep us somewhat in the background, and yet fill our coffers, as it were?" There was merriment in her eyes, and a smile on her lips. He replied, "Sister, the sky is the only limit we shall know!" to which they all laughed, and nodded their agreement.

When they had first had conversations on the *Neptune* after being reunited, Connor had said to them, "I have come to realize that I am skilled in numbers, and in business principles. Somehow I know that, but not the why of it. Can any of you ladies enlighten me as to why this is so?"

"Well, I should say you are!" Aunt Sadie had exclaimed. "You helped your papa run the plantation for years before the war, and you can do anything there is to be done there, including keeping the accounts, that's what!"

To this Victoria had lent her affirmation by saying, "You also went to Kentucky to buy the horses multiple times, and made many of the shipping arrangements for the cotton and rice through out the years. Truly you were papa's right hand," she assured him. "Yes, indeed, Connor. Our papa depended upon you for so many things. It was a real hardship for him when you went away to war. Why, Papa said it was like the army had amputated *his* right arm when they summoned you up. That is when he began to tutor me to run the place in your stead, not that I ever measured up to your knowledge and confidence, but I did learn enough to help get us through some really hard times, and be of some help to Papa."

"What little I know of you at present, Victoria, I'm sure you were a huge help, and no less a comfort. If only I could recall our parents," he lamented.

But today, here in sunny San Francisco, not wishing to inflict any shadow on the cheerful party, he laughingly intoned, "I'm sure that day is near when I shall remember all that I once knew about business, and I can assure you that I will be vigilant about looking out for opportunities to refill our coffers. I know investing in such growing concerns that are all around us here will be profitable. There is wealth untold in this place and making much money is happening to ordinary, common folk, to hear Miss Maude tell it. We shall learn more about it and I'm sure our coffers will be full, because only the sky is the limit, remember!"

He got the smiles he had intended, and put his memory loss aside. This was not the day for anything but joy.

The city was an amazing place to discover! The architecture was interesting and impressive, and the daily noises of hammers and saws could be heard in many quarters, as the building projects were numerous. People of many tongues and nations were seemingly everywhere. The ladies were so excited to actually be on a busy street, and see all the wonderful things in the storefronts. Only natural, as the only vistas they had known for so long had been water and sky. The many and varied street scenes were so exhilarating and welcomed.

The ladies told Connor that they would elect to walk several blocks at a time when the milliner or dressmaker shops dotted the streets on either side. Many of the stores and shops were very stylish, judging from what the stores carried back in Savannah. The fashions were changing, and then too, coming from a smaller town where fashions were expected to be somewhat confined to local taste, the gowns they were now viewing were reflecting the diverse and dense population of the city. Fashions reflected an awareness of what the ladies must surely be wearing back East, and were an indication as to the wealth and affluence of San Franciscans.

The girls giggled like when they were children when they saw some of the new frocks. They were stylish, to be sure, but one of the coat-type dresses was cut from the same length of cloth from shoulder to hem, giving it a somewhat sac-like look, and having what they called a raglan sleeve, with a web-like underarm, that they found very attractive. They surmised that it might be a few years before those garments caught on.

The bustle was still somewhat fashionable, but smaller and flatter now. Some of the hats, like the sailor hats, were taking on a more tailored look, rather than the exotic, large brimmed, higher crowned, silk shirred and feathered creations of late. Gracious, but the sailor hat looked down right masculine. They thought those would never catch on! They were told that materials and patterns were coming in by boat and train straight from Paris and New York City. It was so much fun to wander and play the ladies of leisure, without a care in the world whether the cows on the plantation back home had been milked or not, yet nevertheless, knowing that they would have been.

Thinking of the cows back home served to remind her of the first few days after her parents' deaths. Victoria was in such a muddled state of mind after the funeral, it was as plain as plain that Summers Bluff had virtually run itself. The workers were well trained, and they all knew their jobs and did them, and took pride and pleasure in the doing, as they were freed men and woman.

But now that she was free and on the other side of that pressure, she realized what a state she had been in during the most difficult time of her life. She was still amazed that she could even conceive of such a plan as to how to hoodwink Morgan, let alone succeed in carrying it out. Considering the frame of mind she had been in after realizing that evil man had, nay still, wanted her dead, she realized that, surely a Mind much higher than hers had been doing the planning for her, and she had been merely an actress in that drama. The Lord had given her a clear way out, and she was grateful.

Looking about her on this sunny, fall day in San Francisco, she remembered the fear of the unknown they had experienced at even the prospect of leaving the only people and place they had known and loved all of their lives, to face an unknown, very extended sea voyage, which had been fraught with many dangers and hardships. Now, she could appreciate how lovingly the Lord had cared for them every day of that voyage, not to mention giving her back Connor, and adding to her life the precious jewel that Elizabeth was.

All she wanted to do now was buy some suitable clothing, and putting the past behind her, begin to put her hand to something useful. Since money was not an issue at the moment, they would take the time needed for all of them to be fitted with new wardrobes, get to know their new city, and take some time to see what endeavors awaited them. Then they could begin to mingle in polite society in earnest, and be presented to those who were friends in good standing with Miss Maude, who turned out to be the very pillar of San Francisco society. Leave it to the Lord to place them in the very center of the best place they could have landed in all of San Francisco!

Chapter 8

After having been lodgers at the Stanhope Street mansion for a few months now, it seemed like Savannah was a very long ways away. Victoria's troubles were few, and peace reigned, however briefly. She hadn't known then that it wouldn't last long.

The Christmas season was nearly upon them. They saw very little of Paul Cabot, but decided that he must receive some small gift from each of them, not that they expected any in return. They each decided on a book for him that was popular at the time, as they really didn't know him well enough to pick out a more personal gift. He had not opened up to them since their arrival at the mansion, and was an all around unpleasant young man. Paul was a strange bird to be sure. More than once the women would find his stare upon them, and feel it before they actually saw it. Their opinion of him the day of their arrival had not diminished, but had rather grown stronger.

Miss Maude Killian had grown in esteem among all of the Sullivans, who had come to think upon her as another member of their family, just as she had also come to think of them. It was revealed that evening at supper that Paul was a somewhat distant cousin of Miss Maude's. "But I told you that when you first arrived," she exclaimed.

"No, indeed, Maude. I introduced myself that evening when things were so chaotic, with them just arriving with all the trunks and what not," Paul declared. Seeing as he was kin to Miss Maude finally cleared up the mystery as to why he was allowed to remain a boarder there. All the same, Sadie had to wonder if Maude was any more comfortable with him than the rest of them were. Sadie had been concerned about him from the beginning, and just then he was right in the center of her thoughts.

He hasn't done anything unseemly, except for the looks, but then again, the girls are all very attractive, and he is a single man, she thought. *Still, I can't help but feel something is just not quite right about the lad, but I don't want to be judgmental. It would be disastrous, should I be proven wrong.* On the other hand, she had lived long enough, and had interacted with the opposite gender enough that she had learned to trust her inner feelings about people, especially men.

Thankfully, all of the Sullivan women are prudent and mature. Besides, they all seemed duly on their guard with this young man, she concluded. Nevertheless, she made a mental note to bring up the subject with them at her first opportunity.

Miss Maude was reflecting back on when the Sullivans had first arrived at her home. *I could have sworn that everyone knew that Paul was a distant relative of mine. I wonder what they think of him. He has been behaving himself, true, but he was my only reservation in allowing the family to come here to live with us. I can't put my finger on what it is about him, but I know things are not as they should be concerning him. There is too much mystery. He hides things about himself, and his activities are secret.*

Maude Killian had had a definite check in her spirit that it might not be wise to accept the Sullivans, but she simply could not turn them away. But suffice it to say, Connor kept himself a sentry on those women of his, and they in turn were sensible and discreet. She hoped all would work out in the end.

For some time now, she had hoped that Paul would just move on, but that hadn't happened. Of course, he had it too convenient there for that. She reasoned with herself that she had promised her great-aunt to look after her great-grandson, and Paul had come to San Francisco without a word about him, other than the fact that he was kin.

She wondered if she was wrong in letting things just keep on going the way they were, but she just didn't know what else to do. She didn't want to confront him, especially without any specific accusations to bring. She thought maybe she should discuss it with Sadie. She knew for sure that she needed more information to go on. *Great-Aunt Lizzie needs to be contacted. I will write her on the morrow*, she decided.

Chapter 9

They had all agreed that it might be time to take Miss Maude into their confidence, as now that they were living in her home, she deserved to know that harboring them might mean danger to her some time in the future. They all had come to care too much about her to keep her uninformed about Morgan.

When they had first arrived in San Francisco, the next day while the three women were finding the church, Connor and Elizabeth had taken a constitutional. They proceeded in the direction of the telegraph and postal office where they inquired for a 'will-call' letter addressed to Mr. Brown, as Judge West had told Victoria to do upon arriving in San Francisco.

Judge West had, indeed, written Victoria a letter of credit, and documentation as to their identities, as well as a letter of reference. It was good that they had decided to keep their assumed names, as the papers were all made out in those, taken from the ship's registry. The judge couldn't understand the women being listed in a party of five Sullivans, along with one F. Connor Sullivan and wife, Elizabeth, but assumed that the captain added that for good measure, but was confident the women would have agreed. He simply made the references out in the name of the Sullivan family.

The morning the women had set sail, the judge had stayed to see the *Neptune* ease safely from the dock. Given the earliness of the hour, he had then quickly returned home. Had he but waited a little while more, he would have witnessed the return of the *Neptune,* and seen the passengers that had been taken aboard, and would have recognized Fletcher. He would have known who it had been that had joined the ladies, and would have been thrilled and much relieved. Not having done that, he was still under the impression that Fletcher Summers had been killed in the war, and that the ladies were on their own.

Unexpectedly among the mail, the judge had also enclosed a personal letter of testimony from himself addressed to any officer of the law who might ever hear of charges against Victoria concerning the forged notes. Also included, was a documentation of the testimony of a handwriting specialist connected with the impressive London Constabulary of Scotland Yard, declaring as forged, the notes supposedly signed by one Josiah Summers, deceased, to one Calhoun Morgan, from Savannah.

While this practice of detecting false handwriting had been written about for a few hundred years, the world of police investigation had been slow to explore the process. However, several men in high places had been pushing for this investigative tool to be accepted by police teams in general, but especially those in larger cities.

Hearing that this specialist was working with the New York Police to train them in the technique, once he had finished there, the judge sought to bring him to Savannah before he returned to London. The judge had spared no expense in beginning to prepare a case against Morgan, hopefully to be prosecuted some time in the near future.

Judge West had explained that this testimony had come about by intimating to Morgan that he might want to redeem the notes from him, but had asked if he would submit the notes to legal scrutiny. Morgan had evidently assumed that to mean that the judge had wanted another look at them. As he had already seen them once, Morgan saw no harm in allowing him to see them again, and so had agreed. He had no idea that Judge West had had the cunning to consult a specialist in the new field of handwriting analysis, that was up and coming into the forefront of criminal investigation.

Upon entering the chambers of the judge, Morgan had seen that there was a stranger with him, whom the judge had failed to introduce. Instead, when Morgan handed the judge the notes, he had simply handed them to the stranger. Morgan had been a bit unnerved by that, but was still confident about them. After all, hadn't he practiced the signature of Josiah Summers ever since his father had passed away and the law firm had come under his control?

However, when this stranger began to use a small magnifying lens and compare his notes with other documents, presumably signed by Summers, he began to become concerned. Finally, he asked the judge to introduce his guest, who showed such a marked interested in his business affairs.

"Ah, pray forgive my manners. This is Edward Tarkington. Mr. Tarkington, may I present Mr. Cal Morgan, holder of these notes."

Edward did not offer his hand and merely looked at him and asked where he had obtained the notes supposedly signed by Josiah Summers.

"Mr. Tarkington," Morgan acknowledged. "May I know what you mean by 'supposedly' signed?"

"Indeed, you may," Tarkington replied. "In fact, I insist upon it!" He greatly surprised Morgan with that statement. "You see, I have been involved in criminal handwriting detection for the past twenty years, and I can assure you that these notes have been forged. Furthermore, I will swear in a court of law that Josiah Summers did not sign these notes any more than the judge here did," he finished.

With both the judge and Tarkington staring at him awaiting his explanation, Morgan finally declared that his clerk had prepared the notes and given them to Josiah Summers to sign. He further explained that the clerk was known to be honest and trustworthy, and that he had simply trusted the clerk to finish up the documents on the notes.

"I'm shocked, I tell you, shocked, to find that you would think to find corruption in my own offices!" he hotly declared. Looking at Mr. Tarkington he said, "In fact, I don't care who you are, I am telling you that although I did not actually see him sign the notes, I was merely in the next room with the door opened between us. My clerk came in and gave me the notes the moment Summers finished signing. The same notes you hold in your hand at this moment," he offered. "There had been no time a tall for any shenanigans such as you are proposing!" he vented.

He looked at the two men before him and smiled smugly. "This man standing here before me is merely some foreign, so-called expert. I ask you, what is his word against the word of local men of upstanding credentials, such as my clerk and myself? Good day, gentlemen, and I'll take those notes, if you please," as he snatched them none to politely from the investigator's hand.

Chapter 10

After they had gone to the telegraph and postal office, and had received their letters of reference, Connor and Elizabeth had immediately presented them to Miss Maude. She had known that they had been in a whirlwind of activities since their arrival. She had told them not to be overly concerned about the references in the beginning, but since they had already arrived, they were presented. What they had not told her about was what had been preying on their minds for some time now.

Connor went to the library door and wondered if he could have a word with Miss Maude. He told her that the family had expressed to each other a desire for Connor to speak with her and explain a bit more about their past. She assured him that it wasn't necessary from her standpoint, but he was welcome to do so if he felt it necessary. He took this opportunity to make confession, as it were, to their situation.

He explained to Miss Maude that the one reason for their move west was that a powerful, evil man back home had wanted to marry Victoria, but she had refused him, whereupon he had threatened her life. Connor also explained about the forged notes, and how the corrupt sheriff would back the man in whatever charges he was devious enough to think up about her. He explained that this villain had forced the sale of their home, and that if anybody came to her door looking for them, even if it were a sheriff, she would know that it would be about the notes.

He maintained that Victoria could prove by anybody in three counties of their honest and benevolent lifestyle, and the same people could also justifiably vilify her enemy. He then presented the other documents from Judge West concerning the notes. He also wanted Miss Maude to understand that it was the desire of each of them that she understand it all, and if she felt there was any danger to herself or to her home, they would seek other accommodations immediately. The only thing he hadn't told her was their real names, or from whence they had come.

Miss Maude had been more than incensed upon hearing such news as those dastardly deeds being perpetrated upon such nice, respectable people as the Sullivan's. She assured him that she understood what havoc an evil, revengeful man could inflict upon innocent people, and that they were welcome to share her home without fear of troubling her. She also cautioned Connor not to use the telegraph back to his hometown under any circumstances, as it might be made known where the telegram had originated through bribery or force.

After the first part of the story had been told, Connor began to tell of his own struggle with amnesia. He assured her that he could account for himself in that he had left his home to go to war, was imprisoned, had escaped, during which time had sustained a head wound, and had been left at Elizabeth's to recover.

He assured her there were no deep, dark secrets or unknown gaps in his whereabouts or activities, because all of his time was accounted for. Therefore, he could not have had any criminal past, but rather, just could not remember people or details of his past, even his real name.

Miss Maude assured him that whatever had happened in the past, it was too late to worry about moving, because they were part of her family now. Furthermore, she could tell what manner of people shared her home as well as any judge! She was more than satisfied that she knew these people's character and spirits. The very act of them taking her into their confidence voluntarily, making themselves so vulnerable, had touched her heart and had made her love them even more. She would do all she could to protect them, should ever the need arise.

Yes, *I can handle any consequences of my acceptance of this little, motherless family. I haven't lived this long to cower and be afraid of ruffians now, even if they seem to be on the side of the so-called law! Have I, Maude Killian, or have I not, crossed the prairie with my family, and fought the Comanche in my time, and have I not lived to tell the tale? Indeed, I have! This Southern 'gentleman' Morgan was just a trashy blackguard, and God will help this family in their good fight of faith, and I can do no less,* thought Maude.

Connor reasoned with himself: *The outcome of my conversation with Miss Maude is the favor of God! For that good woman, on such short acquaintance, to know all, and still trust her safety among us is also the protection of God.*

Connor prayed, *Lord, please don't let any of us come to harm, especially Miss Maude. And please protect Judge West concerning all of his interactions on our behalf, too.* Although he had not followed the strict letter of the law, he had followed the spirit of the law in order to spare the innocent lives at stake. *Thank you, Father, for such friends, with whom you have graced our lives!*

Ah, so there is more to this family than meets the eye, eh? Paul thought, excitedly. He had been skulking around ever since their arrival, trying to overhear conversations, or find correspondences to show that they were not the wholesome, respectable people everyone thought them to be.

A man without memories could be blamed for a lot of things, and he really wouldn't know if they were true or not, nor could he prove anything, could he now? And he wasn't using his real name! Interesting! Very interesting! I must find those letters he— whatever his name is— spoke of! Yes, he had to find a reason to expose them when the time came. He was nearly salivating at such an unexpected, titillating morsel as the one he had just overheard.

Paul had thought they were phony, goody-goodies from the first meeting. Greedy harlots! Weren't they inveigling their way into his mansion, trying to seduce their way into his position, and into old Maude's heart, not to mention her will? Hadn't she just told him that they were a part of her family now? No, they certainly were not! He alone was her only relative and heir, beside a couple of distantly related, old people back East!

I will burn this shack down around their heads before I give up one cent of that fortune! Not one cent, do you hear me! I'm the next of kin...the only kin! screaming silently, maniacally, to himself. Continuing his inward rant, *She has already said she cares about them, and even if she hadn't said it, I could tell, as it is plain as plain that she does!*

Paul felt justified in that he had been there first, and they would not get rid of him. He could see it in old Maude's eyes. She wanted him gone. She was afraid of him. He could smell the fear.

Hadn't she written a letter to old Lizzie asking about me? But I got it first before the post. She won't be getting an answer to her questions about me that she asked in that letter. Oh, no, she won't! I am in control now, and they will never know what hit them! He brightened at that prospect. *Old Lizzie had known what she was doing when she sent me here. But Maude won't ever know why. No, Lizzie won't be telling her that. She'd be too afraid Maude might send me back to New York!* he reckoned, with a grin.

Yes, old Maude is afraid of me! he thought, nodding his head in assent. He couldn't help giggling out loud, as he thought: *And so she should be!*

Then his erratic thoughts returned to the Sullivans once again. He thought that none of the harlots liked him, but that was okay with him. He was just biding his time. He knew that they couldn't keep running in packs forever. *If need be, I will take them all out of the way at the same time.* For his unaccountable hatred for them all, he must soon have an outlet.

Their brother needn't think he can protect them all the time! Protect them from whom? Pretty Paul? he asked himself with a devious grin, glancing again in the mirror, where he beheld himself with pride. He straightened his tie, and then tore himself away from the mirror. He calmly strode to the supper table, where he joined the others with a pleasant enough greeting, and a pasted on smile.

*L*illy awakened in a cold sweat around midnight in the throws of a night terror. She was so terrified she could scarcely breathe, let alone scream. She had the sensation of being watched. She had been dreaming something bizarre involving Paul that she couldn't shake off even after she had awakened. She couldn't even remember what it was about, but when she could again find her voice, she went to awakened Victoria. "I'm sorry, missy, but I got me some creepy feelin's this night. I had to wake ye, as sure and I'm standing here, scared as a sinner on Judgment Day!" she apologized.

Once Victoria was fully awake, she noted that Lilly was trembling. "Why, Lilly, come get under the covers with me. You're shaking like a wet hound in winter. Are you cold?"

"In a manner of speakin', but not in the way ye're meanin', miss. Cold in me spirit right enough. Like someone we know up on the third floor just walked over me grave, he did!" she said, pulling up the covers around her head.

Victoria was somber, as she tried to sooth Lilly. She was deep in thought when she realized something was odd about Lilly having the nightmare. Hadn't she done the very same thing but three nights back, and hadn't her nightmare also involved Paul?

She thought she needed to talk to Connor about it in the morning. These were portents that all was not well.

Things were all abuzz across the town due to the soon approach of the Christmas holidays. The house had been a veritable oven, with all the holiday baking, preparing, and visiting, seeing as how the weather that year felt more like late fall than winter. Miss Maude had decided that there should be more festive Christmas celebrations this year than what she normally would do, as this was the first time she had really felt the Christmas spirit since her dear Caleb had passed.

With all of the losses the Sullivan family had experienced in the past year, it was a great relief to be with both family and friends and to celebrate the Christmas season together. Friends like they had made with Miss Maude, Pastor Angelos, who was still an unmarried man, and several other folks they had become acquainted with from church. Pastor Mark had been a welcomed visitor for meals at the mansion several times a week, besides Miss Maude's celebrated Sunday buffets.

To say the least, meal times were always exciting times for Victoria. Mark saw to that. He could be entertaining and funny, but there was a deeper side to him that showed her that for all of his good humor, nevertheless, he was a lonely man. Some of the things he had revealed had caused her heart to melt. He always sought her out to sit with her before, during, and after meals. He was always proper, but not formal. He told her that he was very glad that she and her family had come to San Francisco, as their coming had changed his life. She knew that he had meant it.

Mark and Connor had been on very friendly terms since Connor's arrival at the church and seeing that he had a lot of free time on his hands, Mark had invited him to assist him with some house calls and other ministry endeavors. Connor had been happy to accompany him, as it had afforded him an opportunity to meet, and become better acquainted with, a lot of the church members. He also considered Mark a very good friend, as well as his pastor.

Emma couldn't seem to get a handle on her emotions these days, for pity's sake, as she felt like laughing and crying all at the same time. Sometimes, the melancholy she would feel when she would relive their conversations or shared laughter would unnerve her. It seemed to her that her emotions were all over the place.

It must be the Christmas excitement, she thought. They all had received several holiday invitations to supper, which also served to heighten the festive atmosphere. Three times just that week, they had donned their finery, and enjoyed festive supper parties at some of the finest homes in San Francisco; friends that they had made through their close association with Miss Maude.

There were also activities that had been going on at the church, such as the Children's Annual Christmas Play, which had been a real treat for everyone. The Christmas Cantata was always a very well attended event, and had been deemed a huge success that year.

There had also been many shopping outings that had been going on for the past week, especially since the weather had been so mild. The Sullivans had bought each other only small personal items until they settled in their own home, hopefully long before next Christmas.

As much as they all loved Miss Maude and loved living there with her, Paul's presence was now becoming an oppressive cloud that they could neither understand, nor discount. Maude had failed to speak with Sadie about Paul, and she had not received an answer to her letter to great-aunt Lizzie asking for more information about him. There was just so much going on with the Christmas social season that the talk about Paul had kept being put off. The hustle and bustle of activities all week had also caused the concerns that Lilly and Victoria had about Paul to be put aside for the time being, until after the holidays. It had been so long since they had known the true joy that they had been experiencing for the past few months, that they had not wanted to confront the cloud of suspicion surrounding Paul, fearing it might change the prevailing joyful atmosphere they all were cherishing.

Meanwhile, Paul had little to say about any work position he might have anywhere, or what his actual means of livelihood was. So it must be surmised that it was coming from Miss Maude, unless he had a source from back East, which seemed doubtful. He continued to be gone a good bit of the time, and when he was home he stayed to himself, as usual. Still, something seemed off, even for him.

Yes, Paul read his books, planned his plans, and enjoyed watching what he was sure would be the last Christmas activities the Sullivan family would ever celebrate.

Old Lizzie caught me playing with fire back in New York and sent me here. She knew I burned down that barn, and then the office of the bookkeeper. Ah, those were the days! But those days aren't over. No, no, no! Really, just the beginning, I'd expect.

Didn't I set fire to the stables just last month right here in this city? Makes no difference that they didn't burn to the ground, but I was impatient. He shrugged his shoulders, *I'll be more careful and plan better next time, but I saw the opportunity, and took it imprudently.*

After all, there was an old drunk asleep in there, and he should not have been sleeping on the job, should he now? he snickered in scorn. Then his attitude revealed his malevolence. *Didn't that old drunk get the credit for that?* he thought, violently casting aside his hairbrush. *I did all the work and that drunken dog got all the credit!*

Oh, well, I have one more wee project before the big finale at the New Year's Eve gala here on Stanhope Street, he mused and laughed out loud at the thought. *Be sure the devil is always planning something for the goodie-goodie Christians! And they just go on in total ignorance, while people like me have all the fun planning and executing their demise!* He couldn't help but laugh again at that thought.

Chapter 12

Miss Maude had never had a more fulfilling Christmas season in recent years. It was Christmas Eve, and every one was dressed to the nines, awaiting the arrival of the supper guests. Besides Mark, there were only three couples invited, and all the men were associates of Pastor Angelos. Daniel Foster, the associate pastor, and his wife, May; Jesse Prescott, the head of the board of elders, and his wife, Tansy; and Jeremiah Bentley, the Sunday School and Children's Education Director, and his wife, Polly. The guests were so well acquainted that they obviously appeared to be like family. Only Mr. Foster and May were middle aged, as the others were all around Mark's age.

All of them were having a wonderful, lively fellowship, and the wit displayed all around was both entertaining and refreshing. Miss Maude had certainly planned a feast for the occasion. She had out done herself with the menu for their supper. The cook, and other domestic help from the parsonage, had come to lend a hand, and they all had done a marvelous work.

When the Fosters and Prescotts arrived simultaneously, they said the Bentleys were only a few moments behind. When the door chime sounded a moment later, Victoria opened it to find Mark Angelos standing there in formal attire, looking more handsome than she had ever remembered seeing him. He smiled and greeted her with the customary, "Merry Christmas to you, Miss Victoria," and she vaguely remembered returning the cheerful greeting.

He smiled at her, and then looking somewhat amused, asked, "I *was* expected for supper tonight, was I not?" She knew she had blushed, as she was feeling like a schoolgirl, leaving him standing on the stoop like that.

"Oh, do forgive me, Pastor," she exclaimed. "I suppose I just assumed it would be the Bentleys, as the Fosters mentioned they were right behind them," she said by way of explanation.

Stepping into the dazzling atrium, he relieved himself of his coat and hat, which she took, since the domestics were busy in the cloakroom at that moment, putting away the outer wraps of the other guests who had arrived a moment earlier.

He answered, "Yes, I saw them alighting their carriage just now as I walked up." He started to follow her into the parlor when he said, "And please, just Mark," he lowered his voice for that part, and she felt his breath behind her close to her ear. She was so moved with his tone, she stopped suddenly and turned around to face him. She found him so close that he had nearly run into her. However, he didn't back away and when she looked deeply into his dark eyes, she heard his sudden, quick intake of breath, even as she felt her own breath catch.

She had caught the aroma of the balm he had applied to his face after shaving, and honest to goodness, along with the look she was receiving from him at that moment, it produced in her the strangest feeling that she could ever recall having! And whatever this feeling was, she certainly would have remembered it! That brief exchange was the most intimate show of affection that she had ever received to date, and she wasn't quite sure how to react to it. She finally remembered what she was about, and heard herself stammer, "Of course, M-Mark," as she handed off his things to the domestics, and joined the others in the parlor.

While they were waiting for supper to be served, Miss Maude had asked Elizabeth to set the mood for the festivities to follow with some opening pieces at the pianoforte. They would save the Christmas music for after supper, but now she favored them with a medley of songs that they could sing along with, and finished with a beautiful love song that was popular at the time.

As she began her last piece, gracing the parlor with her pure mezzo-soprano voice, Connor slipped from his seat beside Victoria. He went over and leaned on the instrument, watching his wife while she played and sang, his heart in his eyes. His love was open for all to see, so much so that those who were observing such adoring felt they had intruded upon the sacred gift of married love.

Mark also left his seat, and took the seat vacated by Victoria's brother. When she felt him move beside her, she couldn't even describe the sensation that transpired at his presence. She was fairly sure that he was feeling it, too. She wasn't comfortable enough with her own feelings about what was taking place between them to trust herself to even look at him. Fortunately, just as Elizabeth finished to a round of applause, supper was announced. As she stood, Mark inquired if he might take her in to supper, and once again their eyes met and held. All she could manage was an affirmative nod of her head.

When the Christmas Eve meal commenced, they were all delighted and in awe. What a meal it was! There was a large stuffed, roasted goose, apple sauce, mashed potatoes, and all the other Christmas supper trimmings, brought out and set in the place of honor in the center of the serving buffet. After justice had been done to the goose, next came a rack of veal surrounded by a medley of delicious looking steamed vegetables, topped with melted cheese and butter placed at one end of the buffet, while a baked ham wrapped in a crust was placed on the other end of the buffet.

Also served were sweet potatoes, stewed carrots with baby onions, besides a vast variety of other side dishes. The Christmas plum pudding with hard sauce was served for dessert, as expected, and was simply excellent.

With such an over abundance of food served at the table that night, it was hard to believe it had been a mere five years back, when during the war, and even after, thousands of people had literally starved to death. Small children, the elderly, and once strong and vibrant people alike, grew feeble and waned. They seemed to wither, even from day to day, until so many of them had finally succumbed to the unending hunger. Victoria had always been conscious of, and sympathetic toward, those who were hungry, but even more so since the deprivations of the war that she had experienced first hand. She could do nothing about the past miseries, but she knew that the hungry were still among them.

Immigrants searching for freedom, or a better economic situation, were arriving every week in San Francisco from all points of the compass, and there was always a need to help them get settled. She made a mental note to see if the church was assisting in any of those areas. She needed something useful to do, and the people certainly needed the help.

Miss Maude had arranged the seating so that Victoria was seated across the table from Mark and as the supper progressed, she found that she would have preferred to have had him seated next to her, so that she was not so preoccupied with his eyes, or his long-held looks. Her heart was aflutter, and she had completely lost her appetite.

She wondered if the meal would ever end, as several lingering, intense looks passed between them, that both had seemed unable to break until someone had addressed some comment or other to them. Looks that had caused her stomach not to be able to decide whether to plummet to somewhere beyond her knees, or to travel upward toward her throat, but at any rate, it would not stay put!

Mark apparently could tell that she had been flustered after each one of those encounters, and while it was nearly impossible for him to drag his eyes from her lovely face, he had made it a point to give Mrs. Bentley the most of his attention, for safety's sake, for a good portion of the remainder of the meal.

Victoria did not know it, but the way she looked that night in the candlelight, with those green eyes shining with anticipation that she could not suppress, she was capturing his heart, and nobody before had ever managed that. Maybe others in the household had perceived something happening between them before that night, but she had not. He had always been smiling and appeared to be happy whenever he was around her, but he was like that to everyone, wasn't he?

He always held her hand just so, but then he shook hands with everyone, sometimes holding a lady's hand a tad longer than absolutely necessary, but that was by way of showing concern for what the lady had been saying to him. He was nothing if not a concerned listener.

Maybe she was imagining it all. Maybe it was really just the Christmas spirit that was accountable for what was happening between them that night. But whatever it was, something *was* happening between them. She may not have been courted as yet, but she had seen others in the process, and this was definitely the same kind of looks she had caught between such lovers as she had observed.

In the midst of it all, she suddenly thought of Jake and the Christmas Cotillion last year when she had been presented. However, she would not allow herself the sentimental journey of dwelling on all the other Christmases past or the things lost to her. She was too grateful and caught up in what the Lord was giving her this Christmas. It was enough.

But for all that, she had not dared think over much about the looks of promise she had received from Mark during supper. She really had not imagined them, but she reminded herself that she had received just such looks from another man who had caused her breath to catch, but a courtship had not followed. She remembered that she might have felt like this once with him, but she had never been given the opportunity to find out.

She had been trying to guard her heart from anything like that happening again, but it had become more and more difficult, given that for the past weeks she had been in Mark's very frequent company. In fact, that night she was able to admit to herself that she had lost that battle. Even without Mark's ever having declared himself, more's the pity.

Yes, it was a night to be looked back on, and remembered with reverence. It was the night that Victoria had begun to feel, and to respond, to the wooing taking place like a woman in love. Something long dormant had awakened within her that she could never coax back to sleep, not saying that she wanted to.

Chapter 13

A perfect party, indeed! Miserable, miserable, miserable! Paul Cabot thought to himself in disgust. He liked nobody at the table, and disliked some with intensity. He had plans for that night, but he couldn't get to them until he could safely make his excuses and leave the supper table.

The miserable 'pastor' and his staff are all here at this miserable Christmas supper! Paul sneered with a curled up lip. Miserable was the sum total of his emotions that night, all the while smiling when he couldn't resist, because he was entertaining thoughts of something that none of them knew about.

As soon as they finish this Christmas nonsense, before they all begin their exits, I can make my excuses. I have pretended a slight indisposition all day. I didn't eat much at supper, because I was so excited about my display tonight that I lost my appetite, but that will make my excuses seem all the more plausible.

Then I will be free to slip down the back stairs, and not be seen by any of the carriage drivers. Besides, they will all be busy with their own miserable holiday cheer. He rehearsed his activities yet to come to himself. *It will only be a three-minute walk for me, at most, if I hurry to the church premises, and then I can begin to do a little work*

175

there myself, he thought. *After all, they all work there, why not me?* he grinned at that cleverness.

Oh, night of nights, indeed! I imagine that the church will go up along with the parsonage. I would have started it there, but it's harder to make out a church fire started by itself than in a residence. They will have banked the fires, but I can unlatch the stove front, and afterwards when they find the iron stove with the door open, they will think someone was careless, oh, yes they will! he thought in singsong. *Oh, that will be my Christmas present!*

It was getting late, and still they sang and talked, and talked and sang. It seemed that nobody wanted to leave; it was that kind of a gathering, and Paul was getting more and more agitated by the moment. He had work to do, and he was nearly beside himself to get started. He had been living for this night and could hardly contain himself at the table.

The Christmas presents were all around the tree, making a beautiful sight, and would be opened in the morning. Paul had told them to please excuse him, as he wanted to try and rest later in the morning, but he would open his gifts later that day, but for them to go ahead and open theirs from him in the morning with the others. Surprisingly, he had bought them gifts, probably at the suggestion of Miss Maude.

He finally was able to make his excuses, and headed for his room. But having gained the hallway, instead proceeded down the back stairs, as he had planned for weeks. He had placed his coat there after the guests had started arriving, as everyone in the household would be too preoccupied to notice his old shabby coat by the back door. He hurriedly donned it, and eased the door closed behind him.

When the supper party finally broke up a few minutes later, and the guests had bid their adieus to the residents of the mansion,

Paul had been gone less than a calculated ten minutes. He had hurried to the parsonage, forced his way in, opened the stove door in the kitchen, set the fire, and quickly retraced his steps to the mansion.

Upon entering the back stairway, Paul had gained his room without being seen. He discarded his coat in the back of the closet in case perchance it smelled of smoke. He quickly washed up, donned his nightshirt and cap, and mussed the covers to look as if he had been in bed, just in case anyone came to his door. Because of the street lamps, he could see the smoke now from his third story window. It began to billow upwards, and there he stood, his shoulders shaking with his near delirious laughter, awaiting the blaze that was sure to come.

He was quivering with excitement. He figured the small fire he had started a few feet under the curtains in the kitchen would begin to blaze by the time he reached the house on Stanhope Street, and they had, just as he had planned. *Surely*, he reasoned, *no one would be able stop the flames now!*

When his staff had departed, Mark had said his farewells, and then asked Victoria if he could have a word. She took him aside, and he asked her if he had done anything to make her feel uncomfortable that night. She couldn't believe he was addressing what had just happened between them, proving without doubt, that he had felt it, too. She had begun to believe it had been imagined or at least, one sided on her part. She assured him that it was quite the opposite, in fact. He had made it a most memorable night, and that surely he had not done anything amiss, but suggested they could discuss it fully at a more private time, if he desired. He agreed, pressed her hand in his, and left the house.

As soon as he stepped outside, he looked up and could see a bit of smoke in the air off in the distance by the street lamps. He was only a couple minutes from the parsonage, but he could sense that something was amiss, just as he began to hear the clanging of the fire wagon. He began to head for home at a slow trot. But with his next breath, he knew this was something of an emergency, and began to run in earnest.

Upon arriving at the parsonage, he saw that the fire wagon was just arriving on the scene, as the station was a matter of a few streets south. He found out later that the night watchman on his street had seen someone running from inside the house, and had investigated, found the fire, and had sent for the fire wagon.

Moments thereafter, the staff had returned, and in their formal party dress, joined the neighbors to quickly form a bucket brigade, taking water from the church cistern, as they were commonly located throughout the neighborhoods. What with the few firemen and volunteers, the blaze was quickly put out without doing nearly the damage Paul had intended. As the parsonage was built of brick, the exterior had suffered little damage, other than it had been blackened from the smoke on the backside where the kitchen was located.

The interior was a different story, but the blaze, thankfully, had been contained in the brick-walled kitchen. The stove door stood ajar, and it was assumed that someone had left the door open, and sparks had caught something afire. When the fire had been extinguished, and Mark had a free moment, the domestic in charge of fires, Diego, lamented the fire, but insisted that he had not left the stove door ajar.

He was known as a most diligent man, and in all his years of service had never once caused injury to the home of his employer, and certainly his name and carelessness had never been mentioned in the same sentence. Given the fact that the officer of the law had seen someone leaving the premises, Mark knew Diego had spoken truth. Someone had done this on purpose.

Upon reflection of the fire, Mark could not imagine who would want to fire the parsonage, which could so easily have spread to the church, had the wind been coming from the wrong direction. It was simply astonishing and unbelievable, but he now knew that someone meant harm to him, or one of the others in the church's employ. He had arrived at that conclusion, because he just couldn't believe it was a random, mindless act of a troublemaker or youthful miscreant.

There was simply just too much malice in the act to relegate it to the work of a prankster or to a gang of youngsters bent on mischief. Then, too, the arsonist that had been seen leaving the scene of the crime had been an adult, and a lone arsonist ruled out youthful pranksters. No, whoever that man was, he wanted to destroy Mark's home, and perhaps the church into the bargain. Mark would have to question the staff and domestics to see if any of them could think of a reason that might be the case.

Certainly, people had been made welcome at the church. He knew of no areas of concern that anyone on staff had related to him. But from here on out, until this was resolved, none of them would take anything for granted. It went without saying that they all needed to be watchful.

The residents of the Killian mansion had just changed out of their eveningwear when the alarm had been raised by one of the workers at the church, who had come by to inform them of the fire. Upon hearing the news, they quickly donned their outer wraps over their robes and started to the parsonage, but did not have the presence of mind or the will to change into street clothing before venturing out, once they knew what was happening at the parsonage.

It was only a short time until Connor, along with the ladies, arrived to see if they could be of any help. As the fire was nearly completely out, Mark could only suggest that they retire to the parlor and give thanks that nobody had been hurt, and that no more harm had been done in this untoward event.

The fire being successfully put out, Mark had given all who had participated in the crisis his heartfelt thanks and they had gone home. After everyone had left, he and Connor investigated the area around the stove and then on around the room. Neither of them saw anything at first, but then Mark saw a scrap of cloth that had apparently been caught in the splintered doorframe and had been ripped off. It was a rough sort of material, old and well worn. It appeared to be the type of material that workingmen's coats were made of. He absent-mindedly put it in his pocket, and would later put it in a drawer and lock it away. No doubt, the police would want to see it.

Chapter 14

Despite the deplorable actions of some unknown person the night before, who had tried to destroy the church property, the next morning was another pleasant day in San Francisco. The Sullivans intended to take full advantage of it. It was their first Christmas morning together in San Francisco, not to mention their first Christmas together in nine years.

They enjoyed a delicious breakfast together and felt that under the circumstances, it was appropriate for Connor to look at the newspaper to search for any further news of the fire at the parsonage. There was no new information, except for the description of the man seen leaving the premises. Due to the eyewitness of the night watchman, the fire was formally listed as arson. Unfortunately, the description of the intruder supplied by the duty officer could have fit one of a thousand men in the city.

Clean up work would be started on the parsonage the following day. There would be a full crew sifting through the rubble, looking for any usable items, and removing the debris from the kitchen. Then they would begin to clean it from top to bottom. Therefore, there was little those at the mansion could do to help. It was fortunate that the climate had been so pleasant that they could open all the doors and windows, and receive the warm breezes from the Pacific, to begin to somewhat air out the prevalent burned odor.

It would take several days to make everything right again, and until then, the staff would take meals at the Killian mansion. It was not going to be much extra work, as there was so much food left from the supper party the night before, and some of the domestics from the parsonage would again help with the kitchen chores. All in all, it was a good solution to feeding the pastoral staff. It was felt that would also allow the staff and pastor time away from the work and noise, to be well fed, and to fellowship with the good people on Stanhope Street into the bargain. The results of the fire had been taking up most of their waking hours and meals at the mansion would be a welcomed relief.

Victoria wondered what her first meeting with Mark would be like after the happenings that had taken place between them the night before. After the events of the magnificent supper party they had shared, she had hoped that there might be a courtship somewhere in the near future, but was unsure how it would proceed, if at all. Surely, the fire would be his greatest concern for some time to come.

While her heart was light, her mind was troubled with so much turmoil and confusion connected with the fire. A large part of that turmoil came with the realization that someone wanted harm done to someone at the parsonage. *The most likely person would be the pastor*, she thought. Having faced that fact, her old fear of the unknown came creeping back upon her. Victoria knew that Mark Angelos was not the kind of man who usually created enemies. He was kind to everyone and treated everyone with respect and dignity, not only those in his church, but every one from every walk of life with whom he had to do. She had witnessed that many times when there had been community events, or the members had gone into the neighborhoods to invite people to church. But the evidence was before them. Someone had forcibly gained entrance into the parsonage to do harm.

Upon further consideration, except for an old servant asleep far from the kitchen, the place had been empty, as anyone could have told. Some might think that fact alone ruled out that the arsonist had meant harm to any specific person. However, that fact had not lessoned the conviction she felt that whomever had set the fire intended harm to the pastor.

Perhaps this only served as a warning. Perhaps he would be attacked in another way, as well. Yes, the old uneasiness of knowing somebody wanted her dead, was the same uneasiness she now felt for Mark.

Chapter 15

Savannah 1870

*I*t had seemed a long time since Emma Summers had left Savannah. Calhoun Morgan had envisioned the Christmas galas he would have been hosting that year at Summers Bluff after he and Emma had wed, but the reality of that Christmas was far from what he had envisioned.

He sat alone in his home at Morgan's Creek, devoid of any celebration whatsoever, and lamented his lot in life. He was nigh on to forty years old, unmarried, a murdering liar and thief, a mean-spirited, evil man, and he knew it. But knowing the truth and believing it were two different things. He knew the things he had done, but a man without a conscience could always justify them in his own twisted mind, if ever the need arose, although it hadn't done so far.

The thing that had eaten away at him and stuck in his craw the most for nearly nine months had been the undeniable fact that he had not been able to locate Emma Summers. He had his ways and means of finding out anything he wanted to know, and he knew everything that happened in Savannah. He had a gang of rogues acting as his eyes and ears, who went running to him with every little tidbit of gossip or news they thought he would be interested in hearing.

They had looked for Emma everywhere they had known to look countless times. He had all of his rogues running around asking questions, threatening everyone at Summers Bluff, as well as every nearby farm, let alone the far off places, and nothing could be learned. They couldn't come up with a single clue or a lead on Emma Summers anywhere in Savannah or beyond.

Now he found himself in debt, disgraced and nearly broke, as he had invested a fortune in trying to locate Emma, both locally, and in every major city along the Eastern Seacoast from Savannah to Philadelphia. He hated her to the depths of his soul for what she had done to him. She had outmaneuvered him at the very outset of his own game, using pretense and deception as expertly as any blackguard he knew, and had made a mockery of him openly before everyone. Now, he was alone and in sad circumstances. Yes, he had lost face and fortune over the chit.

The very worst part about it all was that he, Cal Morgan, who had been able to see through every scam ever invented, had never seen any of hers coming. She had arrogantly refused his advances, and faced with the phony forged notes, simply took her money from the bank, sold off the place within the hour, and had run. He wondered where she had come by the intestinal fortitude for such brazenness and cunning, and her nothing but a mere slip of a girl!

No, he had not seen it coming. He thought that he was in total control of the situation back then. He thought that he had her between a wedding band and a grave without any options whatsoever, but she had found several, and had taken them.

He never in his life would have figured she would have given up the place she loved best in the world, as wedding him to keep the plantation had been the whole premise on which he had confidently built his plan. And yet she had up and sold it that very day, and had set off to places unknown with just her aunt.

He supposed that to be the case, as Caroline Summers was also missing. He had sworn a vow that he would find Emma, and exact punishment for her hauteur, whatever it took. Yes, he would find her. He had to find her because she had to learn obedience. She had to suffer if he were to know any relief from his own pain. And he needed relief from his own pain badly. He needed his pound of flesh. He needed revenge!

But even that had not panned out for him. He was allowing his obsession with her to cloud his judgment, not only in business affairs, even to the loss of his fortune, but also to the point that his outrageous behavior in his frenzy to find her, had shut every social door in Savannah against him.

After Emma had disappeared, people had finally seen him for the rogue that he was, no doubt, due to that interfering and influential Judge West. Yes, that old man must have known more than he had let on. Because of him, the wealthy men in that city had given him the social cut and distanced themselves from him, so that his schemes would no longer come to fruition. His plans of deceit had depended upon the men's good will and friendship, and being able to move freely in their society.

Having lived all of his life in the South he had always known how to thrive among the wealthy there. He was a handsome rogue, no doubt about that, but he was also skilled in diplomacy when called for. He was quick witted, a good dancer, and was a delight to those silly women who only looked on the surface, and who had marriageable aged daughters who needed husbands.

All the hostesses had sought him out for their galas, and were very appreciative of the attraction he held with the young ladies. He had also been accepted among the men of the Savannah, too, if not well liked, seeing as some could easily discern the cut of the man, but he knew how to make himself useful to them.

It wasn't difficult to get some of them in his debt, and then he could call in those debts when he needed favors. The men paid him well for his legal services, and he knew with whom he needed to be dead honest, and with whom he needed to do a shady deal or two in their favor. Saint or sinner, it just depended upon his audience, and whatever it was that they needed him to be.

Now he found himself in dire circumstances, more so than he had ever been before. There was such a connection to both the old wealth and new money of Savannah, Charleston, and Atlanta that he couldn't count on any of those towns now offering him refuge. He had been fishing around trying to find a new scam to run to put him back in the money, but now he felt the time had come for him to cut bait and leave town. His quandary was in deciding in which direction to head out.

To Northern cities he was not attracted, nor inclined to go. The Midwest was certainly not offering him any lucrative or tempting options. That left open to him the only place he could hope to rebuild his fortune anytime soon: the mining enterprises out West.

After all, the money had been flowing out there from forty-eight when gold had been discovered, and even more so now, since the transcontinental railroad went straight through from New York to Sacramento. Hadn't thousands made a fortune in the last decade? So he settled his mind on Sacramento, California as the place where he would resettle.

Now, Cal Morgan was the one with no options, except the ones Emma had taken. Like her, he would sell his spread, take the money, and run. For not much cash he could have a first-class Pullman sleeping car on the transcontinental railroad the entire way. No telling how much he would win in poker games, or how many deals he would be able to transact en route. He should meet quite a few first-class men at the tables, and some of them would no doubt stick.

I surely could have used Emma's five thousand dollars I was demanding for the forged notes of Josiah, he thought to himself bitterly. *Ah, well, every good-bye ain't gone! I'll meet Emma again some day as sure as I'm sitting here. It'll cost her a bit more than five thousand dollars when I get through with her!* That thought cheered him considerably.

In pondering his trip, he found that he really liked the sound of San Francisco better, and he could be there in a matter of less than a week. Yes, he had come down a peg or two, but nothing he couldn't restore. Probably he could even do it during the long train ride to San Francisco. Time would be on his side, having a captive audience. It would be agreeable for him to try.

Chapter 16

When Mark Angelos entered the mansion on Stanhope Street, the inhabitants were in the parlor discussing the recent events concerning the fire at the parsonage. Paul was much more animated in the conversation than usual, and seemed to really be taken by what had happened the night before.

Mark was greeted with a hardy handshake from Connor. It was obvious that he and Connor had become close friends and Victoria couldn't have been happier about that. Mark was greeted by smiles and kindly greetings from everybody, save one. Paul said nothing. When it came time to go in for dinner, Connor had said something funny that everyone was laughing at, and as Mark was still looking at Connor, he simply moved beside Victoria, taking her arm. It seemed the most natural thing in the world for him to have done. Victoria smiled to herself with delight, and looked at Elizabeth, who merely smiled at her in understanding. Apparently no one else had noticed anything amiss.

She assumed that nobody had noticed, but she had not been looking at Paul at the time, for if she had been, she would have seen him cringe at the act. He was seething with anger, and because he had been so preoccupied with Victoria, he missed the fact that Miss Maude had been looking straight at him at that moment.

Fortunately, Paul had not been looking at her, for if he had, he would have realized that she had rightly discerned his sudden anger. He wouldn't have wanted to give anyone a warning of what he was thinking...or planning. He needed to be the one in total control, and make events happen his way, on his time schedule.

Miss Maude could not believe the malignant look Paul was giving both Victoria and Mark at that moment! *Why is he so angry with them? Nobody has done or said anything amiss. Mark is merely escorting her in to dinner,* she reasoned with herself. *But then again, the act of taking her arm like that had been an automatic response on his part, without asking her permission, nor fearing her displeasure. Victoria had seemed to have expected it, as well,* she realized. Dawning hit her like bolt of lightening! *Yes, it makes sense,* she thought.

Maude, you old duffer! Where have you been? Those two are in love! Last night there had been a constant current of awareness between the two, she recalled, *but I thought it was maybe the Christmas fervor and all the excitement. I knew they would make a wonderful couple, but I had not noticed any progression along those lines...before last night, that is.*

Now that she recollected, everyone had been so full of life, and she couldn't help noticing Mark as he watched Victoria. After, all, isn't that really why she had seated them across from one another? How could two lovely people like Mark and Victoria not develop a strong attraction for one another? With excitement, she thought about what Mark and Victoria being a couple would mean to all of them in the future, and found it a delightful prospect.

The assessment Miss Maude had been making of Paul's evil look he had given the couple certainly rang true in her mind, and as the dinner conversations continued, it did so without much input from her.

Yes, it actually seemed as though they had an understanding last night. They had seemed to have the air of familiarity about them, like they were already a couple. And Paul had surely recognized it! The more she thought about it, the more she knew that that was the motive for his anger.

Had I been watching Paul last night would I have seen the same reaction to them, as I saw a few moments ago? she wondered. *Yes, without a doubt! That look I just witnessed was more than anger. It was hatred, unless I miss my guess,* she realized, visibly shuddering.

"Miss Maude?" Elizabeth said. "Are you alright?"

Maude started, and taking a moment to recover from her thoughts, replied, "Of course, dear. Why do you ask?" At that everyone at the table laughed, except Paul. "I called your name twice!" Elizabeth said with an amused grin.

"Oh, my! Forgive me, all of you, for my rudeness! I suppose I was wool gathering for the moment," she explained. "What was it you said, dear?" she asked Elizabeth.

"Well, I had merely commented that you have been very quiet thus far through the meal, and haven't said two words," Elizabeth said.

"I suppose it is just the let down after all the holiday shopping and baking, not to mention the lovely time we had last night at the supper party, before the awful fire, that is," she finished.

"Speaking of the fire," Paul spoke up, "are the police continuing their investigation?" he asked Mark.

"Certainly, they have been back around. But at this point, I suppose they have done all they can at the parsonage for the moment. I'm not sure where the investigation will go from here, if anywhere. It might be a bit of a dead end," Mark replied.

"So, no clues to go on? No mistakes of the culprit? No real eyewitnesses? No other place for San Francisco's finest to look?" he asked, in a light-hearted, amused tone. Seeing Mark shake his head in the negative, he hurried on.

"So they have concluded their investigation, have they? No suspects, no one in custody? Pity, that," Paul finished, with an inappropriate look on his countenance, definitely amusement, and being very pleased with himself.

"Well, I wouldn't say that, exactly," Mark looked at him, inquiringly. He had obviously caught the look on Paul's face, as well, and heard his amused tone.

"An expert has been summoned to examine the facts they have collected so far. We do have some more evidence. There is the clue that I found myself," Mark informed them.

Noticing the pallor and agitation that suddenly came over Paul, whose mouth was literally hanging open, and having such a look of utter disbelief on his face, that Mark felt a check not to continue with that line of conversation.

After a moment's hesitation, Paul seemingly recovered himself and said, "Well, man, don't leave us in the lurch, for pity's sake. What was the clue?" he chirped, trying to cover his emotion with laughter and a somewhat casual look.

Mark cautiously worded his reply with, "Well, it may be nothing. I certainly don't want to start any false rumors. Best leave the sleuthing to the authorities, I say," he finished, amicably.

With Paul's laughter being more of a forced nervous giggle, and given his sudden pallor, Miss Maude did not think he had quite captured the façade of nonchalance he had been aiming for. Nor did the others. Yet she couldn't fathom why anyone would be anything but thrilled with Mark having found something to possibly keep a miscreant, who was apparently getting away with a crime, from doing so! Then she again remembered the look Paul had bestowed upon Mark and Victoria just a few moments earlier and shuddered.

Maude Killian has been a fool! Yes, that is exactly what I've been! If anyone needed a better motive than hatred to spark an ugly act of revenge, I'd like to know it. Paul either loves her or hates her, I don't know which, not that it matters. But would he actually go so far as to...I can't even say it to myself, she thought. She was more troubled over the situation at hand than she could remember being over any other actions of another. She felt a helplessness that was gripping her hard.

When the meal had finished and everyone had taken coffee in the parlor, Mark said that he had to get back. Rising, Victoria walked him to the door and out to the gate. She thanked him for coming and he thanked her for walking him out. They couldn't think of anything else to say, but had stopped and had looked at each other in silence without speaking until they each knew what the other was thinking. He took her hand, kissed it and said, "I will see you at supper tonight, my dear." She nodded shyly, but never broke eye contact, while responding with " Indeed. Until then, Mark."

Everyone having dispersed to their rooms for rest after the dinner meal, Victoria quietly slipped down the hall to Connor and Elizabeth's room and knocked softly. Connor immediately answered the door, and seeing his sister standing there, apparently displaying some distress, motioned her inside.

"Connor, I dislike disturbing your time of rest, but thought it expedient to come here to talk with you, hopefully before you napped," she began.

"Yes, of course. No bother at all. What's troubling you, girl?

"That exchange with Paul and Mark at the dinner table!" she was adamant, even though she spoke quietly. "Paul was arrogant toward the police not being able to catch the intruder, rude in his manner overall, and entirely inappropriate in his amusement. Was it just me, or am I picking on him because I really don't trust him?" she admitted, looking somewhat contrite, yet worried.

"Well, my opinion is that you have every reason to be concerned, even as we both are." Connor confirmed her feelings by saying, "I noticed the other women at the table, and from the looks on their faces, I don't think you were the only one making that assessment."

"Fletch, that's not all! Lilly and I have both recently had night terrors involving Paul. There is something I can't explain about him, but I don't like whatever it is!" she said with a shiver. "He seems alright on the surface of things, but underneath, he is disturbing. Lilly and I have felt his stares and when we look, he really is staring," she finished, with a shake of her head.

"I know how upset you are about this, Victoria, as you just called me Fletch!" he said with an understanding smile. "But seriously, Elizabeth has had the same kind of presentiments as both of you concerning his stares. On several occasions now, she has thought to be alone in a room, only to find that he had walked up close behind her to startle her. At those times he has acted contrite, but underneath he was insincere and even laughing at her. He seems to have a mocking spirit about him," Connor spoke the words, shaking his head in perplexity. Victoria stated that he had done the same with her on more than one occasion.

Elizabeth had nodded her agreement with what she had been saying. She spoke up and said, "At first we felt like it might be because he is a single young man, and doesn't have an apparent social life. We thought perhaps he was overcome with the beautiful unmarried women around him. But it has now been long enough to better assess his character," she, too, was speaking softly, apparently wanting no question of being overheard. "He has become more arrogant, as you said, as evidenced by it seeming like he was pulling for the villain instead of the police a few moments ago. It's like he is always looking down in derision from some high loft at the police, and us for that matter. It's as if he knows a secret, making himself superior to all the rest of us," she finished.

Connor picked up the conversation, "That he does not care for us is evident. His secret everyday life and shifty eyes are a real concern, too. When you put that together with how he acted out today, it seems that something is definitely troubling him," he went on. "We need to find out what it is if we can. I think this is something that we need to consult with Miss Maude about. Shall we continue along these line with her after resting?" he asked.

Victoria readily agreed, yet dreaded having to have any conversation that might hurt Miss Maude, all the while, knowing they must.

Chapter 17

Savannah 27, December 1870

Judge West was in a stew. It had just come to his ears, by way of one of his clerks, that a new deed had been recorded on Morgan's spread. He had just sold up and quit the area, and it seemed he had done it in a hurry, and on the quiet to boot. The judge immediately sent private agents to find out his destination. After some investigation by telegraph, he was informed that he had made reservations for a Pullman sleeping car on the transcontinental railroad to San Francisco.

He has flown and gone to California! Judge West thought, with stone cold dread in his heart. After sending telegrams to San Francisco to 'Mr. Brown' and receiving no return confirmation, he was in a quandary as how exactly to proceed. After a quick prayer, he felt immediately that he should seek the advice of another believer. He immediately set out to speak with Pastor Jacob Jackson.

Upon entering the parsonage, the pastor received him with great warmth. He hoped his appearance on his doorstep signaled that there was good news of Emma. He had been keeping in touch with the judge on nearly a daily basis to see if any news of her had surfaced. Much to his pain to admit it, Judge West told Jake that he was sorry to tell him the reason for his visit.

Jake's heart beat like a trip hammer in fear, thinking the worst had been realized and that something had happened to Emma. "Please, Judge! What is it?" Seeing Jake's sudden agitation and apparent fear, he said, "Sorry my boy, I didn't mean to alarm you, but I do have disturbing news. It was not my wish to deceive you all this time, but Emma had exacted a promise of silence from me, and under the dire circumstances of her leaving, I could not risk breaking that promise, even to you," he explained.

"You see, Cal Morgan had forged notes, supposedly from her father, that he was holding over Emma. When she went to the bank to pay him off, she overheard him bragging to some of his cronies to forging those notes. He also said Emma would marry him or die within the month," he finished, but when Jake, who had been listening and trying to show restraint, heard that, he jumped up and demanded to be heard. He wanted his questions answered right then!

"Sit down, my boy, and I will tell you all," he said.

The judge shook his head in the affirmative and said, "That is why I am here, Jake. With this new development just confirmed today, I can no longer hold my tongue. But I need to finish the story first. You need to know it all," he said.

"The day she heard the threat, she sold up to me and left for San Francisco that night, along with her Aunt Caroline, and Kitty on the boat of a good friend of mine, Captain Flynn," he told him. Upon hearing that, Jake again jumped to his feet and bellowed, "Are you telling me, Judge, that Emma is traveling thousands of miles away on a ship with no man to protect her? If that were not bad enough, you're saying that once she arrives, she will be alone and unprotected in a large city?"

"Now, now. Of course, they have safely reached shore. They are there under assumed names for obvious reasons. They have received the documents I sent with legal confirmations for their new names. I also sent documents proving the notes false," he informed him, seeing the incredulity on the poor boys face.

"But just this morning, I have discovered that Morgan has sold up and left town, also. My private investigators have confirmed that he has headed to San Francisco! Why, that's just a journey of less than a week! I have sent telegrams to Emma using our code, but have not received an answer. I'm in a muddle as to how to proceed in getting her the news. She must know that Morgan is headed to her territory! Now, do you have any idea how we should proceed?" he asked Jake.

Jake Jackson was dumbfounded with hearing such an unbelievable horror story as the one he had just heard concerning Emma. Just two weeks from burying both her parents, all this had happened to her besides? How much could the dear girl take? Then making a long ocean voyage of thousands of miles taking nearly half a year to complete, for three lone women fearing for their lives? "My God," Jake murmured. "My dear God!"

While the judge held his peace giving Jake time to think, Jake took only a moment to speak. "Well, it's obvious to me that Emma needs help and I, for one, can't sit idly by and leave her in the hands of the devil, and do nothing. I will be leaving for San Francisco today!" he exclaimed.

The judge looked at him and said, "So, it's like that is it, son?"

"Yes, Judge, it is exactly like that! I had meant to declare myself, and ask her permission to speak with her papa before he took the trip north. However, there were so many ill and needy in the church, and I was so busy with them then, I just hadn't made the time," he explained, somewhat shamefacedly.

"Besides, I hadn't known about the journey to Philadelphia until the very last possible moment, and since I had no time to speak with Emma first, I had no choice but to wait until their return. How I have lamented that decision for the past nine months!" he moaned. The judge commiserated with him, saying he well understood.

He told Jake that he thought extreme caution and secrecy was necessary from there on out, so that Morgan should not receive word of his departure for California. Jake agreed and said he would tell his congregation that he was needed in another city on an urgent spiritual matter, and the head of the deacons could carry on at the church. If fighting the battle with a devil bent on murder, and protecting the innocent wasn't a spiritual matter, he didn't know what was!

"I agree with you that you need to head on out, as time is of the essence. I only wish I were accompanying you, my boy," he said.

"Well, who is to say you couldn't, Judge?" Jake asked him.

"If I didn't think people would ask too many questions about us both going off, knowing that we are both close to Emma, and knowing that I might be watched, I would!" he responded. "But mind, if you run into any trouble out there, any trouble a tall, you just telegraph and I will go directly to the governor of this state to get justice for you against Cal Morgan," he assured him. "He is a good friend of mine and can be trusted. I won't bother with that no-account sheriff!"

Jake Jackson left Savannah on the next train bound for his connection with the transcontinental railroad headed to San Francisco. He could only believe that he would find Emma quickly once he arrived, find her safe, and very happy to see him! He had dreamed of finding her waiting for him, as he had been waiting to hear from her, and had prayed for God to protect and defend her wherever she was. He also prayed that He would also grant her great happiness, into the bargain.

*B*efore tea was served that afternoon, Connor approached Miss Maude's private rooms and knocked. He asked her if the ladies and he could have a moment of her time. She seemed to dread the coming conversation, thereby indicating that she might already have a suspicion of what it might be about.

She readily agreed, and Connor motioned the ladies in from the hall. The women who entered her quarters, and stood before her were a solemn assembly if ever there was one. She had put them at their ease immediately by having them sit down and asked if this had anything to do with Paul's attitude at the dinner table. They nodded and she said, "Well, I thought so, not that I am surprised. In fact, I meant to speak to all of you about my concerns about Paul before Christmas, but so much was going on with the festivities, I didn't want to spoil it with having to confront this issue," she admitted. "Please, Connor, if you will take the lead here, I would appreciate it. I only hope that you will speak freely," she told him.

"Of course, Miss Maude. May I simply lay this out without interruption or comment until I have finished?" he asked them all. When he had their permission he began, "First, allow me to say that we have no desire to cause you any discomfort, seeing that Paul is a relative, however distant, but we do want to find out what you thought of what happened between Mark and Paul this noon at the dinner table.

But as you have asked me to begin, I will let you know that just today we have shared our feelings about Paul with each other for the first time. Since the day we arrived, we have not been able to place any confidence or trust in the young man. We have tried to give him every benefit of the doubt, and have waited until we knew him better to form a lasting opinion, but regrettably, it appears that we know him no better now than the day we arrived," he explained.

"His behavior today, we believe, shows him to be a very troubled young man. He is secretive, withdrawn, and socially unable to carry on a polite conversation with those in close communion with himself. These things might appear as insecurity, or feelings of inferiority," seeing the nods of agreement all around, he continued.

"But while he seems withdrawn and insecure, we believe that on the contrary, he is really arrogant and angry. I am convinced he feels vastly superior for some reason, like he knows a secret that none of us knows," he said, as he watched Miss Maude's face carefully for any signs of disagreement with his assessments. He very kindly spoke the truth in love to her.

"I will give you but one example that each of the ladies have told me just today. One of them will think she is alone in a room, and Paul will suddenly be standing there right behind her, causing a dreadful fright. While he feigns contrition, he's actually enjoying their discomfort, and is laughing at them all the while. That certainly indicates there is something inherently wrong with him," he said as Miss Maude nodded, thoughtfully.

"We definitely feel that he has an intense dislike for all of us. We have thought much about it, but none of us knows why. We only know that this has gone on for far too long, and now the ladies are having nightmares about him. Do you know why this should be, Miss Maude?" he finally finished.

Miss Maude was silent as she took it all in. It only confirmed her own suspicions. She took a deep breath before answering him. She told them that when she had been asked by her great-aunt to give her great-grandson a home, she had been only too glad to do it. He had come to her from New York City without any other information, or anything to recommend him, other than he was family.

She told them that as far as she knew, he did not have any means of employment. What he did with himself all day she had no idea. She was fairly sure that he was not trying to find employment, and when she had tried to find out from him what other jobs he had back in New York, it seemed that he hadn't worked there either. Of course, she was giving him money to live on.

Miss Maude told them she knew that he had been troubled ever since his arrival two years earlier, even though he hadn't communicated anything with her about his life prior to his arrival in San Francisco. That was long before the Sullivans had arrived, but she said that he had definitely undergone some kind of change when they came to the mansion, and that unfavorable.

She felt this trouble seemed to be coming to a head, as she, too, had sensed more open hostility in him and more agitation over seemingly nothing. She told them that she had some idea of the cause. However, it might seem like interference or presumption on her part, because what she had to say was definitely personal to one among them. She assured them that she hesitated to bring it up in open conversation. They assured her in turn that they wanted to know all her thoughts.

She then related the time that Mark had taken Victoria's arm to lead her in to dinner. It had been a completely natural act, without him asking permission, nor believing that he would have been out of line in doing so. "Was that not right, my dear?" she asked. Seeing Victoria blush and nod her agreement, she told her, "I wouldn't embarrass you for the world, but I believe that is at the crux of the problem. When that happened, I had looked straight at Paul, who was looking at you and Mark. I shudder to say this, but that look was one of hatred and fury," she told them.

At this point, Victoria entered the conversation. She told them that she had meditated on the fire and that she firmly believed that whoever did it was wishing to do Mark harm, as he would have been more affected by it than any other. The difficulty in that reasoning had been finding anyone who had a motive. Now Miss Maude was telling her that probably Paul had one, and possibly the oldest and strongest in the world: jealousy.

"Do you feel he is capable of such an act…well, you know, the fire?" she asked Maude outright.

Maude told her that as much as she hated to believe or admit it, she was afraid that idle hands had definitely done the devil's own work the night of the fire. She said, however, that there was no proof and that getting proof would probably necessitate catching him in the act.

"I have written to my great-aunt, to find out more about him, but have not received an answer as of yet."

To this, Connor suggested that she send a telegram straight away asking why Paul had needed a home there with her. Surely, if there had been nothing wrong, it would be a simple enough question to answer. "The very fact that you have sent an inquiry by telegram should alert her that if there is something she needs to tell you, she should do it now," Connor told her. Miss Maude agreed, and asked Connor if he would go immediately and do that for her.

The conversation ended in Connor telling all the women that they were never to be alone in the house, except behind locked doors, or alone anywhere else, for that matter, until this was cleared up. If any of their speculations were true, Paul not only hated them, but he was a dangerous, unstable man.

Chapter 19

After sending the telegram to Miss Maude's great-aunt, Connor went by the parsonage to speak with Mark. After exchanging pleasantries that he did not feel, Connor asked him straight away, on the basis of their fast friendship, whether or not he had feelings for his sister.

Mark did not hesitate one second, but laughed and said, "I hadn't realized it so plainly showed! But to answer your question, of course, I do. I am in love for the first time in my life, and yes, it is certainly with Victoria. Do you have objections to that, Connor?" he asked with a perplexed look on his face, as he could feel the intensity in Connors question.

"No, no, of course not, my brother! Certainly, congratulations are in order, but I also came by today to talk with you about Paul."

Seeing a brief frown of distaste cross Mark's face, he hurried on to say, "I have just come from a meeting between Miss Maude and my family. Everyone is very concerned about him. We all have just shared with each other some situations concerning him. We have always felt that he was an unpleasant mystery that we hoped we would never have to solve, but it seems that is not to be the case," he lamented.

"Miss Maude saw a look of deep hatred and rage on Paul's face when you took Victoria's arm in a possessive way at dinner yesterday, as though you both expected nothing less," he told him. "That is why I asked you how you feel about her. We now believe that is the root of the problem, as Miss Maude thinks he is obsessed with Victoria. With either love or hate, but whatever the case, it has caused him to give the impression that he despises the two of you, most probably through jealousy," he said, watching Mark's face to make sure he was following his reasoning.

"But the worst part is, Miss Maude also believes he was capable of starting the fire here last night. We now believe that he has a firm motive, and while we have no proof, of course, we believe he is capable of the deed. Were you serious when you said that you had found a clue?" he questioned him.

Mark was concerned that Paul would have had the audacity to have done such a thing, but couldn't really say that he was all that surprised. He related that to Connor and said, " I was serious about the clue. I found a small swatch of fabric torn from an old garment, caught in the splintered doorframe, where the intruder entered. It looked as if it could have come from an old coat," he said, and showed him the patch.

"I actually haven't thought more about it, with so much going on around here today. I've been meaning to give it to the police. Now that the arson specialist is coming over, I need to follow through with that," he said, making a mental note to do it that day.

When Mark had retrieved the scrap of material and showed it to Connor, he examined it and said that to his knowledge, he had never seen the material before. Then again, he hadn't usually seen Paul when he had been arriving or leaving, so he didn't know if it was his or not, although he made up his mind to keep his eyes open for it.

Supper was a somewhat somber occasion after all the discussion that had been going on about the situation. Paul had not appeared, claiming whatever had affected his stomach the day before was still holding on. However, his light-heartedness at the dinner table belied that. They wondered what else he was hiding.

Outside of Miss Maude and the family, only the other staff members of the church had been alerted to the situation, as they would be spending some time in the mansion on Stanhope Street until the parsonage had been made ready and was functional again. They had all been shown the swatch of material Mark had found before taking it to the police. Who knew but what the owner of the garment might return to the scene of the crime? It was certainly worth keeping their eyes open.

It had been three days since the fire and the Harbor Mission staff had arrived for supper at Miss Maude's again. That night Mark was seated next to Victoria and across from Paul. They all were more than a bit uncomfortable with the man, and were having a difficult time in not showing it.

Having gotten though the meal, they gathered in the parlor for coffee and conversation. Paul had excused himself on the premise that he needed to get to bed early, as he still was not feeling well.

After they had finished their coffee, Mark wanted to be alone with Victoria. The nights were still mild, and he asked, "Victoria, would you care for some fresh air?"

"Of course, Mark, that would be lovely," she answered, as she fetched her heavy shawl from the hall tree. Mark took it from her and draped it around her shoulders.

Once outside, he held her hand until they had passed out of the gate and onto the paved walkway, then drew her arm through his, keeping her close beside him. Besides an occasional smile or some nonsensical comment that lovers often make while in the first bloom of romance, they walked in silence until they reached the area that overlooked the bay.

Once seated on a bench, Mark turned to her and said, "Victoria dear, we need to talk," taking her hands in his. Victoria nodded her agreement, waiting for him to begin.

"First of all I want to ask you if Connor discussed with you the conversation he and I had today when he dropped by the parsonage after sending a telegram for Miss Maude?"

"No, Mark, he didn't mention anything to me about it," she answered, wondering what Connor had wanted to talk to Mark about that would cause Mark to bring it up to her.

"Well, that makes it a bit harder for me to start," he hesitated a few seconds and then resumed. "Victoria, Connor came to ask me if I had feelings for you. You know by now that something very special has been happening between us, do you not?" he inquired.

"I believed so, Mark. But this is all new to me, and I couldn't be sure how deep it went with you," she answered him, squeezing his hand.

"Well, since this is also the first time anything like this has happened to me… I fear I am not doing this very well," he stammered. Beginning again, he said, "I have been around you much of the time since you arrived at the end of September, and I have admired you so very much. May I continue?" he asked her, wanting some sign that the conversation was not uncomfortable for her.

"May I help you here, Mark?" she softly asked.

"I certainly wish you would, my dear," he said, with a heartfelt smile.

"Mark, I only know how to say this as honestly as I feel it. I adore you, and based on the looks I have been receiving from you, I think that you love me, too." When Mark just looked at her, a flush coming upon his face, she hurried on, "Oh, dear, have I been too bold? Have I spoken out of turn?" she murmured, more embarrassed that she had ever been in her life.

"No, no, my darling, you didn't say anything amiss, merely what I wish I had said. I do love you! You can believe me when I say that, as this is the first time I have ever uttered those words. I was just surprised at you being brave enough to say what I most in the world wanted to hear. I just couldn't seem to get what I feel about you into words! You brave girl!" he squeezed her hands, and brushed away a wisp of hair that the wind had blown across her mouth.

"Well, it wasn't bravery at all," she assured him. "It was just harder to hold it in than to say it. Besides, I never really dreamed that it could happen to me and not to you!" she cried looking at him with all the love in the world.

That look was his undoing, never mind the words with which she had just bowled him over. He wanted nothing more than to hold her in his arms and kiss her until they both had their fill. But he could hardly do that in front of God, and the city of San Francisco!

Looking back at her with dark, sultry eyes, she could hear him take in a long, ragged breath. "Darling, we need to start back," he said, rising rather abruptly and pulling her up beside him. He stood very close to her looking at her face, and then tucking her arm through his again, he quietly said, "Victoria, I am going to have to kiss you soon, love."

She could not believe what was happening to her insides. She wanted to snuggle as close to him as she could get. She honestly could have thrown her arms around his waist and held him close to her bosom, daring anyone to notice, not that many were around. But one just didn't kiss the pastor of the Harbor Mission out in the open, publically, especially for the first time.

Her mama would have been shocked at her, and would have told her that the man did the kissing! Well, she was shocked at herself, and no telling how she had disgraced herself in his eyes, as surely he could hear her erratic heartbeat and read her thoughts.

They walked home arm in arm and very close together. That balm he used after shaving was wreaking havoc with her senses again. Surely, he could tell what was going on inside her, as she could barely walk straight. She could not control the wild beating of her heart, as a fluttering was happening in her stomach. She wondered what in the world would happen to her next!

She couldn't help but recall Lilly talking about the serving girls back in Savannah, and how easy it seemed for them to get into…trouble. She had heard them called trash, and that they were no good, but tonight showed her that it would be very easy for any woman in love to act completely natural, and end up in trouble. She shivered and determined to keep a strong hand on her emotions. Hadn't she already broken the promise to herself that the man would definitely declare himself first?

Chapter 20

When Mark and Victoria arrived at the mansion and entered the front door, it was obvious that the rest of them had gone upstairs, as the parlor was dimly lit and empty. As Mark closed the door behind them, Victoria moved a couple of steps into the doorway to the parlor, not knowing if he wanted to stay or leave, but when Mark came up behind her and touched her shoulders to relieve her of her wrap, she turned to face him and suddenly found herself in his arms, and he was kissing her the way he had dreamed of for weeks.

She reached up and put her arms around his neck, and leaned into him as she kissed him back with a fervor that shocked her. If he thought it too forward, he wasn't letting on! Finally, he brought the intimacy to a reluctant end. She looked at him through dreamy eyes as he rubbed over her lips with his thumb. "My darling girl, this is real, isn't it?" he murmured in her ear.

"Well, if it isn't, it should be!" she said breathlessly and in all sincerity, as he chuckled, moving away to hang up her shawl. When he had again faced her he said, "Victoria, love, we need to talk about our future soon. I haven't a doubt in the world of my feelings for you. If you feel the same, I think I need to speak with your brother as soon as possible!"

Thoughts of Savannah and Morgan sent a shiver down her spine. Mark saw it and said, "Darling, what is it?"

Thinking of Savannah and all that happened to her there, she wondered if it was time to tell Mark the rest of the story. "Nothing, really. I was just reminded of my last proposal!"

"Excuse me, Victoria! Uh… what do you mean your last proposal?" His face had gone pale and he was white around his mouth. She recognized by his eyes that it wasn't anger, but fear. He had thought her totally innocent of any love entanglements, but her comment about a proposal of marriage had hit him hard.

He had realized that the beautiful Miss Sullivan surely had been pursued. But she just wasn't the flirty kind of chit who received multiple proposals from young swains hanging around her front door. If a romance had progressed to the proposal of marriage stage, had she feelings for him still? He had a million questions that he could not ask, but the bewilderment he obviously felt in his heart showed on his face and was actually palpable.

"Mark, this isn't the time or place for me to go into it. Suffice it to say I never considered the proposal. In fact, that is why we moved here, to get away from it all," she told him.

"Was it so painful that you couldn't stay in the same town with him?" he inquired.

"Oh, Mark, not at all. She studied his face a moment and then said, "Sit down, please. It isn't fair to leave you with so many questions," as she began her story.

"You see, my parents died in a horrible fire outside Philadelphia just nine months ago. A mere fortnight after the funeral, Cal Morgan, papa's solicitor, brought forged notes to me showing that papa had borrowed more than five thousand dollars from him." He could sense her anxiety in having to discuss it all with him, especially in light of all that had just transpired between them.

She hurried on, "When I arrived at the bank to pay them off, I overheard him in the next room bragging about forging them. Then he said that I would either marry him, or lie beside my parents before the month was out," she shuddered again as she remembered that harrowing day. "After I withdrew all my money from the bank, I decided not to pay him. I intimated that I would await his next move. Instead, I sold the plantation to papa's best friend, Judge West, that very day. Aunt Sadie, Lilly, and I left Savannah that same night. I knew if he ever found me he would kill me for leaving. Not only for selling the plantation out from under him, but because I used his own flimflam against him, and made him look foolish," she said.

"Thank you not interrupting to ask questions, as there will be plenty of time for those. Anyway, it was there, as we were leaving, that I saw Connor on the deck of an arriving vessel, after the army had declared him dead six years earlier! He was suffering from amnesia, and still cannot remember anything past when he and Elizabeth met. Perhaps you have noticed that we seldom speak of the past. Anyway, the captain of our vessel returned to port, and Connor and Elizabeth came aboard. We began our voyage that night," she said, as she watched a range of emotions flash across his face. He was utterly speechless! "There's more, Mark. We are all using aliases to prevent Morgan from readily locating us. You must think us awful deceivers!"

Mark was sitting in astonishment. Those vile happenings only happened to other people, not to his Victoria...Victoria!

"I never thought I would have to ask this, love, but what *is* the name of the woman I love and plan to marry?" That earned him a tumultuous smile as she replied, "My name is Emma, Emma Summers of Summers Bluff plantation in Savannah, Georgia. Connor is Fletcher, my aunt is Caroline Summers and my cousin is in truth my friend, Kitty Thornton." Seeing his astonishment, she said, "Again, you must think us awful deceivers!"

He sat looking at her a long moment and then said, "Contraire, my dear, I think you are an amazingly brilliant and brave woman, and God has certainly protected you. Emma. Emma. I like the sound of that. Come here and let me hold you, Emma," he said, as she moved closer to him.

She leaned her head on his chest, and allowed the tears of happiness to flow, as she really wept for the first time over all that had happened to her with Cal Morgan. Other than when she found her brother and wept tears of joy, she had not wept like that since the funeral. He held her and let her weep, as he lovingly stroked her auburn hair that he loved so much.

They would work this out, and he, who stood for truth and goodness, favored her righteous cause. After all, to change one's name to save life is not the same as to change it in order to deceive and for the sake of deception alone. He thought he would have to make discreet inquiries about one Calhoun Morgan. One thing he already knew about him, was that he would never, ever marry Emma Summers.

Never was he so relieved than to know that she had not harbored feelings for the man. He, Mark Angelos, really was her first and last love. He would see to that. Yes, he would have to talk to Connor.

She's in there with him, now. I can't get close enough to hear her clearly, he thought. He had caught the words proposal, Savannah, a judge and another name he couldn't make out. *I knew they were from somewhere in the South with that disgusting drawl of theirs,* Paul thought to himself.

So, she was on the fly from Savannah, was she? Fleeing from someone she was afraid of. So, somebody there hates her and wants

*to see her dead as much as I do! Maybe I can help him out with that!
Yes, just maybe I can be of service to the Southern 'gentleman'! After
all, we have so much in common.*

Mark had paced his library floor for the past hour. He had
a lot of thinking to do. He knew he wouldn't sleep until he had
gone over the things that Victoria had shared with him earlier
that night. Unbelievable things swirling around and around in
his mind, and even though he had meditated on them, he still
couldn't seem to take it all in. He knew he loved her with his
whole heart, and the outrageous situation she was in was just
incredible, but there it was, proving truth was often stranger than
fiction.

Of course, she would have to keep the name she was using,
for the reasons she had chosen it to begin with. He wanted to
protect her and keep her as close to himself as possible. He would
talk to Connor tomorrow. There was no need to wait another day
without at least an engagement settled.

He didn't know if Victoria wanted all the frills of a large
church wedding, but without scandalizing themselves, they would
have to be married in the church. Knowing if Miss Maude had
her way, it would be the social event of the season. He didn't care
what kind of wedding they had as long as it was soon.

He couldn't help thinking that Victoria was still in real danger.
After all, who would be obsessed with the beautiful Victoria
Summers, and then merely let her walk out of his life, especially
after she had thwarted all of his plans, not to mention making
mockery of him? Not the evil man she had described! That man
would follow her to the ends of the earth to exact revenge!

He got on his knees and began to pray.

Chapter 21

Cal Morgan had joined the society of the transcontinental train headed west. He had met several well-to-do businessmen from Sacramento, but only a few from San Francisco. They were all full of themselves, and their silver or gold enterprises, and talked freely about them, trying to impress each other.

For the most part, those fellow travelers were originally from the large Northern cities on the East Coast, and while they were talkative, they really weren't giving away much. Those he knew to be working the crowd. They were there to make shady deals, and he avoided them like the plague. He didn't want any scandal attached to him. No, he needed a clean slate to make his own flimflam work once he reached San Francisco.

Most of the Californians aboard were of new money, while there were only a few elegant gentlemen from back East around Richman and Charleston, who were surely of old wealth. He felt that he had to keep a surface relationship with them at first, until he learned of their business acquaintances in Savannah, as they might know people who knew him from past transactions. It had been awhile since he had pulled any flimflam in Richman or Charleston, so maybe they would not have heard of him. Yes, he would have to be careful with what he said and did with them; pity that, as they were the only decent company onboard.

He felt that maybe he could impress them with his assumed Southern graciousness and charm, when compared with the boldness and brashness of the other Northerners in their company, which would, no doubt, put him on a better footing with them. If the obviously genuine articles would accept him, he reasoned that the new moneymen would take note of that, and gladly open their society to him. Then he could use them to get some of that new money of theirs when the old gentlemen weren't around. He wanted to keep the gentry safely guarded for his entrance into San Francisco society, once he had worked his schemes, and was back on top and in the money again.

Yes, there were many good prospects of future deals right there on the train, especially if he could get them in his debt. When that happened, for some of the new moneymen, he would squeeze any debts hard, as he certainly needed their money more than they did. But for the old wealth, he would forgive the debt of money in exchange for the debt of gratitude and obligation of a true Southern gentleman. After all, he could afford to be generous, as it was an investment in his future, which he was sure to get back with interest.

Jake Jackson was trying his best not to worry about Emma—rather Victoria— being alone anywhere near Cal Morgan. Knowing that he was headed her way just as quickly as he possibly could mattered little when he also knew that Cal Morgan was ahead of him, and would arrive in San Francisco a day or two before he would. While that was concerning him, he knew he was on the fastest route to her. He would just have to sit back and let his faith carry him the rest of the way. After all, he had had a lot of practice doing that, like every day for the past nine months!

He was doing all he knew to do, as he studied his small Bible, and reread the promises of protection, and the ones that declared that nothing was impossible with God. He knew that meant that God could do anything, but he also realized that it meant that it was impossible for God to do nothing! Nothing was absolutely impossible for a God who was always on hand, always working His plan. He was always doing something! He had to believe that God's perfect will would be done and that He would perfect those things which concerned him, as he sat on the train in a state of impotence to do nothing more than pray and believe. Yet, all of God's promises assured him that in so doing, he was doing the one thing that would help.

Paul Cabot was about ready to make his move back in San Francisco. Tomorrow was New Year's Eve. He would wait until the gala was in full swing and then spring the trap. He knew the ball would be held in the second story ballroom. There would be too many people in attendance for anyone to notice his activities. He was so excited he would periodically shake himself like a wet hound.

The double doors at the entrance of the ballroom would remain open, but the doors at the far end would be closed and locked. When the time came, he could set the fire, escape in the ensuing panic, and close the front doors. By slipping a bar through the iron handles it would lock them all in. The balcony doors would be closed, due to the cold night air, he would see that those would be locked already. There would be no escape for the Sullivans or '*him*'!

Tall, dark and handsome preacher and dead at twenty-eight! he thought with delight. *But one bad thing would be that there wouldn't be a lover to mourn his death. No, she would die right along with him! Wasn't that tidy?*

A telegram from New York City was delivered and placed into Miss Maude's hands that morning. It read: Paul loves fire Stop Forgive my silence Stop No proof Stop Still known to be dangerous Stop Keep me apprised Stop Affectionately, Your great-aunt Lizzie

Maude could scarcely believe it, although it was exactly what she had expected to hear. They had hit the nail on the head when they knew he had set the fire at the parsonage! She tucked the telegram into her pocket and made her way to Connor's door.

When he opened the door, she found the rest of the family with him. He ushered her in and she took a seat. Withdrawing the telegram, she handed it to Connor. There was a mingled look of relief and concern on his face.

"Well, that much is settled. At least we know who the culprit is, but now the question is, what are we supposed to do about it?" he asked the others, as he handed the telegram to the ladies. There were intakes of breath from that quarter and they handed the telegram back to Maude.

Connor said, "I would advise you to give that telegram to Mark as soon as possible. He needs to advise the authorities. And we need to be extra vigilant for the next few days," he impressed upon them. "I have been studying on this," he began. "We need to watch for any change in his normal attitude, whether he's happy, sad, excited, things like that. I think his attitude at the table the other day is typical of when he is making his moves," Connor told them.

"When he claimed to be indisposed all day on the day the fire was set, he didn't eat much. But I would presume that was because of his excitement, not illness, as he claimed. Looking back it is easy to see that he was agitated, as though the party was delaying his plans, which we assumed was because of the claimed indisposition," he told them.

"We now know the indisposition to be a lie. He fabricated that, using an indisposition as his alibi, because he did not go to bed, he used the back stairs and went to the parsonage, where he started the fire," he continued.

"Also noted, he waited for a time when we were all occupied. We were paying him no attention and that left him free to roam. Now, we have another gala coming up tomorrow night, only on an even grander scale!" he exclaimed, as he looked from one to the other of their faces, and knew that his face mirrored the concern he saw on each one.

"We know that there will be many more people here for him to hide behind. Therefore, I propose to keep eyes on him every moment of the evening. No telling what that diabolical mind is devising, but I feel in my very bones, that there is something planned, and it has to do with the gala," he finished.

Maude spoke up and asked, "Do you feel I should cancel the ball? I could claim a sudden indisposition, and with how I feel at the moment, it would be the honest to goodness truth!"

Connor replied, "Actually, I think that more would be accomplished by allowing him more freedom, not less. But I suggest we hire detectives to act as more servants, and some to be posted inconspicuously, but unfalteringly at each door, posing as guests."

If the doors were ever shut, they couldn't watch him, leaving him a free hand to move about freely to carry out his diabolical plans. Maude thought that a good idea, and said that she would see to it. She would send for Mark to come to read him the telegram and be advised of the plan of action to be put to the detectives.

Should a large crowd of people in their finery be trapped in a second floor ballroom, there would be no escape. Measures must be taken to avoid that at all cost, and not only anticipatory measures be taken, but actual firefighting measures would also have to be somewhere close at hand in case anything should go wrong and the worst should happen.

It was unfortunate that a suspected fire would be planned for such a night in a place where city wide celebrations were to take place, as legitimate fires were apt to break out in other parts of the city, as well, and their best laid plans of fire fighters being near by might not succeed.

And even a very devious mind like Paul's might even set perimeter fires for that purpose, to occupy the fire fighters away from the main event. Also, in the event that they were off course and the plan was not the mansion, then guards would also be stationed at the church and parsonage.

What a terrifying thought, that they were discussing a possible planned destruction of many of their friends, and of they themselves, and at the hand of a man in their own household!

Mark arrived at the mansion fifteen minutes later. He joined the family in Miss Maude's private quarters. One of the church staff accompanied him, but waited in the foyer outside her quarters, to be sure no one lurked at the keyhole. Paul, however, had been busy and had not realized they were all there. It might have given him pause had he known.

There was to be somewhat of a vigil from 11:00 o'clock until midnight New Year's Eve. That was when the dancing would be stopped, the music stilled, and thoughts turned from the gaiety of celebrating the blessings of the old year, to give way to thoughts of what the New Year would bring to them in the year 1871. Mark would give a small devotion, and they would spend time giving thanks for this year's blessings, and for their prospects for the coming year. Then at midnight they would be dismissed with a blessing to go their separate ways, hopefully with each one reflecting on God's goodness to them.

During that hour, it would be more difficult to keep an eye on Paul, if he had not made his move by then. All would be still and the detectives couldn't follow him as inconspicuously as in a moving crowd. They would have to be posted inside and out. They would have many obstacles to hide behind outside, but decidedly less on the inside.

Chapter 22

A New Year's Eve celebration is usually connected with a riotous, strong-drinking crowd, but the guests of the gala at the mansion on Stanhope Street that night, were mostly the members of the Harbor Mission. They would have an evening of music, dancing, and entertainment. There would be soft refreshments, lively fellowship and conversation, and spiritual reflection to welcome in the hopefully wonderful New Year of 1871. The heart of every invited guest, no doubt, would be light at the prospect of the festivities to come that night. Especially Paul Cabot's.

Mark had spoken to Connor and received his blessings on his engagement to Victoria. The couple planned to break the news that night at the ball. Their love would be their best blessing that they had received that year. The wedding would be as soon as the festivities were over and people had settled down once again. When the gown would be ready, all else would be, too. They had never been happier! They knew their congregation would be delighted for them, as well.

The mansion was a busy place that day, as delivery men were in and out, and new servers arrived to help with the preparations and decorating to be done. It seemed even the third floor was to be decorated, as people would take advantage of all the balconies on what turned out to be a mild New Year's Eve. That was Paul's first fly in the ointment.

Paul didn't like people on his floor. He didn't like people on his balcony. He needed free access to move along the balconies as needed. He had gathered the things he would need for the fire and had carefully stowed them in the back of closets in unused rooms, where there was not the slightest likelihood of them being discovered.

He made himself scarce throughout the day staying in his room, and as expected, picked at this food during meals, attributing his lack of appetite as the same lingering indisposition. When questioned about his symptoms, he gave out that he felt it was his nerves at the upcoming celebration. Then, too, he told them that he was uncomfortable with so many people coming and going.

While he was at the table during mealtimes, the detectives took the liberty to search his rooms. While they didn't find anything amiss relating to fire that would probably be set that night, they did, however, find an old coat with a piece of cloth recently ripped from it, as they had been advised they would.

They then turned their search to scrutinize other rooms not in use. Finding the apparatuses Paul had hidden, exactly what they had been looking for, and as far as one could tell, they had left them entirely untouched. They did not want to give warning they knew what he was up to, as they would need proof to put him out of reach of harming others again. Knowing that he could be spooked at some unforeseen happening, he was watched all the day, lest he panic and act prematurely, without the best defensive team in place.

The guest began arriving at eight o'clock in the evening at 117 Stanhope Street and by ten o'clock the gala was in full grandeur. But for the occupants of the mansion, it was a night akin to the night they had left Savannah! Tension was thick and pressure was felt to be mounting.

Paul had gone in and out several times. He couldn't sit still. Therefore, twenty others could not, either. They had hoped that he would be his usual non-communicative, quiet self until the time that he made his move. They should have known better.

The occupants of the mansion realized that they had never really seen him with a genuine smile, except that once on Christmas Day, when he had been gloating over the police not catching the arsonist. But tonight he was genuinely smiling and giggling. He was giddy over what he had planned.

How they hated to not just go and arrest him right then, and put them all out of their misery. But he was a very intelligent man, and without proof he would never admit what he had planned. They had to see it through to the end.

Paul, sick man that he was, was in his glory. He was strutting and laughing, and sometimes was seen to be dancing a few step all by himself. He needed help. He was God's creature, but had been twisted by the devil's own hand. They had all prayed together before the start of the gala, that Paul would be reached by the Holy Spirit of God, and delivered from this sickness. After all, God had done greater miracles!

Paul made his move around ten-thirty. He first went to the balcony and from a corner retrieved a simple wooden stick that nobody had realized was there, as it had looked like just part of the woodwork.

He quietly began to close the door, when a 'guest' asked him not to, as it was too warm in the ballroom. He hesitated, but the others around him took up the cry. In the end, he gave it up. Another twenty minutes went by when he again tried to close the balcony doors, but again he was foiled in his attempt. He was frustrated, but too preoccupied with his plans to be overly concerned. A short time later he decided he had given those fancy dressed peacocks plenty of time to enjoy themselves, and now it was his turn.

He glance around him in all directions and seeing nobody paying the slightest attention to him, he immediately went to the upper, unused rooms and gathered his small, but beautifully wrapped 'gifts', and brought them back downstairs. He began placing them on shelves around the ballroom. Nobody seemed to notice. At least, nobody interfered. After all, this was a gala affair, and if anyone had noticed, perhaps they would surmise that the mistress of the house had a special surprise in store for them. When all the apparatuses had been placed exactly where he wanted them, in all four corners of the room, he attempted to close the balcony doors a third time, only to be thwarted yet again.

He next went to the front doors and closed one of those. Just as he was closing the second one, a few 'guests' had come back through the doors and had stood in the middle of the doorway, talking and laughing with each other. Paul had to accept that he would not be closing the doors. His only regret is that he would never have a chance to use his rods to lock them all in. That being the case, some few might even escape. Oh, well, such was life.

Not being one to quit while he was ahead, he simply went to the next phase of his plan. He knew the astonishment his next actions would cause, along with the confused reaction of the guests, would allow him plenty of time to gain the balcony and get away, long before anyone would even realize what had happened. Therefore, the chance of anyone recognizing where the trouble had started would be slim. There would be great noise and fire, fire, fire! He could watch from the street. Oh, yes he could!

He looked around him and all was just as he had always dreamed it would be. They were all laughing, talking, dancing and having a wonderful last few moments of their lives! Seeing all was well in hand, he made his way through the crowd, and went straight to the dais, where he was elevated enough to see all the packages that were placed on shelves higher than a man's head.

He withdrew a pistol and in rapid succession, fired into all four of the packages. His actions merely left a small bullet hole in each of the packages, hardly noticeable. Wondering what his point was of creating such a noise, when everyone had stopped what they were doing, they only saw an agitated young man with a mustache surrounded by guests, who had disarmed him, and was leading him away.

The young man began to curse and scream, "What have you done with my beautiful gifts? What have you done? You have ruined everything! You have ruined my surprise for you," he ranted.

He looked at Mark, and Victoria and spit out, "It was you! I know it was you! I hate you both! I hate you! What have you done to my bombs?" He was finally led away, still ranting.

All of the invited guests were astounded at the happenings. To see another guest shooting inside the ballroom, and causing such a disturbance was unlike anything any of them had ever witnessed at a gala event before. Most of them stood in shocked silence while trying to make sense of what it all meant.

After the young man had been led away, and they realized it was over, they all began to chatter excitedly about what had happened. That night would surely go down in history as quite the most unusual gala New Year's Eve ball they had ever attended.

Chapter 23

*S*ince the ball had turned into a shouting of obscenities, it took a while for the real guest to settle down. When they had quieted, Mark explained the situation, that the man was mentally unstable. He told the guests that Paul had been the one to set fire to the parsonage, and was suspected of setting others around the city, and had been trying to destroy the mansion that night.

The 'gifts' were his small, hand made bombs that would have exploded, and although small, they would have been enough to cause a fire. Had not the San Francisco detectives been alerted, and had they not searched the premises for just such things as they had found in the upstairs rooms, the outcome would have been a tragedy. They had disarmed the simply made, but deadly bombs, and had rewrapped the 'gifts'.

But once order was restored, they moved on into their vigil. They were ready for a refreshing of their spirits.

Just before the midnight hour, Mark asked Victoria to join him at the dais. When he took her hand to guide her up the steps, he did not let it go. She had never looked lovelier. Her flowing gown was of the best deep green velvet with a front panel of sublime champagne colored, shirred satin faille. She wore her mama's pearl pendant that lay perfectly in the hollow of her delicate looking throat. My, my, but Mark was a smitten man!

He told his congregation that his greatest blessing of 1870 had been the Lord bringing the lovely Miss Victoria Sullivan into his life. He publically told his congregation of his total commitment to her, and declared his great love for her, and that she had consented to become his bride in the very near future.

There were gasps, and smiles, and then laughter all over the ballroom, as his beloved congregation rejoiced with them, breaking out into enthusiastic applause!

Aunt Sadie, Lilly and Miss Maude were jubilant! If any of the young maidens in the room were heart-broken that night, they had the good graces not to show it! The same went for the young unmarried men in attendance.

Connor and Elizabeth were also elated and pleased at Mark and Victoria's engagement. They were romantics at heart and the announcement had reminded them that they were still on their honeymoon! Ah, the party would soon be over.

Earlier that evening, as the news reporters hanging around the police station house that particular New Year's Eve, had been waiting for a report of some fracas or other that they could write about in tomorrow's newspaper, they recognized some of the toughest police detectives in formal attire, heading to some gala event.

When they heard the address they gave the cabby, they recognized they were headed to one of the mansions belonging to a Nob, and since that didn't happen, they knew something was afoot. They followed them to the New Year's Eve gala at 117 Stanhope Street.

Later, when the formally attired detectives brought out a demented man screaming his bombs had been ruined, and the fires hadn't burned, the police had no choice but to give them a story. Between the police bragging, and the exaggerations, the story was the sensation of the town for the next few days. The arsonist involved with the church parsonage had struck again, and had been foiled in his attempt to kill a ballroom full of San Francisco's elite society. Days later they were still discussing how intricate and well organized the police surveillance had been. The results brought many accolades to the police detectives.

Paul finally got the credit he craved, but his mind was so twisted by that time, he hardly knew his own name. Her great-aunt Lizzie had been notified, and the family was having him brought back East under private guard, and under the care of a physician.

It was an interesting story, even to new comers to the town, who knew nothing about the prior antecedents of the story. Even Cal Morgan, who was interested in everything that happened in San Francisco, found it interesting. If the people were talking about it, he wanted to know all about it.

The story was also interesting to Jake Jackson, who had just arrived a couple of days into the New Year 1871, and after finding a place to stay, he had formed a plan on finding Victoria, as that was the name in which he would have to search for her. He knew her heart. He knew that she would seek a church as soon as she arrived in town. His best chances were to check the hotels and churches for her. No doubt, her aunt and Kitty would be with her, too.

The judge had given him the names they were using, and he would check with the banks for clients with Victoria's name if the other two sources failed. Yes, he had a plan, and hopefully it was a good one. Judge West had also given him a letter of reference and introduction, and had also wired ahead a letter of credit for Jake at the largest bank in San Francisco. That would allow him to question if this was the bank where his good friend, Victoria Sullivan, had an account.

It was only a matter of time until he found her, seeing as he had the information already, and Cal Morgan would be merely seeking her by description only, should he decide to look for her, as he no doubt did everywhere he went. Hopefully Morgan would be too busy for a while, setting himself up, as he still did not know she was even in San Francisco.

The hotels had not yielded any results on Victoria Sullivan's whereabouts. He had been visiting churches during the day looking for her without success, but tomorrow was Sunday and he would try the fourth church he had on his list. He had walked past it that night and it was a large, two-storied affair made of red brick, just the kind of church any man would be proud to pastor. It was also same church that had been named in the newspaper as where the arsonist of the New Year's Eve Ball had also set fire to the church parsonage a week earlier on Christmas Eve. He had decided he would try there that Sunday morning, and had dressed with care, as he fully hoped and expected, to find Victoria there. If not there, he would keep looking.

When he entered the church, he was impressed with the congregation. It was large and the only empty seats were the ones in the far back. Usually, they were the ones in the front. Taking a back seat, he couldn't see past all the people, but when the service started, he momentarily forgot about Emma and concentrated on the happenings before him.

God was certainly in their midst that day. Jake had appreciated, and joined in with, their enthusiastic worship, and then was certainly moved by the message. It was a very good sermon from the heart, and powerfully delivered by a handsome man, who knew what he was about. There was no doubt as to his sincerity, or of his walk with the Lord. The anointing truly rested on the man bringing God's word.

Jake recognized that this man, like himself, had the fire of God shut up in his bones, and could not help but preach. He carried himself with confidence and with the authority of a man close to God, and had earned Jake's respect before the sermon was finished. He had reminded him that God was on His throne, and that He would have His way, no matter what. Jake knew enough to believe that!

When the service was over, the pastor immediately descended the platform, and headed for the back of the church, while a deacon stepped up to deliver the closing prayer. The pastor stopped when he had reached the first row, and then held out his hand to a beautifully dressed, auburn-haired beauty. In fact, she looked a lot like Emma, or rather Victoria.

That must be his wife, he thought. They were a beautiful couple. But as they started down the isle, he would have known that walk anywhere. God in Heaven! What was he doing with Victoria and why was there such an unmistakable air of familiarity about them? That they were definitely a couple could not be denied! His heart slammed against his chest, and hot tears sprang unbidden to his eyes, as he made his way out of the church and away.

Victoria was thrilled at the way Mark was possessive of her in a sweet, undemanding, yet authoritative sort of way. There was no doubt that he wanted her by his side all the time. She had already finished with most of the wedding plans, which were now full blown. True to Mark's presentiment, Miss Maude wanted to give the bride her wedding. When he held out his hand to her that morning after the service, she was the happiest person on earth to be his woman.

When they stepped out into the isle, he squeezed her hand, and then tucked her arm through his, and continued down the isle with his hand on top of hers. When they had gone a few rows, a man stepped out into the isle, on his way to the back door, but honest to goodness, he looked the world and all like Jake Jackson! Yet, it couldn't be, but when he strode down the isle, she knew it *was* Jake. She had known him all her life, and she knew him from the back, front, or side!

She quickened her step, much to Mark's surprise, but he kept pace with her. When she got to the doors, she had a clear view of Jake getting into a cab, and when he had sat down, he looked back and directly into her eyes. The church set close to the road, and she could plainly see the pain on his face. She lifted her hand to him, and he nodded his head to her in acknowledgment, and tipped his hat.

Mark watched the scene play out between them, with an air of utter disbelief. Who was the handsome, impeccably dressed man, who had quickened Victoria's steps, and caused the look of pain that had passed between them? Sensing Mark behind her, she turned around to face him, and he could see the difficulty she was having in trying to pull herself together. She could see the questions on his face, as his congregants were descending upon them to shake their hands.

Chapter 24

When Mark and Victoria walked the few blocks to the mansion, there were a thousand unanswered questions between them. All Mark wanted to do was to take her somewhere they could be alone and talk. She didn't want to try to explain her feelings for Jake. She was so shaken by seeing him so unexpectedly again, that she really wasn't sure what she felt; nor did she want to hurt Mark by clumsily trying to explain something she didn't understand herself.

Since neither of them had an appetite, sitting through Sunday buffet at Miss Maude's with everyone there, was more than they wanted to face right then. They stopped in to tell them not to wait, as they were going to the Hotel Pacifica for a quiet tea.

They found an alcove that afforded them plenty of privacy and ordered the tea. It was a busy and well-known tearoom and would take a while to be served. They had time. Mark simply waited for Victoria to remove her glove, and then reached over and took her hand. He held it in both of his and simply said, "I love you, darling." He waited until she was able to respond.

Finally she began. She asked him not to interrupt her until she had finished and then she would answer any questions he wanted to put to her. "I want you to know that I have known Jake Jackson all my life. He was my pastor back home. I believe that he was in love with me and I was very attracted to him. I knew that I really cared for him when I was presented at the Christmas Cotillion last year. I had assumed a courtship would follow, but he had not yet declared himself."

She watched his face and could see the pain, but she had to continue. "Jake is a wonderful pastor, who cares so much for his flock. All last winter there was one sickness, or one death after the other, or something happening so that his time was not his own. Whenever he traveled a good ways to visit a shut-in, he did whatever he needed to do to care for them. He sometimes cooked meals, washed clothes, chopped wood or whatever they needed done. We saw each other at services, and at gatherings, but always in a group. He had made a point to tell me that spring would clear up a lot of his time. He had expressed his hope that I would be free then as well, so I had assumed he had meant we would court then. Probably, he did as well."

She watched as Mark passed his hand over his eyes. When she questioned him if he were all right, he assured her he was and to please continue.

"When mama and papa died, Jake was there. The only time he touched me was when he held me and let me weep the night before the funeral. A fortnight later, without so much as a word of good-bye, I was gone and on my way here. What he is doing here, I haven't a clue. If anything were wrong, Judge West would have let me…Oh, no! I haven't checked the post office for 'will call' mail lately because of the holidays. Maybe he sent him here to tell us something! Should that be the case, it would be of monumental importance, or he would never have broken his vow of silence to me," she exclaimed.

Knowing she had to finish the story, she began again. "Anyway, when I was leaving it all behind, the thought struck me that I had been wrong about two things. I had been wrong when I had thought I was leaving everything I had ever known behind. I had not left my faith in God behind," she told him.

"I had also been wrong when I told myself that I had not married because there was no one I could see myself married to. But I think I told myself that because he had not spoken the love words to me. As I had been looking out the porthole on the ship, I realized that I could have pictured myself married to him, but since he had not declared himself, I would never know.

The reason I did not turn to him instead of leaving is that I knew he would try to help me, but Morgan would never have left us alone. He would have killed us both," she said with a shiver. "Therefore, I accepted the fact that any future Jake and I had together died on the deck of the *Neptune*. I had a definite, painful void in my life after that, but then you came into my life, and you know what we have. That is as honest as I can be with you, Mark," she finished.

The tea was being served and it gave Mark time to breathe and figure out what he still needed to know from her. The bottom line was obvious. *Where does that leave us?*

When the waiter left the table, he saw that tears had sprung to her eyes. It literally broke his heart. He didn't speak until she had taken her handkerchief out and dabbed at the corners of her eyes.

She offered him a little smile and asked him if he could tell her what he was thinking.

"Darling, drink your tea first, then we can talk more. I know that was difficult for you. You have been through so very much in this past year alone, not to mention the war deprivations and thinking your brother dead, and then Morgan, and all he has put you through. Drink you tea, my dear girl."

He moved closer to her until she could feel his warmth, and it was like a blanket wrapping her in safety and peace. "Mark," she whispered. We are alone in this cove and even more secluded by these plants. Will you kiss me, darl—?" The words had not left her mouth yet until his lips were on hers. He wanted it to be a kiss of comfort, but it turned into a kiss of passion and need, wet and wild. It only lasted a moment, but a moment was all it took to wipe away any threat of disharmony between them.

Where had that come from? he wondered. Her eyes shone with love and pleasure. "I do so love you, Mark. I do!" she smiled. That was all he needed to hear!

Chapter 25

After they had finished their tea, Mark simply said, "What do you want to do about this, my dear?"

Taking a deep breath, Victoria replied, "Well, I think something important has brought him all this way. I can't believe he just happened to travel all the way across the country to merely visit San Francisco! I know he is here because of me in some way. The fact that he left after clearly seeing me, tells me he was very upset. He wouldn't leave his flock, nor would Judge West have told him anything without cause. I think we need to find him and find out what has brought him out here, don't you?" she queried.

"I suppose I knew you would say that. Yes, I think we need to at least talk with him. Do you want to do this alone, or am I part of it?" he asked.

"I guess we should see how it goes. You being a man, you will know better than I what will be the easiest for him," she told him. "You will know whether to leave or not. I suppose we need to start searching the hotel registries. What about here?"

Just then, Jake Jackson entered the tearoom. They both saw him at the same time. She couldn't even put into words the emotions that ran rampant through her heart and mind just then. All of the precious memories of her life, before the trouble with Cal Morgan, flooded her memory. Her life as a youth, for all the years she had lived joyfully at the plantation while growing up with Fletcher, Jake, and her friends. Everything that was good and home to her had just walked through the door.

"Are you ready, love?" Mark asked her.

She swallowed down unbidden tears, and tried to overcome the shakiness her insides wouldn't seem to turn loose of, but the tender look of concern, mingled with fear, on Mark's face gave her the courage she needed. She nodded and Mark stood and walked across the room to Jake. He extended his hand and Jake took it. As they shook hands, Mark said, "Jake, I am Mark Angelos, Victoria's fiancé. She would like to speak with you, if you would like to follow me?" he asked.

Jake could feel the thump of his heart in his throat. His mouth went dry, so much so that he had difficulty in swallowing. Walking toward the love of his life, he prayed he would not embarrass himself or them. When he reached the table, Jake stood before her and extended his hand. She took it and he said, "Thank God, Emma! Finally, I can see with my own eyes that you are all right! I have been in the depths of hell itself worrying about you...we all have."

"Jake! Jake! It's so good to see you again, my dear, dear friend. Sit down, won't you?" she said as she moved over, and he slid in beside her, Mark taking his seat on the other side of her in the rotund alcove.

"I couldn't believe it when I saw you at the church! Would that you had stayed. We have so much to talk about. What are you doing here?" she asked.

"To start with, Judge West has told me everything about why you are here, and I only wish I could have helped you back then when you needed someone so desperately," he spoke quietly and sincerely to her. She remembered those dark brown eyes so well. Hadn't she seen them often enough in her memories, and truth be told, her dreams? If only he had come sooner. There would have been no doubt in her mind that it would have been him who would have been kissing her a moment ago.

"I am so sorry I wasn't the first one you came to!" he lamented. "If nothing else, as your trusted pastor," he said, watching the play of emotions that were crossing her face. Realizing how difficult this must be for her, he hurried on.

"Judge West came to see me a couple of days after Christmas. He was terribly upset and told me everything that had happened. I realized then why you hadn't said good-bye," he spoke tenderly to her as he began his story.

"I try to be a man of faith, Victoria, but when a woman like you has to hie off to parts unknown, in the dead of night, fleeing for her life, alone…well, you know what I'm saying! It is almost more than a man can carry. I praise the Lord you are all right!" Jake exclaimed and then took a deep breath to steady his nerves.

"Anyway, when the judge learned the day after Christmas that Morgan had sold up and left town, he had him investigated and found out the same day that he was coming out here."

"Coming here!" she exclaimed. Mark laid his hand over hers. "Don't fret, Victoria dear. This isn't Savannah, and we know he is here. He doesn't know you are."

"Of course, you're right. Go on, Jake," she asked him with a tremble in her voice.

"Well, the judge sent you telegrams, and when he didn't hear back, we didn't know how else to reach you. Perhaps the judge has learned something more since I left, but we felt that time was of the essence. I boarded the train the same night, a couple of days later than Morgan. I got here a couple of days ago," he said. "Of course, neither the judge nor I knew that you were not alone. We thought you to be unprotected," he looked at Mark.

Victoria shook her head in understanding. "Yes, it was a devastating time in all our lives. Jake, something else you should know," Victoria said, "the night we were leaving Savannah, we discovered that Fletch is not dead!"

"What! You're serious? Of course, you are! Well, glory be! Oh, my dear, that is wonderful. I am so happy for us all. But you know, the judge didn't tell me that," he said.

"He doesn't know. If he had stayed to see us return to port, he would have found out why, but he had gone by then, and I didn't trust sending such news by mail or telegraph. I was not supposed to contact him, except in case of emergency, " she said, watching the pleasure Jake had felt to find Fletch alive, play on his features. They had been the very best of friends, nay brothers, all their lives. His joy had to be close to what she had felt!

She told him excitedly, but with a touch of sadness, "Fletch has amnesia from a head wound sustained while trying to escape from a Yankee prison. But he got away, and was nursed back to health by his future bride. But he's alive, he's here, and he's now married! You see, as our boat was leaving the dock his was coming in, and we saw him on the deck of the other vessel. We went back for him, and we all made the trip here together. He is at home waiting for us now," she said.

"Emma, that is wonderful news. I'm sorry. I should use the name Victoria. I just want to say that I have had a bit of time since the service this morning to think and to pray. Yes, and to do some soul-searching, too. I want to tell you both that I am genuinely happy for both of you. I mean that!" he exclaimed.

Looking at Mark, he said, " I have to say that every thing I prayed for Victoria while she was missing, I can see that God answered every thing I had asked Him for. Just not in the way I had imagined."

Continuing, he said, "Mark, I was very blessed and refreshed in the service today. Your message was from the heart, and God has truly anointed you. I have prayed one prayer that has sustained me in all of this, and that is that God's perfect will be done in Victoria's life," he said and bowed his head for an agonizing moment. Raising his head again he said, "I know in my heart that Victoria is in good hands with you, and that this is God's doing!" he finished.

"Thank you, Jake. Bless you for your kind understanding. I knew at the church from what I witnessed, and also from what Victoria has just related to me concerning the two of you, that you both had deep feelings for each other at one time. But as it has turned out, I, too, believe this is God's will for all of us, and that is why the two of you never really got together. I have never loved before, but I assure you that I certainly do love this woman, and I will cherish her as long as I have breath," he finished and noted the tears that had sprung to her eyes.

"I understand that, as it is clearly there for all to see," Jake replied. "But if you have no objections, for the years we have known each other, I want to stay here until I have had an opportunity to speak with Fletch, meet his wife, and contact Judge West to see if he has any more information on Morgan."

"Of course, Jake, of course. Where are you staying? There is room for you at the parsonage with me, if you'd care to," he told him. By the look on his face, and seeing that he was absolutely sincere, Jake agreed. "Well, that would be perfect, if you're sure it won't be a bother."

"No bother at all. There, that's settled! Done and done." Mark declared.

'Do let's go home and see Fletch. He will be so surprised to see you!" she allowed, and then remembered that he probably would not be surprised; he probably would not remember him at all, more's the pity.

Mark left them to pay the bill. Jake looked at her and asked, "Why didn't I tell you that I loved you back in Savannah when I had the opportunity?"

Victoria sat quietly looking into his sad eyes a long moment before responding to his question. "Like Mark said, I suppose it was God's will that you didn't, Jake" she told him softly. "But when I left, I didn't want to involve you. You had the church responsibilities, and Morgan would have found a legal way to kill us both. I knew that the night I left Savannah, as well as I know you are sitting here today."

Mark returned to the table and they left for Jake's much anticipated reunion with the others.

Chapter 26

Victoria, Mark and Jake arrived at the mansion to find Connor and Elizabeth chatting with the other women in the parlor. They were all free from the recent oppression that Paul's presence had created, and that freedom was expressed in much joy and gaiety.

When the trio arrived, at the sight of Jake Jackson, Aunt Sadie and Lilly squealed, jumped to their feet, and both ran to him. Aunt Sadie nearly shouted, "Well, I declare! Lawsy mercy, it really is you! They both hugged him at once, quite overwhelming him. They blushed, but couldn't help themselves. Jake was introduced to Connor as their former pastor. He took Jake's hand and said, "Nice to meet you. So you are from back home in Savannah?" he asked him, unnecessarily.

"Yes, Connor, and it has been an unbelievably amazing trip to see this huge land of ours all in a little under a week's time," he responded.

"When did you get here, Jake?" he asked him. A dead silence met his question as all the excited chatter the women had been doing suddenly ceased.

Looking around him, Connor simply said, "What?"

Victoria was the first to respond with, "Connor, nobody told you his name. He was introduced as our former pastor. How did you know his name was Jake?" she asked him with an expectancy and hope in her voice.

"I-I don't know," he said, "But I did know his name, didn't I?" the anticipation clearly catching. "I take it we were good friends, Jake?" he asked him.

"The very best friends, Fletch!" Jake assured him, pulling him into a strong embrace. "We grew up together and were inseparable as youths. When the war came, I was in bed with scarlet fever, and did not recover in time to take up arms. Once I recuperated somewhat, I did everything I could at home, which was taking care of the women, children, and elderly. I was too ill for the Yanks to even bother sending me to prison.

By the time I could finally be up and around they had seen that I was no threat to them, as I only usually walked next door to the church or rode with the doc to help him somewhat with the ill and dying. I wouldn't want to go back to those times, would you, Fletch," he knew the answer, but was making conversation to see if anything would break through to Fletcher.

"What are you doing here, Jake," Aunt Sadie asked.

"Judge West and I felt the urgency to let you all know that Cal Morgan is here in town," he said and saw the immediate fear on all their faces.

"Oh, no!" cried Lilly, as Elizabeth took her hand to sooth her.

"Yes, Kit-Lilly, he left Savannah a couple of days before I did. As soon as the judge realized he had sold up and cleared out, he came to see me and explained everything. He was afraid that his actions were being observed so I decided to come and let y'all know. As far as we know, Morgan still doesn't know any of you are here," as they nodded in understanding, and let out a sigh of relief.

"Apparently you hadn't checked your messages in a few days. He had asked you to telegraph him letting him know you had received the message. With Morgan out here, he felt better about using the telegraph. He did not use names, naturally, but said you would have known the meaning of the message. It was, 'Mr. Brown, beware, the wolf is at your door'. Of course, we thought y'all were alone, as he didn't know about Fletch being with you… or Mark, but...," his voice trailing off, and so left it at that.

"It is so good to see you, Jake!" Aunt Sadie interrupted. "We have a wonderful pastor now in Mark, but we have never forgotten you, and your love for us, nor ours for you!" she assured him.

"How are all the folks back home, Jake," Victoria asked him.

"Most are doing well, Victoria. See, I have been practicing your new names," he said with a smile. "I had not known where to turn in finding y'all, as the Judge was supposedly using detectives to do that.

He was the official investigator, but he knew he couldn't let all the information he had be known, so he wasn't investigating, but I didn't know that. I'm just glad you are all safe!" he finished.

"None of us knew of another thing to do except just to run, so that is what we did," Aunt Sadie lamented. "How we hated knowing the fear and heartache we were leaving behind. But we felt like anyone we involved would have met the same fate we would have had we stayed. Since everyone couldn't run away, it was better for us to leave and do it the way we did, even though we might not have been thinking clearly at the time," she finished.

"Well, that is all in the past. Where do we all go from here?" Connor asked the room in general.

"Fletch, the judge has hired a growing detective agency to stay on Morgan and try to find some evidence of wrong doing that would be enough to convict him here in California," he said.

"He will show his hand soon, because he always lives the high life. That takes money and he is short of that right now. His spread didn't bring as much as it would have if he hadn't left so suddenly. So he will bamboozle somebody soon and they will have him.

I talked to the judge when I arrived, and he is gathering evidence back in Savannah, and has already found out that three people has been done to death at Morgan's own hand. Now that he has left town, with no sign of returning, the people will be sure to tell all they know," he told them. "As to where that leaves all of you, well, that pretty much leaves Victoria in the same predicament as when she left in the first place, from Morgan's point of view. I'm sure nothing has changed about him, except his location. However, there are three important changes to that situation now. He looked at the other men in the room and said, "We are here, and we all know what is going on this time. Victoria is not facing him alone. We will be watchful, diligent, and constant in watching over this household."

Miss Maude spoke up and advised them that her husband had used that detective agency before, and that they had a close friend in town, retired from the agency. She was sure he would be agreeable to becoming a temporary boarder at Killian House, and others besides, if he deemed it necessary.

"This has been a wide open town from the beginning with the Barbary Coast ruffians. We decent folk didn't have the law on our side back a few years ago, but now that people have made their fortunes, they want to live better, and protect what's theirs, so the town has changed a lot from those wild and wicked days," she told them.

"They still they have their dens of iniquity that are enslaving men and women night after night. But men like Morgan will always collect the ruffians to do his dirty work that will give them power through violence, coercion, intimidation, and fear. However, we have the upper hand now. We know he is out there, and the best minds in criminal detection are watching, and are ready for him. It's true that Victoria needn't fear like she did the last time. She also has the best hearts inside this house looking after her, as well!" she finished.

"Well said, madam. Well said!" Jake responded.

"What a day this has been," remarked Aunt Sadie, and they all voiced their agreement, and thanks to God. Surely, He was keeping an eye on them, as evidenced by Jake's safe arrival, and giving them warning for what was sure to happen in the near future.

Chapter 27

There were a few men moseying around the outside of the tavern that day, but most of them were inside drinking while their rich and entitled employers were shut up in a private room upstairs listening to the men talk. Men who were supposed to have the inside story on what was available to be bought cheap, and sold high dollar later on, and where to buy.

In reality, they were fraudulent agents of the railroad, supposedly selling land close to the railroad route in order to establish towns between the East and West Coasts, with the supposed blessings of the government, and with a lot of tax exemptions to sweeten the deal.

Their flimflam would be an organized scam covering several states, through which the railroad passed, where men claimed to be railroad agents for their particular states. They would sell the land, giving false certificates to the buyers, and by the time it was discovered, the scammers would have closed their trunks and disappeared.

This would be the perfect scam for this time and place, because everyone knew the railroad had been given lands on which to build the railroad. Not only for where the rails would be, but also for miles in every direction of the railroad, since it was not known exactly where the rails would lay, given all the variables the railroad would have to take into consideration. Given the fact that the real agents of the railroad had begun to sell off the lands, now that the railroad was completed, their scam would be completely believable.

The key to the entire scheme would be secrecy, and secrecy is always the hardest thing to keep. If the railroad knew what they were about, they would be swinging from the end of a rope. Their whole premise was built around the greed and arrogance of the wealthy.

There had been extreme fortunes made through investments in buildings and land sales to the thousands who had been coming into the city of San Francisco for the past twenty years, and most of them had stayed on whether or not they had made their coveted fortunes. Cheap land was becoming scarce.

Prosperity had been seen on every hand, as new mansions had been going up all over San Francisco. The city had been expanding on every side, but there was still opportunity to buy land. However, it was now becoming expensive. But the new deal that the men in the room were discussing that day was the concept of rich, entitled men going somewhere other than San Francisco, and starting their own towns.

In their conceit of being honored as the richest and therefore, worthiest to be sought out by these supposed land agents, and naturally supposing that they were getting first refusals of the land, they had sat up and taken notice. They were informed that their decisions would make the difference in the great state of California being settled quickly, with detailed organization, and a web of networks that only their wealth, influence and wisdom could afford. Of course, they had been sought out for the obvious reasons, being as they were the wealthy elite, therefore, undisputed leaders of that generation.

Obviously, since their fortunes were already made, they would be free to choose any area of any state that appealed to them. They could set up their own town, and begin to govern with sovereignty over those men of lesser means, but who were needed for the services they would be providing for the town.

The wealthy barons would begin these towns having banks, hotels, restaurants, mercantiles, and anything else that would entice the people from back East to settle in their towns. Their money would be returned hand over fist. Logically, whoever owned the land and started the town, would control the best lands for miles around it. They knew that it wouldn't take long for several towns to spring up, as thousands of people from the crowded cities back East were coming to California on the railroad every week.

In turn, obviously whoever held the land could control the businesses, saloons, sheriffs and every other activity in town, as they chose. Once those men chose a town in which to settle, they would be pressuring their other family members and friends to join them, as their hook would be the benefits they would derive of having the power man as a member of their family and inner circle. They would also discover freedom of owning their own spreads, inexpensively, and working for themselves.

Thousands more would continue coming from Eastern cities, and that would be a self-perpetuating cycle. Each and every week they would come, and would continue to do so, as long as those cities remained as they were. They were so overcrowded, dirty, crime-ridden, and only had low-paying jobs to offer workers, and no inexpensive land to offer the citizenry.

Working the mines would hold little to no appeal for them. Yes, they would be coming with skills to provide those services that their towns would need; laborers, teachers, blacksmiths, shop keeps, dressmakers, accountants, and any other service one could imagine. They easily could be enticed to move to their towns instead of the overcrowded, expensive San Francisco.

The tycoons would settle towns within easy traveling distances to a railroad all across the nation, and could ship and receive goods wherever they needed to, from coast to coast. Settlers would be willing to take the risks of moving to a new, unknown town if it were advertized correctly back East. Even down South, for that matter. When one considered how the war had killed so many Southern men, and decimated so many of the towns, and what with the high property taxes that couldn't be paid, it left many homeless. Many of those who had become adults since the war, were the ones enticed to strike out for greener pastures. As a further incentive to move to the unsettled West, they would be able to leave such horrid memories, and happenings of the war behind them. To start a new town rather than try to rebuild a destroyed town appealed to the younger generation, who having no real roots or adult relatives to consider, were free to roam where they pleased.

Men who had made their fortunes in gold and silver, but had no idea how to invest it were lining up for some of that land. In San Francisco, they were just another rich man. But if they could get enough land to start their own town, they would be *the* rich man. They had made their fortunes by hard work, but the prospect of owning their own town, and gaining another fortune off the work of others, appealed to them greatly. After all, one could never have enough money, nor could the newly rich believe they wouldn't run out unless it was continually being replenished.

Most of the men who had made their fortunes working the fields or mines had not been businessmen, and their naïveté had led them to make some unwise investments. But so many were the stories of men who had invested wisely, that these men without business acumen would still be willing to take the risk.

Those who had made their legitimate fortunes had as much trouble holding on to their money as they had had in making it in the first place. Unfortunately, but true, among the rich was a counterfeit element, the pseudo rich, who had all the airs, lifestyles, graces, self-importance, and self-confidence of wealth. Their main goal in life being to part the rich man from his coin, and if they were successful, do it without being able to be accused of the crime.

To this element of society, the concept of selling land for towns was a perfect way for them to sell forged deeds to railroad owned land, and to sell them fast enough, and all at the same time to multiple cities. This would be done among the rich behind closed doors in secret, as the wealthy were used to dealing.

Knowing these wealthy investors would hold their investments close to the vest until such a time as they would be able to travel to the sites, make their plans, and survey the land, which would give the owners of the scam time to scatter after they had made their fortune in the phony land sale.

Yes, all of those preparations would take considerable time before the land could be offered for sale to settlers. The rogues would be long gone after the sale of the land, leaving behind wealthy men to deal with the railroad, once they learned of the towns that had sprung up on their government granted lands.

The bamboozler that had come up with the concept of bilking millions in gold from this scheme was none other than the trusted Southern gentleman and solicitor, Mr. Calhoun Morgan. He had been in town for four weeks, and had moved freely in society, and had seen the lay of the land. He had found himself in the middle of private conversations, fortunately for him, when men's tongues were loosened with strong drink, or sometimes over a poker table. He had heard things not meant for his ears. In turn, he had gathered rogues from Savannah, Charleston, Atlanta, and the Eastern Seaboard to learn the ins and outs of his scheme. A printer was among them, and he had been sent one of the real land grant certificates that Morgan had come by dishonestly. They would have authentic certificates, just not authentically owned by them.

They would also double cross the rich men who would start the towns, by selling land in the major cities from coast to coast to the people who were stifled and hemmed in. They would sell them the idea of easy travel on the exciting new railroad route, and as further enticement to resettle, stressing that it was just a matter of days to reach their new towns, rather than six months or more of hardships, dangers, and the deprivation of traveling overland by wagon, or even the long way round by ship.

Since all the land sales was set to begin a fortnight hence, a telegram had been sent to agents across the nation saying only that date, nothing else. Secrecy was of the essence, and should even one agent speak out of turn, the entire scheme could collapse.

One of the agents of Morgan's was Madison Monroe. He had decided to branch out on his own in secret, and thought to recruit his own sales force on the side. He was sure he could manage at least a baker's dozen, given time, but six should do well to start.

Two of the first half dozen he chose were Dan Wade and Yancey Pierce, who were working for the very well known detective agency Judge West had sent to keep an eye on Morgan. With the agents having extensive knowledge of criminals, their pursuits and plots, they were able to add fuel to Monroe's fire. In the end, Monroe decided that the two new men were better than the whole other four put together, and so had cut them loose. He laid out bits and pieces of the scheme for them, and felt confident that it was a good decision on his part to let them into the inner circle in small ways.

He had to keep them away from Morgan, because they were too sharp for Morgan not to want them. He would also have been furious with Monroe, had he known of his sideline, and he probably would not have lived to carry out the scheme. Because Monroe wouldn't let them meet the others, they feigned a suspicions of him, like maybe he wasn't playing straight with them. As a result, he sought to ally their fears by giving them more and more information.

With their knowledge of deduction, they could assess the information, and ask relevant questions that would extract even more of the plan, until eventually everything Morgan had planned had been laid in their laps. It was really too simple for them, but they played well their parts of greedy, but submissive, potential rich men.

Jake, Mark and Connor had spent significant time together and had become fast family friends. One day out of the blue, Connor asked Jake what he knew of a red cart. Jake was surprised, but pleased at the question. He answered with, "When we were about eight years old, your Grandfather Summers brought over a red cart for you. It was useful for hauling needed vegetables from the garden up to the house for the day and such. You were told you could hitch a pony to it, and ride all over the plantation common grounds, between the house and the out buildings, but no farther.

One day you decided that we could take it to town. So we did. By the time we got there that poor pony was plum puny! The sheriff caught us and knew we were off the plantation, so he stopped a wagon going our way and tied the pony in one corner, and the cart behind, and they carried us home. You went home and confessed to your papa that you had been 'rested by the sheriff!' You were just a bawling," he told him as they all laughed.

"That's why I kept seeing a badge with that cart!" he exclaimed. "I nearly remember that. I do remember parts of it. I remember being hungry, too!"

"Well, we missed our dinner and Granny gave us what for. We each ate three biscuits and some cold chicken. You are going to remember everything, Fletch! Don't worry! I know you use Connor, but sometimes when you are on the verge of remembering, maybe hearing Fletch will help you! Connor was excited that surely the Lord was lifting the veil on the past and allowing him the precious gift of memories once again!

Chapter 28

The wedding gown was finished and never had the girls seen anything as lovely! It was a gorgeous creation fit for the most regal, crowned heads of Europe. The wedding plans were finally all in order awaiting the big day. Jake had asked if they had decided who was officiating at their wedding. They hadn't asked anyone yet, but had always assumed Dan Foster, the associate pastor, would do the honors.

"I may be way out of line here, but the more I think of it, the more I would like to have that honor," he quietly told them.

Victoria was shocked at the magnificent gesture of love and friendship—and even in a way— forgiveness. For surely Jake's behavior had proven his heart attitude to everyone, especially to her and Mark. "You would do that for us?" she asked in a reverent tone.

"Of course I would, Victoria. I only want the Lord's best for all of us. I believe, like the two of you, that he has more than shown us what that is. If you will both have me, I would be happy to officiate," he finished.

Mark took the initiative and said, "I'm fairly sure I know Victoria well enough to speak for the both of us. We would be delighted for you to do the honors. I admire any man who could step aside in such a dignified manner, as graciously as you have, and with such sincerity of heart. Bless you, Jake. I mean that, my brother! Maybe I can do the same honors for you one day!"

"I wish you would! And soon!" Jake said, and they all laughed, knowing that their friendship had stood the test of deep heart pain and survived.

Victoria, Elizabeth, and Lilly were on a shopping spree for some small last minute essentials for the wedding. They would finish their purchases in the next emporium and be finished. They had planned to go to the finest hotel in town to take advantage of the scrumptious fare at their tearoom, and celebrate the completion of all things needed for the wedding.

As they entered into the large, well appointed lobby of the hotel, with its beautiful plush furnishings, including areas with South Sea Islands motif, lush greeneries, palm trees, and ferns set amongst quaint little tête à tête areas, they were a carefree lot. They marveled at their gracious surroundings, as there were also areas with screens, crafted with images of beautiful island birds, adding to the privacy for people to meet, and have undisturbed conversation.

One had to pass through a portion of this beautiful lobby area and go through large French doors on the left side, to enter the Ladies Tea Room, while on the other side of the lobby was located the Gentlemen's Lounge.

It was through this gorgeous lobby that the Sullivan ladies passed on their way to the tearoom that fateful afternoon. Exiting the gentlemen's lounge at the same time was one Calhoun Morgan. He had certainly suffered a tremendous shock at discovering Emma Summers with Kitty, and another unknown woman. He had the presence of mind to hold his tongue and not cry out to her.

259

His planned formed as he watched her go through the French doors opposite. He turned to his companions, two of his cronies, and told them to follow the women when they left and find out where they lived. He could not very well grab her out of the hotel lobby in broad daylight. He could scarcely believe this was happening. After all these months of desperately searching for her, to come to the very city where she lived and to find her sashaying through the lobby of that establishment, as though she had not a care in the world!

Ah, the beautiful Emma. She seemed more beautiful than ever. Her grief had passed it seemed, as the year of mourning had not been fulfilled, but there she was as big as life and not in mourning clothing, either. "Little hypocrite!" he said under his breath.

He watched her as she laughed and chatted with her friends. How long had he endured life without her? What she had done to him, well, love or no love, he would have to teach her better. *Not only am I sitting on a fortune, but the winds have also blown her straight into my waiting arms!* he thought. Yes, life was good and he was back on top!

When Jake arrived at the mansion, he brought news from the judge. According to the reports he had received, it seems as though the detective agency had infiltrated Morgan's setup, and if he didn't change his plans, they had those, too. They knew the places, the scheme, and the date of the proposed sales.

The problem was, trusting law enforcement in those areas. For that reason, the agency had decided to send agents to every city they had information on. They had a large force of trained men, and could easily manage it. It didn't matter to an agent what the cost might be, nor did it matter what subterfuge they had to use to get their desired results.

Even the Title Office of the government, and certainly the railroad, would be kept in the dark about the forged land certificates until they had successfully completed their operation, and recovered the certificates. Then the railroad would pay the price to keep the forged certificates out of the wrong hands. They had successfully worked with the railroad many times before.

O'Brian and Devon reported back to Morgan on the whereabouts of Emma Summers. They correctly deducted that she lived in a ritzy part of the city where the swells lived, as the women's cabby drew up in front of a mansion. They asked the driver of their carriage if he knew anything about the mansion, and he reported that it was operating as a boarding house. The women went in and did not leave again, so presumably it was their home.

Morgan took the information with great pleasure, but then again, not exactly pleasure. Maybe perverse delight was more accurate. He left them and went into his private office. He thought out his plan to the last detail. He would leave nothing to chance this time. She would not bewitch or outwit him again! No, things were looking up for him to such an extent that nothing could stop him now. Nothing!

Oh, yes, he had the upper hand again, just like in Savannah in the beginning. He knew exactly where she was, and she did not know he was within several thousand miles of her! He thought the best thing to do was to send Devon to the house in search of a room to rent. He was a Southerner, and had a gentlemanly comportment and looked the part. Yes, Devon would do nicely. He would send him round right then.

James Devon showed up at 117 Stanhope Street at six o'clock in the evening of the same day. He was admitted by the butler and asked to have a seat in the atrium. Miss Maude was notified, and since she had been conversing with Victoria at the time, she asked her to accompany her to greet a new prospective boarder.

When they approached Devon, he stood and graciously introduced himself. The interview went as follows:

He was from the low country of South Carolina. No, he did not have family in the great state of California. They were all back East. He looked forlorn at that disclosure.

No, he was not a married man yet, said with a hint of a blush.

Yes, he was a God-fearing man, said with a straight face.

No, he did not imbibe, nor use tobacco products. He couldn't stifle a cough he used to hide his inward humor.

Yes, he was a quiet individual, and kept moderate hours. Surely his pants were on fire.

He was self-employed in financial enterprises. How he had cheated and schemed his way up to lowdown.

Yes, he could provide references in a few days. Morgan would see to those.

Yes, he would prefer to take meals with the rest of the boarders. No, he was not a fussy eater.

How many boarders reside here? Eleven presently? Oh, that many?

Have they been with you long? Oh, a few months now. I see, a family of five. Southerners? No, not from the South, but from the Northeast, you say? Six single men reside here presently. I see.

Well, Ma'am, it is a beautiful establishment and I am looking forward to moving in. I will return to the hotel and bring my things.

Oh, I misunderstood. You would rather wait for the references. I quite understand and will try to obtain them for you on the morrow.

Good evening, ladies, until tomorrow. And thank you for your gracious reception of me. I am quite thankful for this opportunity. Good-bye again.

"Well, what did you think of him? Miss Maude asked Victoria.

"Unless I am greatly mistaken, I saw that same gentleman in the lobby of the hotel when we were taking tea. I noticed him still around when we left, and as we were there quite a while, I wondered at him being there so long, but assumed he had been awaiting someone," she explained.

"But as we were getting into the cab, I distinctly saw him emerge from the hotel and also summons a cab. Since he had obviously given up the wait, I remembered thinking that he must have been stood up. When we arrived here and exited the cab, I saw another cab draw to the curb at the corner and just sit there. Now I see him here in our vestibule? I need to call the men, that's what I think!" she exclaimed.

Jake, Connor, Mark, and the detective friend of Miss Maude's, along with his friends, who had moved in temporarily, came to the parlor. Victoria told them her story. It didn't take the detectives long to figure out that somehow Morgan had seen her and she had been followed home. Now he was making his move with trying to plant someone on the inside to either do his dirty work, or to open the door for him to gain entrance at a time of his choosing.

Upon pondering the situation a few minutes, they decided it best to allow him to move in and be given a room between two of the agents, and directly across the hall from a room Jake and Connor would occupy for the evening. One detective would feign sleep in Victoria's bed in a woman's gown and nightcap. Nothing was left to chance with these agents, and no camouflage too difficult or ridiculous!

Mark was not leaving Victoria alone for a minute, with such imminent danger at hand, and insisted on staying with her in Miss Maude's private rooms, along with Aunt Sadie, Lilly, and Elizabeth. The women would take the two inner sleeping quarters, and he and the remaining two agents would keep watch in the outer room. It was located in the turret that was part of Miss Maude's quarters.

This was agreeable to all the men and so they settled down to see what the night would bring. They were sure that nothing would happen until Morgan's flunky had actually moved in, but it was possible that he might return that night with references, in which case they would be ready for him.

True to that premonition, Devon did return to the mansion with a small grip and references. He apologized for the lateness of the hour, it being nearly ten o'clock. He was shown his room, and he asked which were the other guest rooms, as he entered the hallway on the second floor. He claimed he just wanted to know who was close at hand, as he had met but one, Victoria, and liked to know who was around him.

He was told which were the ladies' rooms, and which were the men's. He seemed satisfied that he was next door to Victoria's room to his right. He was given a latchkey to the front door, and was told he would have a tour of the home on the morrow, but for now everyone had retired. He expressed his satisfaction to everything, and again expressed his delight at being taken into such a fine establishment as the Killian House.

Connor, Jake, Mark and all the agents were on full alert. The Killian House mansion was as quiet as a church on a Monday, and every moving branch outside was startling. The house was darkened except for a dim light in the upstairs hallways. However, not one of the men let down their guard for an instant. They all assumed that when Morgan came, he would not come alone. He was too much of a coward for that. They also assumed that he would not come before three or four o'clock in the morning when the night was the darkest, and sleep was the deepest.

In that assumption they were wrong. At half past midnight, they heard a noise. It was almost like a tinkle of ice in a glass. But then no sound was repeated. One of the agents shook his head 'no', indicating not to move yet. Across the hallway, Jake shook his head 'yes' at Connor. They had rigged a tall table with a blanket over it and had taken a broom with a long handle, and tied a mirror to the head. When standing on the table, Jake could hold the mirror and view what was happening in the lighted hallway through the transom.

When Jake held the broom up, he could see four men in stocking feet outside the door of Victoria's room. One of the men was Morgan. Jake held up four fingers to Connor, who went to the window, looked out, and saw no one watching the house. It was a clear night, and as his sash was already up, he put his head out, and looked to his left.

Connor held up four fingers, then a full hand facing the lookout. The lookout in the turret of the front room of Miss Maude's quarters saw the signal plainly due to the street lamp outside. Connor's signal was received and understood. Mark and one man stayed with the women, while the other man prepared to move. They knew the flat hand meant wait. As soon as the men cleared the hall, Jake would give the signal, and they all would move out.

Jake watched the men through the transom, as three men entered Victoria's room, while one stayed in the hall. Jake flashed one finger. Connor repeated it to the lookout, and by the time Connor was at the door, Jake had gotten down from his perch, and was right behind him.

As Connor opened their door, both men went at a full run across the seven-foot hallway at the remaining lookout man, and they never stopped. Hitting the man with the full force of their bodies, breaking the doorframe, and carrying the man well into the room, where he was out cold.

From the light in the hall, they could see Morgan was in the process of bending over Victoria's bed, when a fist of the agent in the bed caught him under the chin, and he staggered backwards. The other agents were right behind Jake and Connor, and never hesitated to enter the fray. They had downed the two startled accomplices of Morgan, who were inside the room, while Jake and Connor took on Morgan. He put up a good fight like the wounded, cornered animal that he was, but they got him to the floor and subdued him.

He finally calmed and they let him up. He rubbed his chin, looking with hatred at the person who had hit him, probably wondering for a moment if it could have possibly been Victoria. When he saw the detective in the gown that had got up out of bed, he looked furious. The agent looked at him, and laughed saying, "Guess you've learned a lesson here tonight, my friend!"

Morgan looked at him with derision and said, "Oh, and just what would that be?" he asked him. "And I'm certainly not your friend!" he added, the statement dripping with sarcasm.

Still laughing, the agent answered him with, "Ever' shut eye ain't sleep, is it now?" at which all the detectives, Jake, and Connor laughed. It served to relieve the pent up tension in the room, as all the men were very keyed up. The agents had tied the hands of the three men on the floor behind their backs and were lifting them to their feet. Then they came to Morgan, and trussed up his chest and arms like a chicken, and none too gently.

The detectives had taken them to the local police calaboose. The nightmare was over and Morgan was going to be put in a place far from Victoria. Judge West was trying to get him brought back to Savannah for trial for three killings, that witnesses were now willing to testify about. He was sure California would let them take him back. Finally, they could breathe easier. The first time they could in ten long months.

They were having refreshments in the kitchen, as nobody could sleep yet, when the door chime sounded. Connor and Jake went together to answer it with the others following behind. It was two of the agents coming back to inform them that when they were attempting to take Morgan from the cab to the station house, he had broken free and had run right in front of a fast moving dray. He had been mangled by the wagon and trampled by the horses. He had been killed instantly. The others had been safely locked away.

Other detectives were already at Morgan's office and were sure to find the stash of forged certificates of land sales. Yes, the agency would be well paid by the railroad for this case.

Victoria had not been told that as they were leading Morgan away, he had looked at Fletcher, realizing that he was alive and standing before him. After a moment, understanding dawned on him and he said, "Well, well, well! F. Connor Sullivan, I presume. That is why she was listed in a party of five, under the Sullivan name. The F. would be for Fletcher? Come back from the grave, have you? I hope your family doesn't make a habit of that," he laughed, sarcastically.

"Now what on earth could you possibly mean by that, Morgan?" Fletcher asked him.

"Well, if your dead folks were to pull a stunt like that, they would certainly have a tale to tell! It didn't take much to burn that old inn to the ground!" he bragged and laughed a bitter laugh. "He said I never would wed his precious daughter. That's when I knew they had to go! I still didn't get your sister, though, did I now?"

At that callous confession, Fletcher saw it all in an instant. He saw his mother's dear face as she held his cake for him to blow out the candles, while she wished him a happy birthday. He saw his father lifting him onto the back of his pony. Old Granny was giving him cookies, hot from the oven. He saw Emma, chasing him around the oak tree in the front drive. He had a flash of Jake slapping him on the back when he had just assisted a mare in a difficult labor, as he had helped her successfully deliver her first foal. It all came flooding back when he realized what Morgan had just confessed to.

He started screaming, "No!" over and over. He ran at him and would have done him harm, had he not been restrained. He shouted, "Mama! Papa!" at the top of his lungs. It brought the women running, and found him slumped in the floor completely undone, Jake holding him in his arms, and shushing him like one would a baby. He kept saying, "Mama! Papa! No, God!"

Jake looked at Emma and said, "It's all over, Em. He remembers everything." They had taken Morgan away before he could say anything more. Emma hadn't known what shock had brought his memory back, and they saw no need to enlighten her, causing her even more grief. It was assumed by the women that the night's ordeal had done the deed.

Thankfully, out of all the worry and chaos, they had Fletcher back in his entirety! The Morgan nightmare was over. They could go on with their lives without the constant fear they had known for so long! They could, and would, all go back to using their real names. God was being praised all over the house that night, and with good and sufficient reason!

Chapter 29

*I*t was simply a perfectly gorgeous day in San Francisco, 14 February, 1871. The weather was a warm sixty-eight degrees and rising. There was a perfect, balmy breeze off the Pacific. It was *the* day. Emma Summers and Mark Angelos would be wed that day, providing nothing untoward happened.

The mansion at 117 Stanhope Street was ready for the wedding reception, and looked marvelous. Parts of the front of the home had been draped in a sheer fabric of mauve and dusty rose that had been gathered into large blooms. Rose petals had been strewn all around, awaiting the reception guests once the ceremony was over.

All of the cooks at the mansion, along with those from the parsonage, had been very busy of late, and now delicious fare was awaiting the wedding guests, who would soon to be arriving. Many of the women from the church had insisted on bringing over pies, cakes and other desserts, as well. It would be a sumptuous wedding feast, to be sure, and certain to be remembered for years to come.

Just then the front door opened and Fletcher Summers stepped out. He handed his wife out the door, then his Aunt Caroline, followed by Miss Maude Killian, Miss Kitty Thornton, and finally his lovely sister, Miss Emma Summers. As they walked arm in arm down the steps to the wedding carriage, they were all smiling with much anticipation and joy.

It was a lovely, roomy, open carriage and even with the gowns, everyone fit beautifully inside, with Fletch riding with the coachman. They were headed for the Harbor Mission for the wedding ceremony. The entire congregation was waiting to see the elegant and beautiful Emma Summers exchange vows with their pastor.

Those early mornings Emma had been enjoying in her garden at Summers Bluff had been a year ago now. Today, there were birds singing, just like then. The sun was shining, and they were together with loved ones, just like then. They were filled to overflowing with love, happiness and a godly anticipation for what would lie ahead for each of them, just like then. But 'then' seemed a lifetime ago. Much loss had occurred since 'then'.

True, they were on the other side of many trials now, most of which had been huge. The war, the death of loved ones, the loss of their name, their roots, and their inheritance, a long sea voyage to an unknown city, the pursuit of two madmen, and the dead come back to the living twice, with Fletcher returning from the supposed grave, and his lost memory regained.

Not much had been easy since 1861, but this was the beginning of 1871, a new decade, and they would rejoice and be glad in it. This was a most triumphant day! This was a day when God was surely on His throne, and all was well with the world!

Once inside the sanctuary, the wedding attendants had taken their places. Elizabeth and Kitty had gone down the isle, and the wedding march that Emma had chosen had started, announcing the bride's entrance. Everyone saw Emma enter the sanctuary on her brother's arm.

Truly, Jake Jackson had been Emma's almost certain love at one time, but it had never really had an opportunity to bloom for them, but Jake understood. A small part of him would have loved to be standing in Mark's shoes, with Mark doing the officiating, but truly, he had come to love Mark nearly as much as he did Emma. They had all been through so much, and with Fletcher regaining his memory, that lifelong fellowship between him and Jake had been renewed. That alone had healed many of Jake's hurts.

As wonderful as it had been to spend the last weeks in San Francisco with those he loved most in the world, he would be headed back to Savannah soon, even though they had all begged him to stay, and Mark had even offered him a position at the church.

But this was their dream, and he had his own. His dream had been tested and had seen him through many hard losses, and had stood the test of time. Yes, he would go back to his flock, his real mission in San Francisco accomplished. He had been compelled to come west, thinking he was coming to find and marry Emma Summers, but his true mission had been to find Emma, to see that she was safe and happy, and to give her up for good. He had done what he had to do, and therefore, it had released them both.

Surely, the loveliness and happiness that was visible before his eyes at that moment would be waiting for him back in Savannah some day. He had to believe that. Emma had been walking down the isle during his reverie, and had nearly reached the front. She was simply gorgeous standing there in her gown of ivory satin.

She had been truly loved by two men in her life, and that was more than enough.

Fletcher was placing her hand in Mark's, and then kissed her cheek. He smiled at Mark, glanced up at Jake and winked, as if to say, you can do this! And he could. God had gotten him this far, and He would take him the rest of the way.

Yes, these are my best friends in the world, and I am officiating their wedding ceremony, he thought. *God was on His throne, and all was, indeed, well with the world!*

"Dearly beloved," he began, "we are gathered together in the sight of God, and these witnesses," and his eyes met theirs and held, and they all paused for a moment, as they shared a very memorable and meaningful smile.

The End of Part Two

Part Three

Jake

Dedicated to the memory of my dear, sweet Mother who gave me life, and to my God who sustains it.

Chapter 1

*J*ake Jackson sat in his seat on the train and gazed out the window. His thoughts wandered where they may, as he was taking in hardly any of the scenery, although his eyes saw it all. He was looking at the great, vast expanse known as the West. It was a time when it was plenty wild enough that the Indian wars were still raging, Queen Victoria was still on her throne, and he hoped he never heard her name again. The name Victoria was an affliction to him, and best forgotten.

He didn't like to think of all that Emma had endured while using the name Victoria. Yes, it was all best forgotten. It had been an unbelievably painful time in his life, as well as hers, and now his future seemed bleak with her out of his life, probably forever. She was now married to someone else. While he understood why and how it had happened, that day found him in the painful throws of loneliness.

He was on his way back to his home and church, and was reflecting on the difference a few weeks had made between his trip out West, and his trip now going back home to Savannah. As he sat there on the train that day, he realized it had only been about a year ago that Emma had suddenly sold her plantation and left in the middle of the night. Yes, she had left with just her aunt and her maid without so much as a good-bye to him.

He had gone out West to save her and God had already provided her with safety. He had thought her alone and probably afraid, and it had tormented him. He hadn't known that God had provided her with a man who obviously adored her, a church full of congregants who loved her, and she had been anything but fearful.

No wonder during those long months of frantic worry, his Bible had opened to so many verses that had told him not to be afraid; verses that had told him over and over to take it by faith that God was in control.

And now he didn't need faith for that, for he could see with plain sight that He was, and always had been, in control. Even to the dastardly Morgan, who had meant her harm, but God had turned it around for her good. She would have no use for a plantation in the South, as the wife of a pastor out West. She had made a quick cut and had left it all behind. The best way, really, all things considered.

She probably would never have left the plantation other than in fear of her life, so Morgan had provided that fear. Since the pastor she was meant to marry was in San Francisco, she had to get there somehow, and God had arranged that, too. The judge had a sea captain friend whose route was Savannah to San Francisco. Not to Florida, or South Carolina, or Argentina, but to San Francisco. Now he could see it all as plain as plain.

He thought he had been going out West to find, save and marry Emma. In reality, God knew he would never give up on her, and move forward with his own life, not knowing about hers. Therefore, He had sent Jake to find Emma, see that she was taken care of and happy, and that was exactly what had happened. Then he had been able to give her up for good.

He had been sitting there pondering some things. He had been wondering where all of that left him. After some thought, he had decided that for one thing, it left him right in the middle of God's will for *his* life. After the wedding, they all had begged him to stay on in San Francisco. Mark had even offered him a position at the church, but after all was said and done it was their dream. As Jake believed in it as much as they did, he was free to go back to where God had called him.

There he would live his own dream. Hopefully, some day with a woman as wonderful, as beautiful, and as full of life, as Emma had been the day she had walked down the isle at her wedding. God was just that kind of God, and he had to believe that. He did believe for the big picture of his life to come together, but figuring out the small, individual parts was what was giving him the most trouble.

Jake knew enough of life to know that there would be highs and lows in his spiritual ebb and flow. Highs come and go. Lows come and go, but sometimes they stay. Today found Jake Jackson feeling more low-spirited, and more alone, than he had ever been in his entire life. He felt it would take an honest to goodness, hand delivered miracle for him to ever feel whole again, or to find someone he could ever love as much as he had Emma.

So while sitting on the train listening to the steady clack of the wheels passing over the rails, he was in a frame of mind that miracles can and do strike as suddenly as disasters. He was certainly in the mood for one—a miracle, that is; he'd had his unfair share of disasters. Yes, he had lived through it all, and was able to tell the tale. After all, where there was life, there was hope. And where there was hope, miracles tended to follow.

Chapter 2

*A*s the trip drew on, Jake found he was looking forward to be nearing home. He was becoming excited to see everyone, and knew that they would be anxiously awaiting his return. His simple plan for the future was that he would throw himself into his work and pray that would be enough to sustain him in the days ahead. It always had been enough in the past, but in the past, he had always had the hope, and the assumption, of one day he and Emma Summers would wed.

Now he had no such assumptions. His mind and will were both clear of any romantic entanglements of any kind. In fact, he wondered if his heart was even beating. The fact that he was still breathing belied the seemingly empty wasteland where his heart had once been overflowing with love and hope.

Yes, he would work hard to feed the people in his church the bread of life, and that would nourish his own soul into the bargain. What else could he do?

Savannah was a beautiful city, but seeing the Italianate style homes that had been built before and after the war reminded him a bit too much of San Francisco. Still, it was good to finally be home. He would soon get back to his normal routine, and the sooner the better. Since the only insight he could come up with was to keep going forward, he knew it might take some time, but he would get on with his life.

He lived at the lovely parsonage next door to the church with his long time housekeeper, Mattie Hawkins. Mother Mattie, as everyone in his family had always called her, had been there long before he had been born, and would probably be there for some time to come.

She had been more like a mother to him than a housekeeper, especially ever since his mama had died. She had kept him amply fed, clothed, and headed in the right direction. She was full of humor and wisdom, giving him whichever she felt he needed the most of at the time.

She was the only person he had told where and why he was going when he had lit out for San Francisco. She wouldn't know what to make of the Jake who was coming home without his bride. More specifically, she wouldn't know what to make of the Jake who was coming home without Emma as his bride. She had loved Emma and Jake equally, and it would be a blow to her, as she had always been finding ways to get them together. She wanted so much for him to be happily married and have a family.

Mother Mattie reckoned she had been with them long enough to qualify as family. When Jake called her Mother now it was like she really was his mother. She knew she loved him like a son. She felt she had to get him married before she left this world; it wouldn't be right leaving him all on his own. One thing was certain: she wasn't getting any younger.

Jake reckoned when she learned the whole story, and how blissful was Emma's marriage, she would be so happy for her. Especially after all the worry she had known while Emma had been missing.

Jake had never considered himself a prideful man, but knowing that the whole church, and community, would soon know about Emma's marrying another man, he realized that would be hard for him to deal with. Everyone had known they were a couple, even if they hadn't reached the full courting stage yet. Putting himself in their shoes, he knew they would be feeling sorry for him, and he certainly didn't intend to be a victim in all of this.

He had made up his mind to cheerfully share his adventure with his church. He would tell them of his mission, and its outcome, and how God had planned it all from the beginning. He would tell them why Emma had left Savannah, why she had not said anything to him or any of her friends, and what God had done for her in her new city. He knew they would understand. Everyone would know that she was not to blame for any of it, but rather had handled what she had been forced upon her with grace and good sense.

He had sent a telegram from one of the depots to Mother Hawkins advising her of his expected time of arrival. He should have known better. He had been welcomed home like a war hero. A banner had been hung at the train depot, and at the church. Mother Mattie had been at the depot to meet him, and was delighted to see him safe home.

As he had figured, she had a definite question in her wise, old eyes, wanting to know, no doubt, where Emma was. He knew plenty of questions would come his way later when they had time alone.

As he was due in on a Sunday morning, there was a fellowship dinner planned to welcome him home after the service, so he had been taken straight to the church. Fortunately for him, he had traveled by sleeper car, and was refreshed. His expectation at finally arriving home and seeing loved ones again had helped him to shake off the aloneness and weariness of travel. He looked forward to some of the best home cooking to be had in Savannah at the reunion dinner.

He found the church doing well, with no dire news awaiting his return. He was pleasantly surprised to find that three new families had moved to town, and had sought out the Savannah Chapel as their new home church. Three new families added to their numbers were most welcomed.

Harry and Bessie Adams, a middle-aged couple with grown children, had one unmarried son, Todd, still living at home. They seemed to be a very friendly, sincere couple. They loved the church and were very glad the meet the pastor upon his return.

They had recently moved to Savannah from South Carolina to be nearer older relatives, who were ranchers, and who needed help with their ranch.

Todd was a handsome man of around twenty-five, who carried himself very well. He had a way about him that was very wholesome and attractive. He was a hardworking man, and had always been a rancher. Jake was sure he would do well out at the old Ferguson place, and that he would be able to bring it back to its former state. Todd seemed like a man who would work and play equally hard, and Jake had the impression that he would surely go far in life.

The Borellis were a Yankee family from New York City. Carmen had been in Savannah for quite some time. He worked in affairs that had to do with the reconstruction that had been going on in the South since the end of the war.

He had grown accustomed to the mild winters, and had decided to make Savannah his home. He had then brought his wife, Abigail, and their children down to be with him. They had been seeking a home church, and had settled on his. The family consisted of twin boys, Joey and Jamie, who were around twelve years of age. They also had a daughter, Carmel, who was twenty-three.

Carmel was a beauty with black hair, green eyes and olive complexion. Not that Jake had met her yet, but her mother had described her to everyone who would listen, as Carmel was the apple of her mother's eye. She was also the sweetest, darling girl that ever drew breath, to hear her mama tell it. Carmel had stayed behind enmeshed in her studies, as her schooling would not be over until her graduation in May. She was studying to be a medical doctor, of all things!

Jake was standing there talking with the couple, but his mind was wandering to his thoughts of their daughter. He couldn't imagine the people of Savannah submitting to the medical administrations of a woman, even though they were becoming more frequently heard tell of. She had to be a very strong willed, pushy woman to have survived medical school with all male professors and students, no doubt unsympathetic to her cause.

As Abigail had been describing her precious daughter, he had been thinking that he had not been overly fond of any Yankee women he had ever met, and there had been several after the war. He felt pretty sure this one would be no different, if she were anything like her mother.

Abigail was sweet and friendly, but also extremely talkative and could say more in one minute than a Southerner could say in five. She was just a bit over loud, too, as some Northerners tended to be. But she seemed a goodly soul, for all that, and Carmen seemed a quiet, strong man. They would make a good addition to the church, and Jake was more than glad to have them.

Bert and Jenny Abbot were from over Jonesboro way. They literally had a houseful of children, six he thought they had said, from ages four to twelve, and all of them boys. Jake thought that would be very interesting drama to watch so many youngsters, mostly boys of around the same age, grow up in their midst! Remembering what all he and Fletcher had done as youngsters reminded him that chickens do come home to roost. No doubt these new youngsters would find ways to try his soul.

A single woman and her younger brother had also started coming to the church. They were Marcy and Timmy Jennings. She was a real beauty, with flaxen hair, having green eyes, rather than the blue usually seen in one so fair. She carried herself very well, and was quiet, but friendly, having a ready smile for one and all. She seemed to be an all around fine woman.

She worked as a social secretary for the Savannah mayor and his wife. There was just something about her that he found soothing and attractive. He was always very careful and circumspect around the single ladies, but he had to confess that Marcy was certainly thought provoking. Her brother was around the same age as the Borelli twins, and seemed like a very nice sort of youngster.

It was very exciting for Jake to see so many young lives becoming intertwined with the family that was the Savannah Chapel. He had been given a great work to do with his congregation of one hundred fifty souls, and he did not take it lightly. He recognized that it truly was good to be back where he belonged, come what may. He needed to be needed, and as he helped others, surely it would help him forget his own troubles.

Chapter 3

With the reunion over and the church empty once again, Jake had sat down in one of side chairs on the podium and looked out over the empty pews. He had been doing that during the long months that Emma had been missing. He could remember exactly where she had always sat.

Today, as he looked out over the church pews, he couldn't really see her sitting there like all the other times. When he thought of Emma now, it was always in the Killian House mansion, or the parsonage, or somewhere else in Mark's company. He supposed that was as it should be.

He bowed his head and asked the Lord for wisdom and guidance once again. He needed to know just how to put the past firmly in the past, and move forward to lead his flock in the paths of righteousness for His name's sake.

When Jake arrived home after the party, Mother Hawkins was waiting for him. "Well, my boy, I am glad to have you home. You look a bit peaked for all your troubles, but better than I had hoped for!"

"It's good to be home, Mother," he said and realized he was telling God's own truth. He was home and that was a wonderful word. He had a bit of an uneasy spirit still, for all that he had prayed the whole way home. He felt at loose ends. He soon realized that being home and being *at* home were two entirely different things. At least he was home where he could begin to work and adjust to his new life. He would need to learn how to be at home with himself, and his lot in life again. It would take time, but time was all he really had.

His thoughts turned to his best friend, Fletcher. There had been a telegram waiting for him upon his return, and it simply said, "God will provide." Fletcher was a blessing, and he was being used to help Jake make it through this alone time. Fletcher had known what he would have been feeling had he lost Elizabeth, and could easily commiserate with Jake. He thought of when Fletch had been in the dark tunnel of amnesia, and how loose-ended he had felt when he couldn't remember his past. Now Jake felt that same loose-ended way, but it was because he couldn't forget his.

Well, Fletch had eventually remembered and Jake had a hope that as surely as Fletch had remembered, he would some day truly be able to forget. No, not forget, exactly. He would never forget all the good, and all the love he had for all his friends in San Francisco. His hope was just that soon he wouldn't have any pain along with the memories.

Mother had come in the parlor and Jake shared the telegram from Fletcher with her. She was delighted when Jake had shared his San Francisco experiences with the church, and she had learned that the boy hadn't been killed in the war as reported. She had been so pleased to know that he was happily wed. She just wished Jake could fine someone to love like Fletcher and Emma had.

They reminisced about how Jake had been at the plantation with Fletcher, or else Fletcher had been at the parsonage nearly every day before he had gone away to war. Usually it was Jake at the plantation, helping Fletcher with chores, so they could have time to ride for pleasure.

Jake's father had been the pastor before he suddenly was taken away with the influenza around the time of the outbreak of the war back in '61. Both of their lives had dramatically changed then. Fletch went away to war, while Jake had been in bed with Scarlet Fever.

He had come down with dreaded complications, and had been laid low for months. When he had miraculously recovered, somewhat, he had been able to amble to the church next door for short periods of time. He had never recovered enough to take up arms in the war. The war and the reconstruction of the South had been such trying times for Southerners, but things were getting more and more back to normal.

Jake showed up at Judge West's office Monday morning. The judge had not been in town to greet Jake, as he had been in Charleston for the past week, and had just arrived back late the night before.

Judge Joe West was very glad to see him. He asked his clerk not to disturb him for a while. Then he asked Jake to tell him the whole story. Jake told him first about finding Fletcher alive. The judge was awe struck at that news! It took him a moment to respond.

"Well, Emma never would accept that he was dead, would she?" he asked Jake.

"No, sir," he agreed, "she surely wouldn't! I'm so glad that nobody ever discouraged her from believing he was alive. Speaking of Emma, Judge, I was never prouder in my life, than I was when Emma and Mark allowed me to officiate at their wedding ceremony. It made all the difference in feeling left out, or being a part of my best friends' lives."

"Son, I never doubted for a moment that you could face anything that came your way. You are just that kind of man. I have to say that I was floored when I got your telegram announcing Emma's wedding to Angelos. I know you must have gone through a lot. But you handled yourself very well during everything you went through in San Francisco. You acted like a true man of God and I'm proud to know you, Jake, and I mean that."

To lighten the moment, the judge said, "You know, I never told you about the time Morgan came in here to ask me if I knew where Emma was. I put on the performance of my career and I still chuckle at how that little slip of a girl bamboozled him with his own flimflam!" he said as he laughed out loud.

"Why, you should have seen the look on his face when he realized that she was gone and had sold the plantation to me before he could place a lien on it. So he didn't get her money, or her plantation, nor did he get Emma! You would have been proud of her, my boy!" he assured him.

"Yes, she is a stronger woman than any of us realized. Judge, you know, I can certainly see that the Lord led me out there, not for Emma's sake, but for my own. I know now that if I had spoke up and told her how I felt, she would have been my wife today. She told me that in San Francisco," Jake said, as the judge just let him tell his story without comment.

"But, I hadn't spoken the words that I had wanted to say, and that she had wanted to hear at the time. I know now that it hadn't been me, but it had been the Lord who had been restraining me from declaring myself, because she was meant for Mark. I can see it plain as plain now," he finished.

"Son, the same God that made Emma Summers, has made a Mrs. Jake Jackson. He will bring her to you right on time, as surely as he brought Emma to Mark. Just you believe that and hold on to it," he declared. "You will see it with your own eyes some day!

Summer was nearly upon them and the calendar was filling up with the end of school recitals, plays, and commencement exercises. Jake was always present at those affairs, and was usually asked to open or close them in prayer. He had to say that his church members were still keeping him plenty busy, but nothing like during the winter months. He was now rested and felt better about so many things. All in all, he really was becoming contented with his lot in life.

How many married men could say that, he asked himself. His answer was a chuckle. He was a pastor and he heard some of the troubles that frequented married couples' households. He knew that life was not all love and roses, just because a man had found someone to love, even if the woman loved him in return.

Such was life, and he was no stranger to life, but he could honesty say that he was no longer a victim of life, either. He had picked himself up, brushed himself off, stood on his own two feet, and had wondered at all the fuss he had been embroiled in but a short while back. It had been over a year now since Em had left and with the Lord's help he could stand tall again, as he was beginning to know his place in the scheme of things.

It was the first Sunday morning in June and a lovelier morning could not have been found in all the earth. It was one of those mornings that Emma used to say that you were sure that God was on the throne, and that all was well with the world.

The chapel bells had been ringing for a couple of minutes now, and the church was filling up. The boys were making a general nuisance of themselves, but they were in the carefree days of summer, and Jake had understood. He could almost see himself and Fletch doing those same things down those same isles years ago when they were boys.

He truly loved this place and always had done. It was one of the reasons he could never have stayed out West. These were his roots, and these people were his family, and he belonged here, no question about it. The organ swelled and the worship was beginning.

He took his seat on the podium. His thoughts were only of God's goodness, and of the sermon he was eager to preach that morning. The words had simply flowed from his pen, as he had taken notes for his sermon. He prayed that the people would receive them exactly as he had.

He closed his eyes and allowed the vibrations of the music to wash over him like a cleansing tide. He felt a lump in his throat, as tears filled his eyes. Had he been alone, he would have wept and shouted his praise to the Lord, or perhaps even danced a bit. As he wasn't, he lifted his hands and merely wept. Not much he could have done about that, even if he'd tried.

When the Lord lifted His hand from Jake just a little, he was able to dry his eyes and saw that many others were doing the same. Surely, this was a day to be remembered. As he looked out over the crowd, his eyes automatically went to the seat where Emma had always sat. His wondering eyes couldn't seem to pull away from a young woman sitting with Abby Borelli.

After a moment, dawning hit and he realized just who she was, as he thought to himself, *Ah, so this was the paragon daughter I have heard so much about. And why was she sitting in Emma's seat?*

He pulled his eyes away from her and thought to himself, *Emma's seat? Lord, help me! I cannot believe that silly thought just hit me after feeling the presence of the Lord so strongly! The devil surely was a persistent cuss.*

After the service was over, he made his way to the back doors to say farewell to his people. When Abby Borelli appeared before him with her daughter, she made introductions.

"I'm pleased to meet you, Miss Borelli," he said, taking her hand momentarily.

"Thanks, I'm pleased to meet you, too," she said. "Nice sermon."

Nice sermon? Wonder where she came by her manners, as if I didn't know, he couldn't help but think.

"Well, I'm glad you enjoyed it," he answered.

"Now, I didn't say I enjoyed it. I said it was nice," she said, with a twinkle in her eye. Her mama patted her hand, and giggled. "Now be nice, dear."

She is goading me. What cheek, Jake thought in disgust.

"My mistake, madam. I will not repeat it in future. Hopefully you will come back and give me a chance to do better next time," he smiled, but was sure it wasn't believable.

They moved on and he continued to shake hands with the next person in line, probably a little more firmly that they had been used to!

Chapter 4

*J*ake Jackson was normally a very mild mannered man, but something about Yankee women turned him around in circles. He wasn't used to, nor did he want to become used to, their brash, outspoken ways. It was unfeminine, and if there was anything he wanted in a woman it was femininity.

His feathers were smoothed somewhat just then by the presence of Marcy and Timmy, who were just stepping forward to shake hands. She was femininity itself. But for all that, she had a firm handshake, and a bit of steel in her eye. She was impeccably dressed and her eyes were sincere, and not flirty in the least. He saw amusement there, like she was full of life should anyone care to find out.

Working for the mayor and his wife, and having seen a good bit of life in high society, she was used to carrying herself well. When asked about the rest of her family, she told him that her parents had passed on many years ago, and that she and Timmy lived with their grandmother, Grace Jennings, who wasn't able to attend services. Grace had decided to move to town from the country so that Marcy could be near to her work. Marcy related to him that her grandmother had wondered if the pastor would be free some time for Sunday dinner. She had wanted to get to know him, and if it wouldn't be too much trouble, would he serve her communion when he came to dinner? He assured Marcy that she only had to name a date, and he would be pleased to attend. She named the next Sunday and was gone. Jake realized the moment the words were out of her mouth that he would be looking forward to next Sunday all the week long!

When he got home, Mother was waiting for him with a good meal, as usual. She had taken the liberty to issue dinner invitations to Harry, Bessie, and Todd. She often did that, as it had always been fine with Jake. He loved fellowship, and she saw to visitors, as he had a lot on his mind of a Sunday morning. He would forget to invite anyone, like as not.

The more Jake talked with them, the more impressed he was with Todd. He was intelligent, reasonable in his thinking, and showed a huge heart besides. He had asked if anyone was taking care of seeing to the elderly getting to services, especially for those who did not own buggies. It had been his experience that since the rest of the family could walk, the shut-ins thought that it would be easier all around for them to just stay at home.

Jake was impressed with the concern Todd was showing for the elderly and infirm. He told him that he knew of one shut-in whom he had heard about just that morning. He asked Todd if he had thought about it enough to have come up with a plan.

He responded by telling him that he had heard about the trams, the horse-drawn cars they had in the big cities that ran on rails. He wondered if they could afford one, if the car was more simply made. Perhaps having regular carriage wheels made from wood, with simple seats inside. He thought if they could get one of those, it would be perfect to bring the people in all at once, since time was of the essence on a Sunday morning.

Jake thought that was a brilliant idea and asked him if the church could raise the funds, and could find one such conveyance to buy, would he be willing to do the honors and chauffeur the car. He responded affirmatively. An idea that had been just a little thought, until Todd had spoken it out, had now become a set plan. Once he had spoken it, he had given the thought a life of its own.

He was not surprised when Abby Borelli arrived at the parsonage with an invitation to Wednesday night supper after church. She wanted to get to know her pastor better, and for him to get to know all of them. He accepted her invitation, but wondered if she could sense his reluctance. Probably not, as she had stopped talking only long enough to hear a 'yes' from him, and then was off and running again on another topic. It would be a long supper.

Then he learned that Mother Hawkins had also been invited, as well as Todd Adams. Hearing Todd would be there, he thought to himself, *Well, shame on you, Mr. Negative Lips; there would be a bright spot in the evening after all!*

Wednesday night proved to be fair of weather. After the service, the invited guests walked the few blocks to the Borelli residence. There was a festive atmosphere at the home, in spite of Jake's negative energy, as everyone else seemed very pleased to be there.

Carmel was a beauty and no denying that, and she carried herself well enough. It was when the female opened her mouth and spoke that ruined it all for him. The boys were full of themselves as usual, and for that matter, so was Carmel. It seemed that she was full of fun, as she laughed and teased a lot, especially with her brothers and Todd, who seemed to appreciate her sassiness.

Oh, well, to each his own. Thoughts of a comparison between Carmel and Marcy caused his heartbeat to quicken, as Marcy's face came to remembrance. Considering his reaction to remembering that lovely face, he thought, *Very interesting, that*!

The meal progressed and he found the food tempting and delicious. They were having spaghetti and meatballs, and it certainly wasn't your typical Southern cooking. He was more than a bit surprised when he learned that Carmel had prepared the main dish. He had finally found something that he admired about Northern women; at least that Northern woman.

Trying to find some table talk to include her, Jake said, "I understand from your mother that you studied to become a physician. That is both amazing and interesting. What caused you to decide on that undertaking?"

She looked at him apparently trying to decide if he really wanted to know, or if he were merely making conversation.

Very perceptive, I'll give her that, he thought.

Supposing that others might have a genuine interest she answered him, "Well, I would like to believe that I received a calling, not unlike yourself, to a life's work of usefulness. Certainly, I will be able to help meet a great need. Women notoriously do not care to see a male doctor for certain things," she said without so much as a hint of a blush. The others at the table were doing enough of that for her.

"They have expressed their need and desire for women to administer treatment to women. If there were not so much prejudice against women in the medical field, the common man and woman would see the logic for it, and receive it gladly. Women like me see that logic, and we choose to step up and speak out, as it were, never mind the stones that are thrown in our direction," she spoke with conviction and more than just a bit of passion.

"I see," said Jake. Put that way, he supposed he could see her point of view. He had to confess that he had never spent any time whatsoever in pondering the situation, but called to his attention, he could see her logic. If he were a married man, he knew he would want his wife have this obviously capable, and self-confident woman take care of her medical needs, rather than old Doc Wilson. Nodding his head, he repeated, "I see."

She could see that he really seemed to be studying about what she had just said. He didn't give any indication as to whether or not he agreed with her philosophy. It did show that he thought her point of view worthy of consideration. More than most men, who held any position of authority, seemed to do.

On a lighter note, she said with a chuckle, "And in case you were wondering, the stones I just mentioned were literal!" Jake was amazed that she could take a thing like that into her stride and just keep going, even laugh about it.

"Well, Miss Carmel, what do you intend to do next?" he queried.

"I'm glad you asked, because maybe I can use your help with my plans, if you're willing" she replied.

Interested, but unable to fathom anything he could help her with in the medical arena, Jake asked her what she had in mind.

"Well, I propose to start a free day clinic for the poor women and children among us. Even though the doctors in this town feel nobody will come, the free part will still infuriate them. They will no doubt rise up. They will tell the women not to come, because I couldn't be any good, or I would charge for my services like they do.

However, if you will speak to the women you know, and ask them to give me a try, they will see that I am a good doctor and they will spread the word. Especially those you know to be poor, as they will be getting the treatment they need at the same time," she finished.

Jake could not help but be impressed. He supposed he couldn't have thought of nearly as good a plan, and told her so. She seemed pleased that he approved.

A thought was forming. He asked her, "What do you think about me introducing you in church Sunday so you can speak to the congregation directly. How about right after the service?"

Carmel was amazed. "You would do that for me? You don't even know if I am a good doctor or not. What if you recommend me and then I make some awful mistake. Won't the women blame you?" she asked.

"Well, do you plan to make some awful mistake?" he asked her with a chuckle.

"No, of course not, but one never knows! That is why they call it a mistake!" she voiced.

"Well, my dear girl, don't make a mistake! But eventually you might. Again, as you just said, that is why they call it a mistake. However, it has been my experience that if one is diligent and caring, as you seem to be, the people will forgive a lot of error done in good faith," he advised her.

She seemed taken aback somewhat by his genuine feelings about introducing her, and lending his generous offer of assistance. She had assumed that he would be like all the other men in positions of authority, worrying only about what it may mean for them down the road.

She extended her hand across the table and said, "It's a deal. I'll be there Sunday. Mother is allowing me the downstairs study as a consult and surgery. I can have everything ready for Monday morning!"

All in all, a better evening than I imagined. She may be brash and immodest for a Southern lady, but I suppose she's normal for a Yankee doctor, Jake allowed to himself.

Well, I am somewhat surprised. I thought I had him all figured out— a prude and judgmental to boot. I must say, I am definitely pleasantly surprised, Carmel thought.

Chapter 5

*I*t never failed to surprise him how little he knew about women, especially after his conversation with Carmel over dinner last night. He couldn't figure out if she were just bold, immature, or just plain didn't care a fig about the opinion of others, when those opinions concerned her.

He would have to study that one for a while, as he couldn't seem to get a handle on just who she was. She certainly wasn't like any Southern belle he had ever met. He just didn't understand her. But then again, she wasn't a Southern belle, was she?

Mother Mattie had told him that she had invited Timmy and Marcy Jennings for tea on Friday afternoon. Timmy would be out of school and Marcy left early on Fridays. Mattie Hawkins knew everything about everybody! She also knew Jake would be available. So she was up to her matchmaking endeavors again, but he couldn't honestly say that he minded. He found himself very much looking forward to Friday. Life was becoming much more interesting of late.

Todd dropped by the parsonage and wondered if he could have a sit down with the pastor. Jake was happy to oblige him. Todd began by saying, "Pastor, how well do you know Carmel Borelli?"

Jake was a bit taken aback, but realized it was because it had been an unexpected question. "Well, I have only been around her the same as you, at the dinner Wednesday night. Why do you ask?" he said.

"Well, I just find myself thinking of her quite a bit. She is different than any of the girls around here."

"She is that," Jake allowed.

"So you don't really know her either. But what do you think of her?" he persisted.

"Todd, I really haven't been around her enough to form a real opinion. It takes time to know what to think about someone. Especially a woman, as first impressions can be deceiving. She is different, like you say.

She is much more professional and independent than what Southern men are accustomed to. That is neither bad nor good, just a fact. So it seems you may be smitten with her, my friend?" he asked, good-naturedly.

"I wouldn't say smitten, exactly; maybe more like just curious. I admire her fortitude and ambition. She certainly knows how to go about getting things done her way," he noted. "And she's pretty as anything!"

"I agree with that!" Jake laughed. "I certainly agree with all of that. Since we are speaking of newcomers, what do you think of Marcy Jennings?"

"Marcy? Well…" he said, with a flush creeping over his countenance, taking a moment before he continued. "I can't say. Like you just said, I haven't been around her enough to know. I do know she is a beauty. She is graceful and dignified. She carries herself well, and seems to be a very sincere Christian. Way too elegant…I guess I don't have an opinion after all."

Jake laughed out loud. "For someone who doesn't have an opinion, you sure found a lot of adjectives to describe her!"

Todd laughed right along with him and it did them both good. But truthfully, Jake was a bit disconcerted after Todd had gone home.

From the flush on Todd's face, it seems to me like it is Marcy he was really here to find out about, he thought. If he were to be honest right then, he would have had to admit that he really didn't like to think of either of those two women with any man.

Why ever would I think that? What was that attitude all about? he wondered. He needed to get a grip on his thoughts and emotions. Had he searched his soul a little deeper, he would have discovered that each of those women held an attraction for him. Since it was too soon to know what he wanted, or which of them that he really might care about, he shamefully hoped they both remained unattached, at least for the time being.

Friday afternoon teatime came around. Marcy and Timmy appeared at his door, right at the appointed time. They were literally like a breath of fresh air. Timmy was a bright boy, and was interested in everything. One thing he especially wanted to ask Pastor Jake about was if he knew anything about horses. Jake related to him all about his friend, Fletcher, being a connoisseur of horseflesh and that he had shared a lot of that knowledge with him.

Jake asked him if he knew how to ride, but Timmy didn't. Neither, it seemed, did Marcy, but both indicated that they would love to learn to ride. He told them that could be arranged, and if they had the time, they could go to Summers Bluff to ride the very horses that Fletcher had cared for.

They had been in church when Jake had shared with the congregation what had really happened to Emma. They knew about the plantation belonging to Jake's good friend, Judge West, who would, no doubt, love for them to enjoy the horses.

A date for the following week on Saturday was set for their outing. He could see the unrestrained excitement on their faces. He knew that if he could have seen his own face, he would have seen that same excitement in his eyes. The only problem was that Saturday week was an entire week away!

Chapter 6

*S*unday service went especially well, and there had been a couple of male visitors. That was always encouraging to see. They were well dressed and suave, probably due to being from a larger city than Savannah. When they had arrived, Todd had taken them under his wing and introduced them around before the service.

Jake had studied them throughout the service and decided that maybe they were just a little too suave. He didn't like to a make snap judgments, but the gift of discernment took him where it would, and that is where it took him concerning those two.

Another thing, he had seen them both watching Marcy. He had assumed that they had pushed Todd into making introductions, as they had made a beeline to speak to her after the service. It surprised him, but she actually had greeted them as if she already knew them. Since she worked for the mayor, she met all sorts of people as a matter of routine. Still, them knowing the mayor certainly didn't relieve his not feeling comfortable about them.

After the service, Todd had accompanied them to Jake and made the introductions. They were handsome, sophisticated and suave, indeed, no doubt owing to having a bit of wealth. All in all, they really seemed out of place in his congregation, and he didn't know why. He couldn't account for that assessment of them, as he had wealthy professionals in attendance, as well as farmers, and common laborers.

For one thing, they seemed to be looking down their noses at him, which is not the impression he normally had when meeting any visitor he'd ever had before. That feeling served to cause him to draw himself up to his full six-foot height and meet their assessment head on.

"Nice congregation you have here, Pastor," said Bill Boyd, as they shook hands. Then it hit him that he knew exactly what he had been feeling about those two. He felt like they were wolves amongst the sheep!

"Yes it certainly is Mr. Boyd. Where do you boys hail from," he casually inquired.

"Oh, we're from up Richmond way," he answered smoothly.

"Great city, Richmond. I have a couple of pastor friends up there. What church did you fellowship with up there? Maybe I know it."

It didn't take spiritual discernment to see their amused faces at his suggestion that they attended any church. He didn't let on that he had understood their looks.

"Oh well, we went to a new church just starting up. Maybe like a Presbyterian offshoot. Can't say as I recall the name. It escapes me now," Hoyt Davison said off-handedly.

"Well, no matter," Jake told them.

He questioned them a bit further and found out that they had been in Savannah for a while on business. They said they would be back to church in the near future, and would look forward to meeting others. That struck him as odd, as it didn't seem like they would have anything in common with any of his church members. In fact, them mixing with his congregation seemed to remind him of oil and water.

"If there is anything I can do for you, you will let me know, won't you?" Jake asked.

"Right neighborly of you, sir. We will surely do that," as they walked away with somewhat of a smirk. It looked to Jake like they were smiling exactly like someone with their hand in the cookie jar, and could already taste the cookies.

Jake Jackson was an amiable man and a benevolent pastor, but he was a deadly foe. He couldn't count anyone as such presently, but he had put those two men on his watch list just the same. Jake made two declarations to himself then and there: *it is not sheep shearing time, and when it is, it won't be my sheep that get sheared!"*

After the service, Mother and Jake walked to Mrs. Jennings home with Timmy and Marcy. Marcy had told them a bit about her grandmother on their walk to her home. She said her grandmother never complained of her infirmity, but rather was long-suffering, patient, and always kind.

Jake and Mother Mattie was presented to her, and soon realized that she really was a suffering angel. She had a personality that made them feel like family immediately. She was so very appreciative of him making time to come to Sunday dinner that she was quite beside herself. He could readily believe Marcy's assessment of her grandmother after spending just a few moments with her.

She seemed hungry for Christian fellowship with someone who would speak to her of the Lord, and give her some nuggets of faith and encouragement in her trials. She said she loved to fellowship around the Word of God and a good meal. Well, she had been provided with both that dinnertime.

She asked them to call her Grace and they agreed. She wanted to talk some about Marcy. She related to them that she and Timmy had lost both their parents by the time Marcy was eight and Timmy was a newborn. They had been staying with her ever since. She had sent them to school, and while Timmy was still going, he was now old enough to basically care for himself. That was fortunate, as she was having a hard time walking and getting around.

Marcy had graduated from school at the top of her class, and then been sent off to the Boston Secretarial Finishing School for Young Ladies. There she learned familiarity with high society and business organization and structure. She could serve as secretary to male or female in the business arena. She had a natural common sense, and could anticipate needs. Therefore, she was invaluable to her employers.

She helped the mayor with his social engagements, and his wife with her more complicated one. Sometimes she was called to help him entertain important people when there was a wife or other lady present. She was also asked to sit in on private meetings to take notes, as she was proficient in the art of shorthand.

She was probably the highest paid assistant in the city. She moved in elegant circles, including the homes of the pillars of Savannah society. That was probably because she was without guile and was completely trustworthy. Jake believed that absolutely.

Marcy was pursued by anyone wanting the mayor's ear. Jake could appreciate that, too. He wondered where the two wolves in church that morning fit in. So he asked her.

"They are acquaintances of the mayor," she told him. "They are pushing some business deal, but I don't think the mayor is really interested. Not at the moment anyway, but they seem unwilling to give it up. They keep coming up with better sounding terms. I just hope he doesn't give in and accept them," she finished.

"Why do you not want him to accept their deal," he asked.

"I don't know why, but I just don't trust them. Maybe that's because they're too smooth. I'm not sure of their entire plan, but what bits and pieces I have over heard, their deal seems too good to be true. Whatever their game, the mayor would be playing it with taxpayer's money." She hesitated, and then chastising herself, declared, "Dear me! I have gone to talking out of turn."

"I'm sorry, I shouldn't have asked such a direct question, but rest assured, I am honor bound to silence. Whatever you tell me about anything in future, please know that it stays between us," he assured her. "I will remember that, Pastor, and I trust you to forget what I have just said," she implored him.

After serving Miss Grace communion, they all said their good-byes. "We have had a lovely time, Miss Grace, Miss Marcy, and thank you for inviting us," Jake said.

Marcy walked them out the gate, and then on to the corner, as they were still talking. Then he watched her until she was back inside the gate. He lifted his hand to her and she returned the salute. They both smiled.

He wondered what lay in store for him with regards to Marcy. He thought he was beginning to see the hand of God move, and it was just a bit disconcerting, now that it was finally happening.

Chapter 7

*I*t was the middle of July and the day for the church picnic was upon them. It was always well attended, and even visitors were made to feel at home among them, as they sang, played, ate, and fellowshipped.

They were having a quilt and bakery auction with the proceeds meant for the horse drawn car Todd had suggested. They also had boxed dinners for auction, which Jake had always refrained from bidding on. He couldn't risk offending any of the single ladies at church. He blessed the food, and the auction began.

He was quite surprised, a few minutes later, at the sight of Carmel bidding on her own box, of all things. No woman had ever bid on a boxed dinner before in the history of boxed dinners, especially her own box!

What could the chit be up to, pray tell? he wondered. When she won the bid, the people thought she must either be shy, or that she just had not wanted to sit with any of the young bucks during dinner. They forgave her Yankee ways. Apparently, she just did not know the proper etiquette for boxed dinner auctions.

Everyone had noticed that she had gone straight to Jake, and having a blanket in hand, handed him the box and proceeded to spread her blanket on the ground. She then graciously sat down upon it. He was so flabbergasted at her audacity that he just stood there holding the box and staring at her.

"You do have to eat, and you certainly can't embarrass me by refusing to eat my dinner. Not after I prepared it for you, and then bought it for you, too!" she said with a look that dared him to challenge her. He sat down.

"Well, Miss Carmel," he said when he had found his voice. "I thank you for thinking of me. Although, I must enlighten you on bidding, as it is usually the man who does the bidding," he said softly.

She looked at him and giggled saying, "I know that! But you were just standing there with your hands in your pocket, not bidding. I certainly didn't want some one else to eat your dinner!" she said in a tone that clearly said, 'You silly man!' She laughed at his dismay.

She looked around and noticed the people staring at them, so she asked him, "Are you worried what people will say?"

"Well, there is that!" he replied, but not unkindly.

She is outrageous! Who in the world would have that kind of nerve? Is there anything she wants to do that she denies herself? How does she even think these things up?

Again she laughed, as though she hadn't a care in the world. "Pastor, pastor! Don't fret yourself. People will see that we are just having a bit of fun, not a romance," she assured him. Then he had to laugh, too, at her audacity, if nothing else.

"I do thank you for the food. It is simply delicious," he assured her, as he cut into his noodles for another bite. "Ummm. What is this stuff? Tell me, did you really make this, too?" he asked. "I already told you I prepared it for you, and I bought it for you, and it's called lasagna," she said, laughing.

To change the subject, she asked, "How do you think my invitation to the women for free health services went this morning?"

He answered her saying, "I watched their faces as you presented your proposal to them. I could see a bit of confusion at first. They looked at their husbands a lot, but since I had presented you to them, I know they were willing to at least listen. I think you were successful. How do you feel it went?"

"One young lady came to me quietly after the service and asked me again of the charge. When I reemphasized no charge, she asked me if she could come in the morning! So I have my first patient. Thanks to you, Pastor! I really appreciate it!" she exclaimed.

"No need to thank me. I am glad the women will get the care they need, and that you will be doing the work you need to do, also," he told her sincerely.

All he could do was shake his head and laugh. He hoped he didn't have too much explaining to do. When he looked across the way and saw Marcy sitting with Bessie, Harry and Todd, he wondered what they were thinking of Carmel's escapade. He wondered what Marcy was thinking of Todd. When he looked at Carmel, he realized that she had been watching him watch Marcy.

He could feel his face flush. Without saying a word she got up and left the blanket, having a wistful smile. He knew he had somehow offended her. He was trying to figure out what he should do, since she had up and left him sitting alone on her blanket, when Todd had come over. He told him that the tally of the auctions had been good and that they had enough to buy the car, and now only needed to find one.

Just then Carmel reappeared with two slabs of chocolate cake. "I didn't have time to bake a cake. I hope you don't mind. I got this from Mother Mattie," she explained with a smile, as though nothing had happened.

The woman was simply unfathomable! Who knew how her mind worked? Seeing him lingering far too long on Marcy had bothered her, he could tell, but she hadn't caused a scene. She hadn't said anything, nor had she acted out, even to him. It made him feel weak and ashamed. He had no idea what she was about, or what he was about when he was with her.

They finished their cake and he declared that it had been a very satisfying meal. He thanked her for her concern for him to fix his dinner, and to share it with him. All in all, he had forgotten about the people around him and had ended up enjoying their time together. He was pleasantly surprised to realize that.

He was also surprised that she could cook so well, and didn't seem to mind doing it. He had her pegged as a suffragette all the way, but she did have some un-suffragette, wholesome characteristics, not that he knew much about the suffragettes. She went to church, and she could cook. That was a start!

Jake was thinking that he would have to return the favor. In the near future, he felt that the fair thing for him to do would be to ask her out to supper. He had a policy not to date the women in his church to keep from anyone feeling slighted, and it had cost him Emma. Although he planned to be circumspect, he didn't intend to let that happen again with a woman he cared about. How that would work out around his feelings for Marcy, he had no idea.

Whenever it rains, it pours. Things seem to go along just fine, and then up jumps the devil, literally. It was a rainy night and nearly ten o'clock when someone had twisted the chime at the front door of the parsonage.

It was Marcy and she was wet to the skin. She didn't want to come in for fear of wetting the rug. He ushered her in anyway. He called for Mother Mattie, and seeing Marcy dripping wet, fetched a towel for her to dry off.

She told him she was concerned for her grandmother, who seemed to have taken a turn for the worse. She explained the situation as best she could, and said that Miss Grace had wanted Jake, so she had come to fetch him. Upon hearing that, he grabbed his coat and umbrella and they left for her home.

When they got there, he could see at once that Miss Grace had, indeed, taken a turn for the worse. He held her hand, and prayed for her, and she acknowledged his presence. He told her he would be right back, and then took Marcy out of the room. He had instinctively hugged her just for the briefest moment, quite before he thought, and told her not to worry. He would be back with the doctor. He also reminded her to get some dry things on as soon as he left.

He headed for the Borelli house at a trot, and rang the bell. The maid answered and he asked for the doctor. Carmel came quickly to see what the trouble was. When he had explained, she donned her raincoat, grabbed her doctor's bag, and followed him. He fairly ran, but she had kept up with him.

Arriving at the Jennings' home somewhat out of breath, Doctor Borelli was shown immediately into Miss Grace's room. She took her pulse and listened to her chest with her stethoscope. She asked Marcy for some hot water to prepare some willow bark tea.

When the tea was ready, she asked Jake to help bring her patient up in the bed a bit more. Miss Grace had a slight drawing of the left side of her mouth and the tea dribbled down her chin a bit. She took Miss Grace's hands in hers, and spoke softly to her.

She asked her if she could pray with her, and she readily gave consent. Carmel said a simple prayer asking God to take care of

Miss Grace and make her well again. At the time, she had asked that out of force of habit, and had momentarily forgotten that the pastor was there and could have done it. *Oh, well, a prayer is a prayer if it's heartfelt.*

When Carmel squeezed her hands, Miss Grace responded with a squeeze of her own and Carmel had noted a slight weakness of the left hand. She felt her lower limbs and asked Miss Grace if she could feel her hands on them. She shook her head to indicate 'yes'. She asked her if she felt any difference between them. She said that she did not, that they were the same as always. Carmel told Miss Grace not to worry, and that she would be back. She asked to see Jake and Marcy outside.

She had explained to them that Miss Grace had suffered a stroke and that she could not determine the full extent of the damage right away. They would have to wait and see how she progressed. She explained that she really couldn't treat it, except with exercises for her muscles a bit later on, and the willow bark tea, 'nature's aspirin'. She did not want to excite her with any further examination at the moment. There would be plenty of time for that later. While bloodletting was the normal course of treatment for any and all diseases, Carmel refused to employ such means.

She asked Marcy if she could afford a nurse to watch her for a few days, and she responded that she could. Carmel told her she would arrange one to be sent to the house the following morning, if that was suitable. Marcy agreed and thanked her for everything.

She told them she would stay for an hour or so longer. If there was no further change, they could believe that she was stable for the time being.

Jake asked Marcy if she needed anything, but she said she was fine. He could see that she was upset, but that she was handling it as well as could be expected. He took her hand and patted it and told her he would be glad to get her some tea if she wanted some. She apologized and rose immediately to make a fresh pot for them all.

Jake turned to Carmel and asked her how she was doing. She assured him that after seeing the things she had seen in the hospitals in New York, there probably wasn't much that she could see that would really upset her.

He just wasn't used to seeing Southern women exposed to such things without the strong support of a man. But then again, hadn't they seen plenty, both during and after the war, when their men had come home maimed and crippled? Hadn't some women even bravely served in the make shift hospitals?

He personally had seen it all when he had sometimes helped the doc in the hospitals when he was able. He supposed he had formed those images of the helpless Southern woman before the war. Once the war was over, he somehow expected the genteel life to continue as though nothing had happened. He knew he still thought of them as genteel and needing protection. He understood his concern for Marcy, but was mildly surprised to find that he had felt the need to also protect Carmel Borelli.

He told her that he had seen her with Miss Grace and that he was very impressed with her bedside manner. "I would trust your knowledge and skill with any infirmity," he told her. She knew that was the best compliment she could have been paid, and knew he had meant it.

He didn't know how appealing he was, giving her the compliment about her skills that she had craved from men in the medical profession, without ever getting any. No, they were selfish with their praise. It only went from one to the other of them.

When Marcy returned with their tea, Jake was glad to have something to do with his hands. His gaze wandered to each of these beautiful women and realized for the first time that he was attracted to them both! Lord above, he was afraid he wouldn't ever have anyone to love after Emma, and now he could see himself in love with either of these women!

Surely, a normal man can't be having these kinds of thoughts. Certainly, a godly man wouldn't be having them. What is wrong with me anyway?

He had always been a simple, uncomplicated man. What you see is what you get. How could such a thing be possible? He had steered clear of women up until Emma. What's more, he had always been in control of his emotions. For the life of him, he couldn't understand such a predicament in which he now found himself!

Carmel, with her long black lashes over green eyes and having the classic and timeless beauty of the European woman was very appealing. She was also a qualified, professional physician and a sweet, thoughtful, caring woman at heart.

Marcy, the height of femininity, yet a profession woman, with her blond hair with the curly wisps escaping and framing her lovely face was also very appealing. She was both loving and caring to everyone.

This was definitely not what he had bargained for. Both were believers, both desirable, both adorable, and both available. He lowered his eyes to his cup and asked again if there were anything he would be able to do to help either of them.

"You can see me home in a few minutes. I think it's still raining," Doctor Borelli said to him.

"Of course. I intended to," he quickly assured her.

He couldn't tell if the women knew of his predicament or not. He assumed the perceptive Carmel probably did, as she always seemed to be two steps ahead of him. When he looked at Marcy again, she was giving Carmel a look that he couldn't read. It was a cross between wonder and suspicion.

Oh, could it get any worse? he thought to himself. He just didn't know then that it could— and would— get a whole lot worse!

Presently Carmel got up and left them to check on her patient. Marcy looked at Jake with gratitude in her eyes, and thanked him for coming. He told her that if she needed anything else that night, she could send word by her neighbor. Under the grave circumstances, he would understand, and would come and get him.

She assured him that she would be fine, but acknowledged his concern. She gave him her hand. He squeezed it tenderly, and then said his good-byes. Carmel came back from her final check on Miss Grace, and they made their departure.

On the walk home, gratefully the downpour had stopped and the night was now pleasant enough. Carmel had said little to him after leaving the house, and with the state of his emotions, he didn't find much to say, either. He supposed it was just as well, and the less said the better. He tended to get lost in his own thoughts wherever something was on his mind, and tonight was no exception.

He didn't like this feeling of going up into the boughs and then slamming back into the depths. He loved a nice, steady, even keel. Too much to either side was vexing for him.

He was a natural problem solver, but mainly for other people. However, it seemed like all he had done for the past several months was search his own soul to better understand himself, and his own feelings. He had worked through a lot, to be sure, but he knew he had farther to go.

"Did you hear me, Jake?" she asked him. Coming to himself, he wondered when she had taken to calling him just Jake. He didn't mind, but it was uncommon to hear it from a single, young, Southern lady. But, again, she wasn't Southern, now was she?

"Pardon me, Miss Carmel. I was wool gathering I suppose. Please forgive me?" he asked. "What was it you said?"

"I said, what do you think of the price of eggs?" she said with amusement.

"The price of eggs? That is what you asked me?" he asked her in bewilderment.

"Actually I didn't, but for all the attention you were paying me, I might as well have done," she said, with a lighthearted attitude and a smile.

"Do forgive me, I was being rude. I apologize and promise never to be so obtuse in future," he said. "Now, what was it you said?" he wanted to know.

"It really was unimportant, as I was just chatting, but I don't mind the silence, really. I just couldn't help teasing you. You're so serious!" she added.

"I guess I am fairly serious at that. I have always been turned more like that, and never felt the need to be the life of the party," he assured her.

"But I am assuming that it is not your wish to be the death of one, either!" she said with a laugh that he joined in with.

Growing serious once again, he told her, "My life has taken some unexpected and drastic turns this past year. It seems to be taking longer to shake them off than I would have expected. But I love to have fun, and to see others have fun, too. So give me time to finish shaking the dust off. Then I will fill your presence with laughter," he promised.

"That's a deal, Pastor. You have a nice laugh, what little I've heard of it!" she teased.

My, but she was a daring little thing!

Chapter 8

*J*ake and Mother Mattie had gone to call on Miss Grace and found Dr. Borelli attending her patient. They all exchanged greetings and then Marcy made tea. Carmel gave instructions to the nurse, said her good-byes to Miss Grace, and went to join Marcy and Jake in the parlor while Mother Mattie visited with Miss Grace.

Immediately, Marcy began to speak, "Pastor, I need to ask your advice. I need to speak of the two men you asked me about the other day, Mr. Boyd and Mr. Davison. I know that both a pastor and a doctor can keep a watch on their conversations. I believe the mayor is in some kind of trouble with those two."

"What makes you think so, Marcy?"

"He is anxious, confused and downright fearful," she told them. "He isn't saying anything, but then he is a politician. I've seen him in times of crisis before, and yet I've never seen him quite like this. He is dealing with something entirely new to him. He is thinking long before he says nothing." She was perfectly serious, but that statement drew a smile from Jake. He couldn't help thinking that pretty much summed up most politicians.

"He won't let on like anything's wrong, but I know it is about that deal that they have been trying to seduce him into, and no mistake about it! He has purposely not allowed me to see the paperwork that exists, so I know they have reached some kind of agreement. In fact, he has actually bypassed me. He assigned it to a junior clerk at the office," she related, shaking her head in disgust.

"I'll go further and say that I know he is ashamed, because he can't look me in the eye. He is spending more and more time away from his duties. I get the impression that he might even be trying to keep me out of it on purpose so that they can't hold anything over me like they obviously are doing to him," she finished.

"Marcy, maybe I'm not the best person to help you with this," Jake told her as soon as he got the gist of what she needed. "I am out of my league here, but I know an honest and trustworthy judge. Maybe you've met him in church, but he is a believer and a powerful ally. May I take you to see him about this?

"Well, if you think that would be best. If you trust him, then I do," she said, without any doubt showing on her features.

"Very well, I will call on him this morning - on second thought, I will have him come here so you don't have to leave your grandmother," Jake told her. They left it at that for the time being.

Jake looked at Carmel and realized that he wanted to know what was going on in her life. He asked her how she was doing. She told him, "Regular. I have had three patients from the church. Fortunately, they were simple cases to treat, so there should be some good reports being circulating soon. Nothing much else is going on. But at least nothing bad, either!" she exclaimed, always in her vivacious way. At times like that, she was so appealing that he had no idea what to make of her.

Mother had left Miss Grace to rest and had entered the parlor moments before. She spoke up and said, "Son, if you've a mind to,

I could stay here while you take Marcy to get whatever's bothering her off her mind right now."

He looked at Carmel again, and then he suggested to Marcy that they go right then. She agreed and they set out to see the judge, leaving Carmel and Mother Mattie watching after them.

The judge was just coming out of court and motioned Jake and Marcy into his chambers. He said he was sorry to hear about her grandmother, and hoped that she was recovering well. She thanked him and got right down to her story, knowing that the judge was a busy man.

After she had laid it out for him, he said, "Do you know exactly what this is all about?"

"No, Judge, not exactly," she admitted. "It could be any number of things. But I do know they are rogues. There is no doubt about that."

The judge steepled his finger tips and thought a moment. Then he said, "I'm going to send some friends of mine over to the mayor's office looking for work," the judge informed her. "I will need you to tell the mayor that with your grandmother ill, you will need some time off your job to care for her. The men you will introduce to the mayor will be qualified men looking for the same kind of work as you do. Never fear, the men I send will be qualified in short hand, etc." he assured her.

He went on, "Tell him you would like to train them for a couple of days, and then they can take over for you. Tell him that both of them can only give him part time work, but between the two of them, they would still keep his needs taken care of.

As an added incentive, the figure that they will quote they both would need for the job will be less than he is paying you alone. He will have no choice but to accept. That way it won't seem unusual if their time overlaps some at each of their shift changes or at dinner time, so one can search while the other one watches," he explained.

"The boys I have in mind are sharp enough to pick up on the people the mayor deals with, and probably even the deals they are making. Jake, you might know them. I think you worked with some of their agents in San Francisco," he told him. He went out and sent his clerk to fetch the two men.

When they arrived, they were none other than Dan Wade and Yancey Pierce, the same detectives that the judge had sent out West to get the goods on Morgan. They had been part of the agents that caught him in the final act when he had tried to kidnap Emma.

"Dan! Yancey! Good to see you both again!" he said rising to shake their hands.

"Good to see you, too, Preacher," Wade responded, slapping him on the shoulder, while Pierce nodded his assent. "Guess we got us some more bad guys to work on, eh?"

"Yeah, Wade, that's about the gist of it."

The judge laid out the plan, and it suited the agents. They would appear in the mayor's office first thing in the morning. All of them were excited, as the game was afoot!

Chapter 9

*I*t was a perfect morning, with the sun being mild and the sky a beautiful blue. Jake was in route to Summers Bluff Plantation. He was a happy man that morning. He was taking Marcy and Timmy for their first lessons in horseback riding, and they were all excited about being together that day.

The first one he saw there was Big Joe, the stable master. The man stood near seven foot in his stocking feet and Jake couldn't believe his eyes.

"Big Joe!" he exclaimed, shaking his hand and slapping his back.

"Howdy, Preacher man!" Big Joe responded. "Good to see you again, son!"

Jake asked him when he had returned to the plantation. He told him that he hadn't been there too long. He said as soon as the judge had heard that Morgan was dead, he had telegraphed for Big Joe to return. He had been back there within the next week.

Jake introduced him to Marcy and Timmy. Big Joe got them fixed up with mounts, and took Timmy to the coral to show him some moves before he got started. Timmy took to it like he had been born to a saddle. He was also old enough to pay attention and not get hurt.

Marcy felt a bit awkward at the whole process, but she had taken his advice and had dressed sensibly. She wore a simple white shirtwaist and a plain navy skirt. Her sleeves were rolled up to mid-forearm and he had never seen her look more stunning. Her slender figure was well defined in her choice of outfit, seeing she had left off all but the one required petticoat.

When he placed his hands on her waist and lifted her into the saddle, he could not resist looking into those emerald eyes. They were on his face, and she was smiling, trusting him not to drop her. Her eyes were reflecting a radiant spirit within. His breath caught, and it was a good thing she was so light, as his sudden, momentary weakness was a new feeling for him.

He quickly looked away. He concentrated on getting her settled, then mounted his own steed. It was decided that they would ride on for a few minutes around the common grounds of the plantation, while Big Joe was instructing Timmy. He had decided it would be best if Timmy would ride in the coral the first time.

It was a perfect day for a ride. The sun was still rising in the sky, so the air was still fresh. Where Jake had chosen to ride had plenty of intermittent shade trees, making for a very comfortable ride. She was asking him how he had become a pastor. He told her of his father's ministry before he had assumed it as his own upon his father's passing. It seemed as though they were both orphans, and that both their fathers had been very special and influential in their lives. Now, neither of them had a father, except their heavenly One.

Marcy was easy to talk to, as she wasn't making eyes at him, or giggling like a schoolgirl every other breath.

Why did women do that around men? Did they really think men liked that?

It had done nothing for him except make him determined to run from such nonsense. He didn't have to worry about Marcy being bold, immature, or brash. Marcy was as modest as Emma.

Had he been comparing her with Carmel? He chastised himself about comparing her to anyone. Marcy certainly fit his standard. She was nothing short of a paragon for his idea of a perfect pastor's wife, just like Emma had been.

The more he knew her, the more he liked her. The more he liked her, the more he wanted to be with her. But the more he was with her, the more unsettled he had become. He supposed that was the way of romance. Miserable with it, or miserable without it, he assumed.

Wade and Pierce arrived at the mayor's office just after opening that Monday morning. Monday was always a busy time. Everything needed to start back up so they could pick up where they had left off the previous Friday noon. Everyone was in the process of that when the detectives appeared.

True to his word, the judge had sent men qualified in office skills. She tested them so she could show the results to the mayor. She took her salary figure and deducted ten percent. She then divided it in half and gave that figure to the men to ask for as their salary.

Marcy asked them some history of where they had worked and made shorthand notes while they spoke. They handed her their letters of reference, which she knew had been arranged, and should anyone check, she knew they would be verified.

The judge had told her not to fret about her pay, because she would be given the reward from any monies the detective agency found to be gained by crime. The judge would see that the salary she was losing would be forthcoming from the mayor's office when all was said and done, maybe even a nice bonus.

She then went into the mayor's office and made her appeal. In a few minutes, she opened the office door and asked them to please step inside. Their clean cut appearance, along with their decent clothing and gracious Southern manners, to say nothing of their asking salary, made them acceptable to the mayor as her temporary replacements.

She knew that within a few days, when the office cleared out for the dinner hour, it would find them deep into investigations. The thought made her cringe on several counts. She cringed at the possible detection or recognition of the agents. She was concerned greatly at what they would or would not find. She wondered just how deeply the mayor was involved. She knew that the fur would fly soon.

Wade and Pierce didn't find anything their first week. There had been many people in to see the mayor. They could always tell when they weren't legitimate callers, as the mayor would flush and fluster when they appeared, and he would be secretive afterward.

Once Wade knew their names, he had ways to check out their banking transactions, as well as the mayors. He found some interesting facts in that search. Unfortunately, they were all circumstantial, however questionable their methods.

They had time. They would keep looking. One place they would need to look was in the government contracts issued for the reconstruction. The local authorities would decide on a needed project, present it to the government in Washington, and if approved, the government would settle the debt when the work was done.

However, it was known that many variations of fraud were being perpetrated all the time through that means. Sometimes the government would be grossly overcharged. In some cases, the government official would approve projects, and then the local officials would decide to issue bonds to get the project started.

They would then promise to return the purchaser's money with a good interest when the government paid off the work.

Many times, the criminals would take the money for the bonds and run. Sometimes they would see it through, but after sufficient time for approval, the project would never be done at all and the money would disappear.

Wade and Pierce were inclined to think that the fraud they were looking for would fall under that category. What they were hunting for specifically was the fraud where the local government would also issue bonds to raise the money to get a project started, claiming it was an approved project when it hadn't been approved at all. Once they had the money from the citizens and businesses, the money and rogues would be long gone.

That kind of fraud was especially facilitated should the mayor have an inside man in the government in Washington. He would verify the project had been approved. Never in writing, mind, or if it happened to be, it would be signed by a man who was later said to never have been employed by the government.

They suspected that Boyd and Davison were preparing to sell the bonds for a fictitious government approved project. That was why they were ingratiating themselves into the church, seeing the people as buyers of the bonds. It shouldn't be long until the agents found what they were looking for, since slowly but surely, they were gathering proof they needed to prove corruption. They had recruited other agents to back up their leads by keeping some of the visitors watched, and figuring out how the pieces went together.

In turn, the judge kept Jake informed as to the happenings going on at the mayor's office. He needed to know so he could counter any attempts to sell his church members bonds without tipping the rogues off that they were onto the scam. With all the subterfuge and spying he had been involved with in San

Francisco, and now here, he was wondering if he had missed his vocation! That fleeting thought merely amused him.

It was the first of August. The blistering Savannah heat was staggering at times. It was downright uncomfortable in the church that Sunday. After the service, when the Borelli's went by to shake hands with the pastor, Jake saw over Abby's shoulder that Carmel was staring directly at him. The look she was giving him was disconcerting, to say the least.

The next time he glanced at her she was looking past him and giving something or some one a sour look. He turned and glanced to his right and saw Marcy watching him with adoring eyes. He kept talking with Abby, or rather listening to her, but his heart was doing flips.

Why did Marcy watching me seem to bother Carmel? he wondered. As he glanced back at Marcy, her eyes had left him and had locked with Carmel's. He looked back at Carmel and noted that both women had smiled at each other, just like he would have thought two women would have done, who had spent as much time together as those two had. But their eyes were anything but smiling.

What have I done to make those two—enemies? Surely, enemies had to be too strong a word. Carmel doesn't give one hoot who looks at me or who doesn't. She doesn't look at me with adoring eyes, so why should she care who does?

He was at a loss. He had seen a similar look at the church picnic, but he attributed that to Marcy's reaction to Carmel's outrageous behavior.

Had it been more than that? Women! Now see, that is just the kind of sticky situation I have tried to avoid ever since I became a pastor! he nearly moaned aloud.

"Well, can you, Pastor?" Abby was asking him.

"Uh, Miss Abigail, uh…"

"Well, if you can't come to dinner today, what about supper?" she asked.

"Let me check with Mother to see if she has invited anyone for dinner at the parsonage," he answered. He didn't know why he had hesitated, as the food was always exceptional, and the company was not bad, either. But the looks he had seen pass between those two women made him not want to be around either of them for a while.

When he had found Mother Mattie, he asked her about dinner. She informed him that she had accepted an invitation to Marcy's.

Oh, mercy me. Here we go! he thought.

He went back to the Borelli's and explained that Mother had already accepted an invitation for dinner for them both.

"Well, whoever it is, maybe they would like to come, too!" she said, all enthused at the prospect of more guests.

"I'm afraid that wouldn't work," he told her. Just then, as fate would have it, Timmy came up and asked if he could walk home with him, as his sister and Miss Mattie had just walked home together. At that question, Jake looked immediately at Carmel, who was, of all things, shaking her head in derision at him, as if to say, "Jake! Jake! What are you doing?"

Timmy was still waiting for his answer so he said, "Of course, Tim, that would be my pleasure," but was looking at Carmel while he said it.

Jake wasn't good at any aspect of deceit and this felt deceptive. He failed to see how it could be deceit, though, because he normally hadn't cared what anyone knew about him. Hadn't he always been circumspect in his dealings? Therefore, he had nothing to hide. Why anyone should care where he ate, he couldn't fathom. He certainly didn't want to hurt anyone else, but it was starting to look like he might be in danger of doing just that.

He didn't know how to fix what he didn't know for sure was even broken, but he figured that until he had committed to some one, he felt his life and times were his own. Surely, he was free to explore all avenues the Lord might present to him to find out what possibilities existed for happiness.

The looks he saw from Carmel might have been nothing, as who could ever tell what she was thinking? She might have been laughing at him, or maybe just amused at a budding romance between Marcy and himself. It might not have been personal for her at all.

So now he had to wonder why her look had upset *him* so much. Yes, it had upset him. He felt embarrassed and unhappy to think he might cause pain. Well, he couldn't do anything about it now.

They were nearing his home, when Timmy said, "Pastor Jake, are you mad at me?"

That brought him out of his reverie. "Certainly not, Tim. Why do you ask?"

"Well, you are frowning, and you haven't said a word to me all the way here," he said.

"I'm sorry, old man, I was deep in thought, I suppose. Do forgive me," he asked, and realized they had reached the house.

Dinner was sure to be a scrumptious affair, and he was glad that he had come. Marcy was obviously happy to see him, and relieved him of his hat. Mother Mattie was already visiting with Miss Grace. Marcy told Timmy to wash up, and then led Jake into the parlor.

She surprised him when she asked, "What have you been doing all week?"

"Well, I have met several times with Judge West. Things seem to be progressing as well as could be expected at the mayor's office," he responded. "Pray tell, what have you been up to?"

Miss Grace was improving, but still needed a nurse to follow Carmel's orders for muscle exercises, and to teach Marcy how to do them. Now that she was home from the office, she could oversee them for her grandmother. She was used to being extremely busy all the time and now that she was off work, she wasn't content to sit and do nothing. The sewing and mending was finished and she had done a fair share of baking. Her grandmother and Timmy were always asking for sweets and Marcy didn't disappoint.

"Just busy things," she answered. "I am not used to idle hands. I have caught up all the sewing needs, and have attended to early fall window cleaning. I've spent a lot of time with Grandmother reading to her, and singing to her, and doing her treatments. We pray together, and she rests a lot these days."

"I didn't know that you sing. Why haven't I seen you in the choir, missy?" he asked her with a laugh.

"I didn't have time after Grandmother had the stroke. I did sing a lot up North at concerts and such."

Jake saw the piano and asked her if she would please favor him with a tune. She looked at the watch she had pinned to the front of her shirtwaist, and decided she had time. She lifted the piano lid and stretched her long, slender fingers. Then she gave him a beautifully romantic rendition of a lovely old song.

Jake could scarcely breathe. Her green eyes piercing his, and those curly wisps framing her face was nearly his undoing. She was simply a vision of loveliness and womanliness sitting there. She was looking and sounding for the world like a woman from a storybook land, and not from this world at all.

When she had finished, she simply looked at him, as he looked at her. Obviously they were having the same feelings. Neither could say a word, and both startled when Timmy came bouncing in, telling them the cook said dinner was served, breaking the tender moment between them.

He moved over to her and took her arm, assisting her to stand. He took just another moment to look into those emerald eyes and had an unmistakable feeling of familiarity and comfort, as he held out his arm, asking if he could escort her to the table. She smiled and they went to the dining room, neither having any appetite at all.

As Mother Mattie and Jake walked home together, she asked him, "Son, what's troubling you?"

"What do you mean, troubling me?" Jake asked her.

"Well, dear, you didn't eat enough to warrant dirtying the plate. What's wrong with you, is what I'm asking."

"I don't know, Mother, honestly. I have a few things on my mind is all. You always know me, don't you," he commented more than questioned.

"Well, since you won't bring it up, I reckon I will. What do you feel for Marcy?" she asked him the question he was trying the most to avoid having to answering, even to himself.

Jake signed heavily and slowly responded, "I don't know. I suppose that is what is troubling me the most. I am very attracted to her, but is it love? I can't believe I would even hesitate after losing Emma for not speaking out. But the truth is, I just cannot do it yet. I'm sure I could love her, hold her in my arms and kiss her breathless. I believe I could be happily married to such a kind, beautiful, wonderful woman as Marcy. But the very fact that I am hesitating shows me not to start something with such a woman until I am sure. Why do I hesitate, Mother?" he asked her, really hoping for an answer.

She took in his statement in wonder, without comment. He was smitten with Marcy, as she had known he was, but something was scratching his spirit.

"Son, if you don't know your own heart yet, then you best do just what you are doing now. Wait. The Holy Spirit leads you true and you know His leading. He has proven time and again that you can trust Him. When He says wait, you wait. When the time is right, you will understand why it is that you are hesitating now. Lean on His understanding, because you obviously don't have any of your own right now."

She let it go at that for the moment, but determined to keep her eyes open. No telling what she would see!

Chapter 10

*S*unday dinner at the Borelli's was getting to be something of a routine. He wasn't complaining because he was comfortable now with all of the occupants of the lovely old place, including Carmel, and always enjoyed his time with them.

Jake was making table conversation with Joey and Jamie. He asked them what they liked to do for fun.

They both answered in unison, "Ride!"

He asked them if they knew how and they laughed. Joey said, "Pastor Jake! What an idea! We've been ridding all our lives, until we came here!"

He felt it best to change the subject, so he looked at Carmel and asked her, "What are some of the things you enjoy doing, Miss Carmel?"

"I love to ride, too. We all do," she told him. "And would you try to drop the Miss and just call me Carmel? After all, we are all family friends now. Of course, I learned to ride up North and was pretty good in the saddle, so I would have to say that riding is my favorite pastime. Oh, and reading. I love to read."

"What about you?" she asked, surprising him. People tended not to ask him the same things he asked them, for some reason.

"I, too, would have to say riding. My best friend had a plantation, and was a connoisseur of horseflesh. He taught me a lot of what he knew. We rode together nearly every day, as we had opportunity. He lives in San Francisco now," he told her.

"It sounds like you miss him," she said thoughtfully.

"Well, Fletcher was reported killed in action back in '64 and when I got to San Francisco a few weeks back, I learned that he was not dead. We have had a gloriously great reunion!" he told them.

He went on as everyone seemed interested in his story, "He had been in a prison camp up North around Philadelphia, but he'd escaped. He sustained a head injury during the escape and his comrades left him at a farmhouse some miles from the camp. He ended up marrying the woman who owned the farm, and now they are blissfully happy. Yes, I do miss him, to answer your question," he told her.

Jake felt odd about inviting Carmel to ride at Summers Bluff after taking Marcy there. He wondered if he could simply invite her to join Timmy and Marcy the next time he took them. He wasn't sure about that. He needed to talk with Mother about it first. She knew everything, didn't she?

Jamie piped up and asked Jake if it were true that he was giving riding lessons to Timmy Jennings. He knew his face flushed as the entire table waited for his reply.

After he had taken a drink to dislodge the bread he had just choked on, he told the boys, "Seeing as how both of his parents have passed away, and they haven't been in town long, he had expressed an interest in learning to ride. So I offered to teach him. He has done very well, too, I must say," he said.

Hurrying on, he said, "Since Miss Marcy didn't know many people in town and worked most of the time, she was looking for a way to spend more time with the lad, so I invited her to come along. Now that I see y'all ride, why not consider joining us? I'm sure you boys would make it much more fun for Timmy. That would give us adults more time to get acquainted," he finished.

The boys took up the cry and finally Carmel said, "We wouldn't want to intrude, Pastor." He could see she was back to calling him pastor. She must have used his given name before just to get his attention, since he had been in reverie at the time.

"Why, no intrusion at all!" He realized as soon as he said it that it was the truth. He would like to have them along. In fact, he was almost sure his eyes were pleading for her to say yes.

Suddenly, she laughed and said, "Why not! It would be lovely to get out of the city heat and have some riding fun!"

A date was set for the next Saturday and he already felt better thinking about all of them being at the plantation together and couldn't have told himself why. Mother Mattie said she would be glad to stay with Grace. She saw a lot more when she looked at the situation than apparently her boy did!

Judge West sent a message to Jake to come around to his office. He was right when he figured it was about the situation with the mayor. The judge told him that they were making headway down at the courthouse. The new government department that was looking into fraud contacted the detectives working for the judge. They informed them that they seem to be working the same case. Since they had already infiltrated the mayor's office, the suggestion was made that they work together.

The two men who had showed up at Jake's church had been the same two men who had brought on the investigation in the first place. They had been involved in several other frauds, especially concerning the railroads. They were known to be dangerous, and had been facing murder charges in San Francisco when they had escaped from jail.

They knew they could get them on those charges anytime, but they were trying to discover the identity of the inside man in Washington. They felt certain there was some one. They thought they were getting close to taking out the entire Savannah gang.

Saturday dawned clear and warm. The Summers Bluff outing was to take place at eight o'clock in the morning. They could get in some good riding time, and still be back in the city by dinnertime.

But when Jake was ready to leave, he had been handed a blanket and a nice dinner basket with enough food in it for all of them. Leave it to Mother to think of everything. As Jake was taking the buggy, there was plenty of room for it and everyone else.

When he got to Marcy's he cautiously advised her that he had invited the Borelli twins to join them. While Timmy was expressing his gladness over that, he slipped in the fact that their sister would be joining them as well. He had watched her face, and other than a quick blush, she said nothing, simply nodded her head in agreement while giving him a smile.

Lord above, but she was beautiful!

When they stopped at the Borelli residence, Jake got down to greet Carmel and the twins. The boys came romping out of the house and climbed in the back seat with Timmy.

Since Jake was still standing on his side of the buggy while saying his hellos to the boys, she simply went around to his side and slid into the middle position of the front seat. She was laughing and talking and seemed totally unaware of what she had done, other than to find the only empty seat in the carriage. He thought that she appeared outrageous, even when she wasn't trying to be. Jake had assumed that most women would have approached Marcy's side, allowing her to move to the center. Carmel wasn't most women.

When she had seen the picnic basket and Jake had confirmed his intentions, she sent Jamie back in to let them know not to prepare dinner for them. She chatted most of the way, breaking the initial tension. She told them how good it was to get out of the city and enjoy the sunshine and fresh air. She expressed her thanks to Jake for the opportunity. She said she could hardly wait for their ride.

Jake Jackson was a good man, but even good men make mistakes! The lovely day of riding and fellowship he had imagined certainly did not turn out that way. Well before they were to the plantation, it seemed the ladies were suddenly wishing they were anywhere except with Jake Jackson… or each other.

Since Carmel had carried most of the conversation, she suddenly didn't have anything more to say. The silence between the adults was deafening. They were polite enough to each other. Oh, brother, were they polite! If he had to take much more of their politeness he might have to take someone over his knee!

He wondered what he had done, but thought it only right to act as if he wasn't aware of any under currents. It seemed they certainly weren't intending to confront what was bothering them. *What else could possibly go wrong with what I once had thought a superb plan?*

When they arrived at the plantation, Big Joe had their mounts ready for them. Jake assisted Marcy onto her mount, and when he did so, he naturally looked into her eyes. She smiled and it was an intimate moment, however brief. When he went over to help Carmel, she had already mounted and was in the process of dismounting again. He assisted her to the ground, but she didn't look at him when she thanked him. She told them to please go on, as she was not comfortable with her saddle. Jake informed her that they would wait. She told him there was no need, but rather to please get the boys started. He finally agreed and left her there, since she was an experienced rider.

They had been gone less than ten minutes when they heard her galloping up behind them. The cheeky girl had changed her sidesaddle for a regular one! She had on a split skirt of some kind and was actually riding astride like a man! She called a hello as she neared them, but told them Big Joe had wanted her mount exercised. She had promised him she would be happy to oblige, and so did not stop.

As she rode off, the three boys took off behind her. Jake called for them to have a care, but it was like calling back the wind. He looked at Marcy, somewhat embarrassed, as if he had been responsible for her far from lady-like actions.

He thought he detected just a bit of miff. She said nothing about Carmel whatsoever, which was more poignant than if she had verbally criticized her. About that time, he was looking forward to getting this shindig over with. He didn't know what to do or say. Therefore, he ignored the situation and said nothing about the incident himself.

He proceeded to tell Marcy what Judge West had told him about the detectives linking up with the government fraud agents and that they thought the scam would soon be over. She expressed her delight to hear it, but on the other hand, realized it would possibly mean jail for the mayor, and unemployment for her. Another mayor might not want her services.

Jake assured her that as talented as she was, she would be pleaded with to stay on and help any new mayor adjust to the demands of his new office. That seemed to calm her fears about her job, but she bit her lip as though there was more bothering her than just the situation with the mayor. Jake saw it and asked her what was troubling her.

She stunned him when she simply asked him, "Jake, where do we stand?"

It was such a brave question for her to ask. She certainly had every right to know. He looked at her for a long moment.

"Marcy, dear, I just don't know," he said as tenderly as he could. "I haven't said anything to you about feelings that either of us might have, because until I knew, it wasn't fair to speak to you about it," he told her.

"Well, that answers my most important question," she told him.

"What question is that, Marcy?" he asked.

"It doesn't matter now, Pastor," she told him.

"Of course, it matters, Marcy!" he exclaimed.

She merely looked at him and said, "I think it would be best if we don't carry this on any further. Timmy is getting far too attached to you, not to mention myself. Distance is a good thing, until such a time as you do know. Are you agreeable with that?"

He could see the party of other riders a little ways ahead. He said, "Marcy, if you are more comfortable with that, then I am certainly agreeable. You are so delicate and fine. I certainly don't want to bring you any pain. Do you believe that, my dear?"

"Of course, I believe that! You know I do," and smiled at him as only she could.

The others had joined them, but they were riding too slowly. They were joyful, exuberant, and loving their experience. He looked at Carmel only to find that she was simply ravishing. She was mussed and flushed from her gallop, and wisps of her hair was windblown around her face, even though she had pulled it back at the nape of her neck.

He looked away in confusion at what the sight of her had done to his emotions. Carmel saw his look and misread it. She thought he was judging her for riding astride. She knew exactly what she was about. She had fought that battle in the North, and wasn't about to settle for a side-anything again just because she was now in the South.

Carmel and the boys rode on ahead to the barn. The boys could be heard in the distance chattering and laughing in glee. They were just finishing caring for their mounts by the time Jake and Marcy arrived. When Jake started to do the same with his own, Big Joe said not to bother. He had saved so much time in not having to exercise the other mounts that he would have plenty of time to brush down a couple of them. Especially, since they looked like they had hardly been ridden. Jake thanked him, and they proceeded over to where the boys had already started swimming.

The ladies took out the dinner and spread it on the blanket on the ground under the shade trees around the pond. The boys didn't want to stop swimming to eat. The adults were nearly finished by the time they had finally been able to drag them from the pond. They had been famished, and had caught up with the adults in no time. While the boys were enjoying themselves immensely, it was all over the adults that they were eager to return to the city.

Dinner over with, the adults were ready to head back. The boys piled into the buggy, and this time Carmel waited to see where Marcy would sit. She had surprised her by sitting on the far side from Jake where she had sat on the way out, leaving the center seat open as before.

What is her game? Carmel thought. *I know she cares about him. From the looks of it, he cares for her, too. I can't understand what he* is waiting on. *I truly thought that he would have declared himself to her weeks ago. Truthfully, I had expected to hear wedding bells long before now. I wonder why he is waiting?* she pondered the situation, as she certainly couldn't understand any of it.

Lord, it feels like I am between the devil and the deep blue sea, Jake thought. *What am I to do here? Why can't I just marry this gorgeous, blond-haired woman, and put all of us out of our misery?*

Lord, I am so miserable, Marcy thought. *Why doesn't Jake declare himself to me? I know he cares. He knows I care. Everyone seems to have thought we would get married, but we aren't even courting!*

I thought we were beginning to by riding together. For him to invite Dr. Borelli, I just don't understand. Does she care for him? Is that why he doesn't commit to me? Just show me, Lord, and please do it soon, before I get in so deep I can't get out!

Chapter 11

When they arrived back in town, they came to Marcy's house first. Timmy had jumped down as soon as the buggy had stopped, and was handing Marcy down before Jake could go around and do it. They made their thanks and farewells, and were gone inside the house.

When they arrived at the Borelli's, the twins hopped down, thanked Jake, and were off. Carmel sat in the buggy a moment longer. She turned and looked at Jake. "You are playing with fire, Jake. You could get burned, you know," she simply said.

He was astounded at her abrupt honesty. Hadn't he been telling himself that for the past hour?

"What exactly do you mean, Carmel?" he asked her, but she turned around to step down from the buggy. He hurried around and handed her down. Taking her arm, he turned her back around to face him.

"Can we finish this in the privacy of my surgery?" she asked.

When they were inside with the door closed, she said, "I think you and I both know, that you know exactly what I mean," she said definitely, but not unkindly.

Jake said, "I want to hear you say the words, so that there is no room for misunderstanding between us," he pleaded.

"You are falling in love with both of us, Jake."

At those words, his mouth went dry, and he was having trouble swallowing. She was looking at him like she really could feel his pain. Without conscious thought he took her in his arms and kissed her with everything he had inside him. She responded in kind, and the love that she had been storing up for weeks came pouring out.

When he had brought the intimacy to a close, she said, "We can't just leave it like this you know."

Jake waited for her to speak. He was completely in awe of what they had just done. The emotions he was feeling was akin to nothing he had ever felt in the past. He had no idea how to even know what all of it meant.

"Jake, I have never been in love. I know from the way mama said that you looked when you told the story of your trip to San Francisco that you were in love with Emma Summers. You might still be. Yet, you're an honorable man, and you would do all in your power not to love a married woman. You are on what they refer to as the rebound. Any woman who loves you now, is apt to get hurt. But my heart is already in. And I want to love you, Jake," she told him simply and without pretext.

He had sat down on her surgery table, while she stood in front of him. He pulled her to him and put his arms around her and just held her with her head against his chest. He didn't know what to say or do. He could not toy with any woman, but if he were perfectly honest with himself, he could not deny that he held a certain attraction for Marcy. Yet, he had a passion for this woman in his arms.

He pushed her gently from him and stood up. He took her hand and held it over his heart. "What you said was very true. I was in love with Emma. I thought I would never love again. But as hard as it is to admit this even to myself, let alone to you, I have to admit that I have a certain attraction for Marcy."

He feared she might bolt at that statement, but she didn't move or say anything. So he continued, "But on the other hand, you and I both know that I hold a passion for you. I could even call it love, without fear of contradiction. But I don't want to involve any woman until I can do justly by her and give her all my heart," he told her with all the sincerity in the world. He was watching her face, as the different emotions played across it.

"Please know, Carmel, that I have never, ever toyed with any woman's affection. I have not kissed any of the women at church, or anywhere else for that matter; not even Emma. I have never been as intimate with anyone as I have been with you in the last few minutes. I have remained celibate, and will, until I have a wedding band on some woman's hand, but what you do to me, I never knew passion like this existed," he continued on without interruption.

"I loved Emma, but it was simple and pure. Not that what I feel for you is impure, but it's different. This that I feel for you is just consuming me, and it's anything but simple. I know it is not just lust. I care about you as a person. I want to be with you all the time. I want to hold and kiss you, but I want to be fair to you most of all."

Carmel had heard enough. She was back in his arms kissing him and he could only kiss her back. But there was tenderness in the kiss, and a caring, and a joy, for all that.

When it ended, she said that she understood that he had not made a commitment to her. She told him that she was not sorry that she had declared her love for him, and neither should he be. She let him know that she had always been a single-minded woman, and didn't have time for games.

She was looking at him and a twinkle came into her eyes, a forerunner alerting him that some of her outrageous actions were forthcoming. She said that she was sorry for his predicament, and that she understood his plight perfectly. Marcy was a fine and beautiful woman. In fact, she didn't see how he could ever make up his mind between the two of them!

The woman was goading him again. Since she had deliberately tried to lighten the atmosphere, he obliged her with a squeeze, and she giggled.

"I should go, lovely lady. We both have a lot of thinking to do. I appreciate you and your loving attitude toward this messy situation. I will tell you plainly that if I make the step, and you love me, too, I will do everything in my power, which is considerable, to be faithful to you in thought, word, and deed," he assured her.

"This is no way for any man to live, let alone one dedicated to honesty and serving the Lord. I don't like messy. I like clean and above board. I have always done that in every area of my life… until now. But where you are concerned, honesty is the only way I will deal with what is between us, now and in the future," he promised her.

She looked at him with eyes that revealed her heart, and he knew in that moment that she truly loved him. She was a playful, exciting woman when she was playing, but she was a no-nonsense kind of woman about serious things. And this was as serious as it got!

Jake was awakened with the dawning of a new summer's day. He arose and looked out the window and saw the church. He took care of his morning grooming, dressed and went to the church to commune with the Father.

He was feeling a horrible mixture of excitement and dread. He poured out his frustrations to the Lord, and asked him for direction. He seemed to hear that a double minded man was unstable in all his ways.

Well, there was no denying that now was there? The Lord could get a witness from him on that point! He felt as unstable as water, and was willing to do whatever he needed to do to be rid of that feeling.

He just needed to know how to do what Emma had done with her feelings for him. She had made the decision that it was over, regardless of how she felt, and then had reinforced it by willing herself to push down any and all feelings for him. She had succeeded and so would he. His dilemma was in not knowing which of his feelings he needed to push down.

Chapter 12

*J*ake went about his day wondering how the women were—both of them. He had decided he would go and find out. He called Mother Mattie and told her to get her hat and gloves, that they were going calling.

She told him to give her a couple of minutes. She went out into her garden and cut a bunch of flowers for Grace, and wrapped them in a damp cloth and then in newspaper.

When she came out with the bouquet, Jake asked her about the flowers. "Well, we are going to visit Grace, aren't we?" she asked him. He never got over her knowing everything. "Yes, we are visiting Miss Grace," he said.

Marcy answered the bell. She was her lovely self and Jake's heart seemed to skip a beat as she greeted them and ushered them in. She took Mother Mattie's things, and Jake's hat, and asked them to please go on in and see her grandmother. Miss Grace looked a lot better to Jake than she had done for the past week. She said she felt much better, too. The three of them had chatted for a couple of minutes, when Carmel entered the doorway carrying a tea tray and invited them into the parlor for tea.

Mattie collected two cups for her and Miss Grace and continued her visit, while Marcy and Jake joined Carmel. She had set the tea tray down on a table between two chairs. Jake pulled up another chair, as Marcy poured. He hadn't seen her all week, but she was poised and delicate as she poured the tea, and every bit as desirable as he had remembered.

They chatted about Miss Grace and Carmel confirmed that she was doing much better. She was happy and cheerful, and could sit in the garden for a few minutes each day now.

Jake paid attention to them both, and to neither, really. He was feeling once bitten, and now was twice shy. He wanted to keep his relationship with both women purely platonic for a while, especially after what had happened between Carmel and him last week. Until he knew which woman he truly loved, he couldn't move forward with either of them.

He spent as much time with Carmel's family as he did with her. That way, he could still see her, yet not be alone with her. Not that Carmel minded. Jake confused her. She didn't deal well with confusion. She was one to see through subterfuge or deception and get to the bottom of things. She couldn't find the bottom with Jake.

When she was confused, she didn't know how to proceed, and she prided herself that she always knew what to do next. At least, she had until Jake had come into her life. She had always done what was honest, to her way of thinking, and had always just let the chips fall where they may, so to speak.

With Jacob Jackson, she spent too much time trying to pick up the chips and put them all back into order. It was tiresome. She was too old for foolishness. At least the foolishness of playing games with people's hearts.

She was too young to care about what didn't concern her. Apparently Jake didn't concern her, from his perspective, as nothing had changed since the intimate time they had shared last week, when he had kissed her.

She wouldn't waste her youth like some chits who waited by the front door for some young lover to come calling. It was her own fault, really. She was old enough to know better than to love a man who hadn't worked to win her heart, but she was too young to care. The heart was such a fickle thing!

As each of the three sat taking tea together, thinking their private thoughts, Mother Mattie had come into the room and stood in the doorway. She saw the emotions playing across each face and saw the glances that they had been giving each other. She knew if she kept her eyes open long enough, the Lord would show her why she had needed to. She let them know that Grace was resting now, so they all made their farewells.

As they were walking down the street, Mother suddenly said, "Jake, I've known you a long time now, and I've known you well, but you have me all in a tangle right now," she told him.

"What do you mean, Mother?" he inquired.

"Which one of them are you falling in love with?"

"Whatever do you mean by that question?" he asked her in bewilderment of how she would know what he had just recently become aware of.

"I mean, which one of them are you falling in love with, Marcy or Carmel. I can see plain as plain that they both care for you," she advised him. "What's more, you are not the same around them any more, and you certainly aren't happy. You are more solemn now than when you returned from San Francisco, for everything you went through out there."

"Mother, do you *ever* miss *anything*?" he wanted to know. He became serious once again and said, "I really can't answer your question, because I don't know myself."

"Is that right? So that's how it is, is it?" she asked him not expecting an answer. They could do that, talk about something without saying just what they meant, but the other knew anyhow.

"Yes, I have an attraction to them both, more's the pity. I know it sounds sick and wicked, but I can't pretend that it doesn't exist," he shook his head in confusion.

"Well, I sense the devil's own hand in this confusion, and mark my words, confusion is followed by every evil work. Today you can know for sure which one, if you will ask the Lord to show you and take to heart whatever He tells you. You need to listen to old Mother!" she warned.

Chapter 13

*J*ake went to see the judge. He knew things were moving quickly, but sometimes things went wrong when bringing criminals to justice. He went there just to be sure everything was still progressing well, and to stay on top of any eventualities.

Judge West assured him that all was well, and explained that the fraud agents were just about to move. It wasn't half an hour later when news hit the streets that the mayor of Savannah had just been assassinated!

The judge and Jake immediately headed over to Marcy's, which was on the way to the courthouse, to break the news to her. They were more than a little preoccupied with her safety. This whole mess could be tied to her, since she worked inside his office, and had access to the majority of his business. People who worked with criminals learned to suspect every possible scenario, especially when a trap was being laid. They knew any trap could backfire.

Marcy answered their ring and was surprised to see them both on her doorstep looking serious and worried. She ushered them in and Jake closed the door and bolted it. He asked first thing if Timmy was home. He was. That was good, Jake told her. Then he briskly walked through to the kitchen and bolted the back door, and pulled the shade. He asked her to sit down in the parlor. She immediately said, "It's the mayor, isn't it?"

"So you've already heard?" Jake asked

"I haven't heard anything, but tell me what has happened!" she implored them.

"Yes, my dear, it surely is the mayor," Judge West informed her. "We have just been informed that he has been assassinated!"

"Oh! Good heavens above!" she exclaimed. Shaking her head in disbelief, it took her a moment to respond further. Then she said, "I dreamed about him last night that he was dead because someone had shot him. Do you have any details," she asked.

"Not a one, but you are a sensible, intelligent woman. You worked closely with the mayor," Judge West told her. "Since we don't know why he was killed, we should explore every possible explanation. One of those is that someone wanted him out of the way so he couldn't talk to the government agents or the detectives. He might have been cracking under pressure. The hoodlums might have realized that and silenced him," he said.

"Now, Marcy," he continued, "you brought the agents into the office and introduced them to the mayor. If they have been suspected, they might think you are in on it, too," the judge explained. "You knew the ins and outs of all of his business dealings, except that one, but they might not know that." Marcy was nodding her head at him in understanding.

"You need to stay here until we get an agent to guard you and your family. Jake will go fetch one of them now, and find out more details of what's going on. I will stay with you until he returns. Is that understood, my dear?" he asked her.

"Yes, of course, and thank you both. She took Jake's hand and said, "I'm sorry to be so much bother," as she walked him to the door.

Jake looked at this lovely, brave woman and said from his heart, "You could never be a bother to anyone, Marcy," and he realized that he had dropped the 'Miss'. This wasn't her fault, so she couldn't be a bother.

He told them he would be back as quickly as he could. She had reached the door and opened it. Suddenly, she was roughly thrust out of the way and onto the floor, just as she heard the report of the gunshot. She looked up just as Jake was falling backwards, and was lying there in a pool of blood, a bullet wound to the chest!

Chapter 14

Marcy was in a fog of slow motion. It was like she could see what had happened, but couldn't make any sense of it. As she finally came to her senses, Judge West had been yelling something to her, but she couldn't make out the words. Then she saw Timmy running to the judge with a folded towel, which the judge held over the wound putting pressure on it.

The front door stood open and he yelled to one of the neighbors, who had come to investigate the gunshot, to run the couple of blocks to Dr. Borelli's surgery and fetch the doctor, and tell her it was a gunshot wound.

He also told them to hail a buggy on your way and tell him to get to the surgery and give the doc a ride over here. Have him wait to see if she needs to get the patient to the hospital.

The whole time he was spitting out orders, Marcy had come to the full realization of what had happened. She began praying for Jake not to die, but to live and declare God's goodness! She was holding his hand, but there was no movement to indicate he was even alive. Grace was praying at the top of her lungs, as she could see into the hallway, and saw what had happened. Timmy was crying, and asking God to spare his good friend.

Dr. Borelli alighted from the buggy and ran up the steps. When she saw who it was, she stopped dead and threw her hand to her mouth and gave a frightful moan. She immediately collected herself, and went to work on her patient straight away.

She handed Marcy her instruments and ordered her to use just enough water to cover them, and then boil them, and told her for how long. She told her to put on another large pan of water and keep it boiling.

She told the judge to send the cabby to the hospital with a list of what she needed, and to ask for Dr. Hershel. She said to tell the doctor to drop whatever he was doing, and bring those things she had named, and to be prepared to operate on a gunshot wound to the chest that was bleeding profusely.

The agents Wade and Pierce, had arrived on her heels to make sure Marcy was safe, only to find Jake shot. Pierce took down the list of things that she needed, and jumped into the waiting buggy to fetch the supplies and Dr. Hershel.

Carmel told Timmy and Wade to fetch all the oil lamps they had in the house and take them to the sideboard and light them. She wanted them to move the table as close to the sideboard as they could get it. She ordered the judge to get some of the men to fetch a wide board or a door to move Jake on, and to come inside and do the moving. She didn't dare wait to move him further than the next room because of all of the bleeding.

During all her giving out orders, she had cut away his clothing so she wouldn't have to disturb him with the removal. She had supervised the judge holding the pressure. They were ready to move him. They got him on the board, and moved it gently to the table. Timmy had the lights going, and the instruments had been boiled.

She quickly washed her hands and forearms, and then had Marcy to rinse them with water. Then she instructed her to pour carbolic acid solution over them, taking less than a minute for her ablutions. It was the most she dared do. She then swabbed Jake's chest liberally with the carbolic acid solution.

By the time Wade had arrived with the doctor and the supplies she needed, she already had Jake sedated. The judge was administering the chloroform with a half way steady hand.

Upon his arrival, Dr. Hershel went to the kitchen and washed quickly. He told Marcy to pour some of the remaining water over his hands that had boiled the instruments. Quickly finishing, he told her to pour the carbolic acid solution over his arms and hands. He also told her to boil more water and to keep it covered. Once it cooled, it would be used for washing the wound afterwards.

His hands scrubbed and ready, he approached the patient. He told one of the agents to stand by Jake's head on the other side from the judge, and to use the earpiece to listen to the patients pulse at his throat. He was to count how many beats, while the other agent watched the second hand on the clock and tell him how many beats he counted in one full minute. He was to do that every five minutes, or as told to.

Dr. Hershel had helped Carmel open the chest around the wound. She had found that the bullet had barely nicked an artery, but had done damage to several other vessels. She found the main bleeder first and clamped it off. She then had taken catgut that had been placed earlier in the boiling water with the instruments, and then sprayed with the carbolic acid solution, and made the necessary sutures.

Releasing the clamp, she mopped up the blood in the chest cavity. When she was sure that she had the bleeding stopped, she was able to find the other vessels, and did the same to them. Next, thankfully, she was able to extract the bullet.

She repaired as much of the damage done by the bullet as best she could. She removed most of the bits of gunpowder and clothing, rinsed out the cavity of the wound with the boiled water using gauze to gently cleanse it. She then mopped up the excess water with more gauze. She applied gauze soaked with carbolic acid. When she was satisfied that the bleeding was completely stopped, and the wound cleansed as best as she could get it, she closed his chest with the help of Dr. Hershel. The bandage was drawn tight and secured.

Once the surgery was over, Dr. Herschel complimented her on her skill and declared the surgery a very fine piece of work. He commented that her patient was one blessed man to have had such a trained and skilled physician so close at hand. He said that his colleagues would certainly hear of this day's work, and was pleased that she had sent for him.

She and Dr. Herschel had attended medical school together, and he was one of the few fellow students who had ever helped her during her training. She had met him again when she had applied for, and been denied, a position at the hospital upon her arrival to Savannah.

She expressed her appreciation that he had come and brought the supplies she needed. She knew that if Jake lived, she wouldn't be leaving his bedside for some time to come. Therefore, she advised Dr. Herschel of her surgery a couple of blocks north. She told him of her patients, and asked if he would consider donating some time to see to their needs, especially any emergencies.

She assured him that she had everything in equipment and medications that the hospital had, and that he would be doing a great service to the women and children of Savannah. He knew how to find her surgery.

Now came the vigil. The worst part had been done, but the immediate need would be to wait and see if her work had all been in vain, or if it had given him at least a fighting chance. When she finished, she wanted them to leave him where he was for a few hours. If anything troublesome happened and she had to go back in, God forbid, he would be in place. She had her instruments washed and re-sterilized in case of that untoward event. She kept water on a low boil, too.

She realized her terrible weakness, nay exhaustion, once the terrible trauma was over and her adrenalin had calmed down. She thought of Mother Mattie, who would be beside herself with worry. She went to the parlor to sit down and speak with her, only to find that probably as many of Jake's church members were there as could get in the room.

"Mother, come here please," Carmel took her by the arm and led her into the hall. She simply told her that Jake was alive. Mattie put her arms around her and they both wept openly.

Marcy understood now. She saw the love in Carmel's tormented eyes. After all, hadn't she seen the same love in her own every time she looked in a mirror?

Well, Lord, Jake is precious to everyone in this room. He needs life. He also needs a wife to share it with him when he recovers. He will recover. He must. Whatever You decide, I will abide with it, and love You just the same, Marcy prayed.

Jake's bleeding had thankfully stopped altogether. His tight bandages remained relatively stain free from frank-red, fresh blood. Only serum seepage was now seen, and that was to be expected.

She had Marcy brew some strong tea for everyone, and told her that if she could rest, she should do so now, in case she was needed later on. Marcy knew that was sensible and followed the doctor's orders.

Everyone had gone, except the agent friends of Jake's. They had some other federal men and detectives they had called in for backup in looking for whoever had done the deed to Jake and the mayor.

They were also very concerned for Marcy, as there was no doubt that the bullet had been meant for her, and would have killed her had Jake not reacted as he had. The assassin would know by now that he had missed his target, meaning that Marcy was still alive and could testify against them.

He would be back. They always were. Now, besides Grace and Timmy, they had Jake and the doc to worry about. They would move Miss Grace and Timmy to the Borelli household by cover of darkness, before the dawn broke in the morning. They would stay until this was over. They had their men in place watching the Borelli house now, so they would know if anyone else was watching it, too.

They didn't want anyone to follow them, or to know where they were, lest they use them as bait to get to Marcy. Marcy would stay here and help the doc. That way they could better watch over the three of them. It could be a long vigil.

Chapter 15

ake Jackson was a sick man. He had been critical since the moment he had been shot, but now by the end of the second day, Carmel realized the dreaded fever was upon him. She gave him willow bark tea at intervals and called for Marcy to bring tepid water, cloths and towels. She called Wade to help gently roll him enough to put the towels in place beneath his shoulders and hips.

She asked them to bring her ice from the icehouse. She wrapped them in cloths, and placed them in each armpit, and on his groin. Then she began her vigil to keep him bathed in the slightly warm water. She changed the water to keep it cool and changed the ice when needed. When he chilled, she covered him with more blankets.

His fever would wax and wane. She asked them to send for a nurse to assist her, as she was exhausted after two long days and nights at his bedside. She was terrified that in her exhausted state, she might miss something, or make some error in judgment that would cause Jake to suffer. She would sleep only two hours at a time. But when Jake was in the throws of the fever, she slept not at all. There was only so much she could do, but what she could do had to be repeated over and over.

She knew Jake was in the throws of delirium now, and she was afraid he would fall out of bed or hurt himself when in that state. She spared him much suffering by gently restraining his arms close to the bed so that he couldn't wake up and try to get up in a panic of pain and fever.

He would call out for Emma at times, or Marcy. He was heard to be saying, "Let me go, she's in danger! Let me go." He was trying to free himself from his fetters.

She gave him doses of morphine when he was at the worst of the pain. She was thankful he hadn't fully regained consciousness. But it wouldn't be long before he was fully awake. Then he would know real suffering.

Marcy was holding up as well as could be expected, since she was blaming herself for Jake's condition. It was she whom they had sought to kill, and yet her pastor had willingly taken the bullet. She doubted she would ever get over the guilt!

She did all she could to help Carmel and never once even thought to resent her close proximity to Jake. She looked upon her as the physician that she was, because she handled herself so professionally. One didn't question her orders, or her right to give them. They just obeyed them.

Marcy admired how a young women of twenty-three could be so well educated, self-confident, dedicated, have strong faith, and still be beautiful, charming, witty, playful, and wise, all in the same person.

In turn, Carmel wondered how anyone could be so gorgeous, self- controlled, talented, educated, kind and womanly, and have such strong faith, all in the same person. They could have been fast friends if it weren't for both of them being in love with the same man.

It seems amazing that he has not committed the love words to either of us, and now he might not ever speak them at all—no! Where did that negative trash come from? As if I didn't know! Certainly not from above! Carmel thought.

Wade and Pierce had been relieved by two more agents and were upstairs asleep. This was the third day after the shooting. They wouldn't ever be far from Jake or the ladies until Bill Boyd and Hoyt Davison were brought down.

The rogues had already escaped from a jail in San Francisco that was very tough to break out of, but they had managed. Wade thought to himself at the time of their escape that had the jail been guarded by his detective agency, they wouldn't have successfully made the jailbreak. The agency didn't loose their men. If they did, it would only be a temporary oversight.

It started at around three in the morning. Carmel had been sitting at Jake's bedside. He was quiet at the moment, but was still feverish, and Carmel was uncomfortable. She had pulled a chair up to the small fire, which had been lit to remove the damp night chill out of the air. It was storming outside, and the wind had been making a racket.

She wasn't dozing exactly, but suddenly was startled and immediately checked her patient. He was lying there with his eyes open looking at her. She hurried to his side and checked his pulse and asked him how he felt, but he couldn't answer her. He merely moaned.

She patted his arm and told him that he had been shot three days back, and now he had a fever. He only gave a little nod and was back to sleep.

She was so glad that he was finally coming to. She had kept a critical eye on his wound. It had some infection, as she hadn't been able to clean everything out of it. She had started silver washings after the carbolic acid, and it seemed to be working better than just the acid alone. Still, he had a ways to go before he was anywhere near out of the woods.

Carmel was soon deep in her own thoughts again. She was thinking about how her life had changed since arriving in Savannah. She had been prepared to show the whole world what a great doctor she was. Or at the least, she thought she would show Savannah. Her work was all that had ever been important to her. Until Jake, that is.

She never thought she would fall for a Southerner. She thought one of her colleagues from the North would be the one with whom she would wed, if at all. Now she knew that wasn't going to happen. Even if Jake Jackson wasn't her man, she had found that she liked the mannerisms of the Southern gentleman. When she was with a man, she wanted to be the center of his attention.

She wanted to feel safe and guarded…that is when she heard it. The wind blowing tree limbs around are loud, and don't care who hears it. This was a sound of stealth. It was coming from the back of the house, and she didn't have much time to act.

When all the trouble had started, she had asked her father to purchase her a handgun. Since Jake had been shot, and she had learned that their lives were most assuredly in danger, she had kept it at Jake's bedside.

She cautiously reached for the weapon and cocked it. That act sounded monumentally loud in the stillness. She didn't know whether to go see about the noise or to make enough noise to awaken the agents upstairs, then immediately wondered what Jake would have done if their places were reversed. She decided that she wouldn't look for trouble, but would stay and guard her man, as he would have done for her.

She decided to go ahead and close the door closest to the back. That would make it more difficult for anyone to reach them, as whoever was out there would have to open the door first. He couldn't do that on the sly without her seeing him. Then she would close the other door to the room closest to the stairs.

Just as she was pushing the back door up, she was accosted from behind with a hand firmly placed over her mouth. She began to struggle in earnest, but a voice whispered in her ear, "Doc, it's me, Wade!"

Carmel stopped her resistance, but as she turned around to face Wade, she fired her pistol. Her aim was deadly, striking the man in the heart. A body fell at the other entrance of the room. Wade spun around and realized that she had just saved both their lives, and probably everyone else's in the house into the bargain!

"Thanks, little lady! If this doctoring thing fizzles, you can always find a place with us!" he chuckled softly.

He hurried over to the man, but to his chagrin, it was neither Boyd nor Davison. It had to be another thug from their gang or a hired killer from Washington.

His partner was coming down the hall making enough noise to ensure he didn't get shot, but still he put his flat hand into the doorway first, indicating to stop and not to fire. He identified himself and came into the room.

"The rest of the house is clear of traffic," he announced, "and the broken glass we heard was in the back library. It's a good thing we lived up to our motto tonight!" he laughed. When on the job, someone was always awake.

Marcy was right behind Pierce. He ushered her into the room. She was very distressed at seeing a dead body in her parlor. The other two agents picked him up and carted him to the back porch.

Wade and Pierce went back to bed, satisfied the other agents were alert and on the job, leaving them to tell Marcy what had happened. They then advised her to return to bed. They all had left the room, as Jake had become restless.

Jake had been disturbed by the gunshot, so Carmel took advantage of it to check him over. She knew nothing had happened to him, but she had to convince herself with evidence to back up that knowledge. After all, she didn't know exactly how long that man had been in the room before she had shot him!

Chapter 16

*M*orning dawned in Savannah bright and beautiful, just as though nothing at all was happening to the pastor of the Savannah Chapel. Jake Jackson had been shot five days ago. That morning, he was an angry young man! He wanted his pants, and he wanted to go to the bathroom.

All good signs of recovery to be sure, but he had to behave so that his sutures would be safe, as they already had begun the process of dissolving. They would not have the integrity to withstand a lot of undue pressure from him thrashing about trying to get up. She told him she would try to get him up to the side of the bed to see how he tolerated it, but he had to calm down first.

"Jake, you have been shot in the chest. You can't be moving around like this. I can't untie your arms until you are calm and reasonable," Carmel explained to him. That must have been understood, as he quieted his thrashing.

"You have not been up since the shooting, and we have to take it slowly. You are much weaker than you think, but Wade and I will do a couple of moves first to get your limbs working and to stimulate your blood pressure to rise. She folded back the covers and draped him modestly. She showed Wade how to first gently squeeze his lower extremities and then gently bend them at the knee before lifting them.

She had done this regularly, but this was the first time he had been awake at the time. Wade did a few of those moves and then prepared to sit him up. She told Jake to take some deep breaths. It produced a cough that she provided resistance against. She could tell he was already breathing hard, but she pushed him a bit more so that he could perceive his own weakness.

She instructed Wade in what she wanted him to do with Jake's lower limbs. As she sat him up, Wade swung them around and off the side of the bed, so that they sat him up all in one smooth motion. He was swimmy headed and nauseated. She left him sitting up just a few minutes with her bracing him on one side and Wade at the ready on the other side.

She then left the room while Wade saw to his personal needs. She was glad that he was able to make water. She knew that he was in no real hurry to go to the bathroom, as he was very dehydrated due to his blood loss and high fevers, but she had been giving him constant sips of water for the past couple of days.

She returned to the room, and quickly washed his back and arms. She then took advantage of him being up so she could change his sheets, while Wade held him on the other side of the bed.

She cleaned his mouth, much to his displeasure, and soon he was back in bed, utterly exhausted, and in a lot of pain. But having been given more morphine was soon asleep.

She was sitting beside Jake's bed watching him sleep and giving thanks to God for leading her into her medical training. If she never treated another patient, she could have been content just to know that she had been in a position to contribute to saving Jake's life. Repairing the damage and caring for him during his recovery would probably be the greatest thing, in her opinion, that she would ever accomplish in her career.

They all were still in danger, but she couldn't worry about that every waking moment. She had wiped Jake's face with a cool cloth and was putting honey on his lips. She couldn't resist leaning over and tasting that honey, but when she leaned over him, he opened his eyes. She didn't know if he was alert or in his feverish fog—until he licked his lips and smiled saying, "Honey, eh?" She couldn't restrain a laughter that just rippled somewhere from deep inside her.

"What… day is it,… Doc?"

"Why, do you have someplace you need to be," she laughed again. "Actually, this is your fifth day. You have gone in and out of fever since the second day. Your wound looks as good as can be expected," and feeling his head said, "yes, your fever has broken. How do you feel?"

"Like something… hot and heavy… is on my chest," he said, trying to see what that might be.

"I have a tight bandage over your wound, but the swelling is adding to the tightness you feel. The burning is your injury… but… you have come through the worst of it, Jake," she tenderly whispered the last part, feeling close to tears.

He studied her face and could see the signs of fatigue and softly said, "Carmel… tell me…you've not…been… here four days," he managed to say. "You must be… worn to a…frazzle," he finished, and she could see that he was trying to commiserate.

"Not a bit of it," she smiled at him tenderly. "We Yankees are tougher than to be frazzled over losing a little sleep. Didn't you Rebs learn anything about us?" she teased.

Giving her a half way smirk, he closed his eyes again. Wade entered the room and pointed to him as if to ask if he were actually asleep. "He is awake, Wade," she informed him.

Jake opened his eyes again and seeing Wade, he asked him what the shooting had been. It seemed to him like it had been just a while ago.

"Oh, that little fracas we had here last night? Well, it wasn't much of anything," he assured him. "Our little woman here just bagged us a mountain lion," he told him with a laugh.

"I have ... fever again?" he asked her. "Didn't.... follow that."

"What I meant was, one of Boyd's bunch sneaked in here last night and the Doc here put him out of his misery. He would have got me for sure if her aim hadn't been true. That would have left the rest of you at his mercy, and I wouldn't have counted on him having had any of that. Boyd and Davison are still at large," he finished.

Jake had been looking at Carmel the whole time Wade had been talking. Marcy had come in and was watching Jake looking at Carmel. She noted the look of appreciation and admiration he held for her. She understood. She felt the same way about her.

Her foresight of being prepared with a handgun, her quick action, and ability to hit her intended target had most certainly saved all their lives last night. It was good to be alive, but it was very tedious to live under a threat. She had begun to realize what Emma had gone through running from Morgan.

Marcy was thankful for Todd spending so much time with her grandmother and Timmy over at Carmel's home. He had come by to check on Jake every day, too, and to see if he were needed for anything. He always stayed for tea, sometimes with both the ladies, but usually with just Marcy. He had held long conversations with her, as Carmel spent most of her days and nights in the sick room with Jake.

Todd had taken over the pastoral duties while Jake was recovering. He was doing a great job, to hear Mother Mattie tell it. Marcy had a maid for cooking and caring for the clothing, while Mother Mattie had stayed to help with the meals. It was felt the danger was worse at Marcy's at night. They didn't want anyone there that didn't absolutely need to be. Apparently the rogues didn't think Jake knew anything. Neither did they find his maid of any importance. It was only Marcy they wanted.

Chapter 17

The detectives were at their wits end turning over every rock to hunt for Boyd and Davison. They had called in every favor Judge West had coming from anyone. They had scrutinized every ward and square of Savannah. Using every police informer, rumormonger, or mole they knew, yet had not yielded the first lead as to their whereabouts.

Between the government agents from Washington, and the detectives flooding Savannah, Boyd and Davison had begun to fear they would not get out of town with their skin intact that time. Their gang had disbanded and had flown unto all directions, mostly anywhere out of town, leaving them hold up on a mean street down by the wharf.

They had laid in enough canned food and drink the first day the mayor had been murdered. Of course, they ate it cold, as they didn't dare start a fire. The old warehouse they were in hadn't been used since long before the war. Unfortunately for them, the place had rats the size of a man's forearm from elbow to wrist.

The windows were boarded up from the inside and Boyd had a couple of his trusted men see that the main entrance was heavily locked and enough old, moldy trash put in front of the door to make it look like nobody had opened it for years. They were pretty sure even the detectives wouldn't bother to look there.

Just when they were feeling pretty safe, howbeit miserable, a man came around pecking on one the boards covering a back window. They startled at the sound and were dumbfounded that somebody knew they were there. They didn't answer, but they clearly heard him say, "McGee sent me!"

Not only did the man know that someone was in the building, but he also knew who it was. Davison started to the small door that they could open and get out if need be, even though it was nearly hidden with brush on the outside. Boyd restrained him with a finger to his mouth indicating silence.

McGee was the name of their inside man in Washington. Boyd certainly wouldn't answer the summons then. They had not killed the mayor, nor had they had a hand in it. They didn't even know who had, but with many wasted hours of sitting awaiting their fate in an empty warehouse, they'd had the time to think it through.

They knew the mayor was getting antsy, but not to the point of fearing he would change his mind and want out. Not at first, anyway. As time went by, they knew there had been a new development, as they could scarcely get hold of him, and he was as agitated as a cat living in the middle of a doghouse.

At one point, they had thought he had been on the verge of revealing something of what was going on. When one of the part-time secretaries had entered the room and handed him a message, he had clammed up, but not before his aid had mentioned the word 'capitol'.

They had thought nothing of it at the time, but on reflection, perhaps the Washington man had something to do with his nervousness. Now that the mayor was dead, and someone was snooping around here, they had come to some quick deductions. It didn't take a genius to add two and two and get four.

The Washington man had probably become scared off when he had received the mayors frantic messages about the famous detectives being in town. The mayor had probably caused McGee to fear his connection to what was going on in Savannah, and he knew the mayor had to be shut up before he spilled the beans.

McGee had probably sent one of his killers to the warehouse searching them out. He had probably dressed like a bum to avoid attracting attention. No doubt, someone in his gang had notified McGee, advising him that all of them had left town. Everyone had been on the lookout for Boyd and Davison, so trying to leave town had not been an option for them. He probably told McGee where they could be found. No doubt, he had signed their death warrants by divulging that information to the very one who was behind all the trouble in Savannah presently, and theirs in particular.

When they had ascertained that the man had left, they reasoned it all out and Davison saw Boyd's point. Where that left them Davison had no idea, but it seemed a plan was forming in Boyd's corrupt and devious mind.

Chapter 18

Carmel had moved a cot downstairs to Jake's room the day she had sent for the nurse. She had been taking her two hours rest each night in his room since the fevers started. Mother had encouraged her to let others help. She told her that she would be happy to remain with Jake to allow Camel to get a full night's sleep, but after the break in she wouldn't hear of it.

Carmel was adamantly sure that she was needed at the bedside at night, convinced that she would awaken at any sudden noise if she were in the same room with Jake. Mother Mattie had been helping to look after Jake during the day to allow Carmel to sleep during that time.

Jake had been resting better. He had taken to sitting in a chair long enough for his bath and his bed change. He was in his senses enough to be embarrassed with his first bath. He had asked Carmel to please have Mother come and do it from then on. He could manage the worst of it by himself, but that was all. She had understood and agreed. He would have done it all himself, but he was still as weak as water, and didn't care if he were washed or not. Admittedly, he did feel better afterwards.

Jake had had plenty of time to think about all that had happened recently. Of greatest concern to him, he had begun to wonder what all this had meant spiritually. He knew there had to be a reason for it. He had lain in the bed asking the Lord to show him what was behind all of this suffering. Not in a questioning way, simply wanting to understand the reasoning behind it all. But when no answer came, just as he understood about Emma afterwards, he knew he would understand all of this one day, too.

He was grateful to be feeling so much better, even if the weakness persisted. His hands would shake holding a glass of water after he had been placed in the chair or after he had gone back to bed. It seemed any movement took a few minutes to recover from.

He had gained a whole new perspective of being bedridden. He had taken no solid food, just water and a few sips of beef or chicken broth for a few days now. Carmel said it was time for him to be started on soft gruel and cream soups.

His mind was ready for a man-sized steak! He had no idea when the good doctor would permit that. But he had realized that, in all probability, he couldn't have gotten more than the first bite down. He had heard nothing but rave reports about the care he had received from Carmel, so he was willing for her to make the decisions on food matters, too.

Judge West called again now that he was awake and feeling better, but Jake couldn't remember his former visits. He told Jake he was amazed at how much better he looked. Jake assured him he was grateful that the pain had lessened and that the wound was healing well. He said if he could just get his strength back, he would be as good as new. He told Jake not to rush it, as he had seen plenty of men relapse from being impatient.

The judge went on to tell him of the day he had been shot. Nobody had really done that yet. He told him how he had pushed Marcy out of the way, taking the bullet instead.

He said that people came out immediately to see about the gunfire, and how he had sent for Carmel. He told Jake how she had taken complete charge, sending for supplies, another doctor, told everyone in the house what she wanted them to do, and even had him holding and administrating the chloroform!

"It was touch and go whether or not you were going to bleed to death right there on the table, but she was precision itself," he told him. "Every move she made counted. I had a bird's eye view of the whole proceedings. She was something else! She had sent word to one of the doctors at the hospital to drop whatever he was doing and bring what she needed, and that he was going to help her operate…and he came!" the judge chuckled in remembrance of how she had taken charge.

"That was Dr. Herschel and it seems they had gone to medical school together. She knew he was here in the city. He came right over and saw it all, and he couldn't praise her enough. Jake, surely that woman was sent here to Savannah by the Lord for such a time as this!" he proclaimed. "You would be in the cemetery if not for her, my boy! Yes, sir, in the cemetery!"

Jake was sobered at the account. He remembered nothing past going to the door that day. He was glad to know that Marcy was unhurt, and that he had taken the bullet instead of her. He couldn't imagine that dear woman suffering the pain he had survived.

Just then Marcy appeared with the tea tray and sat it on the table at the foot of the bed. The judge moved his chair around closer to the table and she took her place to serve. Jake thought he could watch her movements all day. She was so graceful and elegant.

Carmel came in behind her, and pulled up a chair next to the bed. She accepted a cup for Jake and herself, handing him his. She sat down beside him and looked at him as if to ask if everything was all right.

He smiled and said, "The judge here has been recounting the events of that day, and how wonderfully well you handled everything, Carmel. I am one very blessed man to have had you so near that day. He even thinks had this happened outside the hospital doors, it wouldn't have had the same outcome as with you doing the surgery. He even said Dr. Herschel was impressed with your work."

"Hershey, yes, he came and helped me. He was at the hospital when I applied for a position there upon my arrival to your fair city, but I was denied."

"You knew him from up North?" Jake casually asked.

"Yes, we went to school together. He was one of the only men who gave me any help at all in school. At times I would cook him some of my spaghetti, which he loved, while we worked on projects.

After I saw him at the hospital here, I invited him to the house for a few suppers and he has taken me to the tearoom in Savannah a time or two before I set up my surgery," she volunteered.

Jake Jackson was stunned at that news! Here he had been thinking that she thought him to be her all in all, while she had been out with another man, even taking him into her home on several occasions!

She suddenly got up and looked at him closer and said, "Jake, what is it. Do you have pain? She felt his forehead, "You haven't a fever," and was looking for him to answer.

"What do you mean?" Jake asked.

"Well, my good man, you have gone as white as your sheet, and your breathing has increased. What is it?"

"I am suddenly feeling exhausted, but I didn't want to break up the tea," he allowed.

The judge, having finished his tea anyway, stood up and prepared to take his leave. He thanked Marcy for her kind hospitality, and Carmel for giving such good care to his friend. He shook hands with Jake and was gone. Marcy took the tray to wash up in the kitchen and Carmel simply looked at him waiting for another explanation.

"Out with it, Jackson! What's going on with you?" she bluntly asked him.

Jackson? Jackson? He had never in his life heard a woman call a man, any man, by his last name let alone her pastor! *What do they teach a woman in the North, for heaven's sake?* he wondered.

"What is that supposed to mean, my dear woman, and for your information my name is Jake, should you be interested in using it in future!" he informed her, shaking his head.

"I'm not playing games with you, Jake, and I want to know why you suddenly went white and couldn't catch your breath!"

"Hershey? Did you really call him Hershey?" he flung back at her.

On hearing that, she just looked at him a moment and then she threw her head back and laughed and laughed. All of the worry and tension was released in that one act! She laughed until she actually had tears streaming down her cheeks.

Jake didn't even smile, which made her laugh all the more. So that was it? She called a friend Hershey? Was her pastor jealous? He certainly hadn't committed anything to her, so what right did he have to be jealous. Well, on the other hand, truth be told, she was jealous of Marcy. Very jealous. Emotions seemed to have a mind of their own and did what they pleased, without rhyme or reason.

Catching her breath, she responded with, "Well, a lot of people called him that at school, as I recall. Why did you ask about Hershey?"

She certainly didn't pull her punches. She asked the direct questions no man wanted to answer, especially if he had just made a complete fool of himself, as he certainly just had.

"Well, that's not all," he said, trying to justified his irrationality. "Supper dates out on the town…you cooked for him?"

Ah, now they were getting down to it. He *was* jealous! Jealousy was good in moderation. It had angered him enough that he had lost his perspective and blurted out what he would probably regret later, if he hadn't already. Nevertheless, it showed her his heart. She didn't feel like laughing any longer. If she knew herself at all, she knew he would see that she had gone white around the mouth, and that she had difficulty catching her breath, too!

Mother Mattie had arrived and they no longer had freedom to finish the conversation. But something like that could not be left hanging in the air for long. She needed to know exactly what he had meant and this interruption would give him time to figure it out for himself before they took up the subject again later that evening. They certainly would be taking up the subject later that evening.

When all of the agents and federal men had been around town looking for Boyd and Davison, they had been taking advantage of rounding up the drunks and street dwellers, in an attempt to clean up the town. They might as well be doing something for the town, since all visible traces of the rogues had vanished.

While talking with them, the police got a report from some winos living on the streets around the dock area that they had been robbed of their clothing and other items, like that was ever going to happen. It seemed that with the detectives scouting around the city, and a roundup in progress, everyone seemed more riled up than usual.

Boyd and Davison were still at large. The police also got a tip that they were hold up in an old warehouse down by the wharf. When they raided the building, nothing could be found that indicated they had ever been there. However, a few articles of fancy clothing were found outside close to the building; two shirts and two vests with a bullet hole in them around the area of the heart and blood around the holes.

Since neither hide nor hair of the rogues had turned up, they were inclined to believe that someone had done them to death and thrown their bodies in the Savannah River, given the close proximity of where they had found the elegant clothing, sure to be theirs.

After no trace of any of the scammers had turned up, after an intense citywide search, most of the federal men and the detectives were nearly all gone, with just a few men still looking. They would be the two agents that the judge had hired, along with a handful of others. They had assumed that Boyd and Davison had either escaped early on, or that the vests and shirts they had found had belonged to them. The most logical answer was that they were dead.

Meanwhile, they were still working on finding whoever had shot Jake and the mayor. The judge reckoned they would work until it was discovered, them being the cream of the crop at the agency and all.

Meanwhile, they were still living at Marcy's, as was Carmel and Jake. All of them wondered how long they would have to continue that arrangement. Jake was somehow diminished in his own eyes, having to recover in front of two beautiful ladies. It was an absolute nightmare for Jake. He didn't like the ladies to see him bedridden in weakness, or dealing with the pain. It was working out for the best, as far as the agents were concerned, as all three of them being together made it easier for them to be watched over, but not from Jake's point of view.

There had been another attempt on Marcy's life the night before. The would-be killer had fired into the front windows of the house from horseback, but got away clean. There were no longer any lights burning at night in any of the rooms where the occupants were. They only lit them in the hallway and that showed just enough light for anything they had to do.

The front door window was covered with a blanket after dark as well. All of their meals and the clean up was done well before dark, preventing them from becoming an easy target in the light.

When the house was quiet for the night, Marcy had gone to bed. Carmel had gone quietly to Jake and had sat down beside him.

"Can we talk, Jake?" she asked him.

Jake looked at her and wondered at the wisdom. Sitting there with her in the semi-darkness, she was the most beautiful creature he had ever seen.

"Yes, Carmel, we can talk. What do you want to know?" he asked her.

"It's what I need to know, Jake. "What do you need to tell me?" she said and left it with him. "Please just say it plain."

He took a deep breath and began. " I have thought about my reaction to Dr. Herschel and I suppose I was uncomfortable knowing you were so familiar with him, as you were seeing so much of him," he told her honestly.

"Why did that bother you, Jake," she wanted to know.

"Carmel, I'm not sure we are ready to discuss this after all. Surely, you understand?"

"No, how would I understand unless you say the words?"

Thinking back, Jake asked himself, *Are those not the very words Emma used to me? You never spoke the words, Jake.*

"Very well, I will speak the words. I was jealous of him spending time with you, and to have felt jealousy, I have to have very strong feelings for you, and I do. I do have strong feelings for you. But….." not finishing, he let the words hang.

"But what. Are you saying you have feelings, but not love?" she asked him.

"You say it straight, don't you, Carmel?" he asked her.

"Is there any other way to say these things, Jake," she wanted to know.

"No, there is no other way. It's just that I am very attracted to you, but I don't know if it's love. I think sometimes it is. I know it could be love if I let it be. What I feel for you is different from what I have ever felt before. Emma was my first love and I suppose I have…," again he couldn't finish.

"Well, I think I may as well say it if you can't or won't. You have the same feelings for Marcy that you did for Emma?" she flung at him.

His first reaction was to deny it. As he thought of it, he realized that was exactly what he felt for Marcy. "Yes, my dear, I am afraid that about sums it up."

"And where does what you feel for me fit into all of this muddle?" she asked him.

"I am sorry to admit that I don't know. I think about you all the time. But when I am with Marcy, I am attracted to her, just like I was with Emma. That I cannot deny," he said and weariness of not knowing what to do about Carmel or Marcy overcame him.

"Oh, it's too much for me to ponder or discuss right now. I don't want to hurt you and I know I have," he said, but then began to think. Maybe she wasn't that hurt. "Or have I hurt you? You haven't said anything about any feelings you might have for me, or Hershey, or anyone else I might not know about. What are those feelings, Carmel?"

"Jake, I can honestly say that I deeply care for you. I believe it is love, but whether it is or not, someone with a higher power than I will have to decide that. I do enjoy my time with Hershey. I enjoy being wooed.

I will admit that sometimes when we were together, I have wished that it could have been you that I was with, but Hershey is a good man, a handsome man, and a fine doctor. I would be proud to be his wife, should it ever come to that. We have good times together. Naturally, we have so very much in common," she said.

"I believe he is falling in love with me," she watched his face while she explained what she knew of her heart's feelings. "I am very attracted to him, and since you have been so ambiguous on what you feel about us, I confess I have no confidence in us right now. Even if I knew you loved me, at this point, I don't even know if that would change Hershey and me or not. I don't want to let him love me if I am meant for another man. On the other hand, I don't want to loose him if I'm not. That is all the truth I have about this" she finished.

"If you feel like that, why do you still want to know how I feel?" Jake enquired.

"I felt we both should clear the air since there is evidence that we do care for each other. What has happened to you should prove that life is too brief for us to beat around the bush about important things like this," she opined.

Jake was dumbfounded. How he could speak so freely about such deep things, as he had just done, amazed him. That she had felt the liberty to speak of her deep emotions to him amazed him even more, especially after he told her he did not know if he loved her or not. One thing about Carmel Borelli, you would always know where you stood with her.

He now had to deal with the fact that even if he discovered his love was for her alone, she might not be in love with him. Dr. Herschel certainly had much to recommend him, and he had a history with her, having spent a lot more time alone with her than he had.

She took his pulse once again and squeezed his hand as she went to her bed. She laid down fully clothed, pulling a cover partly over her. Sleep would be a long time coming to either of them that night!

Chapter 19

*J*ake continued to improve and except for the agents wanting him to remain there, he was ready to go home. He wondered if Marcy could join the others at the Borelli's with Carmel, and he would be free to go. He brought it up to Carmel, who thought it was time, also.

Truth be told, he could have gone home a couple of days earlier, but she hadn't wanted to turn him loose yet. Since their conversation the night before, she felt the tension between them. She knew it was time. She knew Carmel's mother would welcome Marcy with open arms, especially if it allowed her daughter to go home as well. She considered it settled. They would speak with Wade tonight.

The agents were adamantly against it. They knew there were too many people there to try to protect, never mind three young boys to try to watch over. With their strong objections, the arrangements were left as was.

Todd came to see Jake and give him another update on the church. He told him that things were going well and that everyone sent their love. He also told him that a simple horse drawn car had been heard tell of over Atlanta way. Supposedly, having carriage wheels, a roof, windows, and with multiple passenger seats all ready to go.

From what he had heard tell, the car could be had inexpensively. He had an address to write and find out all the particulars if Jake approved. Jake definitely approved, and told him to go ahead and find out about it.

To Jake's surprise, Todd also told him that he had felt led to have a service there in the house for the three of them before he left. They all were thrilled that he had thought of it.

When they had taken Jake off the operating table, his bed had been put in the parlor where the piano was. So they put the chairs around the piano and Jake joined the others.

Todd opened the service in a short prayer and asked Marcy if she would please come to the piano and lead them in worship. Jake wondered how he knew that Marcy could sing and play, but apparently their time together, during their long talks while Jake was recovering, had yielded that information.

Marcy played an old hymn and they all just listened. The music was so beautiful they thought it didn't need words. Then she lifted up her voice and sang a song that she had written, *Need I Say More, Lord*. The women were weeping when she finished. Jake was moved with both her song and her voice. His mind flew to the first time he heard her sing at that very piano. She was an amazing woman, no doubt about that.

Jake listened in wonder when Todd began his sermon. *Where had that boy learned to preach?* he wondered. To his knowledge he had never done so until Jake had been shot. But the few services he had missed could not have given him the expertise that he was displaying before them now. He reminded him of someone in his delivery and style. Todd had carried the anointing to preach that night, that was certain.

When it was over, he laid his hands on each of them and prayed for their safety. He had always prayed with them before he left the house, but that prayer surely reached the throne of God. It was heartfelt and Todd believed it. So had all the others.

Jake shook hands with him and told him how much he had enjoyed and appreciated the service. When Jake looked at Marcy, he was surprised to find her looking wistfully at Todd, with tears still shimmering in her green eyes. Todd had blushed, but he was holding her gaze just the same.

Well, now. That's interesting, Jake thought. Surprisingly enough, it didn't bother him nearly as much as it should have.

After Todd left, it was time for bed and everyone had said goodnight. Jake was just dozing off and suddenly he startled completely awake. Amazingly, he saw a truth staring him in the face. Todd had reminded him of none other than a young Mark! And Marcy had reminded him of Emma! Was he in love with Marcy, or with the memory of Emma? The heart was a deep, tangled mystery—who could know it?

The next morning, Jake awakened and recollected the thought he'd had last night about Todd and Marcy reminding him of Mark and Emma. That thought had been very disturbing. The mind was deceptive. Had he been transferring his old love of Emma onto Marcy to make it somehow more acceptable to himself, so that he didn't have to give her up?

He thought he had dealt with all of that in San Francisco, but now he didn't really know. What he did know was that it was a puzzling mystery for him to solve. It appeared that could be exactly what he had been doing subconsciously.

Just then the doorbell chimed. Wade answered it, after checking the window to see who stood there. He admitted Dr. Herschel, who had come to call.

Carmel heard the bell and was coming down the hall to see who it was. When she saw Dr. Herschel, she quickened her steps and went to greet him.

"Isaiah!" she said, holding out her hands to him. He took both her hands in his, and drew her to him for a kiss on each cheek. Jake watched the exchange with a heavy heart. That they made a handsome couple, he couldn't deny.

"Jake, may I present Dr. Herschel. Isaiah, this is Jake Jackson, my pastor.

Jake had never hated that title before, but on her lips to that man, he hated it. *Not my friend, not the man I love, of course, but my pastor.*

Dr. Herschel came forward and offered his hand. It felt vaguely familiar, like when Mark offered his hand for the first time and introduced himself as Emma's fiancé. This was the same feeling as then. His mouth went dry and he couldn't swallow.

He took the man's hand and said the right words. He thanked him for his part in the surgery that had saved his life.

"Oh, nothing I did would have made much difference to you. Carmel did all the skilled work, and work it was. Sheesh! At the blood! When I first entered this home the last time, I had my doubts as to ever seeing you on the green side of the grass again. Thankfully for you, Dr. Borelli is probably the best surgeon I have ever worked with, or have had the privilege of watching operate. I think her cool head keeps a steady hand in her case," he gushed. "I am well pleased to see her patient looking so well now."

"Well, I certainly am glad that you came, since she thought she needed you anyway," Jake told him.

He looked at Carmel then and told her that he really couldn't stay, that he had just wanted to check on the patient, and on her. He said his good-byes to Jake, and Carmel took him toward the library.

Her pastor? Her patient? Jake thought just a little irritably. *Carmel had been right. Herschel was handsome and distinguished looking. He was impeccably dressed and looked very professional. And me lying here in a nightshirt with my whiskers showing a five-day growth!*

Somehow, that just did not seem equitable or evenhanded to him. *Lord, what is happening to me?* Jake thought. His self-confidence and self-esteem had been taking a beating lately. First Mark, then Todd, and now *Hershey.* God surely knew how to humble a man!

Lord, I really need some spiritual discernment as to what is happening to me. Is this painful for me because my pride has suffered or is it deeper? Do I love Carmel? How did I ever get into this mess? Jake asked the Lord… and himself. Neither one answered him.

When Dr. Herschel and Carmel came back to the front door, Wade was there to make sure the front was clear before he opened it for him to leave. He had waved at Jake as he passed his room on his way out, and Jake had responded respectfully.

Carmel came in and wanted to know what he thought of her friend. Jake forced a smile and told her what he really thought of him. He was everything she had told him about the man. She seemed pleased that he saw him in a favorable light. Jake was nothing, if not a truthful man. He would like nothing better than to get on with his life, whatever that meant, forget this tension, and find peace once again!

Chapter 20

Wade came in just then and told him that he had just picked up the oddest tip. He wanted to pass it by Jake and see if it rang any bells for him.

"What's the tip?" Jake asked him.

"Look to y'alls own house," he answered, with a confused look on his face. "What do you suppose that means?"

Jake thought about it a moment and asked, "Do you think he means your literal home? How would he know that?"

"Exactly so," he said. "He has no way of knowing where my home is, nor any of the other agents. So does he mean my office, the agency office, what?"

Jake said he didn't have any idea on that. Carmel had entered the room and had heard the question. She spoke up and said, "A house is where someone lives, not works."

"That is true, but that doesn't enlighten me any," Wade responded.

Jake said, "One thing that stands out to me is the word y'all's. Not an individual. Who could be included in y'all? All of you. You, who? All of you who are looking for the rogues? Could he mean all of you detectives, or all of you federal men, or all of you police?" Jake had answered his own question.

Carmel spoke up again and said, "A home is where one lives. What does one do to live? They eat and sleep. Put that together with what Jake just said. He said, "You agents, you federal men or you police. Where do you agents eat and sleep and bathe? At hotels, so it isn't that. The same is true for the federal men, as all of them are here from out of town," she continued to lay it out for them, understanding dawning on her as she went.

"Who does that leave?" she asked. "The police. Where do the police stay, eat, sleep, etc? Not at the police station, but their house. Now there are people who do eat and sleep there. Who does those things at a police station?"

"Prisoners!" they all said at the same time. "Look to y'all's own house. What else could that mean?" she asked Wade.

"How could looking at prisoners gain us whoever shot Jake?" Wade asked himself and the room at large. "Guess I'll round up some of our men that are still in town. We need to find out just who is in that jail!"

Wade came back to the house in record time. He was excited and asked Carmel if she had considered what he had told her the night she had shot the intruder. They both laughed. Jake had not been let in on what happened, so Wade enlightened him.

"I told her if this doctoring thing fizzled out, she could work with us. Now I know I want her to! You know Boyd and Davison? The ones we wrote off as shot and thrown in the river? Those scoundrels were in jail! Here's their story," he said.

"They admitted right enough their involvement with the bond deal, but here is where it gets interesting. They told us their lives wouldn't be worth a plug nickel if we left them in jail, now that the police knew their identities. They were simply terrified. For that reason we believed them. So we got the judge to give us custody, and took them to a safe place," shaking his head, still excited about what else he had to share.

"But the thing we have been holding out for is to learn who their inside man is in Washington enabling them to make the frauds work. His name is McGee unless that's an assumed name, but it's probably his own since he's killing people to shut them up. Boyd told us that the mayor had been getting anxious. They thought he had sent messages to Washington concerning his fears when we infiltrated this town, and even more so when the federals got here," he said.

Marcy spoke up and said that surely was the way the mayor had been acting. She also confirmed that he had sent several messages to Washington.

"They had reason to believe that since they didn't have anything to do with the mayor's death, that McGee would have been the only one with motive enough to have done the deed.

You see, when their gang lit out, those two held up in a boarded up warehouse with a lot of old, moldy trash piled in front of the door making it look like it hadn't been opened in years," he said. He told them how he had remembered seeing that very warehouse and had thought that very thing! It was another crook's trick to be stored away for future reference.

"They said that nobody knew about the warehouse, but a couple members of his gang. One of them had to have called on McGee to report that they had split up, and that the deal was off. They must have told McGee that it had been too hot for Boyd and Davison to get out of town. They must have also told him where they had left them, probably not realizing they had just done them in by giving McGee that information," he told them.

"The other night a man came around looking for them and called out that McGee had sent him. They knew then that it was a trap and that McGee was silencing everyone who knew anything about it that could talk. The others got out clean, so McGee wasn't worried about them. Besides, he would need them for other scams. Because those other two couldn't get away, he had sent a hired killer to silence them before we caught them. No doubt the same man who shot you and the mayor," he told them.

"After McGee's man had come to the warehouse, they had come up with a plan. They left the warehouse before dawn that next morning. They shot a hole in their shirts and smeared it with blood they got from killing a rat. They removed any trace of them having been there in case McGee's man came back. Then they robbed some hobos taking their clothes. Remember those guys who had been rousted in that city clean up? They said they had been robbed, and we laughed at them.

Well, Boyd and Davison were the ones who had done the thieving. Those men actually thought the safest place for them hiding from McGee would be in jail. It almost worked and would have if not for the tip. We wouldn't have understood it if it hadn't been for missy here," he said, looking at Carmel.

"Now we have our men in Washington checking out their story. If we can find McGee and break him, we will know who is after Marcy," he finished.

Todd had arrived in the middle of his story and when he heard the part about Marcy, he moved over to her side. They had passed a knowing look at each other. Jake knew exactly what that look meant!

Chapter 21

Carmel had gone home for some more supplies for caring for Jake's wound. It wouldn't be long before it was completely healed.

Marcy came in and sat beside Jake, as he sat in a chair by the window. He seemed deep in thought, but she wanted to talk with him.

"Oh, Marcy, I didn't hear you come in," he told her.

"I didn't mean to interrupt your thoughts, but I wanted to talk," she said.

"Well, as a matter of fact I was thinking of you, he told her.

"What were you thinking, Jake," she said.

"You first, my dear. What did you want to talk to me about?"

"I wanted to see if you were clear yet on how everything stands between us. I need to know rather than wonder," she told him.

Suddenly, Jake had a knowing. He had the answer to his question about how his feeling had become mixed up with Marcy in the first place.

"I want to tell you something that I believe the Lord revealed to me just yesterday as a *possibility* of an answer to your question, and just now it has come to me as a *reality*.

When I heard Todd preach, he reminded me of someone. I awoke that night with the realization that he reminded me of a young Mark Angelo, the man Emma married. I knew in that moment that you reminded me so much of Emma," watching her face for pain or sadness.

Seeing neither, he continued, "I suddenly had the knowing of sorts that I had transferred my love for Emma to you, thinking unconsciously that would have been more acceptable than to have feelings of love for a married woman. I wouldn't have had to let my love for Emma go that way. The heart is so deceptive, but the Lord has given me a clarity that I haven't had since we met," he finished.

"I understand, Jake. You see, Mother Mattie had told me quite a while ago how much I reminded her of Emma. Not so much in looks, but that I have a way about me like she does. With your hesitancy in declaring yourself to me, I wondered if the reason for that was that your main attraction for me had been that I reminded you of her. I understand what you just told me. I agree that it is most logical that you might have mixed us up in your emotions when one considers it."

They shared a smile and Marcy showed her sense of humor and good will when she said, "When you told me just then about Todd reminding you of Mark, and me reminding you of Emma, I couldn't help but think that if Todd and I were to marry, just like Mark and Emma did, it hit me that both of those preachers would be marrying women you had cared for. What are the odds of that happening?" she laughed at that thought and so did he.

"Marcy dear, you need a man who will love you completely for yourself. You are woman enough for any man. With everything that has happened in my life over the past year, you are simply too good to have my confused heart hurting yours," he finished. She nodded her agreement.

"I am leaving today, Marcy, and I think you need to go ahead and move in with Carmel, just for a few days. I think the agents will have this cleared up in just a short while anyway, and Carmel needs to go home, too," he said.

She stood up and impulsively she leaned over him and hugged him just as Carmel entered the room. Her sudden intake of breath alerted them to her presence. They looked at Carmel, and she just stood there looking at them. She had gone pale and Jake stood up and walked over to her.

"I know what that looked like, love, but its not what you think," he said. She whirled around without a word and was gone.

Well, this is a fine mess. One tells me good-bye and another doesn't even do that! I am probably right back where I started when I returned from San Francisco! He hated that she had misunderstood. *What else could go wrong,* he thought. He was soon to find out!

Marcy felt awful that Carmel had misunderstood. She was sure she could explain it all to her, as it certainly wasn't a hug of romance on her part. She hurried after her and Jake realized her intentions just as she ran and opened the door. He shouted and Wade came running. He just said, "Go!"

Wade realized that Marcy had left the house when he saw her hurrying up the street. He shouted and she stopped. He saw a movement out of the corner of his eye, and told her to drop to the ground, as he pulled his weapon and fired. At the same time, he heard the report of another gun going off. Jake had reached the sidewalk just in time to see Marcy fall, as well as another man, who fell from his position of being partially hidden behind a tree. Wade reached Marcy and only saw the blood.

Carmel heard Wade yell for someone to drop to the ground. She turned around just as she heard the shots and saw what had happened. She took off at a run. Her bag was at Marcy's, so she screamed for Wade to get her bag from the house, as she was running to Marcy. Marcy was just coming around when Carmel reached her.

Carmel saw the wound and tears sprang to her eyes. Thank God, it was slight, and only a flesh wound. She spoke tenderly to her, telling her she would be fine, and not to worry. She said that the bullet had only grazed her shoulder.

Wade reached her with her bag. She taped gauze over the wound until she could get her to the surgery to clean it properly. She and Wade got her up. She said she could walk, but Wade picked her up anyway and carried her to Carmel's surgery. A few moments later, Jake hailed a cabby to drive him to Carmel's. He was frantic with worry.

When he entered the surgery, Carmel looked up. When she saw it was Jake, she told him not to worry, that she would be fine. Jake went over to her and took her hand. They smiled at each other and he stood by her while Carmel cleansed and bandaged the wound.

Carmel was quite surprised when Todd came rushing in and Jake quietly moved aside, and gave him her hand. He took it and the look that passed between Todd and Marcy could not have been more loving. She looked up in shock at Jake expecting him to be upset by that look. He was watching her. When he saw that look on her face, he laughed and said, "I told you it was not what you thought!"

When she was finished dressing the wound, Abby had brought in some strong tea and cookies. They all needed it. They let Marcy rest on the fainting couch, while she sipped her tea. When tea was over, Todd took her home. Timmy and Miss Grace went with them, being as the threat to Marcy was sure to be over. They were just hours away from arresting McGee.

Jake looked at his cup. He then looked at Carmel. She gave him a knowing smile. He returned it and wondered if he had really held and kissed her less that a fortnight before!

Chapter 22

*J*ake was back in the pulpit. He had just finished his first sermon since he had recovered from the gunshot wound. The sermon had been full of thankfulness for him being well again, and back in their midst. His sermon was full of compassion for his sheep. He had praised Todd for taking charge of the services, and for attending to their needs during his time of trouble.

He told the church that he had a very special announcement to make, and would Todd and Marcy please join him on the podium. When they came up, he told them that Todd had found, and bought the horse-drawn car, which they had raised the money for at the picnic.

He related that Judge West had donated the horses to draw it. Come Sunday next, there would be transportation especially equipped to accommodate bringing the elderly or infirm to services. Everyone broke out in applause and rejoiced with them over the good news! Several families had the elderly and infirm who would now be able to attend worship service with them.

He heartily commended Todd for a work well done. He thanked him for his vision in starting a new arm of ministry. He told Todd that the people had praised his sermons, and also for all the time and love he had poured into the people in Jake's absence.

Jake also shared with them that the deacons had come to him asking him if he would recognize the fact that Todd had been ordained by God to be a minister. Jake had assured them all in the service that he most certainly did recognize the Lord's hand upon Todd Adams.

Turning to the couple he said, "Now with Todd's permission, the church would like to also recognize God's ordination by the laying on of hands and administering the prayer of ordination into the ministry of the Lord Jesus Christ before he starts his ministry route."

The people had stood and applauded. A hearty "Amen!" had been heard from all quarters. Todd waited for them to sit back down and then told them how honored he was to have their vote of confidence, and that he would do all in his might to live the life he believed in.

Then he said, "Yes, of course, I will accept Pastor Jake's ordination!" But Jake wasn't through. He told the people, that before they prayed for Todd, there was another matter that needed their attention first.

He stepped over to Marcy and took her hand in his and then stepped between the couple. He looked at Todd and commenced, "Todd, you are entering a very exciting time in your life. But a minister's life is never his own. We all know that, even as we stand at the door and prepare to enter through anyway.

You have to also know that you will have some of the best of times and some of the worst of times. You will know heartache and loneliness, regardless of who shares your life. You will give to your people, and then give more. But you will take, too, because your flock will give, and give some more, just like you will.

As God is my witness, I have endured many empty days and empty nights, even being in the center of God's will. You will experience those times, also.

But in your case, my friend, God has given you a means to avoid much of those times, by giving you Marcy to love and to be your wife," he said. Looking at her, he continued, "You need to be ordained along side your fiancé today, because you will be called upon in the future to pastor a church as much as he will.

You are both two of the finest people I know. Surely, the anointing and favor of the Lord rests upon you both. He has ordained you Himself. We merely recognize that ordination, and I want you both to know that I am proud to be your pastor and your friend. Do you both agree with the church?" he finished.

There was not a dry eye in the house, including Todd's, Marcy's and Jake's.

Jake put Marcy's hand in Todd's and the prayer was offered to the Lord. After the prayer, he asked them when the wedding would take place. He was surprised that it would be but a fortnight hence. The church applauded, showing their approval.

Jake was also happy to tell them that with such a growing membership that he needed an associate pastor. He had discussed it with the deacons and they all had felt that Todd was the man for the position, if he would accept it.

What Jake didn't tell them was that he had a wife to marry and that, of course, would take a bit of time to woo and court her, as Carmel Borelli enjoyed being wooed! He would see to it that he had the time to do that, with his whole heart in the center of it all.

Chapter 23

When Jake called at the Borelli house, he was surprised to find Carmel out. He had wanted to take her to the best restaurant in town. He wanted to get on with the wooing, so that he could marry her. He wanted to woo her as a husband, not just a fiancé.

Abby told him she didn't expect Carmel until late, as she was taking supper with that nice Dr. Herschel. Jake couldn't believe his ears!

What was she doing? Taking supper with that nice Dr. Herschel? What was she thinking? Those thoughts surged through Jake's mind at that moment.

Abby insisted that he come in for tea, so he obliged her. He wanted to see what else she might tell him that he didn't know, not that Carmel wouldn't have gladly told him anything he wanted to know. He knew that here was not a deceptive bone in her body. Deceptive and outrageous were two different things. She could be outrageous in a second, but she couldn't be deceptive in a lifetime. He honestly couldn't imagine why she was out to supper with Herschel!

Yes, what she was doing out with Herschel was what he needed to know. Had she not told him that Herschel was in love with her, and that she would have been proud to be his wife? So many things in common, she had said. He had to get out of there. He was feeling weak and nauseated. Enough tea. Enough talking. He had to think!

He hated to do it, but he knew he had to wait for her. He had to see them together. He had to know. Maybe she was going through what he had been. Maybe she didn't know if she loved him or Herschel. If he saw them together maybe he would be able to discern the truth.

He waited around the corner like a callow youth until he heard a buggy pull up in front of their house and stop. Ashamed, but determined, he watched Herschel hand her down and when her feet touched the sidewalk, he pulled her into an embrace and kissed her. He felt like screaming for him to stop, but instead, he turned around and headed for home.

Never in his life would he have expected to see that overt a display on the public street, even with Carmel, as outrageous as she could be. He just didn't understand it. He didn't understand her. He knew she loved him, or did she? That kiss changed a lot of things. He had only kissed her on one occasion after months of loving her, and not two weeks later, she was kissing Herschel!

The upcoming wedding of Todd and Marcy was on everyone's lips. He was asked to officiate and it was sort of like he had been through that before. Here he was soon to be officiating at the wedding of another couple. A couple that totally reminded him of Mark and Emma. Was he always to be the minister, never the groom? Not that he wanted to be Marcy's groom, of course, but still the thought had struck him. He was feeling as dejected as he had sitting on a train months ago when leaving San Francisco and Emma behind.

It was Sunday morning and it had been a week since he had seen Carmel. He couldn't bring himself to talk with her to hear her speak the words she no doubt had for him. But he knew he would have to sooner or later.

When service was over, he stood at the back to say good-bye to his people. Abby and Carmen were next in line to shake hands. Jamie and Joey were somewhere around, because he could hear their peals of laughter. Where Carmel was he had no idea, as he hadn't seen her in the service. Apparently she didn't want to talk to him, either.

Abby asked if he had plans for dinner and he told her that he had. "Pity that, as I really wanted you to come home with us. I especially wanted you to join us because Carmel and Isaiah will be there and all of you could have had such a nice visit!" He was floored, but responded that he had assumed that Carmel was not in church because maybe she was not feeling well.

"No, she's as healthy as a horse!" she said and offered no explanation as to why she wasn't in the service. He didn't ask.

After the nooning meal, Jake lay down on his bed with his hands behind his head, staring at the ceiling. He supposed he no longer had to worry about talking with Carmel, as her actions made it plenty clear that there was obviously nothing for them to talk about.

He was miserable and that was putting it mildly. Again, he had waited too long to say the words. Now she had apparently chosen Isaiah, while he was having difficulty concentrating, or studying, or even praying, truth be told.

He had been able to practice self-control since he had been in his teen years, but now that he was twenty-eight, he wasn't sure if he was coming or going. He had heard those awful stories about men being lovesick, and he thought it so much nonsense. Now he was the king of lovesick.

I don't know what to take for it either, because I'd have to see the doctor to find that out! He chided himself for his sarcasm. No, sarcasm didn't become him. He had always faced things head on, good or bad. He had never thought of himself as a coward, but apparently that was exactly what he was when he couldn't face a mere woman.

Mere? Who was he fooling? Carmel Borelli wasn't a *mere* anything. She was lightening and fire, sugar and spice, and certainly everything nice! And he missed her!

Jake was home alone and still thinking about Carmel when someone twisted the door chime. He answered it and was surprised to see Carmel standing there. He stood and looked at her for a moment and found her to be simply gorgeous! He could scarcely take his eyes off her.

"I did think you would ask me in, at least, if for nothing else than for old times' sake, seeing as I did save your life once!" she finally told him, her sassy mouth showing.

"Oh my, Carmel! Please forgive me! I was just thinking how well you looked!" he explained as he took her hand and drew her into the house.

"How have you been," he asked as casually as he could manage.

"You know, regular. Some good, some bad," she answered. "Et toi?"

"Well now, I'm just fine. If you don't count misery," he said, not really meaning to get into it.

"What are you miserable about, Jake?" she asked like she didn't know.

"Oh, well now, I would have assumed you of all people would know that. But then I stopped assuming about you just about a week or so ago!" he said with a chuckle that sounded hollow.

"How would I know, Jake, when I haven't seen you for a week?" she asked. "You have been conspicuously missing from my doorstep, you know."

"Come in and sit down," he told her.

"I don't want to sit down, Jake. I came her for serious answers to serious questions. Where have you been?" she wanted to know.

"I came by your house last Monday night, but you were out," he told her. He could tell when she figured out where she had been that night. She looked guilty, plain and simple.

"So, Carmel, maybe a better question would be where have you been?"

"Fair enough, Jake. I was out with Isaiah. Didn't Mother tell you?

"Of course, she told me. You were out to supper with that nice Dr. Herschel. Just like she told me you two were together yesterday."

"Well, obviously it bothered you that I was with him."

"If I took Marcy to supper would it bother you?"

"Yes, it would, Jake. So I take it you were angry about me going to supper with Isaiah. I'm sorry, but I would have explained had you called."

"What I saw when he brought you home needed no explanation," he insisted.

She hesitated for just a moment and then said, "Jake, you saw him kiss me, didn't you? Then it dawned on her that he had spied on her. "Did you wait for me so you could see what I was doing?"

"Yes, love. I'm ashamed to admit that I did," he was looking down at the floor, and had admitted it so quietly that she could feel the sadness in him, the earlier anger gone.

"Jake, it was a mad impulse on his part, because I had just told him good-bye. I told him about you over supper. It was not that long ago that I was told that it wasn't what it looked like, and those same words would serve me well right now."

"And yesterday?" he asked.

"Yesterday, I missed hearing you preach, because Isaiah brought a young woman in labor to my surgery. She was having a lot of difficulty and he felt that maybe I could help her. He worked with me, of course, and Mother wanted to feed him before he left. She knew he would stay until the baby was born. That's why she wanted you to come and get to know him better. She didn't know that Isaiah and I were ever anything more than colleagues," she finished.

She still stood and was looking at him. He felt like a fool. He knew he had acted like one.

"I should have confronted this like I do everything else. Head on. But my heart has never been invested like it is now. I am playing a game and I hardly know the rules. I certainly am not skilled in the sport. Forgive me?" he asked her with the saddest brown eyes she had ever seen.

Mother Mattie came in just then and found them still standing in the hall by the front door. She came in before he got his answer.

Chapter 24

There was a whirlwind of affairs going on at the church. Jake was taking a break, and was on his way to see Carmel. Todd and Marcy's wedding was in a couple of days. He wanted to see Carmel before then. He had to speak with her, as she was helping the ladies with the wedding reception, just as was everyone else in the church. All the ladies wanted it to be potluck. The women in his church could not have been put to shame on anything they prepared to serve. Everything would be delicious.

Arriving at the Borelli house, he could smell the spaghetti sauce cooking, reminding him that he hadn't eaten since breakfast. He didn't notice it until he smelled the sauce. He went to the surgery first. There, through the window of the front door, he could see Carmel at her desk with her head resting on her arms. When she heard the bell announcing a patient, she stood and seeing it was Jake, she moved forward in greeting. Jake took one look at her and quickly crossed over to where she was and put his arms around her. She responded by wrapping her arms tightly around his waist and laying her head on his chest.

"Carmel, Carmel," he murmured in her ear. "What are we doing, love?"

She pulled her head back from his chest and looked into his eyes. They were smoldering with his emotion. She fit so nicely in his arms!

"What do you mean, Jake? What are we doing right now or…"

He interrupted her by kissing her until they were both weak. He couldn't believe that his second occasion to kiss her would surpass that of the first! Finally breaking the kiss, he said, "I know exactly what we are doing right now, love" he said with a smile. "But what are we doing tomorrow, and the day after?" he asked her.

"What do you want to be doing, Jake?" she asked him.

"What we are doing right now, darlin'!" he assured her.

She wrapped her arms around his neck and leaned into the kiss. After they had held each other for some minutes, and when Jake could speak, he whispered, "Marry me, love, marry me!" he exclaimed.

She took a long moment and then said, "What has changed? Why are you sure that this is what you really want?" she asked him, watching his face carefully.

"When the Lord showed me that I did not love Marcy, but had transferred to her the feelings I'd had for Emma, I realized that was exactly what I had done. I did not love her. I admired her and thought her a wonderful, beautiful woman, who had so much to offer.

But you and I both know that there has been love between us from the very beginning. I fought it, simply because you were not like Emma and Marcy was. When the Lord showed me I was doing that, I knew I was free. But then I saw Hershel kiss you…" he didn't have to finish the words.

"Will you?" he asked her. She looked at him and said, "Will I what?" with all the innocence of a newborn babe.

"Are you teasing me, woman?"

"Ah, you did notice! My only question for you is, when?"

"Then you will marry me?" he asked her.

"Well now, that depends," she smiled. "It depends on how long you propose to make me wait around before you do right by me! If you are going to drag around like you have been doing up until now, even getting yourself shot so that you wouldn't have to marry me, I might as well let you know right now that I decline!" she said with a grin, as she watched his face.

He chuckled at that and told her, "My dear, if it were up to me, I would call Todd and we would do it right this minute!"

She looked at him and he saw that twinkle that always announced that the game was afoot. "You would?"

"Well, that was just a statement meant to show that is how anxious I am to marry you!" he exclaimed.

"Back peddling already, are we Jackson?" she asked, giving him that same look.

"Darlin', we would be in total disgrace if we did not have a church wedding so all the church could be invited! Surely, you see that, don't you," he asked.

"Of course, I do! I just wanted to watch you try to get out of it!" she laughed. "Let's go announce it to Mother and Daddy. They will be so pleased!"

"Sweetheart, would you be terribly upset if we wait on that for just a bit longer?

Well, here we go, Lord. Life with Jake Jackson was sure to always be some kind of hurry up and wait! she thought.

"Why do you want to wait this time, Jake?" she said and there was definitely an attitude of miff there.

"It's just that I would like to give the spotlight to Todd and Marcy until after their wedding. Then I would like to have the spotlight with you, love, for ours" he explained. "We could announce our engagement the first Sunday after their wedding, if that would be agreeable," he said.

She thought again of what a wonderful, caring, fair man she was in love with.

"Oh. That's different. Of course, we'll wait," she agreed. I would tell Mother alone, but I know that it would be like telling the newspaper!" she laughed.

Jake had received word that McGee had been the real name of the Washington inside man, and he had played into a trap the detectives had set for him. Of course, another would take his place the same day he left office. One could only hope that that man would be honest.

Boyd and Davison had been sent back to San Francisco to await trial for their crimes there, once it had been learned McGee was out of the way. Wade and Pierce escorted them via the transcontinental railroad. They had plans to stop over in San Francisco to see the Summers family.

Reaching San Francisco, Wade and Pierce showed up at the mansion on Stanhope Street where they were welcomed with open arms. They all had shared many memorable moments together, and had become fast friends. Emma and Mark had come over from the parsonage to be a part of their visit. When Wade told them about Jake and Carmel's wedding, they were ecstatic.

After thinking on it for just a very few minutes, they soon made plans for all of them, even Miss Maude, to attend the wedding as a surprise for Jake. After all, Mark had promised to do the same for Jake's wedding as Jake had done for theirs, and a promise was a promise!

Emma, Fletcher, Aunt Caroline and Kitty were terribly excited about their trip to Savannah. They would take the opportunity to once again wander over their beloved Summers Bluff plantation, the work of a lifetime of their great-grandparents, grandparents, and their own dear mama and papa. They would once again clap eyes on everyone who had lived with them from the day that they had been born until Emma had left. They would take that opportunity to acquaint Mark, Elizabeth and Miss Maude with the old home where they had been born and bred.

It would be wonderful to fellowship with Jake's again and to meet his wife. They would celebrate his happiness and visit with the people at the chapel, whom they had known and loved so well. They looked forward to seeing Judge and Isabelle West, Big Joe, Bessie and Jessie May. The judge had mentioned in his letter that they were all still there on the plantation.

They would look again upon Fletcher's horses. Emma would see her bedroom, her flower garden, and all the familiar things in their home. How precious, after thinking never to set eyes on them again. They would ride again, and would swim in the pond. Mother Mattie would certainly be a sight for sore eyes. Just to get one of her hugs would be like hugging her dear, sweet mama again!

Aunt Caroline would get to see the old Summers' home place where great-grandfather Summers had grown up; the same old home place that Aunt Caroline had lived after her parents had passed, up until the fire had taken Emma's parents. They all had spent many happy days and nights, including most holidays at her great-grandfather's old boyhood home. Emma and Fletcher had spent a lot of their youth there visiting with their grandfather's sister, great-aunt Arabella, and her family. They had such tender memories of the place. They would renew their happiness in the former things and visit with the family one more time!

Oh, it would truly be wonderful to again see the sights, and hear the sounds of the plantation. The singing of the hands, the laughter, the lowing of the cows at milking time, would serve to bring back the memories of that place. They would be reacquainted with all those memories that had been stored up in their hearts.

Yes, those memories would come to life again, as they looked at the banister in the great hall, which they had slid down so many times without getting caught, all the Christmas Eve's they had sung around the piano, and listened to their grandfather tell them the Christmas Story. When he had passed, her father had taken over that part. Then there were the hayrides they had so loved every fall.

Yes, they would go back home for a little while and refresh their spirits. Indeed, they would do all those things and more. The game would well be worth the candle!

It would no doubt be an amazing time in all of their lives, never to be forgotten. It would be a healing of sorts, given the state of affairs, and soul misery of the last time Emma had seen it all. It would do them all good to be in touch with their youth, and all the good times they'd had, and they would be able to share them with each other, Mark, Elizabeth, and Miss Maude.

Yes, thankfully, they would soon be heading back home to Savannah and the day they started their trip couldn't come too soon for any of them. It would be a time well spent, and the journey would be one of a lifetime!

The End of Part Three

Part Four

Sentimental Journey

Dedicated in memory of my Grandmother,
Clara McWilliams Brown,
to whom I owe so much!

Chapter 1

$\mathcal{A}$fter the hustle and bustle of the morning, and the final call for all visitors to leave the East-bound train, the congregants of the Harbor Mission had stood on the platform waving good-bye to their beloved pastors, Mark and Emma Angelos. Besides Mark and Emma, their traveling party consisted of Emma's brother, Fletcher, and his wife, Elizabeth; Aunt Caroline Summers; lifelong friend, Miss Kitty Thornton; and their good friend and landlady, Miss Maude Killian.

The Summers family was taking a spur of the moment trip back to their childhood home in Savannah, Georgia in the spring of 1872. It would be a relatively short trip, less than a week, considering the distance they would be traveling from San Francisco to Savannah.

It would probably seem like a lifetime aboard the bumpy, smelly train, even though they were traveling in the coveted luxurious sleeper cars. In their high state of expectation of what awaited them on the other end of the journey, it would no doubt make the trip seem even slower than it actually was.

They were so excited to be able to make the trip, as they knew their arrival would surprise and please Jake enormously. He would be so proud and grateful to them for going to that much trouble to be with him on his special day. Not only would they get to meet his bride and attend the festivities, but would also get to renew their old friendships, and visit Summers Bluff plantation once again.

Since Fletcher had gone away at the start of the war, it had been eleven years since he had clapped eyes on his plantation home. At the sight of all that he had left behind, and had expected to find awaiting him upon his return from the war, would no doubt thrill his very soul.

He had loved his time with his family in San Francisco, but that had not been the same as loving San Francisco. He had not been able to find a niche into which he had fit there, so he had been content to do nothing for a while, except to enjoy his wife, and get to know his family again.

He thought of all the friendships he would be able to enjoy once again in Savannah, even though it would only be for a little while. He had been more than excited to be able to see his beloved horses once more. He felt like a schoolboy at the end of the school year, and about to start the carefree days of summer.

Now that Fletcher had regained his memory, the trip would be a wonderful experience for him. While he had certainly enjoyed the sea voyage, or rather where they had made port, seeing the Western frontier first hand would be a lifelong memory. Not only for Fletcher, but for all of them, as it would be their first trip over land. They watched everything until the days began to blur into each other.

The trip was especially hard on Elizabeth. She was expecting their first child and had been experiencing morning sickness. She had been praying for strength and stamina for this long journey that was underway. Just a few more days and, thankfully, they would be in Georgia.

The tired and weary travelers reached Savannah, without incident, late in the evening of their seventh day. While their bodies were fatigued, their spirits were rejoicing to be home again. As their arrival was to be kept a secret until the wedding, their party had not arrived to a fanfare at the depot. Just as well, as they would still have a ways to go to reach the plantation.

Nevertheless, some of their best friends had been there to meet them and take them home. Judge Joseph and Isabelle West had been on hand to drive some of them home in their carriage, as was a couple of deacons from Jake's church, who would be discreet. It had been a wonderfully short, but sweet, reunion!

As they had arrived at night with hardly anyone around the depot, the judge had given strict orders to the agent and the porter not to breathe a word of the return of the Summers family. They would happily obey the judge's wishes in the matter, as they were very happy to see young Fletcher alive and well. He had gone off to war at the very start of it, and it had saddened all who had known him to receive the report of his death.

The whole town had heard how Morgan had done Miss Emma, thanks to the testimony of Judge West, and everyone had been grieved for the young miss. For them to see her well, happy, and back in Savannah would be a joyful occasion. They couldn't wait to see why they had been cautioned with silence about their return, but knew if the judge were involved, it would be a good story.

Fletcher had made arrangements with Judge West for all of his family to stay at the plantation while they were home. When the plantation had been sold, each and every one of the workers had elected to stay on. Clayton Kean, the judge's nephew, was the only occupant of the plantation house, besides the servants who had always worked and lived there, and he had elected to reside in the servant's quarters. The large home had more than enough rooms for them and a host of others besides.

Fletcher would be more than happy to help Clay with the plantation chores while he was there. He was itching to jump right back in where he had left off helping his father run the place. It was the only work he had ever known, apart from soldiering, and the brief time he had spent farming at Elizabeth's. He was probably the most excited of them all to return to Summers Bluff, however temporary the visit.

When they reached the plantation and neared the house, every worker had been on hand to line that portion of the driveway to respectfully receive the rightful heirs of Summers Bluff. It had certainly been a very tearful reunion. They could well remember when the news had come of the young master's death, how his mama and papa had grieved, to say nothing of his younger sister.

Oh, what a different reception it would have been had only Master Josiah and his misses been there to see their boy safe home. To see Miss Emma safe from that devil, Morgan, had been a huge relief, too! How they all had worried about her for the past two years, and how they rejoiced with her being home again!

Bessie and Jesse May had been wiping tears of joy from their old faces throughout the reunion. Knowing they were tired, they had quickly ushered them on into the house. Fletcher and Emma wept afresh at the loving memories that swept over them as they gazed around and saw all the lovely, familiar things that had made up their former home.

Mark and Elizabeth could scarcely recognize their mates, as they were jubilant with interacting with all of the people who had known them since they had first drawn breath. They had come back home, and it was truly cause for joy like that home had not seen since the beginning of the war.

From then until the wedding, none of them would be going to town for anything they might need. They would be sending one of the servants or asking the judge to see to it. No doubt, that would please him to be of service. The others would have been spotted before they had gained one block, and would have ruined Jake's surprise.

Fletcher had elected to stay in his old room, so Emma and Mark had taken her parent's larger rooms. Before retiring, Emma had made her way down the hall to her room. She found that nothing had changed, as it was just as she had left it that night when she had fled from Morgan.

In her exhausted state, Emma simply sat down on the side of her bed and wept again, as memories flooded over her from all the seasons of her life lived in that room. They were tears of joy mixed with bittersweet ones. She remembered all the grieving she had done there, first for the news of her brother's death, and then when the telegram had come about her dear parents' death. If only news of their deaths had turned out as wonderfully well as Fletcher's had! But she was home again, and the hour was late. She was grateful for what she had. It was enough.

Emma had arisen at dawn, as usual, and after she had made her morning toilette, couldn't resist donning one of the lovely morning gowns she found still hanging in her closet that had been left behind when she had fled. Then she had headed down to see her flowers that she had thought never to see again. Surely, some of her favorites would be in bloom.

When Fletcher had looked for her and found her about to go to the conservatory, he asked her if she would mind joining him on his way down to the stables instead. She knew how much this moment would mean to him, as he had talked of little else since they had made such hasty plans to return. She was glad that he wanted her with him, and had readily agreed.

They chatted together about the horses, like old times growing up. She laughed out loud as she watched Fletcher's face when he had gone inside the stables and had realized that a few of the very horses that he had left behind were still there in the stables, along with those that had foaled in the meantime. The ones he had cared for had been taken into the deep woods and sheltered there during the war to keep either army from conscripting them.

They had been cared for all those years and had been fattened back up after the war. They were incredibly dear to him. He had quickly gone to each of them and offered his hand and sugar cubes, as he spoke words of greeting, and was rewarded when they snorted and nodded their heads at him in recognition.

Oh, how he had missed this place! He had never had the same feelings for any other place he had ever been as he had for Summers Bluff. He and his sister had been the fourth generation to set their hand to both the work and the pleasure of the place.

After Big Joe had readied Emma's horse and Fletch had readied Rampage, they set off for a ride around the plantation. They spent a couple of hours riding and sharing memories, recalling things that had happened in better times before the war. They couldn't remember a time in recent memory when they had been happier. Finishing their ride, they reluctantly returned to the stables, where a hand cared for their mounts.

Upon entering the house, they found the rest of the family just beginning to stir, as they went to the kitchen to have coffee with Kitty. Breakfast would be a delightful time, as everyone was full of enthusiasm and excitement about being home!

That morning, as Jake was at the church, the judge had swung by and asked Mother Mattie to take a ride with him. He had asked her not to mention it to Jake. She was surprised, but knew the judge would have had his reasons. She put on her bonnet and donned her gloves, and when she had gone out to join him in the buggy, lo and behold, there sat old Granny Thornton! She had hugged and kissed the old woman, and they both had been just beside themselves with joy.

The judge didn't say anything about it, except that Granny had been aching for the plantation, so Big Joe had gone a few days ago and fetched her home to Savannah. She had stayed with the judge until that morning.

When they had arrived at the plantation, it was just ten o'clock in the morning. They entered the house by the kitchen entrance and passed through to the morning room, where they found the entire family at breakfast.

When she caught sight of Granny, Kitty's cry of delight could have been heard clean into Savannah, not to mention how Fletcher and Emma reacted! They could not believe they were seeing the dear, old soul. Seeing her in such good health and spirits brought them all great joy, as the judge had not mentioned her being back in Savannah.

Emma finally got her hug from Mother Mattie! It had indeed been just like hugging her dear, sweet mama again! All the women were wiping their eyes, and Fletch had tears glistening in his that he was not ashamed of.

"So, young Master Fletcher, ye've come home to us at last, have ye?" Granny quietly asked Fletcher. He had never thought to hear the words "Master Fletcher" again, but when he had, they had seared him to the bone. He had a knowing in that moment that he had no other aspirations or goals for his life, other than what he had always imagined he would one day be—Master Fletcher of Summers Bluff. How that fit into his life now, he had no idea.

He embraced Granny again and told her, "I've been longing to see your dear face, and hear your sweet voice once again, and now here you are! What have I done to deserve such blessings?" he asked the room at large.

"Well, like I've always told ye, son, ever' good-bye ain't gone, is it now?" They all laughed and allowed that they couldn't count the times they had heard her say that.

Mark, Elizabeth and Miss Maude could certainly see the joy that this trip had already produced in their family. Emma and Fletcher were still Emma and Fletcher, but they were a better, completely happier version of themselves in this home place setting.

Oh, could life get any better than this? Emma wondered.

Jake was just entering the surgery of Dr. Borelli. He had brought her a new shingle to review, which he intended to be hung outside the parsonage after they were married. He wanted her to take one of the larger rooms to use as her consult and surgery. They hadn't discussed it, but surely it wouldn't be a problem. Any cases she might have in the night, she would be right there to attend them.

She took it and smiled as she read, "Dr. Carmel Jackson, M.D." She was only mildly surprised that he would have thought of doing such a thing. Jake Jackson was proving himself a very thoughtful and attentive lover. She had told him that she liked to be wooed, and he certainly had been wooing her.

He took the shingle from her hand and laid it on the table by the door. He walked up behind her and put his arms around her and drew her to him. Her back was to his chest, and she leaned her head back against him as she rubbed his arms. She loved his arms. She had never felt so safe in her life as she did when he held her to him in that very manner.

True, they had known a stormy beginning to their love affair, but it had come right in the end. It was just a few days now until their wedding. They could scarcely believe it after everything they had been through. The thought had occurred to them that it was kin to sinning to be that happy!

Jake could well remember the times in the beginning when he was so unhappy with his life. He had struggled with why he couldn't commit himself and be happy with Marcy. She was so lovely, inside and out, and certainly she had cared for him. But holding this woman in his arms, he had understood. Exactly like he had understood that Emma had always belonged to Mark.

All being said and done, this woman he was holding was the absolute love of his life, of that fact he had not a doubt. She had stormed in from the North and whipped him as surely as any Yankee army had done. But he had loved the 'reconstruction' that had gone on in his life recently, after the war the two of them had been engaged in at the beginning had finally ended. She was the only woman he had ever even kissed, and was somehow glad about that. It was a day that God was on His throne, and all was well with the world!

Chapter 2

Emma had risen early, as she had always done at the plantation, and had immediately gone to the garden. Sure enough, there were her daffodils, which had just recently bloomed, the dew still fresh on the petals. It did so remind her of two years ago when she sat in that same place, looking at those same flowers, and feeling that the mornings were somehow significant that spring.

Little did she know then, that three weeks later she would be orphaned by that terrible fire, and less that two weeks after that, Summers Bluff would have been sold and left far behind. When she had heard of Jake's upcoming wedding, she had been so very happy for him. When they had made immediate plans to return to Savannah for the occasion, she couldn't describe what emotions had seized her.

Her senses had been overwhelmed.

Her childhood had been a glorious one, and much love was shared in her family. There had been nothing but peace and harmony in her life up till the time the war had commenced. Even in the trials that ensued after that, she and her parents were even closer than ever, especially after the false news of Fletcher's untimely death. Now, here they were back where it had all begun, and they were living life so tenderly again, for a short while anyway.

Thinking that her Grandfather Summers had been born there in that very house, as had every Summers child since, she thought of the baby Elizabeth was carrying. She couldn't help feeling a sadness that the baby would not be carrying on the Summers' family tradition. This child would be the first baby in four generations who would not be born at Summers Bluff. The plantation would have been a wonderful place for the child to have been born and reared, just like all the generations of Summers children before it.

She wondered when she would find herself expecting and glowed with the thought. She thought of the parsonage in San Francisco, but somehow couldn't picture her child being born there. Oh well, she wasn't expecting so there was no reason to worry about where it would be born when the time came. She would be happy anywhere Mark was, but seeing the plantation again with Fletch had rekindled a longing in her that she had thought gone forever.

Marcy and Todd, associate pastors of Jake's church, had recently been married to a hoopla that had been a very joyous affair! Carmel had been her gorgeous maid of honor and Marcy's brother, Timmy, had marched her down the isle to meet an anxious Todd in front of an admiring audience. The wedding and reception had been a beautiful one with more delicious foods and pastries than the Savannah Chapel had ever spread before. It would long be remembered for the love that the entire congregation had for the couple. They had left for their honeymoon in Charleston for a fortnight and things settled back down to a slower pace.

Now, it was Jake and Carmel's turn. They had announced their engagement a week after the wedding, and now it was just a few days away. Excitement was in the very air, and the couple was in a frenzy to get everything taken care of in time.

Jake had called on Carmel in time to ask her if they could go to the Hotel Savannah for an elegant supper, where he had made reservations in anticipation of her approval. When Jake arrived she was in the middle of suturing a patient who had sustained a nasty knife injury. She had asked Jake to stay for supper with the family, but he had told her of his plans, and she had been delighted. She finished with her patient, and went to her room to change.

When she came back down, Jake was enthralled. Her beautiful, black hair was piled on top of her head with wisps around her face, and having one long curl draping over her bosom. She wore a new, elegant gown that clung to her hourglass figure defining her cinched in wasp waist.

She had totally outdone herself and was absolutely breathtaking. Jake couldn't take his eyes off her. As she handed him her wrap and turned around so he could drape her shoulders, her fragrance was wreaking havoc with his emotions. He had to marry this woman soon! But for tonight, he satisfied himself by kissing her neck, cheeks, eyes and ears.

They arrived at the hotel, and while an attendant took the reigns to the buggy, he handed her down and they went inside. The elegant interior was bustling with patrons greeting each other, some waiting for supper, while others were arriving to be registered as guests of the hotel.

He was thankful he had been able to get reservations. He gave the maître d'hôtel his name, and was told that there would be a few minutes wait. He took them to a luxurious nook, having a screen between them and the next table, providing privacy.

They were seated very close together on a curved seat for two with red velvet, tufted upholstery. Jake slipped his arm around her shoulders and drew her to him. She looked deep into his eyes, and he said the words she loved better than any others.

When a waiter came a short while later to seat them in the dining room, Jake told him that they would rather remain there for their meal, and he was happy to oblige them. They moved just a bit apart so that they could better see each other.

It was a splendid meal, served on lovely cream-colored china with gold and red designs running through them. They were set on a tablecloth of white, having a red topper. The table had been set with crystal goblets, and a small, center candelabra. Everything was so elegant and perfect for a romantic supper. The flickering flames had caused Carmel to look more beautiful than ever. Her emerald eyes sparkled with happiness in the glow of the candlelight, in the otherwise dimly lit restaurant.

They took their time and enjoyed their food and conversation. Carmel thought him the most handsome man she had ever laid eyes on! She was proud to be his woman and to have him as her man. They both just wanted their wedding over with so they could get on with their lives together.

Fletcher, Emma and Kitty were in their element. Kitty was sassy and witty and so was Granny Thornton, to everyone's delight. Mother Mattie had come over every time Jake was busy with something, but as a rule, she never went much of anywhere. She certainly didn't want him to wonder about her leaving the house so frequently all of a sudden. Hopefully, he was so preoccupied with his upcoming wedding that he wouldn't notice. This was her Emma come home. She loved her every bit as much as she did Jake, and she just couldn't seem to stay away.

She was very impressed with Mark and Elizabeth, too, for that matter. All in all she was pleased at how Jake and Emma's life had turned out. While they weren't a couple, they were the best of friends, which meant much to her. There was usually some good in everything, and in this situation, she would have two sets of grandchildren to dote upon! She was so glad that she loved Carmel, and that Carmel had returned her love. She was so grateful that her boy would soon have a good wife.

Clayton Kean was around every day for some of the meals and a few evenings for fellowship. He had been friends with the Summers family all his life, as Judge West had raised him, and the judge and Josiah Summers had been closer than kin.

He was devastatingly handsome in the black-Irish kind of way with his black curly locks, green eyes and light complexion. He stood about five feet, ten inches in height, was well built, and had lived in America since a schoolboy. He also had the natural wit of the Irish and nearly always had a joke to tell, or a riddle for them to solve, and was both smart and funny.

He had spent a lot of time with Fletcher on the plantation growing up. Nearly every summer he had been a constant visitor there, and had learned the way of things, as he had helped out around the place. He had learned how to treat the workers, crops, and livestock by watching Josiah Summers. That is why Judge West had immediately put him in charge as soon as he had bought the plantation, and had decided to hold on to it, hoping one day Emma or an heir might want it back.

The place had flourished under Clay's care. Even though he was a single young man, he had enjoyed being there, no matter the solitude. When Fletcher realized that, he wanted to make sure that he felt welcome. He asked him why he didn't take all of his meals with the family, and why he didn't show up in the evenings. He told him that he hadn't wanted to intrude. When Fletch had insisted he readily complied, and said he would be with them that evening.

The workers had piled up brush that had needed to be burned, and that same evening had been set for the burning. Everyone had turned out for the bond fire. They all were singing and clapping when Clay arrived. He joined right in and when the song was finished he started in on one of the lovely Irish ballads in his clear tenor voice. The couples were sitting with arms around each other, and much love was to be seen all around.

Kitty was the kind of woman who had never felt lonely. She had never been in love and therefore, had not missed it. But for some reason, when Clay was singing she had felt lonely and melancholy. She was twenty-one years old, and had to admit that with everyone marrying off, she had felt somewhat left out of things. Well, she had her Granny back now, and for the most part she was happy and carefree. That would have to be enough. It always had been in the past, hadn't it?

Clay couldn't help but notice the only single woman his age on the place, not that he was just then noticing Kitty. No, he had noticed Kitty for years, ever since he had started noticing girls. But she was so feisty and independent, not to mention her beauty, he had never found an appropriate time to pursue her. When they had finished regular schooling together, he had gone up North to business school, studying accounting and business principles, as well as taking some agricultural studies. When he had returned, it had not been long before Kitty had gone off with Emma.

Now, glory be, Kitty was back, but alas, just for a short while. He couldn't see starting anything with her just to have her up and leave again before they would even have a chance for feelings of love to flourish between them. Not that he even knew if Kitty would be interested in him or not, and he would hate to ruin their friendship if it turned out that she wasn't.

But the poignant way she had looked at him when he had been singing the love ballad had given him pause. He couldn't tell what it was exactly, but she surely had looked wistful, and kind of sad. He decided that while he would guard his heart, and not expect a romance to flourish, he could at least talk with her.

"Kitty, so tell me, girl, what's it like in California?" he asked.

"Well now, the Pacific coast has a much milder clime than here on the Atlantic. I've only ever been ta San Francisco, haven't I, which is a hilly place five times as grand as Savannah. But 'tis newer than Savannah, I'm thinkin', and 'tis noisy, and rude, as things are ever bein' built up all about it. Some wards have a raw, crude look still, I'm thinkin'," she told him. He was listening intently, but his mind was on her dimples when she smiled or laughed.

"But there are fine areas filled with mansions, and gardens, and the such where the Nobs live. That's where we lived with Miss Maude afore Emma married Mark. Then she moved ta the parsonage while I stayed behind, them bein' newly weds and all," she finished with a smile and a slight blush. She then hurried to take up her narrative again, not giving him opportunity to get a word in edgeways.

"Ach, and the people! There are people there from all over the country, and even from foreign parts, tryin' ta make their fortunes in the gold and silver mines. Ever'body knows more of 'em go broke than strike it rich, and that's a fact, more's the pity. Mind, there's a lot of wealth, but it seems to cause as many problems as it fixes, that it does," she rambled on.

"There's much more violence heard tell of there, too. 'Course, with so many people livin' there together, there would be. With all the money that's bein' made, the greed is more noticeable. People are after findin' what someone else has hidden, and people bein' done ta death over it all the time! Savannah is much smaller and safer." she declared.

"With so many Yankees and foreigners there, ye don't have the manners of the genteel South, either," she continued, as he seemed to really be interested.

"So Clayton. What about ye? What have ye been up ta since last we met?" she inquired.

"Well, after bein' at school in Boston, I had just come home ta Savannah and had just got me feet under me just a short while afore ye up and lit out. Ever since then, I've been right here on the plantation as overseer, and she's in good shape right now, that she is. The livestock are healthy, the crops have been good, and there's been no trouble here a tall with anyone wantin' ta leave. We are all of us fine as frog's hair. Ya know, Kitty, it's truly great ta see all y'all again," he said.

"Me eyes can see well enough how good the place looks. Emma and Fletch are beside themselves with happiness at bein' back home now. How they will ever be able ta say good-bye again when the time comes is beyond knowin', and there's the truth, sure as I'm born!" she opined.

"Ah, you can see their joy at being home. Say, Kitty, when ye leave will Granny be after goin' with ye, or after stayin' here?" he asked her.

"Well, I'm thinkin' she won't be after makin' that long trip now that she has just come home. I'm thinkin' Granny won't budge again ever, will Granny!" she told him.

"And when it comes time for ye ta say good-bye ta her, how will ye be able ta do that again? Last time, ye didn't have much of a choice, ta my understandin', but now 'twill be a free choice," he told her as he watched the emotions play across her face.

"I won't be thinkin' that far ahead, for I'm knowin' that I'm not ready to see meself tellin' her farewell," she admitted. "Like ya said, this time 'twill be harder."

Wanting to lighten up the mood, he turned to her and said, "Kitty. Is that yer given name, then?"

"Not a bit of it. I'm Kathleen Moira Bridgette Shannon Thornton," she answered him.

"So, Kitty would be short for Kathleen, then.

"And how would ye be knowin' that? She looked at him and smiled. "I had a wee kitten when I was but three or four, and everybody called her kitty, so I changed me name to Kitty ta be like her. I wouldn't answer ta anythin' else. It stuck, now didn't it, for I'm Kitty ta this day," she laughed.

"Kathleen. 'Tis a beautiful name. For a beautiful lass!" he gushed.

"Clayton Kean, yer a bold, cheeky lad! Me thinks ye've been in kissin' distance of the blarney stone," she teased.

"There's nothin' wrong with kissin' the stone if it's helpin' a poor man loosen his tongue and say what he really means," he teased her back. They laughed and it felt good. Odd, but after that exchange, Kathleen Moira Bridgette Shannon Thornton didn't feel so left out of things—or melancholy, either, come to that.

Chapter 3

Clayton couldn't get to sleep easily that night. Thoughts of a feisty, beautiful, petite woman kept him restless and fitful. He normally slept like the dead after putting in a full day's work on the plantation, but even though Fletcher had been helping out around the place, he still had worked as hard as he normally would have done. He couldn't think what the reason was that he was having such difficulty in getting to sleep, or he told himself that anyway.

Kitty Thornton was a mess. She was wondering why she was so giddy and then melancholy all within a few minutes of each other. She was normally a happy, carefree lass without a quandary in the world, apart from worrying about Granny. But lately she had been feeling testy and couldn't understand it when she had her family about her again. Not to mention that she would soon be seeing Jake, and all her friends at church, and from school. She had so much to be thankful for and look forward to! What then was this business of feeling like some other person?

Kitty had never been one for moods. Other than an occasional flare of temper, which cooled as quickly as it had flared in the first place, this new moodiness was certainly out of character for her and she didn't like it one bit. She liked happy. She made up her mind that whatever was bothering her was an outlaw spirit. She spent time in prayer about it. She even rebuked it. She didn't feel any sweeter, but she felt some better about trying to fight it.

Fletcher and Clay were working together in the stable with the horses when Clay asked him about San Francisco.

"Well, it couldn't be more different than here. City life can't be compared with country living, because it would be like comparing paper with silk, or mules and fine horses," he explained.

"I noticed that in yer comparisons that one thin' was better'n the other. Silk is better'n paper. A fine horse is better'n a mule. Does that mean the city is better'n the country or t'other way round?" Clay asked.

"Well, I suppose that is what I said. True enough, there is no doubt about it in my mind that the country so far outweighs the city, so much so, that a comparison could never be made," Fletcher said as he gave the horse extra strokes with the brush.

"Well now, if that's the way of it, what are ye doin' in San Francisco while I'm here lookin' after yer plantation?" Clay asked in some confusion, as he watched Fletcher's face. He could see the struggle he was having with that same question.

Hearing the question put into words, when Fletch had heard *San Francisco*, it was like a knife being thrust into his ribs. When he heard the words, *your plantation*, it had pushed that knife all the way to the heart! What *was* he doing out there flitting away the days while all of his great-grandfathers, grandfather's and father's work had been here awaiting for him to take his rightful place? He didn't have a ready answer.

He had been pondering it for a couple of minutes when he finally spoke. "So many changes have happened in my life that I suppose I have just been going along with circumstances. While

Morgan was alive, coming back was out of the question. Also, I had not regained my memory until after he was caught. Since then, we have pretty much just lived a comfortable life of ease and getting reacquainted with each other," he told him.

"But ever since our return, I have realized just how discontented I have become with just living the good life. I have felt it strongly at times in San Francisco, but I pushed it away. I didn't want to upset the idyllic life we were living." he said. "But now I feel an urgency in me to get to work and do something for Summers Bluff, something to make my mark like my forbearers did before me," Fletcher explained.

He continued, while Clay thought on what he was saying. "Elizabeth being with child complicates it somewhat. I don't want to upset her by making any sudden moves, but I cannot imagine walking away from Summers Bluff again. I just don't know how I can!" he said, realizing for the first time that voicing the words he had been thinking had given them a force that he would now have to reckon with.

Emma had entered the stable in time to overhear his last statement. "Fletch?" was all she could say.

He whirled around and saw Emma standing there. He knew she had overheard him from the questioning look that she was giving him.

"Oh, Em, I really wish you hadn't heard that, dear. In fact, this is the first time I have heard those words myself! I really didn't intend for anything like this to come up, as I don't really know what I can do about it all myself," he finished, shaking his head in apparent uncertainty.

"Let's saddle up our mounts. I'll have a regular saddle this morning. No one is about and I want to enjoy myself!" She surprised him with her seeming exuberance about riding. Of course, before the war, and before she had grown up and become such a lady, they had always ridden together of a morning, she using a regular saddle.

It was just like old times, with Emma's hair hanging loose and swinging out behind her as she galloped slightly ahead of him. It had always been that way. She always had wanted to beat her older brother and prove she wasn't just a timid, sissy girl. That had been fine with him, as it allowed him to watch her and see that she was safe. He wouldn't have thought of galloping off in the lead, leaving her behind, and merely hoping that she would be safely following.

The real Emma was still in there wanting to ride and play and love life just like before! When they had reached the crest of the hill, they had reigned in, and just sat there looking below, as they had done countless times out of mind in the past. They could see the plantation spread out below them in all of its' splendor. The songs of those working in the fields below were being wafted on the wind, and had reached them, causing an ache in their hearts.

How they had missed all of this! How could they ever turn their backs and walk away again? Neither spoke the words, but the question lay heavy between them just the same. This had been meant to be a healing time for all of them, but was it sowing seeds of discontent instead?

Oh, it had been healing in a way, no doubt of that. That empty place that had been in Fletcher's heart for eleven years was being filled to overflowing. That seemed to be the problem. It had healed him so well, that the prospect of being separated from it again was akin to requiring a surgeon's scalpel to do it.

Truth be told, Emma had felt much the same as Fletcher. However, her life had been too perfect in California to risk any complications of change, especially here in Georgia, with an entire nation lying between the two places!

Indeed, much lay between them that morning as they were thinking their own thoughts while gazing at the plantation from their hill. This was the very hill that they had always ridden up years before. Fletch had laughingly called it Fletchem's Hill for both their names. There was joy at being there together, but their joy was tinged with sadness from already missing it, knowing that it would be but a short time until they would start their long journey back to San Francisco.

Mother Mattie was in the best of moods when Jake stopped and looked at her from the doorway. She was actually grinning to herself and when he spoke to her, she jumped and squealed.

"Sorry, dear heart, I didn't mean to startle you, but what is that grinning all about? It is not the first time I have seen you grinning all by yourself this week. What's got into you?" he wanted to know.

"Well now, son, I have a lot to grin about! You are finally settling down with a wonderful woman. You both love each other, that's plain for all to see. Where there is love and marriage, well, naturally, what would come next, I ask you? So why shouldn't I be grinning?" she wanted to know. "It has been entirely too long since this house heard the peal of children's laughter!" she said to him and laughed at his expression of embarrassment.

"You're putting the cart before the horse, but I know what you mean. Guess I have been doing a lot of grinning myself!" and joined in the laughter.

"She really is a terrific woman, Mother Mattie. She makes life seem other than…well, just life. She glows with happiness and I can't even think how I ever rejected her for an instant in the beginning. She was just so different from anything I had ever known in a woman. I wouldn't have her like anyone else for the world now. She is Carmel! My wife! Well, soon she will be. This Saturday. It's like a dream come true.

"Yes, son, I couldn't be more pleased in your choice of a wife," she said. "I am nearly as excited as you are to think of having her here with us all the time! She has become just like a daughter and I can't wait to see her happily wed and become Mrs. Jake Jackson!" she finished.

Jake grabbed her and swung her around the floor, humming a tune. He swung her into a waltz right there in the kitchen. When the dance was over, she was out of breath, as much from laughing as from dancing.

It was so good to see him so happy. He'd had his share of trials in his young life, but God had seen him through each and every one. She had known that he had come out just a little bit stronger and more humbled each time. Each trial had also seen him come out on the other side just a little more in tune with the pain of others around him. That was part of what had made him such a good pastor, and why the attendance at the church had more than doubled since he had taken over the pastorate.

In the year since he had returned from San Francisco, she knew he had faced some deep waters, but they had not overflowed him. Now he was in the best place she had ever seen him in his adult life. He had stood the test of time and loneliness, disappointment and grief, but his faith had held and grown. What more could be expected from tests and trials?

Chapter 4

Clayton Kean was always up before first light, and today was no exception. He liked to roam from pillar to post first thing and see how everything was doing. The stables were always a stopping place, as he knew Fletcher would either be there, or would be coming in soon. He had not bothered with coffee at the bunkhouse that morning, but had slipped into the kitchen where Bessie had given him a cup of the good stuff she always had on the back of the stove.

He had taken his coffee and headed for the stables, and as he'd figured, Fletcher was finishing the last dregs of his cup when he entered. They called their hellos and commented on what nice warm weather they were having that February. They fell to working on the horses, and did so in silence, each having their own thoughts.

Clay broke the stillness by asking him about Kitty, which surprised Fletcher somewhat. "So tell me, Fletch, what's Kitty all about then?" he asked out of the blue.

"Kitty? What do you mean, Clay?" he answered with a question of his own.

"Well, ye know. Does she have a beau in San Francisco then?" he asked, trying to sound as nonchalant as possible and failing in the attempt.

"I don't think so, but why don't you ask her. You know women, just when you think you know all about them, you end up with the surprise of your life!" laughing as he answered.

Seeing the look of thoughtfulness on Clay's face and realizing he was serious, he offered, "Seriously, I don't believe she has a love interest out there. I have never heard of it, anyway. Why do you ask?" he bluntly asked him.

"Well, ye know…," he stammered.

"No, I don't know, and won't unless you enlighten me. Are you smitten with her," he asked, his interest growing.

"Well, 'tis nothin' new, and there, I've said it. I've always thought a lot of Kitty, haven't I? But then I went up North to school right after the war, and when I got back she soon lit out with Emma. I guess I've always been interested in Kitty. She's as pretty as any girl I can remember seein'!" he finished.

"Yes, she certainly is pretty, and such a good, sweet girl into the bargain!" he allowed. "Have you spoken to her seriously," he asked.

"Just regular talk. But she seemed lonely ta me the other night at the bond fire. At least that's how I thought she looked. But I don't know anythin' about women, so I'm always surprised." he said in all seriousness.

Fletcher could see he was serious, but still couldn't keep from laughing. "Well, I suggest you do some of that Irish sweet talking you men are so famous for and get on with this! You haven't got that long to do it in, either," he advised.

"And there's another thin'. How much can you hope to start when she's got leavin' on her mind?" Clay wanted to know. "I can't very well hie off ta San Francisco, and courtin' by mail is not my idea of courtin'. I feel like I'm somewhere between a shadow and the fog, and I jest can't see my way about with that gal!" he finished.

"You will never know her heart without speaking to her. You need to talk these things out. You both have had a long and good friendship all these years, and she's not the kind of girl to throw that over, even if she's not romantically inclined." Fletcher offered him what he thought was good advice. He hoped for both their sakes that he would give heed to it. Fletcher loved her and wanted to see her happily settled. This would be as fine a choice for her as he could imagine!

Everyone at the plantation was terribly excited that the wedding was soon to take place, and it was growing by the day. They couldn't wait for the time that they could see Jake again and all the others at the chapel.

Elizabeth had been experiencing some morning sickness, but it would soon pass and she would be as right as rain again. The judge had told her that if she had experienced any real difficulty, she should consult Carmel, whether or not it spoiled the surprise for Jake.

He reasoned that anytime Jake saw them would be a great surprise, knowing that they all had come so far just for his wedding. Well, that wasn't exactly all of it, but it certainly was a major part of the decision.

It wasn't two hours later that Elizabeth had experienced low pelvic cramping and a severe backache. Clay was awakened and had sent Big Joe to fetch Dr. Carmel, but not to say who the patient was. When he was back with the doctor in tow, Fletcher had come to introduce himself as she entered the foyer. He took her to Elizabeth.

She was surprised to find that Emma's brother and his wife were at the plantation. She couldn't grasp the meaning behind it. When she entered Elizabeth's room, Emma had been at the bedside holding her hand. When she stood, Carmel somehow immediately knew that this was Emma Summers Angelos!

She had a sinking feeling in her heart as to what the meaning of this was. To find Jake's old flame not but a few miles from him had been disconcerting. Had he known she was there? Had he seen her? Those questions and more had immediately flashed through her mind, but she steeled herself to focus her attention on her patient.

She greeted Elizabeth and those in the room. She asked if she could speak to her patient alone for a few moments. Everyone rose to leave, but Elizabeth wouldn't let go of Emma's hand.

"Surely, she didn't mean you, Em," she said, She looked at the doctor with imploring eyes and said, "This is my dear sister-in-law. May she stay?"

Carmel looked at Emma and said, "Yes, of course. If you want her to." Not waiting for Elizabeth to thank her, she immediately started her assessment. She asked her when the cramping had started. She wanted to know how intense the pain was, if it were constant, or if not, how frequently did it come upon her. She asked if she were passing any fluids of any kind.

She said she would need to do a small examination and proceeded to examine her abdomen for any swelling or knots, or for any pain when she pressed in certain areas. Finding all fairly normal, she finished the exam and told her that she could find no reason for the cramps.

Although she did not want to unduly alarm her, she informed her they were not totally normal at any stage of pregnancy. "However, some women frequently experienced some, along with spotting, during the first three months, without any untoward consequence. To be on the side of safety and caution, you will need to remain on bed rest until this passes," she informed her.

She told her she was not to get up on any account except to use the thunder bowl there by her bed. She was advised that she was to call one of the housemaids for assistance to help her with that. In the event that she experienced any dizziness from being in bed for an extended time, help would be there to steady her. Also, she would speak to the girls and tell them to inspect the contents, and what to look for after she was finished. She also told her to drink plenty of water.

"Let everyone else see to your every need," she told her. "Let them feed you nourishing, non-greasy fare. See that you get plenty of fresh fruit and steamed vegetables, and not the heavy, Southern cooking the fine ladies in the kitchen are famous for. Also, see that you get enough sleep," she told her.

Carmel made conversation and told her that she was not aware that any of them were back at the plantation. She wanted to know when and where had they started their journey. Had they traveled straight through or stopped along the way. Elizabeth thought that was pretty blunt, but answered her anyway.

She was glad to hear that it had not been idle curiosity on the doctor's part as she said, "Well, that answers some of my questions about your problem. You have undertaken a long, stressful journey on a bumpy train. You have probably overdone sitting. I'm sure you have not eaten properly, nor had adequate exercise or rest," she told her. "That certainly could account for the cramping you are experiencing, and further proof that you must stay in bed and rest for a while."

She looked at Emma and said, "Jake will be so glad to hear that you all are here," giving Emma an opportunity to enlighten her on why she was in Savannah. When she said that, Emma said,

"Oh, we wanted to surprise him! You see, we have all of us come home for his wedding. We wanted to surprise him and his bride, but of course, since you are the bride, you already know. I dislike asking you to keep a secret from him, but if you could, we would love to see his face when we all come in." Emma finished.

"How do you know I am the bride?" Carmel asked, surprise showing in her face.

"When the detectives, Wade and Pierce, brought their prisoners out to San Francisco, they stopped by and gave us the wonderful news." Going forward and extending her hand to Carmel, she said, "I am Emma Angelos, a life-long friend of your husband's."

"You mean the woman whom he loved, and who broke his heart?" she had said it in a soft manner and not unkindly, but still it had shocked both ladies into speechlessness.

After a moment's silence, and a deep breath, Emma quietly responded, "Not on purpose, Dr. Borelli. Jake had never declared himself to me, and when I had to leave, I knew then that we had no future together. I successfully rid myself of any feelings for him.

I met my husband in San Francisco. A year after leaving here, we were married. There was no intent to hurt Jake in any way, or to even have reason to think that my marrying my husband would do that. I felt there was more than a good chance that we would never even meet again. I'm sorry if you feel this anger at circumstances that were innocently beyond my control," Emma finished.

"I'm not angry. It just seemed dishonest to introduce yourself to me as Jake's friend when we both know you were so much more to him than that," she replied.

"My dear, now that is getting down to it. *Were*. We *were* more than friends. Now we are *no more* than friends. True, the best friends possible. Jake is a most beloved friend to both my husband and myself. And I sincerely pray that we will be your friends as well, just as surely as Fletcher and Elizabeth are Jake's dear friends, too,"

Seeing Carmel's look of distress, she stepped forward and slipped an arm around her saying, "My dear, it never dawned on any of us that we would upset you by being at your wedding. We wouldn't spoil your special day for anything in the world. If you are uncomfortable with any of us being there, or more specifically, just me being there, Jake will never, ever know we were even here. I promise you that," she said.

"Emma, please forgive me. Of course, Jake will want you all there! I want whatever will please him, and this will certainly please him greatly. I am a very direct person. Even Jake calls me a true Yankee," she admitted with a blush.

Being the direct woman that she was, continued, "I will tell you plainly what is bothering me. You were the love of his life, while I, on the other hand, have not been in his life all that long. I don't mind confessing that I have had a miserable time watching him recently think he was in love with another woman at the church, merely because she reminded him of you. Now here you are. I don't want to tempt him, especially if he isn't one hundred percent certain that he wants this wedding," she finished.

Emma couldn't help but laugh out loud. Carmel took umbrage with that, but Emma couldn't help it. She hurried on and said, "We are talking about Jake Jackson, aren't we? The Jake Jackson I know never did a single thing that he did not want to do, ever. I never knew a more independent man! Go along to get along? Not that man! If he did not want this wedding with all his heart, you wouldn't have tricked him, begged him, or blackmailed him into it!" she laughed again. "Take that from a life-long friend!"

At that, Carmel laughed along with her. Yes, that surely was Jake Jackson right enough!

Emma continued, "Just to be clear here, I have decided on second sight, that it would be better all around if we can show up on say Wednesday night prayer meeting, which will still surprise him and we can see everyone then," she told Carmel.

It was Carmel's turn to apologize and ask for forgiveness. "Of course, I want you all to be at the wedding. If you want to wait until then, that is fine, but knowing Jake, he will be highly disappointed not be spend as much time with all of you as possible before you have to return home. I confess, when I saw you sitting there, I knew who you were, and I couldn't help but be stunned at finding you here. I wondered if Jake had already seen you," Carmel said.

"If Jake had seen us you would have known about it. Jake Jackson is no deceiver!" Emma assured her. "Yes, I know that," she said.

Turning to watch Elizabeth, she said, "I am not sure if I should leave Elizabeth tonight. Why don't we send one of the hands back to let my parents know I won't be home tonight," she suggested. "I can rest on the divan in the study, perhaps?"

Emma called Fletcher back into the room and Mark came with him. Carmel told Fletcher that the trip had, likely as not, caused the cramping, but as far as she could tell, everything was fine at that moment. However, she would feel better staying on until the morning. She repeated her orders.

Fletcher had put his arm around his wife, as he sat on the bed beside her. He assured Carmel that Elizabeth would stay in bed, even if he had to stay in bed with her.

Mark had moved to Emma and stood behind her. He had put his arms around her waist, drawing her to him, and she had rubbed his arm unconsciously. She saw that Mark held Emma exactly like Jake held her. Men in love do some things other men don't. These intimate moments, like Mark and Jake provided, could easily be avoided by men not in love, while they could render the accepted token of affection to their mates.

Carmel could easily see the love between both couples. She knew watching them that Jake was as much in love with her as Mark and Fletcher were with their wives! She never really doubted it, but knew that Emma had always been somewhat of a blemish on their love affair. Not that she felt inferior to Emma, but she had long been a part of Jake's life. She could see that Mark was a fine looking man, and that they made a beautiful couple, but still thought her Jake was more handsome.

When she saw Jake and Emma together for the first time, she hoped that she would be able to tell whether or not there were any emotions still attached to her. She realized she shouldn't need proof, but seeing Emma sitting there had shaken her, if she were to be perfectly honest.

Chapter 5

The trees were beginning to put forth buds and many of the early spring flowers had sprung up about the plantation, seemingly overnight, and Emma's old garden was a riot of color and fragrances. She had taken Miss Maude to see the conservatory soon after their arrival, and she seemed much at home there. Emma told her again how very much she had loved and appreciated working in her conservatory while she lived at the mansion. Miss Maude was in her glory sharing garden duty with Emma during her stay, as she certainly needed something useful to do. She liked to be busy and this was a favorite pastime of hers.

Emma had wondered if Carmel needed any more flowers for her wedding, but assumed that she had everything under control. She had seemed a very efficient woman. She would be ready to offer them in the event something went wrong with her flower order at the last moment, but didn't want to bring any suggestions to her concerning her wedding. Fletcher had wished they could have made plans for the wedding reception to be held at the plantation with a huge barbeque. Of course, it would have been great fun, but the ladies pooh-poohed it for a wedding reception. However, it had given them the idea for having one as a welcome home party when they returned from their honeymoon. They would let Fletcher suggest it to Jake.

The prayer meeting was that night, but with Elizabeth still not feeling the best, they called off going into town. Carmel was much relieved at their decision. They could tell when they watched her with Elizabeth that she was concerned. When Elizabeth was watching her face, she appeared as though everything was fine, but was frowning when she was not looking.

After another examination, Emma followed her out, saying she would bring Elizabeth fresh water, but mainly wanted to speak with Dr. Borelli to see if anything serious was amiss. Carmel said that nothing much had changed, except her blood pressure was a bit elevated, which could be due to the cramping pain, or the forced bed rest that was irritating her, but she couldn't say anything specific. She just wanted to be cautious with her, which was routine with Carmel when caring for her patients. Carmel had left that morning with the intention of spending the night at the plantation again that night.

It was about two o'clock that afternoon when Jake arrived at the plantation. He went straight to the stables and told Big Joe that he wanted to ride Rampage that afternoon. He was a bit surprised when he told him that Rampage was out in the meadow. He hadn't said who was riding him, but he didn't know of anyone but Big Joe, Fletcher, and himself who had ever ridden him. Period.

He also wondered at Big Joe's quietness that morning. He didn't seem to want to talk to him, and kept himself busy while he saddled up a different horse for Jake to ride. Jake thought that was just odd, but he only said, "Lovely day, Big Joe. You feeling alright?"

"No, no, I be fine, Master Jake. Jest fine. Jest fine. Uh-huh, jest fine," he allowed.

"You are not sounding like yourself, and you are as jittery as a June bug in a chicken coop. What's wrong with you this morning?" he asked him point blank.

He looked down at Jake with his eyes bigger than Jake could ever remember them. Something was definitely wrong. "Is something going on here, that I need to know about?" he asked him. "And just who is riding Rampage, I'd like to know?" Jake demanded.

"Well now, son, I can't rightly tell you that, no sir, I can't rightly say," he answered.

"Why can't you say? Do you know who is riding him?" he asked.

"Yes, sir, I knows. But Rampage should be trotting in here any minute now. Go on up to the house and get some lemonade. No! I'll run and fetch some for you. I be right back!" he said starting out.

"Big Joe, I don't want lemonade! Why don't you want me to go to the house? Listen, I know something's wrong! Out with it man! What is wrong here?" When Big Joe just hung his head without answering, Jake started to worry in earnest.

"I'll just go ask Bessie and see what she says," he flung at him.

"No, sir, I wouldn't go up there a tall! No, sir! Not a tall!" he replied, shaking his head no.

At this, Jake took off at a trot toward the house. He intended to enter quietly, as he couldn't fathom what could be wrong. But he didn't want to take a chance that it was any danger he was walking into. He entered the side porch off the kitchen to hear Bessie and Granny Thornton deep in conversation. He wondered just when Granny had returned to the plantation.

"That weddin' will be somethin' ta see, I reckin'. Jake and that young doctor woman should have a hum dinger. With Miss Emma and Fletcher a comin' all this way wantin' ta surprise him," Bessie was saying.

Jake was stunned at what he had just heard. He backed off the porch and trotted back to the stable. He didn't want to spoil any surprise, but what on earth had Bessie meant. Dawning struck and he realized that his friends were there in that house that very minute! That is why Big Joe was so antsy! Fletcher was riding Rampage! He had to get out of there before he got back, even if it killed him to leave before seeing him!

He got to the buggy and Big Joe had been standing in the doorway of the stables watching him, obviously wondering why he had returned so quickly.

Fletch told him, "Well, by the time I got to the house, I realized there couldn't be anything really wrong or you would have told me. But on the other hand, I just don't feel like riding any more, so I figure I'll just mosey on back to town. With the wedding so close at hand, I didn't have time to come here today anyhow, with church tonight and all. Well, it was good to see you, Big Joe. Hope you get over what's ailing you," he feigned bewilderment, watching the obvious relief wash over Big Joe's face at him taking his leave.

Why are they here? They are here to surprise me by showing up at my wedding? Now out of sight of the plantation, he pulled the buggy off to the side of the road. He was so moved at what he had heard in the kitchen that tears had sprung to his eyes. His best friend in the world would be at his wedding! Not to mention his other best friend, Emma.

While he sat there, another buggy was approaching. He wiped his eyes on his shirtsleeve, and was shocked to see it was the Borelli buggy with Carmel driving alone.

449

"Carmel! Where are you headed?" he inquired.

"I have a patient down this way," she nonchalantly answered him.

"Why are you driving alone?" he asked her in a concerned tone, getting down from the buggy and going to her. He reached up and cupped her face with his hands. He gave her a kiss and said, "You are gorgeous today, but I don't like you driving alone. No telling who you could have met on this road."

"Well, my patient is a woman with child. I may have to stay the night. I wanted the buggy to get back in the morning," she said.

"Well, there is no woman with child down this way that I am acquainted with. Who is your patient?" he wanted to know.

"Well, Jake, she is from out of town, that's why you didn't know there was an expectant mother down this way," she lightly threw at him.

"But there is nobody down this way but the Summers Bluff people. Who is your patient," he asked again. When she just looked at him, he walked his horse in a wide circle and came around to the back of her buggy and tied him on. He slipped in beside her and took the reigns.

"Jake, you really don't need to do this, you know. I am used to driving around alone. Like you say, there is nobody down this road but the Summers Bluff people."

"And no stranger could have come out this way by mistake? Seeing a woman like you, all alone out in the middle of nowhere, it wouldn't even have crossed his mind to try anything?" he asked incredulously.

"Well, that is exactly why I carry my gun with me at all times. You might recall that I have been known to shoot when provoked," she reminded him.

"Still, the buggy could have had several men in it and they could have blocked your way, so promise me to never drive yourself again!" he pleaded. She could see he was truly concerned and so had agreed to his wishes.

"Jake, I really don't want you to accompany me to the plantation," she told him.

"Just why is that, Carmel," he asked pointedly. He knew his friends were at the plantation, but if one of the women was an expectant mother having trouble, he couldn't just go on back to town and dismiss it.

She just looked at him and shook her head. "Jake, you will be sorry if you come with me!" she fumed.

"Who is the woman with child at that plantation?" he had said each word deliberately, and had slowly drawn them out, nearly through clenched teeth to show his frustration. He had stopped the buggy and had turned to face her with his question.

"You are not going to let this go, are you?" she stormed.

"No, I am not," he said as he whipped the horse up again. Carmel knew that he was angry, but she could not spoil this for them.

"It's nobody for you to concern yourself with really, Jake," she replied, trying to remain calm.

"We will go to the plantation and I will see for myself who is there that I shouldn't concern myself with!" he told her.

"Do you make such a fuss over all the women on the plantation?" she asked.

"Are you telling me that she is one of the field hands?" he asked.

"No, I am not telling you that!" she fumed.

They had pulled into the drive in front of the house and when he had hitched the horse he helped her down. She flounced off and went inside. He followed and walked into the whole Summers household!

When he saw Fletcher, he flew at him and grabbed him in a bear hug! "What are doing here, man?" he demanded.

"What are *you* doing here?" Fletch replied with a hearty laugh. "The best laid plans of mice and men…" he said to the room in general and they all laughed.

Then he saw Emma and Mark next. Without saying a word, he went over to them and put an arm around each of them and they hugged him back. Then he saw Kitty and grabbed her and twirled her around as she hugged his neck, squealing with joy. Aunt Caroline was next in line, and even Miss Maude got a hug. By the time he had finished hugging her, everyone had wiped their eyes, including Carmel.

"What are you all doing here?" Jake asked again.

"We came for your wedding, my good man!" Mark said. "I remember when you offered to officiate at our wedding what I said to you back then, and a promise is a promise. The least I can do is return the favor!" he laughed and slapped him on the back. Jake hugged him again and said, "Thank you, my brother! You don't know what this means to me!" Looking at Carmel, he said, "But everyone, I want you to meet my bride!" And then he took her in his arms and kissed her soundly in front of God and everyone!

They all laughed and greeted Carmel.

"How did y'all know her name?" he looked confused. Then he realized. Looking around, he asked, "Where is Elizabeth?" Looking at Carmel, he asked, "Is Elizabeth your patient? The expectant mother?"

Fletcher said, "Yes, Jake, you are going to be an uncle!" When Jake had given his congratulations, Carmel had gone to see Elizabeth. She had seen his reaction to Emma and she had been more than pleased. He loved her, not Emma!

Thank you, Lord! Jake told me that when he committed, he would give me all of his heart and he has! she thought.

Then she turned her attention to Elizabeth. She looked fine, but Carmel had an odd feeling looking at her. Her blood pressure was normal, her temperature and other vital signs were all good. Maybe it was just a premonition, but she was concerned.

When she could, she got Jake alone and told him. She couldn't give him a definite reason for her concern, but she wanted him to pray with her anyway. They held hands and prayed for Elizabeth, the babe, for Fletcher, and the whole family. This baby was already the focus of all of their lives, and they could not conceive of anything happening to it now.

She would stay the night again. She asked Jake to go to the hospital very early in the morning before Dr. Hershel got started on his rounds, to ask him to come out for a consultation. It might be unnecessary, but better two good heads than one.

Jake had sent one of the lads to tell Todd that he needed to preach at the prayer meeting so that they could fellowship at the plantation that night until late, no doubt. Everyone was pleased even though it had not worked out as planned, they were glad it had been a private reunion. They would have another reunion with the church, but their reunion with Jake had been just too special to share, even with the best of friends.

Jake had been talking and laughing with Emma close to the doorway, when Carmel, seeing them from the hallway, paused before entering. She overheard Jake ask her, "What do you think of my woman, Emma?" he had asked her in all sincerity.

"Oh, Jake, she is gorgeous inside and out. She is a very dedicated and knowledgeable doctor to boot. You are a blessed man, Jake, but she is blessed to have you, too! I am so very happy for you, Jake. You're a good man and you deserve the best," she told him.

"Well, I certainly agree with you there, I am a blessed man. You know, Em, when I saw you with Mark in the church the first time, I thought my world had ended. But when I had prayed about it, I knew that God had restrained me from declaring myself to you before you had gone away, simply because you were meant for Mark. Even after I returned here, I didn't know what to do with my feelings for you, but I did not want to have them. I ended up transferring them to a woman at church who reminded me so much of you.

When I realized what I had done, I knew that God had given me my true love in Carmel, and I also saw that God had spared you and me both from a life of mediocre love. With Mark you got the best, and with Carmel so have I. I love that Yankee with my whole heart, Em. I really do!"

"Well, that's plain as plain, Jake!" she laughed.

"Yeah, I guess it is, but I never get tired of saying it. Even when I am alone, I talk to God and tell Him how much I love that woman of mine!" he laughed with her.

Carmel leaned up against the wall and let the tears flow.

Chapter 6

*I*t was near dawn when Fletcher had awakened Carmel and told her Elizabeth wanted her. Carmel went in to find her with a strong backache, and she told her that she felt wet but was afraid to look. When Carmel saw the spots of blood she paled. It would be hours before Dr. Herschel would get there. She asked Fletcher to get some wood to elevate the foot of her bed a little. She also put extra pillows under her knees for comfort.

Dr. Borelli had a mixture of camp bark, wild yam, partridgeberry and some other herbs that had been tested and proven to assist in relaxing the cramping. It also stopped the blood flow to prevent miscarriage. Since this was the first time Elizabeth had issued blood, Carmel began the medicine drops. She then had sat down beside her. She held Elizabeth's hand, and told her that as she was still in the first months of her pregnancy, spotting sometimes occurred at the time of the regular menses. She wanted to know when Elizabeth's regular time was, but it had been two weeks before. She extended her hand to Fletcher on the other side of the bed, and when he took her hand, she began to pray.

"Oh, Lord, we know that You knew this time would come to us and that we would be frightened. But since we know You are here with us, we shake ourselves out of any fear and doubt, and we hold fast to our faith. We have seen You work in the past, and we know You will work in our present. We bless this Summers baby with health and long life, as we do his precious mother. We will now await Your outcome with patience and peace. In Your Son's name we pray, Amen."

Carmel looked at Elizabeth and while there were tears in her eyes, there was also a smile on her lips. Her husband leaned down and gently brushed her lips with his own, as they both wiped away their tears. They would trust their God, and He would see them through this time of trouble, come what may! It was a frightening journey, but they had faith in the outcome.

Jake arrived with Dr. Isaiah Herschel at seven o'clock that morning. Carmel was very glad to see him and explained Elizabeth's situation to him. He asked what treatment she had been given and wholeheartedly approved when he heard Carmel's plan. There was little else to do but to give the herbs and let them do their work. He suggested plenty of fluids. He thought it important to keep her as free from worry as they could. Possibly by engaging her mind with something else to think of like the frivolous activities of draughts or dominoes, or something of the kind.

Jake had visited with Fletch while Carmel and Isaiah consulted. Given the history of Carmel and that nice Dr. Herschel, as her mother would say, he would be staying until he took him back to town. Not that he was jealous, mind, but then again, neither did he consider himself a fool. After all, 'Hershey' had tasted Carmel's lips, and who knew when he would have another such impulse!

Kitty was gathering eggs when Clay had stopped at the hen house and called to her. She came out carrying her eggs in a soft basket.

"A sunny good morning ta ya', Kathleen!

"Good day ta ye, Clay. How goes it with ye this soft morn?" she asked.

"If I's any better, I'd think it was a frame up!" he said as she laughed. She thought again what a fine looking man was Clayton.

"What makes ye so cheerful this mornin'?" Kitty asked him.

"Well now, lass, a few mornin's ago 'twas Jesse May gatherin' the eggs. Now 'tis yerself! So jest why wouldn't I be cheerful, I ask ye?" he questioned.

Kitty had to laugh in spite of herself. "Go on with ye, man. What does it matter who gathers the eggs, I'd like to be knowin'?" she asked him in her feisty, happy way.

"Ah, Kitty, ye cut me to the quick. Surely, ye know what I'm sayin'," he told her.

"And how would I when ye've said naught but about the eggs?" she replied.

"Kitty, would ye be after lettin' me take ye ta Savannah ta the Grand Hotel for supper, then?" he asked her, with his heart in his eyes.

"Why, I see no harm in that, if ye be wantin' ta, since ye have ta eat," she said as she blushed prettily. "When did ye have in mind for this grand supper?"

"What about this Friday night? I can send in one of the lads ta make the reservations. If I can't get 'em for Friday, I'll tell him ta see about Sunday night, the weddin' bein' Saturday and all. Will that suit?"

She looked up into the sky and said, "I'd be tellin' Clayton I'd be goin' for that, if I should be seein' himself around, that is," she said, teasing the man. "Seein' as how I'd just as leif go as not, says I." But seeing that he was very serious, she followed with "Oh, alright, then! 'Tis proud I'd be ta be escorted ta supper by the most handsome man in Savannah!" she declared as she took the eggs into the kitchen, but stopping in the doorway to smile at him over her shoulder, watching a blush creep over his face.

*Why Kitty Thornton, you big flirt. If I wasn't knowin' ye better, I'd say ye were sweet on the ma*n, she thought to herself. *What's gotten in ta ye, anyhow? Ye can't even be gatherin' the eggs without wantin' ta swoon!*

Clayton Kean was beside himself with giddiness and joy.

You're acting a bloomin' eejit, he thought to himself. He knew he was grinning like one. He was the same age as Fletcher and hadn't ever had a romance. Come to that, neither had Fletch until he met Elizabeth, and here Clay had known and cared for Kitty for years upon years.

Now she was here and he had been determined in not getting involved with heart matters, as she was leaving soon, but would his heart listen? Not likely! It was too late. She had flirted with him and no mistaking it! *Glory be, if I'm not the luckiest man in the world!* He gloated to himself and the cows!

Chapter 7

*D*r. Carmel Borelli stayed at the plantation again that night and before Jake was leaving, she went to find him. She asked him, "What will we do if Elizabeth isn't able to attend the wedding? None of the rest of the family would be in much of a mood to attend and leave her behind."

It was a bit of a quandary, and would take some adjustments, but Jake didn't hesitate to say that they would move the wedding and the reception to the plantation. The people would understand. They would know of the sacrifice all the Summers family had made to make the trip back for the wedding. Then, too, Jake only had a short time to be with them. Yes, they would understand. Given what was at stake with Elizabeth, that would settle it all.

Carmel was delighted, as that meant she wouldn't have to leave her patient for long, either. With the wedding only two days away, Carmel made the decision that she didn't want Elizabeth anywhere near a buggy for some time to come. She told Jake to have her family informed, and Mother Mattie would see to advising the churchwomen of the change. Some of the boys took notes to the homes of the congregants, advising them, as well. Given the news, the congregants of the Savannah Chapel went immediately into a warrior's mode to pray for the baby and Elizabeth, and to change the wedding preparations.

Abby Borelli had the men and some of the women go to the plantation to make sure the tent that they used for large get-togethers was up and properly adorned. Their friends would bring extra chairs with them from the church. When they arrived, Emma, Maude, and Kitty lent a hand with seeing everything was clean and ready.

Emma told the women there were plenty of flowers in the greenhouse perfect for decorating the porches, gazebos and the arched trellis they would be using for the ceremony, besides what Carmel had planned on using at the church, if needed.

Carmel's mother arrived and took over the direction of the workers from there. Abigail Borelli knew what she was about and everyone took her orders good naturedly and thankfully. There was a wonderful excitement in the air. Everyone was thrilled to be a part of what was taking place for the wedding. This would certainly be a wedding like never before seen at the plantation.

With Dr. Carmel being so involved and concerned with Elizabeth and her baby, she was proud to let the women handle everything for her. She hadn't planned to let them do anything with the decorating, but she recognized God's hand allowing her to keep her priorities straight and simple: to care for Elizabeth and her baby. She admired Elizabeth's spunk and attitude. She had kept a positive, cheerful outlook, while she did what she knew she must to comply with Carmel's orders.

While Carmel felt somewhat left out in the whole production, as far as the Summers family was concerned she was center stage. Not only was she the beautiful and beloved bride, but she was also the skilled physician helping to keep their baby alive! Their gratitude would know no bounds, as she had earned a tender place in all of their hearts in her own right, not just as Jake's intended.

They couldn't help but think that if they hadn't made the trip, Elizabeth wouldn't have had the problems. Then again, if the trip had not had anything to do with it, they were grateful if this had to happen that Carmel had been there to handle it.

Many doctors were too conservative to try the new remedies and preferred to believe that if a woman was having problems with her pregnancy, it was her body trying to rid itself of something not right. Carmel would never believe that antiquated outlook. Doing nothing was certainly not, nor would it ever be, an option for one of her patients!

Elizabeth was resting quietly at the moment, but only an hour hence, she had been cramping. The treatment seemed to be working, but for how long, Carmel couldn't know. There was nothing else medical science knew to do, other than what she was already doing. The thought that it might not be enough was tormenting her, but she would shake herself and replace any negative thought with a positive one.

She would do that by picturing what this precious little one would look like, since his father was as handsome as his mother was beautiful, it simply had to be a gorgeous baby. Then she would give praise for being a part of their lives, and for being able to offer assistance at this time of need. She could see why Jake was so in love with them all. She had managed to love them all fiercely, too, and in a very short time.

The weather had been mild and lovely. The flowers being in bloom and giving off their sweet scent, along with the excitement and flurry of wedding activities, made it seem that love was in the very air. Kitty felt it down to her toes. She wondered why she was being so affected. After all, she hadn't felt this way even when her best friend, Emma, had married Mark. But then again, when Emma married, Clay hadn't been around.

With the wedding upon them, she knew they would be headed back to San Francisco soon, at least, just as soon as Elizabeth was well enough to travel. The very prospect of leaving produced a heavy-hearted feeling that she couldn't seem to shake. She knew leaving Granny would be nearly an impossible fete, should she be able to pull it off at all. She hadn't even thought to herself what it would be like to say good-bye to Clay. No, she hadn't been able to even let herself think about that.

On the other hand, she knew she couldn't bear to be parted from Emma, Fletcher, Elizabeth, Aunt Caroline, Miss Maude or the new baby that was on the way. She felt as though she was in the middle of a tug-of-warring. She simply could not be parted from any of them! Not after all they had been through together. It just wasn't doable.

Sitting in the shade of the old oak in sight of the barn, she was surprised to find tears coursing down her face. It was then that Clay rounded the corner of the barn and spotted her under the tree.

He started to go on with his work, but the slump of her shoulders and her bent head signaled him that she was upset about something. He changed course and walked over to her. He quietly sat down beside her. She knew who it was without looking at him.

He put his arm around her shoulder and she leaned her head onto his chest, as he merely allowed her to weep, without the need of questions being asked. Truth be told, every time he thought of her leaving, he wanted to do the exact same thing as she was doing—bawl until the hurt in his heart was somehow bearable.

She soon wiped her eyes and looked up at him. He had never seen anything so touchingly beautiful. With her eyes glistening with tears and her long, dark lashes wet upon her face, he knew he could never let her go to California and leave him again.

When he sought her lips, he found them soft and willing, and knew that she felt the same as he did. At that moment, he didn't need the blarney stone to tell her that he loved her, and needed her with him always. He stood and pulled her to her feet, and she threw her arms around his neck and kissed the side of his neck, murmuring her love for him. He had to be dreaming! After all these years of loving this woman, she was actually in his arms and declaring her love for him. Miracles really can strike as suddenly as disasters!

Granny Thornton had seen the exchange between Kitty and Clay from the kitchen window, and was surprised to see young Clay kiss her granddaughter. Even more surprising, was to see Kitty put her arms around him and kiss his neck! *These younguns nowadays!* she thought. Nevertheless, she wondered what it could mean. She knew that Kitty would never leave Emma and California, and she knew for certain Clay would never desert the judge or Fletcher in caring for the plantation. Yes, she contemplated what good could come from what she had just witnessed.

Chapter 8

Carmel was still worried about Elizabeth and the baby she was carrying. She wasn't far enough along for the baby to survive should she miscarry, but with the good Lord's help, that would never happen! Elizabeth was doing all that Carmel had instructed her to do, and so far it seemed to be working. She was still cramping, but not as severely as before she had begun the treatment, and she was no longer spotting.

Carmel was still spending nights at the plantation. She just did not feel comfortable leaving Elizabeth without medical help close by. She had closed down the surgery and referred her patients to Dr. Herschel until after they returned from their honeymoon, so she wasn't concerned for her other patients.

She needed time to get herself together to prepare for the ceremony, but more than that, to prepare herself for the future she was so anticipating with Jake Jackson. Life was sweet and all was well with her, except for the trouble with Elizabeth. She was praying and believing for a good outcome with the pregnancy.

Carmel had become fast friends with the Summers women and realized once again why they had always meant so much to Jake. In the short time they had been together at the plantation, she had come to love them completely. She was already regretting that they would soon be on their way back to San Francisco, as she just couldn't imagine life without them now.

She knew Jake would be emotionally devastated at their departure. Finding Fletcher alive had filled the giant-sized hole in his heart that had been created by the news of his death. He was closer than a brother, and to be separated from him again was going to be very painful for them both.

Jake was not saying much about it, but every time he reminisced about the good old days, you could sense the wistfulness, as if he were already experiencing the separation that was soon to come.

It was becoming evident to everyone at the plantation that a new relationship was progressing between Kitty and Clay. It was so sweet and wholesome that it was a pure pleasure to see it developing. Obviously, Clay was devoted to Kitty and vice versa. He had finally convinced her that he had been in love with her for years, and was overjoyed to find she had shared his feelings. With that came a reservation that couldn't be ignored: Kitty was leaving soon. It never even crossed anyone's mind that she would consider leaving Emma's side. One supposed it would turn out according to God's own plan, and that would be best, whatever the outcome.

Jake and Carmel's wedding was tomorrow and the excitement in the air was palpable. Of course, Mark would be officiating the ceremony. Emma would be the matron of honor, while Kitty would be the bridesmaid. Fletcher would serve as best man and Todd would be the groomsman.

Mother Mattie was baking the cake, and the ladies of the church were providing the reception food. The grounds were ready with the flowers in bloom and the crepe myrtle trees in full color. The wedding canopy was gorgeously adorned, and fit for a princess.

The wedding was to be held at eleven o'clock in the morning. Abigail was flourishing in her role as mother of the bride, and had absolutely everything under control. She had a cousin who had married a senator, and they had been included in many political gatherings and high society events. Abby had learned much about what was expected at a gala of that kind.

She replicated many of those things she had seen done at other parties. She had brought to life every idea she had for Carmel's wedding, as nothing was too good for her baby.

Chapter 9

ake had been to lunch at the plantation that Friday and
it was time to leave. Tomorrow was the wedding and he
felt he still had things that were unsettled in his heart.
He knew that once the wedding was over, and Elizabeth had a
few more days to rest and recuperate, they would be headed home
to San Francisco.

He brought up the subject to Fletcher, asking him if he had any
idea of the expected date they would be leaving. He advised him
that everything depended upon how well Elizabeth responded to
treatment. She had been feeling much better yesterday and today,
and everyone was in good spirits about her complete recovery.

Jake was saying his good-byes, but Fletcher asked him if he
would go for a short ride with him before he left for town. Jake
really hadn't wanted to leave yet, and so was happy for the excuse
to spend more time there.

When they reached the open fields, they urged their steeds on
to a gallop, and when they reached the top of the hill overlooking
the plantation, they reined them in. Sensing Fletcher had a reason
for suggesting the ride, he waited for the conversation he knew
was about to follow.

However, Fletcher's outburst had come as somewhat of a surprise to him. "Jake, I just can't do it! I just can't!"

"What can't you do, Fletch?" he asked, amazed to see such agitation.

Fletcher dismounted and tied his horse to the branch of a dogwood tree. Jake followed his lead, and they sat with their backs to the tree, overlooking the plantation.

Fletcher passed his hand over his eyes and around the back of his neck. He looked up at Jake and said, "How in the name of all that I hold dear can I possibly leave here again?" He shook his head in the negative and repeated, "I just cannot!"

Jake wanted to shout his hallelujahs, but he knew his friend was in misery and didn't need levity right then. He measured his words carefully and finally responded, "Fletcher, do you think it is wise for Elizabeth to leave here before the baby comes, given what she has been through? I know Carmel wishes she didn't have to go. Is there anything so pressing in San Francisco that the two of you could not stay here, at least long enough for her to deliver?"

"No, no, there isn't any reason. I have just thought we would all be going home together, but the more I consider it, the more I know San Francisco just isn't my home. But I don't want to be separated from Emma and Mark, and I know for certainty that Elizabeth would probably not want to even consider it."

"Well, everyone's future seems to be at a crossroads right now. I know Emma would not be happy to leave Elizabeth before the baby comes. I also know that Mark will have to get back to his church soon. And from what I can see of Kitty and Clay, that is not going to be a happy parting, not to mention Kitty leaving Granny. Mother Mattie is going to be heartbroken when you and Emma leave, and I can't even bear to think of it! But what's the solution?"

"Well, I think I will have to wait until Elizabeth is better before I worry her with any of this. But I can talk to Emma. Maybe she will have some notion of what's to be done," Fletcher said.

Jake and Fletcher had returned from their ride, and after caring for their mounts, Carmel walked Jake to the buggy and offered her lips for a good night kiss. It would be the last time she would kiss him as Carmel Borelli. Tomorrow when he kissed his bride, she would be Carmel Jackson. The thought gave her much pleasure and surely God was on His throne and all was well with the world!

After Jake had left for town, Fletcher sought Emma so they could have a heart to heart about what was bothering him.

"Em, dear, do you have a few minutes?"

"Of course, I do! Always time for you, Fletch!"

"Then let's walk in your garden. I know you love it there."

"I won't say no to that. I won't have much longer to enjoy it, will I?" she asked him, with more than a touch of nostalgia. "What's really on your mind, Fletch?"

"You know me pretty well, don't you, girl?" he asked her as they meandered to the garden.

"I do. I most certainly do. Something has been bothering you ever since our return here. Does it have anything to do with what I overheard you telling Clay the other day?"

"Yeah, Em, it does. I'm at sixes and sevens. I know my worry about Elizabeth has contributed to my agitation, but this started before Elizabeth started having difficulties. It's as you say, ever since I clapped eyes on the place, I have had a restlessness that I know is due to knowing I will be leaving soon. But in all honesty, I don't want to leave! I don't feel I have anything in San

Francisco to look forward to compared to what I have here. Do you understand what I'm feeling, Em?"

A tear escaped and trickled down Emma's face. "Yes, Fletch, as hard as it is to admit it, I know exactly what you mean, because I'm feeling the same way, more's the pity! I look at Mother Mattie, Granny, Jake and Carmel and I can't imagine me getting back on that train and going thousands of miles away—again. But I know I must. I haven't said anything to you, because I know you have had enough on your mind of late. I didn't want to upset you more."

"I think it is safe to say that the only reason I would hesitate is that after being away from you for so long in the war, and with the years of dealing with amnesia, every minute is precious to me now. I cannot imagine what life without you and Mark would be like if Elizabeth and I stayed here for good!" he moaned.

Emma just leaned her head on his shoulder and told him she felt the same way. "Do you have any kind of plan, Fletch?"

"Yes, after studying this over ever since I arrived here, I know I want to buy back Summers Bluff. I want to raise our children here. I want to spend my life among these people of my ancestry, and of my youth. It's simple, but yet complex. I don't know what Elizabeth will think of it. What do you think of it?"

"Well, we still have your money Judge West paid for the place. I know he would sell it back to you. Fletch, I know that you were out of place in California. It was like the handwriting on the wall that all of us were ignoring. I knew having nothing useful to do was a festering wound that would have to have a release soon," she sighed.

"I know Elizabeth needs to stay here until the baby comes. I'm sure she would dread to board that train again and face that uncomfortably long trip. Who knows what might happen on the frontier without any medical help whatsoever at hand? That needs to be settled in your mind right now. And as much as I don't want to be parted from Mark, I will be concerned for her every minute of every day if I leave her now."

"Well, how do we proceed? That is the question. I suppose the first thing would be to speak with Judge West just to make certain that he would want to sell. Then we need to confer with Mark. Does that suit?" he asked her. "Then I will talk with Elizabeth." She just nodded her agreement.

Chapter 10

*J*ake Jackson was a happy man. More than that, he was a
man at peace. Yes, the morning of his wedding, he was
at peace with himself, his God, his life's work, and the
woman he loved, who unbelievably, loved him equally as much as
he did her. He was also at peace with his best friends.

His had been a hard life, just like everyone else's, what with
the recent civil war and all. Then the fiasco of Emma's departure
caused him a boatload of worry that had lasted nearly a year. Then
to finally find her, but to realize that she was in love with another
man was more than he thought bearable.

It had left an indelible scar on his heart, and yet, God had
taken His finger of love and erased a mark he had thought to be
a lifelong wound. He had persevered, and had never given up on
the destiny he knew he would have some day, and now the day was
here. Today he would begin a new season in his life as a married
man. Yes, it was a good, good day.

Abby Borelli was one flustered mama. It looked for all the
world like rain, and she just wouldn't have that. She had told
the rain so! She went about her business with an attitude that
suggested that if they knew what was good for them, those rain

clouds would just keep on rolling by. The devil surely knew better than to try to dampen her daughters wedding day! What cheek! What cheek, for him even to have threatened it!

Elizabeth had passed a good night and insisted on attending the wedding, howbeit, from afar. They would place her fainting couch on the side porch where she could see the entire proceedings, but would have a measure of privacy. Besides, every eye would be on the bride and groom throughout the ceremony. She would be able to quietly watch the ceremony without being in the throng of the other guests. That way, Mother Mattie would be with her so she would be keeping a sharp eye on her.

Fletch looked amazing in his best man's wedding attire. Elizabeth was so proud of him! He had truly been through the fiery trials of life, and had come through on the other side without even the smell of smoke. The years he had lost through the amnesia, he had counted as meaning little when compared to the happiness he had known before his injury, and since his full recovery. Life does go on and he was living every day to the fullest.

Carmel was a gorgeous woman, but never as outstandingly so as she was on her wedding day. Jake Jackson thought her to be the most elegant and beautiful woman he had ever seen. He was beside himself with thankfulness and joy. Jake did not only have his bride at his side, with his congregation in attendance, but his best friends in the world were sharing his day with him.

He couldn't help his mind going back to a time of bitter-sweetness to Emma and Mark's wedding, and how he had felt as he had stood and officiated their ceremony. He had been believing God that one day a woman as beautiful and loving as Emma, would be standing beside him at a wedding altar, just as surely as Carmel was standing beside him at that moment. The world says, "If I had not seen it with my own eyes, I wouldn't have believed it!" But Jake knew that if he not believed it, he wouldn't have seen it with his own eyes! Yes, the Lord was faithful!

Jake recalled how he had been tempted to remain with his friends in San Francisco when Mark had offered him a position at the church. He was very glad now that he'd had the wisdom and strength of character to return to his destiny, and to the plan God had for his life.

Back then when he had been hurting so badly, it was as if God had reached through a tunnel, and grabbed him by the shirtfront, and pulled him through the tunnel of fear, isolation, frustration, disappointment, and heartache. Then He stood him on his feet on the other side. He had gone through some deep waters, and it had taken some time, but he hadn't gone under. He hadn't drowned. He had a heart of gratitude when he could look where God had brought him from, and what He had brought him to this very day.

Surely, his life was about to change forever, and that for the better. There was not the slightest doubt that what he was about to do in just a moment was exactly in the center of God's will. It appeared that the blessing and favor of the Lord that had always been upon him, even though it seemed dark at the time, was now resting upon him in a mighty way, and he was grateful! He had sung praises to the Lord all the way to the church for his wedding ceremony.

The wedding party was at the altar and Jake was taking Carmel's hand in his. Mr. Borelli had kissed his only daughter and had surreptitiously wiped away a tear with his handkerchief.

Jake felt like he was in a fantastic dream that had become a fantastic reality.

Mark smiled down at them as Jake glanced over at Emma. She winked and he chuckled. He looked at Carmel and the love he saw in her eyes surely reflected the love in his own. Yes, Jake Jackson still had a tomorrow! The Lord had graciously seen to that.

Chapter 11

The wedding over and the happy couple having been presented to the congregation, the reception was in full swing. Never had Summers Bluff Plantation known quite so much festivities as they were enjoying that day! There had been other parties and holiday celebrations, to be sure, but none that carried so much joy, and raw emotion, for the Summers family and friends as now.

Of course, the country was still smarting from the war just seven years over, yet folks were becoming established once again, but days of true joy were still somewhat rare. Yes, scars of the war were still seen everywhere, but the happiness and joy as was felt by every attendee at the wedding gala that day, was not to be taken for granted.

They all were deeply grateful for another milestone in their lives that had been reached as Pastor Jake and Carmel began their journey of married life together amid laughter, music, dancing, and a lot of great food, and fellowship. Only God knew the future, but it looked nothing but bright and hopeful, as these servants of God prepared to face the days ahead with faith in God and love for each other.

No one was enjoying themselves at the reception more than Kitty and Clay. Regardless of the time drawing near of her soon departure for the West, tonight was given to glorious abandonment, not giving a thought to future separations. God already knew all of the tomorrows, therefore, whatever would be, would be, but this night was theirs.

A waltz was playing and Kitty was in Clay's arms. As they twirled as one, he looked deeply into her eyes and spoke the love he felt for her. She could scarcely breathe, but she managed to assure him that she loved him, too. "Ah, Clay. Surely, me own heart is full of love for ye, lad. Here was I thinkin' it was all too good to be true, but this is real," she whispered in his ear, sending shivers every which way.

If only she could throw her arms around his neck and hug him to herself like she wanted to! This love business was truly a bittersweet situation! Valleys and peaks, peaks and valleys!

Carmel refused to leave her patient even to go on their honeymoon! Jake was relieved and frustrated at the same time. He was so proud of his wife. They had made arrangements to stay in town at the Grand Hotel for a couple of nights, and then return to the plantation. Dr. Herschel was on call in the meantime, in case Elizabeth needed him he could be there quickly. So could Carmel, for that matter, but he could ride his horse and get there first. All of the occupants of Summers Bluff were amazed and humbled that Carmel would make that decision. It showed her heart for them, and that she was truly family now.

One thing was certain. When Elizabeth recovered, and she would, she would not dare return to San Francisco until after the birth of her child. She could never risk that long ride again and her even farther along in the pregnancy. Fletcher and Emma had already come to terms about that, but they had not been sure how Elizabeth had felt about it. Hopefully, their tradition of all the Summers babies being born on the plantation would not be broken by this baby. If that were the case, what other plans would change?

It was already becoming very doubtful that Kitty would be able to leave both Granny and Clay in a matter of a few weeks. Their love had blossomed and was plain for all to see, Clay having proposed to her the night of the wedding. She had not yet accepted him, as she just could not see her way clear to do so yet. She was simply marking time to see what plans the Lord might have for her.

letcher stayed at Elizabeth's side as much as possible while she was still confined to bed. He still helped Clay all morning, but the afternoon and evenings were devoted to Elizabeth. She was still having some discomfort, but all in all, was much better. Fletch tried to keep her mind occupied with other distractions. They read their Bibles together, sang songs, played games, and studied baby names. For a girl they had toyed with Tilley Elizabeth, after Fletcher's mother. They would call her Eliza. For a boy it was definitely Fletcher Jacob.

The days passed and Elizabeth had responded to treatment as well as could be expected. She was so very tired of being in bed, but was willing to do everything in her power to give her baby every chance at life.

"Fletch, you do realize that I will not be able to travel back to San Francisco before the baby arrives, don't you?"

"Yes, I know you could never withstand that long trip again. But more than that, I want you to tell me how you feel about it all," he asked her.

"Well, having nothing much to do except lie here and think, I have begun to see just how much this plantation is such a part of you... and Emma. Really, we have nothing to hold us in San Francisco. Emma is settled there with her husband and congregation, but we don't have any real work there. You are needed here. It's plain to see that you adore this place. I know that has been on your mind ever since you returned here," she told him, as she carefully watched his face for any telltale signs of his inner feelings.

"You know me so well, Elizabeth! No, I had no real work there, because here is where all of my hopes and dreams reside. Until Morgan was out of the scheme of things, there was no thought of returning here. But we are here. You can't leave. I think this is Providence, my dear. What do you think?"

"I would have to agree with you. I don't think our baby in danger is part of God's best, but what was meant for harm God is turning around for our good. I can't seem to see myself being away from all of these good people here on the plantation, or Jake and Carmel, or your friends at church. But it is heartbreaking to imagine saying good-bye to Em and Mark, Kitty and Miss Maude. I don't think I could bear to see them ride away!"

"Don't fret yourself, dear. God will work this all out. Just rest and be at peace. We can stand whatever we have to. We are strong people, and we know God is in control."

"Yes, it wearies me to try to figure all of this out," she admitted. "Why should I try to figure this out, when the Almighty already has a plan? I just need to let everything flow on by me just like the Savannah River! I know all will be set right when it's time."

"Now you are talking like the sensible lady I know you to be."

Chapter 13

$\mathcal{E}$mma sat in her garden and tipped her head back to face the sun. It was a glorious day, and she was alive and well. She had Mark, her family was about her, and she was really sitting here at Summers Bluff in her very own garden. So many things she thought never to have again. Truly, ever good-bye ain't gone!

If what she thought was coming to pass did happen, her Kitty would probably not be leaving for San Francisco with them. She had her man and Clay was a perfect match for her. Emma surely couldn't blame her. Nothing had been said, but she knew.

Just like she knew about Fletcher. He was happier than she had ever known him to be. Yes, they would buy back Summers Bluff, but what would she ever do without them? She was growing restless just thinking about it. Of course, she had Mark and she would be pleased to be wherever he was. But still, the melancholy was upon her until it began to be an ache in her heart.

Mark came in the room just then and saw that his wife was close to tears. He had not seen her this agitated since the trouble with Morgan and his bunch trying to kidnap her.

"Whatever is the matter, Sweetheart?" he asked.

"Oh… I was just considering all the changes that seem to be taking place in our lives. You know… Fletch and Elizabeth will not be returning with us. We won't even be here when the baby comes."

"I know what you mean. I have been watching Fletcher and he is a changed man ever since his return here. He is his own man now, he knows what he's about, and he is incredibly happy to be here. I have often wondered myself what is in San Francisco that would keep him there after being back here where he is needed, and his work and lifelong memories are strongest. Jake and Carmel and all of his friends are around him here. I know you don't want to hear that, but that is how I see it," Mark spoke quietly to her.

At that she had finally succumbed to the tears that had demanded release. He moved to her side and held her while she wept. He realized there was more to the story than what had been said. He sensed that she was feeling left out of a life she knew they would have by living there.

He discerned that separation from the plantation yet once again was nearly impossible for her to think about. Let alone leaving her family behind. He would have to consider this whole situation very carefully. A lot was at stake and he couldn' afford to miss the mark on this one. On the other hand, he couldn't say God had directed him to stay in Savannah.

Jake and Carmel had returned to start their married life at the parsonage. She had accepted Jake's suggestion of setting up her consult and surgery in one of the side rooms there. It was plenty large enough and had large windows all around for natural lighting. Jake had it ready to go for her in just a couple of days. She was content to be close to where Jake was every day, all day. It was fitting.

In just a couple of weeks she had seen the wisdom in having her work area there at home, as she'd had several night emergencies. She had been grateful not to have to leave home to attend them.

Her name was circulating around town and women were choosing her services over their long time family practitioners. While the medical colleagues were incensed, the women were pleased with their choice.

It was time to begin to charge what the women could afford to pay for her services. Whatever the charges they had welcomed her administrations. It really came to a head when the wives of some of the doctors had also begun to seek her out for their medical needs. While she was concerned that there might be repercussions, none were forthcoming, to her great surprise and relief.

Elizabeth was still under her constant care and was feeling much better. She was up and sitting out in the sunshine for short periods of time several times a day. That kept her active without undue stress or strain. She looked much healthier than she had for several weeks. While the pregnancy would remain risky for the duration, everyone was praying and believing God for a positive outcome of a healthy mother and babe.

Granny Thornton was spending a good deal of time sitting on the side veranda looking out over the fields that she had looked upon her entire life. She was as strong and healthy as she had ever been, and was enjoying a life that she had long ago given up hope of ever having again.

First, Fletcher had been reported killed, which had grieved her greatly. Then Mr. Josiah and Miss Tilley had perished in that awful fire. Right on the heels of that, her babe had been driven from her home in the dead of night, taking her precious Kitty with her clean across the country to the other coast. She never hoped to see either of the girls again, but here they all were together again, and her Fletcher, back from the grave into the bargain.

Yes, life was sweet once more. She had suffered loss, but her blessings had outweighed the losses. She was grateful to the Lord above for allowing her to live long enough to see them all back where they belonged, at the plantation.

She was so happy when Fletcher had announced that he and his wife would be staying on, even after the baby came, especially after the babe came.

And what about her Kitty and Clay Kean? *What I saw out the window tells me Kitty won't be a miss for much longer, I'm thinkin'. I never thought to clap eyes on the lass again, let alone see her happily wed, but I expect that's what's comin' down the pike, unless I miss me guess. And what more could I be after wantin'? Clay is a good man and ever'one here thinks a lot of the lad. He'll be takin' good care of her, will Clay.*

A day later Kitty announced that she would marry Clay the following week. No use to waste what time they had while everyone was still together at the plantation.

She and Clay had talked everything out. She saw that he would never be happy in San Francisco working as a laborer when Fletcher needed him here. She had agreed to stay with him and make her home where it had always been before Morgan had ripped her from it two years before.

Emma and Fletcher had gone to Judge West about buying the plantation, and he was delighted that they wanted it back.

"Summers Bluff needs to be in the hands of the Summers family," he said. "I knew the time would come when Emma would be able to come back and claim it again. Of course, I had no idea you were alive, Fletcher, but I am so pleased, my boy, to see you at the helm. Your parents would have been so proud of both of you. Will you be returning here for good, too, Emma?"

"Well, sir, we have a church in San Francisco that Mark needs to decide whether to leave or stay on as pastor. The Lord will have to tell us His will."

"Well my dear girl, I suggest you and Mark discuss it! There is enough room for three families to live out there and all of you need each other. The Lord didn't give your brother back to you to leave him and light out again to the other side of the nation!" he bellowed. "Besides, you love that place just as much as Fletcher here does. Surely there is a church here that Mark could pastor. Or he could help Jake. Our church is growing like nothing we've ever seen, and he will need the help. One or two men like Jake and Todd can't do it all, and both of them just now starting a family."

Emma had been stunned at the turn of the conversation. She'd had many thoughts of staying. Rather, her thoughts had been of how difficult it was going to be to say good-bye to everyone, and to the plantation. She just didn't know what the Lord would tell Mark. Oh, but she had some praying to do!

Chapter 14

Emma was again in her garden, reflecting on the many twists and turns her life had been taking. Growing up had been hard after the war, and all the changes it had brought. But life goes on, and people do grow and stretch with the times.

There wasn't a day Emma didn't miss her parents, but thankfully, there were so many good memories of them to comfort her. There were hurtful memories of the times they had all experienced, just like everyone else had in the midst of a civil war. But the good times had far outweighed the bad.

She had come a long way from that carefree lass sitting in the warm sun two long years ago. She could look back and thankfully, she didn't have regrets. She would have done everything just like she had done after her parents passed. Mark had helped her so much. Time, and the Lord, had made life joyful again.

She would have to be considerate of Mark's calling and his desires in the matter of staying on in Savannah. After all, Savannah wasn't his life-long home. She couldn't expect him to share her devotion to the plantation and everyone there. She had prayed and prayed that God would work this out according to His will.

Jake had come to call and was talking with Fletcher. He asked him if there was any possibility of him staying on at the plantation for good even after the baby came. Fletcher told him they had just seen the judge and he had agreed to sell the plantation back to him. Jake had ben thrilled at that news. He had seen the difference in both Fletcher and Emma since they had returned. Fletcher was also saying how much it was going to hurt everyone to see Emma and Mark leave.

Emma had overheard the conversation and she was simply miserable with this dilemma. She knew she would follow Mark wherever he needed to be, but that wouldn't stop her from yearning for home. She was not aware that Jake had already spoken to Mark about the possibility of Fletcher and Elizabeth staying on for good.

Mark was aware of how it would affect Emma to leave again. It was breaking his heart to know how much she wanted to stay, even though she had never said a word to him. But he had no direction from the Lord to stay there. Until he did have, he would be going back to San Francisco in the near future.

He had pondered whether or not Emma should stay at least until after the baby arrived, but then someone would have to escort her back home. He wanted her with him, but she would have to make some hard decisions. It was going to be difficult any way they went. He would be at odds with himself if he were not ministering in some capacity. He loved his church and they loved him. Neither could he bear to think of Emma staying on without him for several more months until Elizabeth delivered. Yes, only the Lord could sort this all out.

Chapter 15

*K*itty and Clay were to be married that day. The church ladies and all the family had pitched in and made ready for another great reception. This time the men had their way and it would be a barbecue. The wedding ceremony would be held at the plantation, just as Jake and Carmel's had been.

Kitty was a vision of loveliness, with her auburn tresses styled in the Godey girl fashion. Her perfectly fitted gown of dark blue satin shimmered as she glided down the makeshift isle beside Granny Thornton, who had declared that she would give the bride away. If that was what Granny wanted, that was what Granny would get!

Fletcher had served as best man and Emma served as her matron of honor. It was a lovely wedding ceremony with Jake officiating. If she had felt left out of things a few weeks earlier, she certainly didn't any longer. They made a lovely couple. With both of them having such Irish humor, they would weather many a storm, and come out on the other side, none the worse for wear!

Early the next morning, Mark received a letter. When he had opened it, he told Emma that it was from his associate pastor. It seemed as though a board member from a seminary in Savannah had been to the church. He had inquired as to whether or not Mark was available, or interested, in a teaching position at the seminary.

Emma searched his face for some sign as to what he might be thinking about the proposal. The furrow of his brow told her that he was at least considering what it might mean to them, should he decide to accept. She waited for him to speak, nearly holding her breath. He was searching her face for the same reason, and couldn't believe she wasn't jumping for joy.

"Well, Em, I don't even have to ask you what you are thinking. I have watched you and Fletcher come alive in this place. I knew it was just a matter of time for Fletcher staying in San Francisco. He's too young a man not to be totally committed to some endeavor or other. From what I can see this plantation is everything to him. Where else could he possibly go to be so instantly connected to his surroundings as he is here?"

At that, Emma burst into laughter and ran to him and leaped into his arms! "Oh, Mark! You knew all the time what I was feeling! The only thing keeping any of us from staying here was the church. I never dreamed you would ever consider leaving it! Would you really consider taking this appointment in Savannah?"

"Well, I would need to meet with President Anderson and find out the terms of his offer. Mr. Bentley said the man who had made the inquiry had been in Sacramento where he had heard the story of the fire in the parsonage, and since he was going to be in San Francisco the following week, had decided to visit the church.

Seems he was impressed with the congregation, the worship, and felt like I would fit the bill for one of their openings for a professorship."

He continued, "Teaching or preaching has always been my heart's desire. To help train young pastors would be very fulfilling.

It sounds like a stable career into the bargain. So I think the way this is coming about, it would behoove me to look into it. Who would have thought any good could have come out of that fire! But without it, he would never have thought to visit us. God does work in mysterious ways! We both have some praying to do, Em."

Mark had met with the Board of Directors of the Savannah Seminary and had been pleased at their offer. He had met Emma at the tearoom after the meeting, and she could tell by the look in his eyes that they were staying!

They broke the good news to the others that they had decided to stay in Savannah. Mark had a true heart peace about it. He never dreamed things could have worked out so wonderfully well for them all. That God! Always working for our good!

Emma had left with Mark and Miss Maude. They had to get back to San Francisco to take care of things there. After all, they had to get their affairs in order before returning to Savannah for good.

The church had understood that Mark was sensing his call to go back East and help train up men to take their rightful place and do the work of the ministry. He had already met other pastors in Savannah, and had preached for some of them, while he had been at the plantation. He felt that in future he would be doing some work of the evangelist, as well.

Miss Maude had fit right in from the first and loved being in the thick of things. Something was always afoot with her Savannah friends, and she had loved it. She had grown close to Mattie and Granny, and even closer to Caroline. The four of them were fast friends, and all of them unmarried, and very contented. They had spent much quality time together during Maude's time in Savannah. She had been dreading the day when they would start back to San Francisco. The most important people in her life seemed to be right there. Life would be extremely empty without them when she was back in her mansion, with just her servants once again. She wondered how people alone survived. She certainly couldn't see how they thrived. But whatever would be would be. After all, there was a plan for every life, and they would have to trust the Lord that He knew best.

Another pastor had been called to the Harbor Mission in San Francisco and Mark had been pleased at their choice. His work done there and his church in good hands, he was free to return to Savannah. As the time drew nearer for Mark and Emma to return, Miss Maude had decided that she was not leaving this family she had come to love so dearly. Aunt Caroline, Mother Mattie, and Miss Maude were all apt to remain single, and since their relationship had been more like family than just friends, she simply did not accept thousands of miles between them. She had contacted her solicitor and had arranged to put her mansion up for sale.

She had no trouble selling it as soon as she let it be known that she was leaving town. Hers was a most desirable property among the elite in San Francisco, and some were scrambling to be first in line to buy it. When Mark and Emma were ready to leave, she would be, too. They were thrilled at her decision to come with them, and knew the ladies in Savannah would be wonderfully excited to see her get off that train with them. It was just one more detail working for their good. It would have been hard to say goodbye to Miss Maude, leaving her there all alone. Now they wouldn't have to!

Chapter 16

Elizabeth was late into her eighth month when she was awakened in the night with a terrible backache. She couldn't imagine what she had done to bring that on, but it was very uncomfortable. Soon she began to feel other stronger pain, and realized it must be the contractions that Carmel had told her to expect, and knew she had to be in labor.

She awakened Fletcher. He was much calmer than she had expected. She laid it up to all the many birthings on the plantation over the years he had assisted with. However, with the trouble Elizabeth had experienced upon their arrival in Savannah, he was much more worried than he had let on to her. He immediately sent a hand to fetch the doctor, and it wasn't long before Jake and Carmel arrived.

Upon examination Carmel told her she was definitely in labor, but that she still had a ways to go. She would help her pace herself so she wouldn't use up her energy before she actually got to the hardest part of the work. They didn't call it labor for nothing.

Jake tried to keep Fletcher distracted for a while so that he wouldn't worry so much. But when they began to hear intermittent moaning coming from Elizabeth's room, Fletcher had insisted he stay by her side, as unconventional as that had been. Even Carmel couldn't reason him out of it. Her pleas for him to see to the plantation to keep himself otherwise distracted fell on deaf ears.

They had all joined hands in prayer at the outset asking the Lord's guidance for Carmel and strength for the journey for Elizabeth… and Fletcher. They blessed the babe with long life and perfect health. Then the vigil began in earnest.

If only Emma were here! But she isn't! I don't know what she could do, but just her being here would help me! Elizabeth thought.

Fletcher Jacob Summers was brought into the world at three o'clock in the afternoon. The birthing was uneventful and mother and baby were both doing fine. Everyone let out a huge sigh of relief. God was on His throne, and all was well with the world. Fletcher was over the moon with pride, joy, and thankfulness!

The next day the parade began. Many of the church members had stopped by to congratulate Fletcher and take a wee peak at the babe. They didn't disturb Elizabeth that day, but in a few days, they would be back to see her. All the workers had gathered on the front porch, as Fletcher had taken the baby out to show him off. He was a fine boy, and none could argue that. Summers Bluff now had an heir to carry on the Summers' name.

Things had come full circle for Emma. This time when she boarded the train, it would be her last journey from the West. She and Mark would begin their family in Savannah, surrounded by her loved ones and life long friends, just like she had always thought to do. The plantation was a busy and prosperous place those days.

The lad from the telegraph and postal service had just delivered a telegram from Mark advising they would need to be picked up at the train depot that Saturday evening. Everyone was thrilled for Emma to really be coming home for good this time.

Not as a visitor, but as the daughter of the house. If only Josiah and Miss Tilley could have been there to welcome their dear girl home. But other loved ones were there, and she certainly would receive a wonderful welcome!

The Lord surely knew how to tidy up a family. He sets solitaries into families, like Elizabeth, Mark, Kitty, Clay and Miss Maude. He binds up the broken hearted, like Emma, Jake and Carmel. He even causes every good-bye to not be gone, like Fletcher from the dead and then bringing them all home again from out West. He even started a brand new generation with baby Jacob—yes, a new beginning.

Granny had her rocker, her Kitty, and all of her loved ones about her. Aunt Caroline, Mother Mattie, and Miss Maude had each other, and everyone else in the family.

Against all odds, He can and does bring loved ones from the north, south, east or west, proving that miracles can and do strike as suddenly as disasters. Oh, yes they do!

They had no way of knowing what they would be called upon to face or endure in the future, but they knew what all they had endured in the past. They knew the God that had brought them safely through war, death, separation, living under Northern occupation, and having to start over alone and afraid. They knew the God of all of their tomorrows, and they each had a very bright hope for whatever their tomorrows would bring!

The End of Part Four

Many, many thanks for choosing this book! I hope you enjoyed my first offerings, the Summers Bluff series. It was a joy to write, another thing off my list. Every blessing on you and yours!

Suz

Email: summersbluff@gmail.com
Web: amazonmedicalmissions.org

CPSIA information can be obtained
at www.ICGtesting.com
Printed in the USA
LVOW11*1937081116

512166LV00005B/7/P

9 781512 745405